THE TWO DEATHS OF DANIEL HAYES

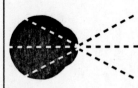

THE TWO DEATHS OF DANIEL HAYES

MARCUS SAKEY

THORNDIKE PRESS
A part of Gale, Cengage Learning

Detroit • New York • San Francisco • New Haven, Conn • Waterville, Maine • London

GALE
CENGAGE Learning

LIBRARY OF CONGRESS CATALOGING-IN-PUBLICATION DATA

Sakey, Marcus.
    The two deaths of Daniel Hayes / by Marcus Sakey.
        p. cm. — (Thorndike Press large print crime scene)
    ISBN-13: 978-1-4104-4008-2 (hardcover)
    ISBN-10: 1-4104-4008-7 (hardcover)
    1. Large type books. I. Title.
PS3619.A4T86 2011b
813'.6—dc22   2011022461

Published in 2011 by arrangement with Dutton, a member of Penguin Group (USA) Inc.

Printed in Mexico
1 2 3 4 5 6 7 15 14 13 12 11

For Scott Miller and Ben Sevier,
who've had my back from the beginning

■ ■ ■ ■

ACT ONE

■ ■ ■ ■

"There is no future without an identity to claim it, or to be obligated to it. There are no caging norms. In its very precariousness the state is pure and free."
— Nadine Gordimer, *The Pickup*

He was naked and cold, stiff with it, his veins ice and frost. Muscles carved hard, skin rippled with goose bumps, tendons drawn tight, body scraped and shivering. Something rolled over his legs, velvet soft and shocking. He gasped and pulled seawater into his lungs, the salt scouring his throat. Gagging, he pushed forward, scrabbling at dark stones. The ocean tugged, but he fought the last ragged feet crawling like a child.

As the wave receded it drew pebbles rattling across one another like bones, like dice, like static. A seagull shrieked its loneliness.

His lungs burned, and he leaned on his elbows and retched, liquid pouring in ropes from his open mouth, salt water and stomach acid. A lot, and then less, and finally he could spit the last drops, suck in quick shallow lungfuls of air that smelled of rotting fish.

In. Cough it out. There. There.

His hands weren't his. Paler than milk and trembling with a panicky violence. He couldn't make them stop. He'd never been so cold.

What was he doing here?

Like waking from sleepwalking, he couldn't remember. It didn't matter. The cold was filling him, killing him, and if he wanted to live he had to move.

He rolled onto his side. An apocalyptic beach, water frothing beneath a shivering sky, wind a steady howl over the shoals, whipping the saw grass to strain its roots. Not another person as far as he could see.

Had to move. His muscles screamed. He staggered upright and tried a tentative step. His thoughts were signals banged down frozen wires; after an eon his legs responded. His feet were bloody.

One step. Another. The wind a lash against his dripping skin. The beach sloped hard upward. Each step brought muscles a little more under his control. The motion warming them, oh god, warming them to razors and nails and blood gone acid. He concentrated on breathing, each inhale a marker. Make it to the next one. Five more. Don't quit until twenty. Goddamn you, breathe.

The boulders the ocean had broken to pebbles gave way to those it hadn't yet, broad stones with moss marking the leeward side, spaced with pools of dark water where spiny things waited. He stumbled from one rock to the next until he reached the top.

As lonely and blasted a stretch of earth as any he'd seen. Black rocks and foaming sea and sky marked only by the passage of birds. No. Wait.

He blinked, tried to focus. Two thin dirt tracks led to a splotch of color, a boxy shape. A car. Legs cramping. Breath shallow. He couldn't force his lungs to take. To draw enough. Air. The shivering easing. Bad sign. His feet tangled and he fell. Inches from his eyes, pale grass spotted and marked by the appetite of insects. The ground wasn't so bad. Almost soft. Easy now. Easy to go.

No.

Crawl. Elbows scraping. Knees. Forearms going blue. Blueberries, blue water, blue eyes.

He reached the trunk, pulled himself up, the metal burning cold. Slouched his way to the door and bent stiff fingers around the handle.

Please.

The door opened. He maneuvered around it and fell into the smell of leather. His legs wouldn't move. It took both arms to pull them in, one at a time. Gripping the burnished handle, he yanked the door shut. The wind's laughter died.

Instead of a key there was a push-button start. He slapped at it, missed, slapped again. The engine roared to life.

The man turned the heat all the way up and collapsed against the seat.

A soft time. Warm air making his body ache and tingle and finally ease. For a while the man stared at the ceiling, head lolled back. Content to watch the drifting spots in his eyes. Tiny floating things that he could see only when he didn't try to look at them. He didn't think about where he was, or why, or who the car belonged to and when they might return, or whether they would be happy to find a naked man dripping on the leather seats.

Just cowered like an animal in his den, the doors locked and heat blasting.

After a long time — how long he had no idea — he felt himself coming back. Surfacing like he was waking from a nap. Words and questions swirling leaves from an October tree, tossed and spinning and never touching the ground.

Gasoline. That was one. Gasoline. What did . . .

Oh. He straightened, rubbed at his eyes. His muscles weak and languid. The fuel gauge read almost empty. He shut off the engine.

So. Where was he?

The car was gorgeous. A BMW according to the logo in the steering wheel, with gauges like an airplane cockpit's. The seats were leather, the trim brushed aluminum, and the dash had a computer display. But the thing was a mess. Socks and a pair of Nikes rested on the floorboards on his side; the passenger seat was buried in maps and take-out bags and soda cups and empty blister packs of ephedrine and gas station receipts and a worn U.S. road atlas and a fifth of Jack Daniel's with an inch left in it.

Hel*lo.*

He opened the whiskey, swallowed half the remainder in a gulp. It burned in the best possible way.

Now that it wasn't killing him, the world outside had a kind of desolate beauty. Lonely, though. Other than the narrow two-track the car was parked on, there was no sign of people in either direction. And while he hadn't been fully conscious the whole time, he hadn't seen anyone since he'd climbed into the car.

So then . . .

How had he gotten here?

Where the fuck was here and what was he doing in it?

Calm. Don't panic. You're safe. Just think about what happened. How you ended up here. You . . . you . . .

Nothing.

He closed his eyes, jammed them tight. Opened them again.

Nothing had changed. Had he been drinking? Drugged? *Retrace your steps. You were . . .*

You were . . .

It was like that terrible moment he sometimes had waking up in a strange environment, in the dark of a friend's living room, or in a hotel, that period when his brain hadn't yet come online and everything was automatic, just panic and readiness and fear, the tension of waiting for certainty to click, for normalcy to fall like a warm blanket. That moment always passed. It passed, and he remembered where he was and what he was doing there.

Right?

He set the whiskey down, gripped the steering wheel with both hands. *Focus.*

Focus!

Outside, the wind whistled. The trees looked like they'd been on fire, dark black trunks spreading to broad limbs marked by a handful of stubborn orange and yellow leaves, the last embers.

Okay. Something must have happened. An after-effect of hypothermia, some kind of shock. Don't force it. Tease it. Coax it out. Like the floaters in your eyes, you can't drag this front and center. Come at it sideways.

Your brain seems to work. Use it. Where are you?

A rocky beach. Cold. He could taste the salt on his lips, knew this was an ocean. Which one?

The question was crazy, but he worked it anyway. Let one thing lead to the next. The dashboard clock read 7:42. The sun was just a brighter shade of gray above the waves, but it was higher than before. Which made it morning, which made that east, which made this the Atlantic. Assuming he was still in the United States. Yes. The road atlas.

Okay. The Atlantic. And cold and rocky and sparsely inhabited. Maine, maybe?

Why not. Roll with that. "This is Maine." His voice cracked. He coughed, then continued. "I'm in a BMW. It's morning."

Nothing.

15

A bank envelope was curled in the cup holder. Inside was a stack of twenties, several hundred dollars. Under the envelope there was something silver that turned out to be a stainless steel Rolex Daytona. Nice watch. Very nice watch.

What else? He leaned over to open the glove box. There was an owner's manual, a key ring with a BMW clicker, three pens, a pack of Altoids, a sealed box of ephedrine, and a large black gun.

He stared. An owner's manual, a key ring with a BMW clicker, three pens, a pack of Altoids, a sealed box of ephedrine, and a large black gun. A semiautomatic, he noticed, then wondered how he could know that and not remember where he had been before he woke up on the beach. Or worse, even his own —

Stop. Don't go there. If you don't face it, maybe it's not true.

The trunk.

He stepped out. The wind whipped his naked body, and his skin tightened into goose bumps. His balls tried to retract into his belly. He stepped gingerly to the back of the car on bloody toes.

Would there be a body in there? Handcuffed and shot in the head, maybe, or rolled in a carpet, hair and boots spilling out.

No: it held only jumper cables and a plastic shopping bag with a red bull's-eye on it. He opened the bag. A pair of designer jeans, a white undershirt with pits stained yellow, crumpled boxer briefs, wadded-up socks. Someone's laundry.

He looked around again. In for a penny.

He shook out the underwear, stepped into it. The jeans were soft and worn, expensive looking. Too fancy for Target, and dirty to boot. Maybe the Target purchases had been a change of clothes. He wriggled into the shirt, then slammed the trunk. Climbed back in the car, the air inside wonderful, stiflingly warm. The sour smell of feet rose as he wriggled into the sneakers.

Then he sat and stared out the window.

How had he known that red bull's-eye was the Target logo? How had he known the watch was a Rolex? Or that Jack Daniel's was whiskey, and that he liked whiskey?

How was it that he knew the BMW key fob had an RFID chip that activated the push-button start, knew Maine was in the northeast, could identify the symptoms of hypothermia, could glance at a stack of twenties and know it was several hundred dollars — he could do all of that, but he couldn't remember his own goddamn —

He reached for the owner's manual in the glove box, careful not to touch the gun. The book was bound in black leather. Inside the front cover was a registration card and proof of insurance. Both in the name of Daniel Hayes, resident of 6723 Wandermere Road, Malibu, California.

Huh.

He climbed out of the car, walked to the back. California plates.

Who wandered away from a ninety-thousand-dollar car and left the key in the glove box? Where would they go in the middle of nowhere?

And the clothes. The shoes fit. The jeans felt familiar.

Calling yourself Daniel Hayes is a start. Try it on, just like the jeans.

Daniel got back in the car, put on his watch, then cranked the ignition and pulled away.

The two-track led to a dirt road. The dirt road led to a paved one only slightly less bumpy. Eventually that intersected two lanes of faded blacktop with a sign marking it US-1, north to Machias, south to Ellsworth.

He pulled to the shoulder and sat watching. A weather-beaten pickup passed heading south. A minute later came a northbound Civic.

"Life goes on," he said, and laughed a little hysterically. Had he always talked to himself?

Maybe. Maybe you chew bottle caps. Sodomize midgets. Kill people for a secret government —

He pulled onto the highway heading south.

The sky was clearing, the gray patchwork not lifting so much as coalescing into separate regions of dense cloud broken by vivid blue. The BMW reduced the outside world to a soft hum. His eyes felt grainy, his hands and head heavy. But he was pleased to note that the license plates read "MAINE" at the top.

So he hadn't lost his mind. Maybe just misplaced it a little.

Assuming that his first conscious act hadn't been to steal a car, and that the insurance was up-to-date, that meant that he'd driven three thousand miles. Three thousand miles followed by a swim in an ocean cold enough to stop his heart. Why?

Daniel rubbed at his eyes. His hands were raw. He could barely keep his eyes open. He needed to find a motel, sleep for a week.

When he woke up, this would all be better. He'd remember who —

Don't admit that. Madness lies that way.

— what he was doing here. It would come clear.

He passed a blink of a town, white clapboard and a sagging church. A girl pedaled a bicycle with streamers flowing from the handlebars. Sidewalks and a town hall and a VFW with a Friday fish fry. A mile the other side, a roadside marquee announced vacancies at something called the Pines Motel, a low-slung cinder-block building huddled along the highway. Fine. Good. Perfect.

The lot was gravel that popped under the tires. He stepped out into birdsong and chilly sunlight, tramped past a handful of dusty pickup trucks sporting rifle racks and hand-painted camouflage.

The lobby was just an alcove off the main hall with a desk tucked into it. No one there. Hanging on the wall was a surprisingly skilled painting of a deer bounding over a fallen tree. The artist had caught the animal's panic, the brushstrokes menacing, the woods turned into the darkest sort of fairy tale. He could sense the hunter beyond the border of the painting, the threat closer and more dangerous than the animal could know.

"Help you?"

Daniel whirled. A woman held a bead curtain half-parted. He couldn't tell if she was a rugged thirty or an attractive fifty.

"Yeah, sorry. Just admiring the painting."

"My husband. Don't know why he bothers, myself. No use to the things. Keep trying to get him to paint over the old ones, but he likes to save them."

"He should," Daniel said. "He's got a lot of talent."

"A lot of time is what he's got. Don't know about talent."

And what a lucky man he is to have you for a wife. "I, ah, I need a room."

"Single or double?"

"It doesn't matter."

"Single's cheaper."

"Single, then. A single will be fine."

The woman sat behind the computer, began punching keys. "Forty dollars. How long?"

"I'm — I'm not sure. What day is today?"

She gave him a look that read *city folk,* but said, "Wednesday."

"Okay. Just tonight for now." Wednesday. Nope. Nothing. He set the bank envelope on the counter, made sure she got a look at

21

it. "You said forty?"

She nodded, and he pulled out two twenties.

"Name?"

"Daniel Hayes."

"Credit card?"

"Huh?"

"For a deposit."

"I lost my wallet. How about I just give you an extra forty as a deposit?"

Her eyes narrowed, but she took the money. "Checkout is noon. No smoking. You're in seven."

"The room has cable, right?" he asked anxiously, and then did a double take. *Huh?* The words had come out of his mouth unbidden. What did he care about — She was staring at him, so he said, "You know, television?"

"Television. The magic picture box?"

"Right. Sorry." He rubbed at his eyes. "I'm a little hazy."

She handed him a key on a heavy brass fob, pointed down the hall. "That way. Ice and vending at the end."

Room seven turned out to be a ten-by-twenty rectangle with a twin bed. The furniture was particleboard, and the remote control was tethered to the nightstand. The windows were draped in yellowed lace, giving the room a funereal feeling. It smelled of chemical air freshener.

Home sweet home.

Daniel dropped the envelope on the dresser, went to the bathroom. He hesitated outside the door, his hand on the light switch.

Probably the moment he did it, everything would come clear. The shock would part like fog. He'd remember everything. Have a laugh, then fall asleep with a light heart.

So why are you hesitating?

It wasn't hard to figure out. What happened if you looked in the mirror and didn't recognize yourself?

Do it.

Daniel flipped the switch. Fluorescent light flickered on, revealing linoleum floors and Formica counters.

No fog parted. No veil lifted. The man in the mirror offered no answers.

He looked exhausted, bruised and worn and dark-circled, but more or less familiar. For a vertiginous moment, Daniel lost track of which was him and which was the reflection, like one was a doppelganger that could break free and act independently, as he seemed to have snapped free from his life.

"I don't feel crazy," he said, and the man in the mirror agreed. "I just don't . . . I don't —"

A sour taste rose in his throat. He slapped at the light. Stepped out of the bathroom, pulling the dirty undershirt over his head as he went.

Sleep. He would sleep for a long time, and when he woke up, he would remember. He would. He had to.

Dear god.

Please.

His dreams were sweaty things full of looming shapes and pointing fingers and the sense of imminent disaster. The context changed from dream to dream — he leaned over the edge of a tall building, he fumbled with the seat belt of a car spinning out of control, he stepped into shadows beneath a bridge where something terrible waited — but the essence was the same. In each of them he was filthy and lost and helpless to prevent tragedy.

The blast of an air horn and the roar of tires woke him, an eighteen-wheeler barreling by. He jerked upright, sure that he had fallen asleep at the wheel again. The sheets were tangled and wet, and the pillow bore a sodden outline of his head.

"Fuck *me.*"

The alarm clock read 4:17 P.M. He'd slept

about five hours. Daniel pushed the curtain aside and looked out at the dreary motel sign and the gas station across the street and the flaming sky beyond. Four o'clock and the sun was setting. These people got screwed.

Weird. You know you don't belong here, and it's not a matter of license plates and insurance cards. You just know it's not home.

Daniel extricated himself from the blankets and padded to the bathroom. Left the light off as he ran cold water and splashed double handfuls on his face and neck.

It was time to acknowledge the facts. Somehow he had forgotten who he was.

So what do *you know?*

He'd woken on a beach, half-dead, naked. Could he have been drugged or knocked unconscious, taken there against his will? But if someone had done that, why leave the car for him to find?

More likely, he had gone there himself. Judging by the contents of the car, the whiskey and the ephedrine and the profusion of crap, he'd been driving for a while, maybe all the way from California. From sunny Malibu to that dark ocean, that hidden bluff, where he . . .

He . . .

Jesus.

He tried to kill himself.

How else to explain it? No wallet in the car, no clothes on the beach, no cell phone. He must have gone into the ocean. He could picture it, the cold light of dawn barely breaking the horizon. Habit might have made him kick off his shoes, take off his watch, then realize how unnecessary the actions were. Walking into the water, wincing at the shock, the bone-snapping cold of the waves. Walking until he could dive, and then swimming, stripping off his remaining clothing as he went. Past the breakers. His mind in turmoil, desperate to die, fighting to live. Diving deep into the womb-darkness, and opening his mouth to invite it inside —

Flair for the dramatic, Daniel?

He didn't know anything like that, not really. Maybe he'd just wanted to take a dip. Hell, maybe he wasn't Daniel Hayes. He couldn't know any of it for sure.

First things first. A shower. And food. He was starving. If he wanted to be more than an animal, if he wanted to believe that he was still a man even if he wasn't a whole one, then may as well start with the simple stuff.

In the bathroom he spun the tap to hot, stripped off the boxer briefs and tossed

26

them on the toilet tank, then, while the water warmed, looked at his body in the mirror. His skin was on the pasty end of the spectrum, and though his arms had some definition, his belly had that early-thirties softness. Scratches crisscrossed his shoulders and back. *I've got a feeling I've looked better.* He stepped into the shower and let it wash over him.

Afterward, a towel around his waist, he explored his room. There was another canvas on the wall, this one a gray outcropping of rock lashed by black-blue waves. Spray flew high, spatters of white against storm clouds. The scene was intensely lonely, all that fury and foam without a hint of humanity to soften it. The only bright spot was in the sky, a tear in the clouds, small and far away.

Yeah, well, if you were married to that woman, hope would look small and far away to you too.

Daniel picked up the remote control from the nightstand, turned on the TV. Five-forty-eight, not time yet. He flipped until he found CNN, Wolf Blitzer myopically paternal. The Palestinians and the Israelis were still going at it, Darfur was still hell, Russia was still backsliding. Daniel hit mute.

His stomach twisted. God, he was raven-

27

ous. Have to do something about that soon. *First, though, let's see if you can get some help.*

The telephone was black and battered. He lifted the receiver, punched 411, and was rewarded by a mechanical tone followed by a mechanical voice. "Welcome to Directory Assistance. For English, please press one. *Para Español —*"

He hit one.

"Please say the city and state."

"Los Angeles, California."

"Say the name of the person or business you are —"

"Daniel Hayes."

"One moment, please."

He waited, twisting the cord between his fingers. After a moment, the silence gave way to the muted buzz of a call center and an operator's bored voice. "Thank you for calling AT&T Directory Assistance calls may be recorded for quality assurance please spell the name you're looking for."

"Hayes, H-A-Y-E-S, first name Daniel."

"Thank you." The clacking of keys. "I'm sorry, sir, that number is unlisted."

"Listen, it's an emergency. I absolutely have to talk to, to Daniel."

"I'm sorry, sir, I can't give out unlisted phone numbers."

28

"Could you connect me directly?"

"I'm sorry, sir, I can't do that."

"Come on," he said, trying to keep the frustration from his voice, "what's the worst that could happen if you connect me? I still won't know the number."

"I'm sorry, sir, I —"

"Can't do fuck-all. Yeah." He hung up the phone hard enough to jar the bell. Five-fifty-eight, almost time. He punched channels until he came to FX, the wrap-up of some cop show. Calling had been a long shot, but he'd been hoping that someone might answer the phone, someone who would recognize his voice. A roommate, a lover, a brother, a wife, someone he could trust to guide him —

Wait a second.

Almost time? For what?

His shoulders tingled like they'd been brushed with feathers. When he checked into the motel, he'd confirmed the room had cable. And earlier, shit, he hadn't even noticed, but as he'd turned on the TV he'd thought that it wasn't time *yet*.

Daniel sat up straight against the cheap headboard. Unmuted the television. Commercials: bad credit, no credit, you could get a loan; a Swiffer made it all worthwhile for a grinning housewife; a Mustang drove

at unlikely speeds across abandoned roads.
And then it started.

INT. MAMI'S KITCHEN — DAY
A stylish West Hollywood café
at lunchtime. BEAUTIFUL PEOPLE
munch organic greens and sip
Chablis, attended by WAIT-
RESSES in chic black outfits.
At a table by the window EMILY
SWEET toys with her silver-
ware. She's a knockout in a
tight T-shirt and designer
jeans.
An appetizer is half-eaten in
front of her. She glances at
her watch and sighs, then
reaches for her purse.

EMILY
I'll grab the check when you
have a second.
WAITRESS
Let me guess. He didn't show?
EMILY
(a tight smile)
L.A. men.
WAITRESS
Don't I know. Too much hair
gel, not enough heart.
30

A handsome man with a jaw that would make Superman jealous pushes through the crowd. JAKE MODINE looks relieved to see Emily still there. The waitress gives Emily a surreptitious thumbs-up.

                    JAKE
Em, honey, I'm so sorry —
                    EMILY
It's fine.
    (standing)
Try the ceviche.
                    JAKE
Wait —
                    EMILY
I'm tired of waiting for you, Jake.
                    JAKE
The reason I was late —
                    EMILY
All this time I've been believing your lies, hoping that someday you'd find the guts to take what you want. And what did that get me?
    (she shoulders her purse)
Warm ceviche.

JAKE

I was late because I was talking with Tara. Yelling, actually.
  (a hand on her shoulder)
It's over, Em.
  (a beat)
I'm leaving your sister.

Emily stares. She can't decide
whether to storm away or jump
into his arms.

A sexy pop song kicked in, synced to a
quick-cut montage: a couple in bed, then a
close-up of the man's fingers tracing the
woman's back. Night traffic on a highway,
headlights blurred and grainy. The flashing
thighs of a girl in a nightclub. People around
a bonfire, the lights of the Santa Monica
Pier behind. A sun-blurred mural of Jim
Morrison on the side of a building. Mani-
cured nails holding the stem of a martini
glass. Finally, three women — blonde,
brunette, and redhead — laughing so hard
that the redhead collapsed on the sidewalk.
As the song wound up, the title *Candy Girls*
glittered across the screen.

Daniel stared. It wasn't the show, which
revealed itself to be a sort of lurid cross

between *Felicity* and *Melrose Place,* a melo-drama about three sisters seeking their fortune in Hollywood, the kind of program that purported to be about learning and loving but was really about fighting and fucking. The writing was solid and the production slick, but that wasn't what caught him. Nor was it the fantasy of eternal youth on the left coast or the stylish editing or catchy soundtrack.

It was Emily.

The middle sister, brunette with a cream complexion and bright eyes, the kind of girl who appeared in ads for skin cream, the kind you could imagine what she smelled like just from watching her smile.

The episode followed her tempestuous relationship with Jake, a producer who had been dating Emily's older sister while pining for Emily. Tara, the blond one, was predictably unhappy about being dumped, and by the end of the episode she had managed not only to split Emily and Jake up, but also to steal a role from Emily by seducing the director. The part was a guest appearance on a show Jake produced, leaving Emily sure that he'd been toying with her all along.

In the last minutes, she walked away from Jake. When she reached the safety of her powder blue VW bug, Emily closed the door and gripped the steering wheel. There were no wild histrionics, just a nicely underplayed swipe at her eyes with the back of her hand, and then she started the car and pulled away, her taillights blending with those of a hundred other aspiring starlets. The credits sprinted past as an announcer teased the upcoming program, something about plastic surgeons. Daniel turned off the TV.

What the hell was that? What did it mean? Who was Emily Sweet?

She's a make-believe character, idiot. What it means is that you're petrified, and right now you'll cling to anything that distracts you from the facts of your life.

Daniel stood, went to the bathroom. Hung the towel on the rack and stepped into his clothing. He needed to eat anyway. No harm making another stop.

He found the drugstore a bit down US-1. The fluorescent lighting was harsh after the deep dark of a Maine evening, but the middle-aged woman behind the counter smiled as she sold him the magazine.

"Anywhere to grab a bite around here?"

"Kingfisher's does a decent burger."

"Perfect." He got directions and hopped back in the car. Kingfisher's turned out to be a diner in a converted house five miles away. Conversation didn't quite stop when he walked in, but he could feel the eyes on him. He spotted an empty booth by the window, slid onto the Naugahyde, pulled a menu from behind the ketchup. Glenn Frey sang from cheap speakers, advising Daniel to take it easy, not to let the sound of his own wheels drive him crazy.

"What'll you have?"

"Let me get a giant Coke and two double burgers, please."

"How do you want 'em?"

"Ummm . . ." *Good question.* "One rare, one well-done."

"Shine a flashlight on one, scorch the other. Got it." She jotted on the tab. "Anything else?"

"Just a question. Where am I, exactly?"

She gave him a bemused expression. "Outside Cherryfield."

The atlas was taped and torn and out of date, but he didn't imagine Maine had changed that much. It took him a couple of minutes to find Cherryfield; it was written in the tiniest font on the map. He wasn't just in Maine, he was practically in Canada. No wonder the beach had been abandoned.

The waitress plunked down a plastic tumbler of soda. The syrupy sweetness

35

tasted wonderful. Daniel pulled out his drugstore purchase, the current issue of *TV Guide.* There it was. *Candy Girls,* FX Networks, running at 6 P.M. eastern. He turned to the next day — same thing. Syndicated, then. A quick scan showed him that it ran five days a week. He flipped back to today — November 4, apparently — and read the description. "Emily (Laney Thayer) and Jake (Robert Cameron) get closer, but Tara (Janine Wilson) has other plans."

"Here you go, hon." The waitress set down the dinner plates. The smell hit, rich and fatty, and his stomach didn't so much growl as roar. He bit into a burger. Amazing. His first meal. Daniel attacked it, throwing it down like he was filling a hole.

"Why do you have two hamburgers?"

A girl of maybe eight stood at the end of the table. Her hair was swept into a ponytail and secured by a pink fuzzy thing, and she wore a T-shirt with a picture of a girl only a little older than her singing into a microphone.

He smiled at her. "What do you mean? I only have one."

"No, you have two." She pointed to them. "One, t—"

Before she could finish, he crammed the rest of the burger in his mouth, his cheeks ballooning out. "Thee?" he asked through a mouthful of meat. "Un."

She laughed and clapped her hands to her mouth. Daniel chewed, swallowed, chewed, swallowed. He coughed and wiped his mouth.

"You're silly," the girl said.

"Thank you." He gestured at her. "I like your shirt. Who's that?"

"That's Hannah Montana! She's a singer except when she's a girl. She's really famous, and everybody loves her, but nobody knows that she's also Miley Stewart. But here she's Hannah Montana. I'm going to be a famous singer someday and do concerts and sing for the president and stuff."

"Wow. I'm lucky I met you now."

The girl nodded sagely. "That's true. I'll be really busy when I'm famous. And I'll live in a big house with a pool and the ocean. And lots of famous people will come visit, and they'll all like me, because I'll be famous too."

"Sounds pretty great," Daniel said. He reached for his soda, took a swig.

"Nadine!" The woman appeared out of nowhere. She ignored Daniel as she snatched the little girl's wrist. "What did I tell you? Get back over there."

"We were just talking," Daniel said. "It's okay."

The woman gave him a mind-your-own-business glare, then tugged the little girl toward a booth at the other end of the restaurant. "I told you to sit still. Now you sit *still,* young lady."

Daniel shook his head. Why even *have* kids if what you wanted was a doll that sat still? It had been good to talk — well, listen — to Nadine. It had felt normal. No questions about who he was or what anything meant. Kids that young were so sure of everything. She was going to be a famous singer, and that was that.

He picked up his other burger. He could feel eyes on him and made a point of eating slowly and neatly. By the time he'd reduced his dinner to crumbs and grease, conversation had returned to normal. When he leaned back, his belly strained the snap of the jeans, and a pleasant sort of exhaustion had come over him. For the first time, he felt almost okay. He had started the day fighting for his life, and since then he had found clothing, shelter, food. He knew where he was and had a name that might well be his.

That's the criteria for okay? Maybe knowing your name?

He had to grip the edge of the table, afraid he might fall out of the booth.

He was in a concrete canyon. Water trickled. The bleeding sun stained everything crimson. Ahead there was a tunnel, tall and broad. The mouth of it was perfect black shadow, but he knew that something waited in that darkness. Waited and watched.

Something terrible.

"Hurry."

The voice came from behind. He spun.

Emily Sweet, pale skin and dark hair spilling in a tangle. Wearing the same outfit as on the show, a T-shirt that hugged her body and flaring jeans. She sat on the concrete, long legs crossed girlishly beneath her. Her feet were bare, the nails painted the color of the dying sun.

She smiled up at him. "Hurry."

"What?"

"You have to hurry."

"Why?"

"They're coming for you," she said.

"Who —" But before he could finish, there was a loud bang and suddenly he was looking at her through the wrong end of a telescope, the barren concrete and the haunted tunnel and Emily all zooming into the distance. Daniel jerked awake. The pounding came again. Someone knocking on the door.

They're coming for you. He struggled against the sheets, adrenaline pounding through his body. "Who is it?"

"Manager."

"What do you want?"

"Money for today. Or you gotta clear out."

"Yeah, ah." Daniel forced an exhale. It was just a dream. His waking mind had heard the banging, integrated it, that was all. Guardian angels weren't on shows called *Candy Girls.* "One second."

He pulled on his jeans and stained undershirt, then opened the door. The manager looked him up and down, took in the funky hair and the pillow marks. "You okay?"

"I just woke up."

"After one." The tone part contempt, part befuddlement.

"Yeah." Daniel rubbed at his eyes. "Is it?" He glanced around the room, saw the deposit envelope. "Forty, right?"

The man reached for the twenties, and Daniel noticed splotches of color under his nails, ocher and chartreuse and evergreen. "Hey, you're the husband. The painter."

"Ayup," he said in the same tone of voice he might have used to admit to stealing from a church donation basket.

"I really like your work. That canvas in the office, and this one." He gestured at the lonely promontory, the salt spray, the shattered heavens. "They're terrific."

The manager's ears flushed red. He nodded, said nothing.

One thing you had to give Maine people, Daniel thought, no one could accuse them of babbling. "You ever have a show?"

"On television?"

"No, I mean an art show. In a gallery."

"I." He didn't seem to know what to say. "No."

"You should. You could probably sell these. They're so vivid, you know? Evocative. They're lonely and sad, but in a distinctive way." He realized he was rambling, but it felt good to talk to someone, anyone. "I bet you'd be surprised."

The guy looked away, muttered something that might have been a thanks. Then he said, "Checkout is noon," and walked quickly away.

Daniel watched him go, this lumbering, quiet man. Living in the sticks, painting cries of desolation he never intended to sell. So shy that a word of praise made him squirm. In bed he and his wife must be about as much fun as a tax audit.

But at least he knows who he is.

41

In the bathroom Daniel splashed water on his face, dunked his head under the faucet. "So," he said to his reflection, "we're a couple of good-looking dudes. What's our plan?"

The mirror offered no suggestions.

Well, okay then. Two options came to mind. He could go to the police and ask for help. Or he could get back in his car and drive to Los Angeles. The police were probably the safest route. But was it that simple?

Daniel grabbed his keys, went to the parking lot. The gun was where he'd left it. He stared for a moment. Glanced around. No one seemed to be watching, but still.

There was a crumpled Wendy's bag on the floor, and he shook it out, dumping a hamburger wrapper and a napkin. Hesitantly, he took the pistol, slid it into the bag, then locked the car and returned to his room.

He turned on the lamp on the bedside table to get a look at the gun. A Glock 17 with the trademark triple-action trigger safety system, no hammer, drop-safe. Tenifer-hardened for maximum scratch and corrosion resistance. He thumbed the magazine release, saw that it was fully loaded with 9mm rounds.

Apparently, I'm comfortable with guns.

That didn't mean anything, really. Lots of people were. Still, there was something ominous in the situation. Waking with, what, amnesia, some sort of fugue? And in the glove box of his expensive car, a high-quality semiautomatic pistol.

He raised the Glock to his nose, sniffed it. It smelled of carbon. *It's been fired. Fired and not cleaned since.*

How long ago? No way to say. It might have been nothing, just a trip to the range. Or it might have been used in an interstate crime spree. What if he had the gun because he was in danger? Or because he was dangerous?

I don't feel *dangerous.*

But the police might disagree. Until he knew what was going on, who he'd been and what he'd done, talking to them was a huge risk.

Which left Los Angeles. There had to be answers waiting there. And yet the thought of returning to California prompted a swell of guilt and shame and horror. He couldn't say why, but the feeling was unshakable. Like waking up with a hangover, dead certain that he'd made an ass of himself during his blackout hours. For some reason, home scared the hell out of him.

So what, you want to just hide?

He set the Glock on the nightstand, thought better of it, pulled out the drawer, and set it atop the Gideon bible. Rubbed at his eyes.

Here's the plan. You already paid for the room. Stay. Get some rest. Stress and exhaustion have to be part of the problem. So take it easy today.

Tomorrow, act like a man.

Deputy Chris Dundridge was raised by *NYPD Blue.*

Everyone said his father had been a lovable guy, quick with a joke, always up for another round of Dewar's, a hell of a baseball player. Of course, Dad had vanished right around the time Chris was starting tee ball, so his own memories were faded photographs. The two of them sitting on the end of a dock, the waves spitting white and green around the pilings. The smell of tobacco and Aqua Velva. That good almost-sick feeling in his belly when Dad tossed him high.

There hadn't been any fights, no screaming or beatings. Dad had just ruffled his hair, boarded a fishing boat, and never come home. No accident, no storm, no letter, just on at Port Clyde and off somewhere else.

So Mom had taken a second job, and Chris had started watching a lot of television. The old shows that ran in syndication after school, *Miami Vice, 21 Jump Street,* even *CHiPs*. After high school, he'd gone to the Maine Criminal Justice Academy, watching cop shows all the while. He loved *The Shield,* he loved *The Wire,* he even watched *CSI,* piece of shit that was. Chris was ready to be a world-weary lawman with a weapon on his hip. He wanted to catch bad guys. He wanted to work big cases, stare darkness in the face and not blink.

Problem was, he lived in Washington County, Maine. They didn't make cop shows about places like Washington County. Not unless you counted *Andy Griffith.*

He steered the cruiser with one hand, popped the last of his bologna sandwich in his mouth with the other, then brushed the crumbs off his uniform. Cherryfield Hardware slid past, and the owner stopped locking up long enough to raise a hand at him. Chris threw back a halfhearted salute.

He had feelers out all over the country, but it was your classic catch-22. Without having worked a high-crime area, he didn't have the qualifications to work a high-crime area. Which left him where?

"Fucked," Chris muttered. "Fucked, fucked, fucked."

"Say again?" his radio squawked.

Shit. He grabbed the radio, saw the button had stuck again. "Sorry about that, Doreen, my mic."

"I hear that language again, I'm going to wash your mouth out."

Chris grinned. "What? I said 'trucks.' "

"Yeah, trucked, trucked, trucked."

"Anything happening?"

"All quiet in our little corner of heaven."

"Spectacular," he said.

Maybe he needed to shake things up some. A tour in the army, he'd be able to write his ticket. It would mean dodging RPGs for a couple years. But that might be better than writing drunk tickets till his eyesight gave, or hanging at the Ten Pin, watching the same girls get older. Chasing jihadis might not be the same as chasing criminals, but it beat the hell out of the alternative.

They'd post him in Afghanistan or Iraq, of course. But what the hell. Get out, see the world. Hear a muezzin's call. Fire a fifty-caliber. Learn Arabic. Maybe even be an MP. Police work with military technology, ooh-rah. Not that he wanted to chase American soldiers, but he'd be after the ones who went crazy, the kind in the news stories, the ones who raped girls or killed innocent shopkeepers . . .

Chris Dundridge was halfway through his nightly tour of imaginary duty when he spotted the silver BMW parked at the Pines Motel.

EXT. ABBOT KINNEY STREET — EVENING
Loud POP MUSIC plays. *Architectural Digest* homes nestle next to ramshackle teardowns. Wet suits are draped over balcony railings.
A convertible rips down the street, turns at the corner.

INT. MADDY'S CONVERTIBLE — CONTINUOUS
The music is coming from MADDY SWEET's stereo. It cuts off midlyric as she pulls halfway into a parking spot and jumps out of the car. Her red hair flies behind her.

EXT. CANDY GIRLS HOUSE — CONTINUOUS
EMILY SWEET stands at the end of the porch, facing away.

MADDY (O.S.)
Em?

Emily stiffens, but doesn't turn. Maddy climbs, pauses, then walks behind her sister and puts a hand on her arm.

MADDY (CONT'D)
Talk to me.
EMILY
What do you want me to say?
MADDY
You could call Tara something that rhymes with "runt."

Emily snorts a laugh. She faces her sister.

EMILY
You heard, huh?
MADDY
Everybody heard, honey.
  (catches herself)
That's not what — I just mean that it —
EMILY
It's okay.
  (it's clearly not)

                    MADDY
Tara's never been concerned
about her karma.
                    EMILY
Not her. Jake. Why would he
tank my audition?
                    MADDY
It wasn't Jake. The director,
he and Tara . . .

Emily stares, understanding
dawning.

                    EMILY
Wow. And I thought a house had
landed on the Wicked Witch of
the West.
   (a beat)
Wait, how do you —
                    MADDY
Jake called. He's upset.
                    EMILY
So upset that he called *you*.
                    MADDY
Life is scary to some people.
                    EMILY
Then maybe they get what they
deserve.
   (shakes her head)
Life is scary to me too.

Doesn't mean I hide from it.
                    MADDY
He loves you.
                    EMILY
So why does he need you to
tell me?

Emily stalks off the porch.

                    MADDY
Wait —

Emily doesn't.

As Emily Sweet walked away and the credits
rolled, Daniel leaned back. His head
throbbed, a wicked headache coming on.

The show meant something. It had to.
Emily talking about life being scary, about
the need to face things — it was exactly
what he'd been wrestling with all day. Like
she could read his mind.

*Sure. You're getting messages from the
television. Tinfoil hat ready?*

It was just his subconscious. Desperate for
comfort, it was fixating on the first woman
he'd seen. A mother/whore thing, sweet Emily Sweet promising to save him, promising
to guide him. Daniel shook his head, then
regretted it as pain ice-picked him. He eased

51

himself flat, rubbed at his neck.

You're losing it, man. If you even had it to begin with.

Daniel closed his eyes and imagined Emily beside him, putting cool rags on his forehead, whispering in his ear, telling him that this would pass. That he was a good guy whose sins weren't worse than anyone else's. That he had nothing to fear.

That it was all going to be okay.

A silver BMW M5, with California plates.

Could it be? Could it be the same car?

Chris stared through the windshield, willing himself to remember. It had been in one of the Teletypes, he knew that much, came in a couple of days back. Doreen printed them all and put them in a wire basket in the break room, next to the coffee machine, the idea being that coppers could check them during downtime. Of course, no one but him did; after all, how many fugitives ended up in Washington County?

They got Teletypes from all over the country, and the details tended to blur, but this one he'd paid more attention to, coming as it had from the Los Angeles Sheriff's Department. Homicide, if he recalled right, though mostly he'd noticed the car, a sweet ride, BMW M5, silver. Just like the one parked here, sporting California plates.

What was the guy's name? It had had an upscale ring to it, he remembered. A little German or Dutch sounding, maybe. He'd know it if he heard it.

So call Doreen, have her dig out the Teletype and read you the info.

Yeah, and if he was wrong, endure a week of jokes, the others calling him Serpico, prank calls on the radio, no thanks. He could drive there himself and check it, but that meant half an hour to Machias, maybe twenty minutes if he ran on sirens the whole way, and likely find the guy gone.

You'd know the name if you heard it . . .

Chris grabbed his radio and climbed out of the cruiser. Northern darkness blanketed the world. He could see his breath as he walked for the door. It wasn't much of a lobby, but the Pines wasn't much of a motel. The desk was empty, and he rapped on it. "Hello?"

There was movement behind a beaded curtain, and a woman came out, her expression wary, the way he'd noticed a lot of people got when they saw a cop. "Yes? Help you?"

"I'm Deputy Chris Dundridge," he said. "Washington County Sheriffs."

She nodded.

"That BMW in the lot. Do you know who it belongs to?"

"What's this about?"

"Police business."

"Don't you need a warrant?"

"You don't want a dangerous guy staying here, do you?" He paused, then smiled, said, "Besides. No one needs to know you told me."

She hesitated, then said, "He checked in yesterday. Paid cash."

"What's his name?"

The clicking of keys. "Hayes. Daniel Hayes."

That was the name, Chris was sure of it. His blood sang. This was the lucky draw he'd been waiting for. Capturing a fugitive for the LASD would move his resume to the top of the pile. He forced himself to keep the joy off his face, nodded, said, "Room number?"

"Seven. But listen, I don't want —"

Chris ignored her, started down the hall, unsnapping his weapon as he went. His fingers tingled. The numbers on the doors ran upward, one, two, three. The floor was linoleum, scuffed from a thousand pairs of hunting boots. Should he call it in? Four, five, six. Regulations were clear, but he didn't want anyone else claiming credit.

Here it was, lucky number seven. The light was on under the door, and he could hear the TV faintly.

The man was in his room. No need for backup.

The ice machine rattled like a spoon grinding in a disposal. Daniel leaned on the button, watching cubes drop one at a time, the racket doing nothing for his headache. But half an hour with an ice cloth wrapped on his eyeballs should. Then grab a late supper, turn in, and tomorrow, make some decisions.

The machine grudgingly hawked up a handful of cubes at once. Good enough. He yanked open the heavy metal door and stepped back into the hallway. Cradling the ice bucket, he rounded the corner. Twenty feet away, someone stood at the door of his room. A cop, broad-shouldered and tough-looking.

Daniel froze. What was a cop doing here?

Before he could think of an answer, the guy took a deep breath and drew his gun, Jesus, *drew his gun,* and with the other fist pounded hard enough to rattle the door in its frame and yelled, "Police! Open up."

Daniel stood with one foot in the air and his mouth hanging open and his head pounding.

"Washington County Sheriffs. Open the door!"

And in his head, her voice, whispering. *They're coming for you.*

"Goddamnit," the cop yelled, "open this door, Daniel!"

At the sound of his name, his knees went wobbly and his hand slipped on the ice bucket. It spun as it fell to the floor, the cubes tumbling out, pinging against the linoleum, skittering silver marbles.

The deputy whirled at the sound. He was just a kid, maybe twenty-four, face pale and pupils wide. For a fraction of a heartbeat their eyes locked. Then the gun started to come up.

Fight-or-flight took over. Daniel turned, heart pumping fire. Planted one hand on the corner of the wall and pushed himself into a run.

"Freeze!"

Do what he says. What are you doing? Stop!

Only he didn't, he went faster, feet slamming into a sprint, headache buried under a surge of adrenaline. For some reason, he found himself thinking of the painting in the lobby. He hurled himself down the hallway. His hands hit the door bar and sent it flying open with a mule kick. Cold evening air that smelled of sap. Behind him, he heard pounding footsteps, and then a screeching sound and a curse. He risked a glance over his shoulder, saw the cop frozen midfall above the dropped ice, legs kicking cartoon circles.

Daniel ran.

Pine trees pressed against the brick wall, needles scratching at his hands and face. He blundered forward, dark shadow and darker ground, then burst around the edge of the building, half-expecting to find the whole police force, lights spinning and guns pointed, but there was just the one cruiser. He sprinted for the BMW, pinballing off the pickup next to it. Jammed a shaking hand in his front pocket, yanked out the keys too fast and lost his grip. He could hear the cop yelling again, not at him, calling for backup, saying words from television shows, *officer needs assistance,* and *all units,* and *suspect on foot,* all muffled as Daniel bent to scrape his fingers across the gravel, *come on, come on, the keys had to be* — there. He snagged them, beeped the alarm, piled in, and was slamming the stick into reverse as the cop came around the corner of the building. Daniel floored it, spinning the wheel hard, then threw it into first without braking. The car jerked to a stop and then surged forward, ten cylinders screaming. There was the crack of a gunshot behind him, holy *fuck,* then another, and ahead a narrow strip of grass with two pine trees and the sad roadside sign for the motel, and he swung away from the trees and clipped the sign, sparks and plastic bursting, block letters flying into the night, a scraping sound and a momentary feeling the car was going to get stuck, and then the tires bit blacktop and lurched and squealed and caught. US-1, two lousy lanes, his heart on fire, running like every frightened thing, the quiet, calm part of himself screaming, telling him to stop, asking him why, Jesus, why was he running?

Because he's chasing.

The BMW shredded the highway, up to 80 in seconds, the road a black ribbon. The nerves in his fingers and feet seemed to connect through the car to the road itself, like he was surfing the blacktop, flying over it, topping 110 now, and behind, far in the rearview, red and blue lights. He had a head start, but the cop was coming fast, others no doubt bearing down from all directions.

Think, goddamnit, think!

He tore around a curve, houses and garages and bridges and trees all blurring into a smear of late-night evergreen, darkness pressing down. Half a mile ahead, a narrow lane pulled off.

Any animal can run. It takes a man to think.

He bit his lip, clenched his fists, and turned off the headlights. Took his hand off the stick long enough to reach the settings knob for the onboard computer system. Twist, press, Options, twist, press, Lighting, twist, press, Disabled. The running lights and headlight halos snapped off. Night swooped down. Gripping the steering wheel with one hand, Daniel worked the clutch and downshifted into third gear. The engine screamed and bucked, the car actually hopping, rear tires skidding. He almost hit the brakes by instinct, stopped himself just in time. The car swerved wildly, but he kept it on the road, forced it into second, the needle plummeting, down to twenty by the time he hit the lane. He spun hard right. The car slewed sideways, the tires leaving the ground.

The world ahead of him was geometries of darkness: triangles for trees, a rectangle that might be a barn. He desperately wanted to turn on the headlights, but didn't, just forced it into first gear and took a chance, aiming at the maybe-barn. The side of the building was fifteen feet away when he jerked the parking brake. The BMW hopped and groaned and shuddered to a stop.

In the fallen silence his heartbeat was impossibly loud. His hands didn't shake, they vibrated. He took them off the wheel, knit the fingers together as though he were praying. Holy fuck. Holy fuck. Holy fu—

The cop blew by on US-1, a frenzied fury of blue and red and Dopplering siren, big as the world and then gone.

Daniel's breath came ragged. He clenched his fists together till the knuckles creaked. Jesus. Why had he run?

More important, why was he chasing you?

Who are you? Who were *you* before you woke up on that beach?

He sat for a moment, as long as he could make himself. Then he turned on his headlights, put the car in gear, and pulled back out onto the road. Outside the windows, the silhouettes of pines loomed, shaggy forms cut from a cloth of stars. Despite the punishment, the BMW seemed okay.

The cop hadn't doubled back yet, but he would. Time to get off this road. Daniel turned at the next intersection that looked like it might go somewhere. Out here, the police wouldn't have many resources — no helicopters, no roadblocks. The key was to get some distance without blundering into them.

He punched up the onboard navigation system, zoomed out on the map. *How come I know how to do this, how to turn off my running lights, but I don't remember* — later. He scanned the map, eyes flickering between it and the road. If he went north instead of west, he could pick up US-9, ride that up to I-95. With a little luck, he could clear the state in four, five hours.

The gun. He'd left the Glock in the hotel. *Want to go back for it?*

He pushed down on the accelerator.

An hour and a half later, Bangor was a glow on the horizon. A sign welcomed him, announced that the population was 31,473; another pointed toward Bangor International Airport. Following the arrow, he found himself in a stretch of low-slung chain hotels, an Econo Lodge, a Howard Johnson, a Ramada. They had the look of places people came to hang themselves. He picked the HoJo at random, pulled around back. The parking lot was only a third full.

His breath was fog. A plane took off half a mile away, the roar loud, red and green wing lights passing overhead as Daniel squatted behind a minivan with a bumper sticker announcing the owner's kid was an honor student at Hermon High. He fanned out the keys on his ring, chose the slenderest one, and fit it into the first screw.

The cold stiffened his fingers and made him curse, and by the time he was done, he wasn't sure the key would be much use as a key. But it did okay to attach the Maine plates to his BMW.

He had a pang of guilt but pushed it down. *You might need to do worse than steal some license plates. Better get used to that idea.*

Boston was about 250 miles. From there he could head west. No choice now. No explaining his condition and throwing himself on the mercy of the police. The only thing left to do was go to a place that scared the hell out of him.

Home.

When her alarm went off, Sophie Zeigler was in her kitchen, drinking coffee and chatting with Mick Jagger like the old friends they were. Not that she knew him personally, but in her flowers-in-your-hair days she'd seen Mick and the boys play a dozen times, and her only lesbian experience had been scored by *Beggars Banquet,* so "old friend" seemed as appropriate a term as any. In the dream, Sophie had leaned over to refill her mug, and when she'd turned back, Mick had unzipped his leather pants and was peeing in her sink. He looked sheepish but didn't stop, and she was thinking how this was the kind of stunt that turned singers into rock stars, and how tiresome it must be to maintain. It was one thing to be twenty-five and beautiful as you hurled a TV out the window of the Chateau Marmont, but once your pubes were curling gray, it was time to call a halt.

Then the drumming of his urine against the stainless steel sink became the droning buzz of the alarm, and the dream evaporated, the aroma of coffee seeming to float in its wake. She slapped the clock to silence. What a weird way to start the day. Everything she was dealing with, and *this* was what her subconscious had for her? Dreams about Mick Jagger's sagging testicles, and memories of clumsy girl-gropings almost forty years gone?

Sophie swung her legs out of bed, rubbed sleep from her eyes. Padded to the window and pulled open the curtains. Early sunlight bathed her garden and the green square of her lawn. Some people griped about L.A. not having seasons, but there were two: "gorgeous" and "absolutely freaking gorgeous."

On a mat at the foot of her bed, she worked through a quick yoga routine. A couple of sun salutations, down-dog into cobra, just to limber up, build some heat. Caught her body in the mirror as she stretched, and smiled. People talked about sixty being the new fifty, but she was shooting for forty-five. In the bathroom, she brushed her teeth while the water warmed up, then slipped out of her panties, kicked them into the hamper, and got in the shower.

God, that felt good. She turned, tilted her head to wash her hair. Okay, so. A long day. She was still dealing with the sheriff's department, trying to maintain a stone wall that got weaker every day. Plus there was her more traditional work. Today she had lunch with a client, a rapper-turned-action-star who released records as Too G, but whose real name was Tudy, and who called his maid to squash spiders. That would be followed by the day's main event, a "friendly chat" at Universal, which had somehow gotten Don Cheadle interested in the script already promised to Tudy. The tricky part was that they hadn't signed papers with her client yet — blaming that on their lawyers, Hollywood Stall Tactic #514 — so technically she didn't have much to work with. And of course, Cheadle was a truly remarkable actor, while Tudy was . . . well, a rap star. But the Universal VP owed her. So, she thought as she turned off the water and pulled open the curtain, if she could remind him of that without overplaying —

There was a stranger leaning against her sink.

Sophie staggered back, fumbling for the wall, her thoughts scattering in different directions, processing the fact that she didn't know the man, that he must have broken in, that she was naked and dripping, that he had something shiny and metal tucked into the front of his pants. Her hand slapped the shower tile, slipped, caught.

"Do me a favor," the man said, "and don't scream, okay, sister?"

Bennett smiled at the woman as she clawed at the wall for balance, her eyes going wide, breath gasping in. "Sophie. Really. Don't."

Her mouth fish-gawped, and he could see her thinking about screaming anyway, knowing she could get a shout off before he could stop her. Then, as her rational mind came into it, realizing that he knew her name, that this wasn't a random break-in. That he had an agenda.

Which was the moment fear really bloodied its claws.

"So," Bennett said conversationally, "I was involved in this thing in Chicago that went badly." He kept his eyes on hers, didn't give her a second to look away. "I know. Who cares, right? Reason I bring it up is simple. My back is to the wall here. And since you spend a lot of time negotiating, I thought I'd make sure you understood that. You know what it means when someone's back is to the wall?"

Bennett had broken in an hour ago and had stood watching her sleep, the rise and fall of her chest, the way her lips were slightly parted. He'd thought about sitting at the end of her bed and waiting for her to wake up, but he wanted her clearheaded as well as vulnerable, so instead he'd gone into the kitchen, made a cup of coffee, and sat at her breakfast nook drinking it and waiting for her to get in the shower. It was all about theater in his line of work.

"Sophie? Do you know what that means?"

Her chin quivered, and it took her a moment to find her voice. "It means all options are on the table."

"Close." He rubbed his hands together so that she could see the white surgical gloves he wore. Her eyes shivered with images of blood and gleaming steel knives. "It means there are no constraints. Do you see the difference?"

She swallowed, nodded slowly. Her arms had settled at her sides, which he liked. Only very stupid people worried about modesty when he came calling. "I understand."

"Good." He pulled a towel off the bar, held it out to her. Basic technique to establish a power dynamic, kick a dog and then scratch his ears. Alpha had control; beta gratefully accepted what was given.

She hesitated. If someone had tried this in the boardroom, no doubt she would have fed them their teeth. *But you aren't in the boardroom, sister.*

Sophie took the towel, wrapped it around herself.

"Now. I'm going to ask some questions. The smartest thing you can do is answer me. You do that, I won't hurt you. You've got my word." He gave her his best schoolboy smile.

"Okay."

"Where is Daniel Hayes?"

Her mouth fell open again. "This is — I don't understand."

"Daniel Hayes. Your client and friend, the one you half adopted when he was still living in a tower at Park LaBrea. Five-eleven, one eighty, likes piña coladas and walks in the rain?"

"Is he okay? What did you do to him?"

Bennett paused, stared for a long time. Then he said, quietly, "You know, you're still a beautiful woman, Sophie."

Her knees almost gave, and a whimpering sound came from deep in her throat. "I don't know where Daniel is. I haven't spoken to him since he left."

"When did you last talk to him?"

"About a week ago."

"What did you talk about?"

"I can't discuss it."

Bennett laughed, honestly delighted. "Really?"

"It's confidential."

"Attorney-client privilege?"

"Well, technically —"

"Let's try again." He slid the Colt from his waistband. "What did Hayes say when he called you?"

She hesitated a moment, then said, "He was drunk. Crying. He sounded terrible."

"I would imagine. What did he say?"

"Nothing that made any sense." For the first time, she broke eye contact. "That he was sorry."

"He say what for?"

"No. Just that it was his fault, he was so sorry. He was slurring a lot, not making any sense."

"Who does he know in Maine?"

"What?"

"Daniel. Maine. Who does he know?"

"I — I don't know. No one."

"Where is he hiding?"

"I don't know. What do you want with him anyway?"

"Do you watch a lot of movies, Sophie?"

"What?"

"I know you represent actors, directors, so you must. You know the scenes where the hero is trying not to tell the bad guys something? Mel Gibson kind of shit? Everyone likes to think that if it was them, they'd hold out. Dig deep, clench their jaw, not say a word. But here's the thing." Bennett leaned forward. "Pain sucks. It sucks worse than you can imagine. It becomes your whole world." He tapped the pistol against his thigh. "I don't enjoy it. But believe me, when pain is involved, real pain? No one holds out."

An effective performance, judging by her reaction. He could see her wondering how he would hurt her, whether it would be rape or something worse. Wondering what she would be afterward, if there was an afterward; all those years of independence wiped away, her freedom caged, loves tainted, triumphs turned to ash. Sixty-one years old and abruptly broken. A victim.

Remember, sister. This isn't the boardroom.

"I-I don't know anyone in Maine."

"Think hard."

"I *am*. I don't know anyone. I don't think Daniel does either."

"Family, friends?"

"No."

"Then why is he there?"

"I — Is he?"

Try something new. "What about the necklace?"

"What necklace?"

"I know you have it. Where is it?" Chances were she didn't, of course, but no need for her to know that.

"What?" The panic was back. "I don't — I swear — I don't have any idea what you're talking about."

Damn. She was telling the truth. There were all kinds of tics when someone was lying. But her blinking was controlled, the emotions in her eyes and mouth matched, she was using contractions. She'd been thrown by the changes in subject, when liars usually embraced them. He'd bet on it: Sophie didn't know where Bennett's payment was, or where he could find Daniel Hayes.

Damn it.

He could always ask more aggressively. But it was risky after the mess in Chicago. That had been a dangerous play from the beginning, but no one could have anticipated the way it would fall apart, the four fucking amateurs getting in the middle of what should have been a clean job. Worse, given the nature of the product, he'd found himself burned completely. A lifetime of staying off the radar wiped away in a week. And not just cops. Homeland Security. They'd have fingerprints, DNA, brass from his old Smith and Wesson, who knew what else.

Which meant that any screwup, any screwup at all, and he was done. Not maximum security done. Not even federal prison done. Twenty-three hours in solitary done. SuperMax done. Hell, maybe Guantánamo Bay done.

Does she know anything worth taking that risk?

His gut told him no. Still, no harm in pushing a little. "You're not helping me," he said, soft and low.

Her hands fluttered at her sides. "I can't tell you what I don't know."

"What can you tell me?"

"The same thing I told the sheriffs. That I love Daniel, but that I don't know why he left or where he is. He called me, I told him I'd be right over, but when I got there, he was gone. Since then I've dialed his cell phone a million times. I've e-mailed him. I've called all our friends. I've talked to the cops. No one knows where he is. You say he's in Maine? That's news to me. I believe you when you say that you'll hurt me" —

her voice catching for just a second — "but it won't make any difference. Because I don't fucking know where he fucking is."

Bennett was coming to like her. Not many people had the stones to talk that way in a situation like this. "Did you tell the police about the phone call?"

"I told them that he called."

"But not what he said."

"No."

"Why not?"

She opened her mouth, closed it. "Because he's my friend."

Hm. "Last question, Counselor." He kept her pinned with his eyes. "If you did know where he was, would you tell me?"

She paused a long moment before answering. "Yes." Sophie pushed her shoulders back. "But not until I couldn't not."

Well, well. We have an honest-to-god human being here. He was almost glad she didn't know anything. Always a shame to break something lovely. "Tough girl." He straightened, tucked the gun back into his pants. "Smart one, too. Since you're so smart, I don't need the speech about not calling the police, right, sister?"

"No. I won't. I promise."

"Good." He started for the door, then stopped, unable to help himself. "And,

Sophie?"

Her breath caught in her throat. Her hair was wet, and the outline of her body marked the towel. She was trembling. Wondering, he could see, if he had changed his mind. If he was going to shoot her, or worse.

"I like your style. I ever need a lawyer, can I give you a call?"

She stared at him, and he laughed, then walked out, back through her house and into bright morning sunshine. He was maybe ten steps out the door when he heard a faint snap behind him, the sound of her locking the deadbolt.

Fifty bucks says she's dialing 911 right now.

Good for her. He did love predictable people.

Daniel was in a concrete canyon.

Water trickled. The bleeding sun stained everything crimson. Ahead was a tunnel, tall and broad. The mouth of it was perfect black shadow, but he knew that something waited there. Waited and watched.

Something terrible.

He turned, but he was alone this time. No lounging vision of Emily Sweet. Her absence made the whole world emptier.

From the darkness of the tunnel, a faint rasping. A movement sound, but indistinct and wrong, like snakes squirming across one another in dark pits, like the slow inhale of some huge beast. His fear was childlike in its perfection. It seized him completely. He wanted to run. Told himself to run. To turn and flee, feet splashing through the trickle of water in this lost basin.

Instead he took a tentative step forward.

I don't want to. Please don't go in there,

don't, stop . . .

He took another step forward. His hands were heavy.

The rasping again. His skin was too tight for his bones. His breath came fast.

Run! Don't go in there, don't go in there, don'tgointhere —

Something moved in the darkness of the tunnel. A shape his eyes couldn't fix, a swirling. Madness made physical.

Runrunrunrunru—

The darkness leapt at him. He threw himself back, arms and legs flailing, foot cracking into the side window of the BMW hard enough to set off the car alarm. A screaming horn yanked him upright, eyes wide, heart slamming against his ribs, hands, fists, and armpits sweaty as he stared around, placed himself, the car, the backseat of the car with the alarm going off, the cacophony hideous, the alarm screaming *look at me look at me look at me* until he fumbled for his keys, finally found them, stabbed the button. The horn died midhonk.

"Fuck," he said, gasping. "Fuck me." Sunlight pounded in the windows, and his skin was sticky. He flopped back against the seat.

Sleep was becoming more trouble than it

was worth. What were these dreams, this feeling of a terrible looming danger? Was it just his subconscious painting a picture of his situation? Electrical signals bouncing around the inside of his very confused brain? Or did it mean more than that?

Something must have caused all of this. Something set him in motion. No matter who he had been, he couldn't believe he just woke up one morning and decided to drive across the country to drown himself.

He closed his eyes, tried to concentrate on the world he'd just left. He remembered a tunnel and an abandoned place. A darkness that loomed. But the details were melting away even as he tried to hold them. He could invent reasons for being there, but that's all they were, inventions, and he couldn't be more certain of them than of anything else.

Maybe I did something horrible. Maybe that's why I don't want to go back.

Daniel rubbed at his eyes, listened to the settling beat of his heart. He'd made some distance last night, all the way from rural Maine to rural New York, long blank stretches of night country briefly broken by shimmering cities. Somewhere east of Buffalo his chin had hit his chest for a second time, and so he'd pulled off into this hideous parking lot of a KOA campground. RVs hunched on concrete pads, electrical cords trailing to junction boxes. Amazing how ugly much of the country was.

We had the whole wide world, and the best we could come up with was McDonald's and miniature golf.

He sat up, pushed open the car door, and went in search of the bathrooms.

Back on the road, he kept to the speed limit. Daniel figured he was safe so long as he avoided notice. He'd swapped plates again last night, trading the stolen Maine plates for freshly stolen New York ones. And the cops couldn't stop every BMW on the road. He should be safe.

Simple as that, huh? So let me ask you, genius. You woke up without your memory once. What if it happens again?

Shit.

Shit.

Another thing. Money. His remaining cash wouldn't even cover gas to Los Angeles. Plus he had a thing about eating, wanted to keep doing it.

Okay, well, so. No one said it would be easy. He'd have to be smart.

He spent the day sliding down the spine of Lake Erie, then across the flat, bland plains of Ohio into Indiana. Somewhere outside South Bend, as the sky began to sadden, he left the highway for a grungy strip of retailers, car dealerships, and gas stations. There was a drugstore beside an Applebee's. Daniel bought himself a school-lined notebook and a pack of pens, then went next door. Bypassed the chipper teenage hostess and took a seat at the bar, a gaudy mess of Christmas lights and televisions tuned to sports. A guy who looked like he'd sampled a few too many appetizers took his order.

"A" — flipping through the menu — "steakhouse burger with everything. Rare." Saying it with confidence this time.

"Something to drink?"

Daniel stared at the taps. God, a beer would be good. Money, though. He should save — "Yeah, gimme a tall Sam Adams."

He uncapped the pen. How to start?

Simple. Start with what you were trying to say. That was the secret to writing. Daniel bent over the page:

Hi.
Your name is Daniel Hayes. At least, you think it is. That's the name you found on the insurance card of a BMW that saved your life. And in case you haven't yet guessed, I'm you.

Let me back up. This starts with you waking on a beach in Maine, naked and very, very cold . . .

His burger arrived, and he ate one-handed, not noticing the taste, getting lost in the process of telling his story so far. He'd only intended the journal in case his memory went on the fritz again, but as he wrote, he found that he was enjoying himself. There was a strange pleasure in stringing sentences together, in trying to evoke the scene as fully as possible with the fewest number of words. Something trance-like about it, and therapeutic, too —

"You look familiar."

Daniel blinked, looked up. The woman sitting next to him had a white blouse and real estate agent hair. He hadn't noticed her arrival, wondered how long she'd been sitting there. "I do?"

"Yeah. I can't put my finger on why, though."

"Me either."

"Maybe you just have one of those faces." She reached into her purse, pulled out a pack of Parliaments. "You mind?"

"Nope."

"Want one?" She held the pack out.

Huh. Do I smoke? "Thanks." The cigarette

felt natural between his fingers. She cupped a match and he leaned into it, then took a deep drag.

His throat caught fire. A thick wave of smoke bellowed out of his mouth. His eyes teared as he coughed and struggled not to gag.

Apparently not.

Massive steel mills blasted flame into the night like something out of *Blade Runner*. Gary, Indiana, Chicago's reeking stepson — cracked earth fronting twisted mazes of pipes and smokestacks. One of them had a Christmas tree on top.

Nothing quite as festive as toxic waste.

Farther west, the south suburbs of Chicago were a blur of strip malls and big-box signs. Modern constellations; instead of gods and heroes, his sky was filled with Home Depot and Best Buy. The clock told him it was after midnight, though his own time sense had gotten skewed. Had it been less than twenty-four hours since the cop hammered on his door, bellowed his name with weapon drawn?

Speaking of which. How about you stop dodging the subject?

During the safety of daylight, he'd concentrated on not thinking. Every time questions had crowded his mind, he'd forced them out by concentrating on practicalities. But now, hemmed in by darkness, he had nowhere to hide.

The Glock, for example. It was one thing to tell himself that lots of people owned handguns, that there was no reason to feel strange about the fact that he knew how to hold one, how to handle it. That it smelled of smoke because he'd taken it to the range. But a uniformed sheriff banging on his door made that harder to believe.

The amnesia, too. Or fugue, or lapse, or whatever he called it. He could call it Roy if he liked, didn't change the facts. It had to come from something. Maybe he was right and Roy sprang from the trauma of his suicide swim. But maybe not. Maybe Roy was a bomb in his head. A brain tumor, for example.

And if that was true, it could have an impact on everything else. Including his personality — or what he thought was his personality. Daniel rolled down the window, let cold air rush in. Took deep breaths.

Really, all of the questions come down to one.

Who are you when you don't remember who you are?

He didn't feel like a bad man. Didn't have

murder in his heart, hadn't wanted to jump the sheriff, or sideswipe the cars that cut him off. Even if he hadn't left the Glock in Maine, the thought of holding it on a clerk and demanding the cash in the register turned his stomach.

And yet the cops were after him for something. It wasn't a mistake. They knew his name, they knew his car, and they had come at him with guns drawn.

What if you were a bad man? A criminal, a killer? Are you that person still?

It was a haunting thought. Part of the point of life was that you looked around, you made choices, and those choices had consequences. Rotten consequences were fair because you had made the choice that got you there. Walk out on your kids, you don't get to complain about gut-deep loneliness on Christmas morning. Tell off your boss, no whining that the promotion goes to someone else. Do murder, and you burn. Maybe not in hell — he didn't feel particularly religious — but in life. Prison, yes, but beyond that, a shadow thrown over every day to come, a separation from every other person.

But this. To just wake up, bang, eyes open, and discover that everything was wrong. That he was suicidal and wanted by the

83

police and maybe a monster, and to have had no choice in the matter.

If the person I was before did something wrong, do I have to pay the price?

And just how high is it going to be?

Daniel hocked the Rolex at a pawnshop west of Des Moines. He hated to do it but couldn't see another way. Maybe in the past he'd robbed liquor stores — hell, maybe he'd killed presidents — but best he could remember, he wasn't that guy, and he didn't want to be.

Perhaps the answer to the question of who you were when you couldn't remember was simple: whoever you chose.

The man behind the counter offered him $325. Daniel countered with $7,500, half the retail price. Where they settled was nothing like the middle, but the man paid cash, a thick stack of worn bills. Daniel celebrated with breakfast at a truck stop and discovered that chicken-fried steak tasted way better than it had any right to.

Iowa in morning light. Sky a pale blue bowl and air just the crisp side of cold. Interstate 80, still. Still flat, still straight, still mind-numbing. Farmland sprawled on either side of the road. Corn, he thought.

Or wheat. Barley. How the hell should he know?

Man, but the country was big. Things were getting bleary. Too much world, and nothing for context. No family to think of, no home to remember. Nothing to do but count the electrical towers looming like metal monsters, Dali animals come to life. The radio was all preachers and country music and one lonely station of teenage pop-tarts with nothing to peddle but firm thighs and the dream of a youth he couldn't recall.

He imagined Emily Sweet in the seat next to him. The window open and her hair whipping in the breeze and that quirky crooked smile on her face. Neither of them talking, just comfortably passing the miles.

Nebraska. More corn.

He passed the time telling stories about people in other cars. The faded Saab was driven by a middle-aged sociology professor; though the love was gone from her marriage, they were staying together for the kids and had settled into the comfortable camaraderie of soldiers on a long campaign. But this morning she had steeled herself against the hurt in her husband's eyes, made a long-distance phone call and a flimsy excuse, and flown westward wild and free, head full of the doctor of Romance languages who was waiting at the North Platte Best Western, a man with thinning hair and an unfortunate chin but eyes that were soft and kind and long fingers that would bite into her skin as he muttered French syllables she couldn't define but understood perfectly.

Choreographing their affair — the professor's husband, it turned out, was not so passionless as she imagined, and would spend tonight pacing, trying not to wake the kids as he sucked a bottle of scotch and planned ways to win her back; only, her Frenchman too was smitten with her, wanted more than an affair, and would follow her east, which brought all of them into a nicely orchestrated conflict on the lawn of their suburban home — carried him into Colorado and the afternoon.

Time to check your head.

Last night he'd wondered if maybe there was something physically wrong with him. It was an uncomfortable thought even in his present state, when discomfort was pretty much the status quo. To think that something might be growing in his head, that some biochemical quirk was the cause of all his present troubles, and that it could happen again, well, it didn't settle the nerves. And yet, he couldn't exactly go to a hospital. No ID, no insurance, not enough money, the cops looking for him — no.

He pulled into the outskirts of Denver around four. The Rockies were just a ghost on the horizon, a blur highlighted by the lowering sun. He stopped at a gas station, filled the tank, bought some jerky and a Diet Coke he could have parked a Jet Ski in. In the hallway by the bathrooms, he used the Yellow Pages chained to the pay phones to find what he was looking for. A three-foot map pinned behind plastic laid the city out. He sipped his soda, found the address, and traced a route with his finger.

The shopping mall, like most of the city, was long and low, huddling beneath the dome of the sky. There was an organic food market, a sushi place, an Aveda salon. At the end, a pale blue sign read CLEAR IMAGE OPEN MRI.

The ad in the phone book had listed the hours as 8 A.M. to 6 P.M. Daniel parked, killed the engine, and tucked a wad of jerky in his mouth.

Early darkness had fallen by the time people started trickling out of the clinic. The patients were gone by five-thirty. The doctors followed hard on their heels, well-dressed men and women heading for expensive cars. At six o'clock, a couple of receptionists in blue scrubs strolled out chatting. Daniel watched carefully, hoping he hadn't been wrong, but neither of them stopped to lock up.

When he pulled open the heavy glass door, a bell dinged somewhere to announce his arrival. Daniel rocked from foot to foot, glancing around the waiting room — comfortable chairs, abstract art, *Esquire, InStyle,* and *Vanity Fair* — and ran through the script he'd written for himself.

"Sorry, we're closed." The man behind the desk had appeared from nowhere. He wore white scrubs, as Daniel had hoped.

He didn't say "Sorry, sir." Take that into account. Go fraternal. "I know."

The guy glanced at his watch. "If you want to make an appointment —"

"This is going to sound weird." He played the pause. The last days had given him the physical appearance he needed, deep pits under his eyes and an air of haggard weariness. "You mind if I ask, is your father still alive?"

The buzzing of the overhead lights seemed loud. "No," the man said, finally. "Lost him three years ago."

"Mine died last week."

"I'm sorry."

"Thanks." He moved to the counter,

leaned on it. "A brain tumor. There was a Latin name for it, but I never wanted to know. That would have made it too real. Not that it mattered in the end." The hallway leading past the desk was dark. "My dad, he was . . . he was the strongest guy I knew. But this thing, it was like he was possessed. It took his memory, messed with his senses, took his speech." Without meaning to, he choked back a sob, and as he did, he realized that he was actually feeling the emotions he was describing. Was he just mourning the memories that had vanished? Or did those memories hold a sorrow he hadn't suspected? "It was awful."

"I can imagine."

"The doctor said that the tumor, it wasn't hereditary."

"Most aren't, no." The guy seeing where he was going. "You should talk to your doctor, but —"

"I did. He told me not to worry. That just because my dad had it didn't mean I would. Thing is, I can't stop. I mean, that's my biggest fear. Losing control like that. Scares the hell out of me."

The tech glanced at his watch. "Listen, I really am sorry —"

"Hear me out, okay? I asked my doctor if he would run a scan for it, and he said no.

89

Said he wouldn't write a prescription because there was no medical need. And I get it" — raising his hands — "I do. I understand that no way do I have the same thing. But I can't stop thinking about it, you know? I haven't slept in days. It's killing me, the fear that there's something in my head right now."

"You could ask another doctor —"

"It would take me a week to get an appointment. And he might say no. Listen. I just need the peace of mind. You lost your dad. You know what I'm talking about."

The guy hesitated. "I don't know . . ."

"I'll pay you five hundred dollars." Daniel pulled the money from his jeans. "Please. I'm going crazy here."

The man bit his lip. Looked down the hall. Checked his watch again.

"Please?"

"If anyone found out —"

"How? I won't tell, and I don't need the film, or whatever it is. I just want someone to look and tell me I'm okay."

"I'm not a doctor."

"The doctor's the guy who makes bank for having his name on the door. But you probably do a dozen of these a day, right?"

"More."

"Please. You'd really be doing me a favor."

He set the money on the counter.

The tech looked at it. Took a deep breath, then a step forward. "Come around that door over there."

Ten minutes later, he was wearing a hospital gown — *no metal,* the tech, whose name had turned out to be Mike, had said; *this thing is basically one big magnet* — and lying on a table in a device that looked like something out of *Star Trek.* He'd imagined a torpedo tube, but this was much nicer. He was sandwiched between two broad cylinders, and the open peripheral vision was comforting. He had his eyes closed and was concentrating on lying as still as he could, trying not to pay attention to the loud clanking and banging, and most of all, trying not to think about what Mike might find.

On the other hand, if he finds something, you've got an answer. If not, you're just nuts.

It was a long half hour.

Finally, Mike's voice came through a speaker. "Okay, I'm gonna bring you out." The tray Daniel lay on slid smoothly, and then he was staring at ceiling tile, aware again of the draft running under the thin gown.

He sat up slowly, blinked. "What's the word?"

91

Mike stood at the door to the room, holding it open with one hand. "I'm sorry to tell you this . . ."

Oh shit . . .

". . . but you're perfectly fine."

Daniel exhaled. "That's not funny, man."

"Sorry. But you knew that, right?"

"You're sure?"

"Come look."

Daniel hopped off the table, followed the tech into the next room. It was dim, and dominated by a broad monitor. The screen was split into quadrants, each showing a black-and-white image.

"I'm not printing anything out, if you don't mind."

"Sure."

The man punched a button, and the monitor switched to a single image, an amoeba of black-and-white. The shape shifted and grew, morphed into the rough shape of a human skull, the cauliflower coils of the brain showing up in high contrast. As Mike pressed keys, the frame jumped, showing, Daniel assumed, different cutouts.

"I don't really know what I'm looking for."

"Abnormalities."

"Unless it's a little cartoon bomb with a lit fuse, I'm not sure I'd see it."

"There's nothing there. The scan is normal."

"You're sure?"

"Man, you want to see a doc, up to you, but this is your brain, and there ain't nothing wrong with it." The tech turned, looked up at him. "Physically, at least."

"Yeah."

"Now, I'm sorry, but . . ."

"Right." Daniel pulled the money out, passed it over. "Thanks."

Back in the changing room, he took off the gown, put on his jeans and undershirt. Trying not to think.

Mike walked him to the door. "You okay?"

"Yeah, I just —" He shrugged. "I started to believe."

"Well, be happy, my man. All's well."

Daniel nodded, stepped out.

"Oh, and hey. I'm sorry about your dad."

"Thanks," he said, and walked through the dark parking lot to his car. Feeling rotten for the lie, but worse for the truth. He was fine, physically, and that should have been a relief.

The problem was, something had made him take this trip the other direction. Judging by the empty blister packs of ephedrine, he might have made the whole damn distance in one brain-rattling sprint, chewing the bitter tabs so they'd kick in faster, washing them down with Jack Daniel's and gas station coffee. The lines in the road blurring solid, trees a green wall, "reality" less dependable with every exhausted moment. A mad dash into the eastern sky.

Which does beg the question: If it's not physical, what is it?

What would make someone run that hard, that fast?

The chunk of shiny pink flesh slipped from his grip and splashed dark fluid all over the table.

Bennett shook his head and gave up on the chopsticks. Stupid invention. Snagging the salmon between thumb and forefinger, he dunked it in the soy again and popped it in his mouth, closing his eyes to savor the way the fatty fish melted as he chewed. He followed it with a sip of sake, gone lukewarm now. When he wiped his fingers, he smeared prints on the linen napkin.

The taste of fall was in the air, but the afternoon was still warm enough to sit on the patio of Takami, twenty-one stories above the stark clatter of downtown L.A. The small outdoor area was packed, mostly men and women in sharp suits and pricy watches. He leaned back, took in the buzz of conversation.

". . . market is overextended. I'm telling

you, we're headed for a double-dip, and that's if we're *lucky . . .*"

". . . it's yoga, but you do it at 105 degrees. Thing is, you're sweating a lot, and then bending over and spreading your legs, and, well . . .*"

". . . shot one pilot, now she thinks she's Jennifer Freaking Aniston . . .*"

". . . the problem with looking for your glasses is that you don't have your glasses on while you're looking . . ."

". . . you know they're sleeping together. Which is so stupid. How does *that* work? I mean, she has everything, and yet . . ."

It was funny how noisy the world was if you listened. So many sounds the human brain filtered out. Talk was the water people swam through, constant, crucial, and un-noticed. There were so many things you could learn if you just listened.

Everybody had multiple identities. They were different people alone than with friends, different with friends than with family. There was the part of them that sinned, that did things they knew were shameful; and then there was the part of them that judged that same behavior in others. The loving wife who had an affair was two people. One of them was carefully constructed. The other was an animal howl.

One feared the chaos of night; the other was desperate to believe the world was hers to light aflame.

That's how it worked. She could be honestly devoted to husband and children, because the woman getting plowed in a motel room was a different person.

People liked to pretend that wasn't true, and that was how he made his living.

"Can I get you anything else, sir? Maybe some green-tea ice cream?"

Bennett shook his head. "Just the check." He pulled his cell phone from his pocket, dialed the Los Angeles Sheriff's Department number from memory, then punched an extension.

When the man answered, Bennett said, "Do you know who this is?"

There was a long pause, and then the man said, "Yes."

"You don't sound happy to hear from me."

"Fuck off."

Bennett smiled. "Well, brother, you've got brevity on your side. I need you to look something up for me."

"And I need a blowjob from —"

"Do you really want to go down that road?"

"The statute of limitations is up."

"Maybe legally."

97

There was another pause, then, "What do you want?"

"I need an inventory manifest from a crime scene."

"Which one?"

Bennett told him. Then he started counting backward in his head. *Five, four, three, two . . .*

"Were you involved?"

"Not personally. This is a favor for a friend."

"You don't have friends, Bennett. You're a cockroach, crawling in and out of everybody's dark places."

"Very poetic. I'll wait." The waitress brought the check, and he nodded to her. He laid down cash enough to cover the tab and 18 percent — leave 10 percent or 30 and you might be remembered — then put his foot up on the opposite chair and enjoyed the view.

"I give you this, we're through."

"Okay."

"I mean it. Don't call me again."

"You got my word."

"Owner's manual. Canvas shopping bags. Jumper cables. GPS. *Zagat's,* Los Angeles, 2007 edition. Sunglasses. Pepper spray. Lipstick. Mascara. Hand lotion."

"That's it?"

"Yes."

"Nothing else."

"No."

"And no purse?"

"Did I fucking say purse? No? So then there wasn't a fucking —"

Bennett hung up. He tucked the phone away, then stood and pushed in his chair. The sound of conversation was replaced by music as he stepped inside the restaurant, some lyricless lounge crap. A pretty hostess thanked him for coming.

He pressed the button for the elevator, rocked back on his heels.

It's still out there.

Let's go look for it.

It wasn't the most expensive block of Malibu real estate. Not even close, really, considering the wealth concentrated in this little section of heaven half an hour west of Los Angeles. But that was a relative way of looking at things. The house, modern and bright, hidden behind a security fence, cost more than something ten times the size in the parts of the country where Belinda Nichols had grown up.

She was parked down the block, sitting in the back of a van she'd bought the day before. The classified ad had described it perfectly: "1995 Dodge Caravan, solid not pretty, $2200/obo." She'd offered $1500, not because she cared about the money but because not haggling would have made her more memorable. They'd settled on $1800; Belinda had counted bills into his hand, he'd passed her the keys, and voilà, she was the proud owner of a piece of shit. "Not pretty" was an understatement; the thing had been used hard, the exterior a dull white except for the crumpled side where a collision had banged the metal inward and left long tears of naked steel glinting through.

She'd bought it as a disposable home, a place to work out of while she settled things. Her main concern had been utility, a place for a sleeping bag so she didn't leave a trail of hotel records. But the P.O.S. was turning out to be a perfect cover. It would have looked out of place in Malibu, except that all these beautiful, expensive homes needed someone to clean them, to care for their landscaping and maintain their pools. The private security firm that covered the area had twice passed while she'd been parked here, and hadn't touched the brakes on either occasion.

Her stomach was tight, her nerves raw, but she made herself sit still, stare out the windshield. Taking time to check things out, to make sure that she wasn't forgetting anything. The importance of preparation was something Bennett had taught her. He was a monster, but he was good at what he did, and there was a lot she could learn from him.

A battered pickup with a yard crew rolled by, Hispanic dudes in the back balancing among lawn mowers and leaf blowers. Four minutes later, someone's security gate opened, and a Saab pulled out, driven by a woman talking on a cell phone. A bit after that, a nanny pushed a stroller up the block. Everything was quiet. No sign of the police.

Flipping down the visor mirror, she took a last look at herself. The port wine stain that spilled across her eye and down one cheek was brighter today, an angrier red. Her features were even, eyes big, nose small, and without the stain, she might have been a beauty. But the birthmark, *naevus flammeus,* was all anyone ever saw. Ask Gorbachev.

She gathered blond California-girl hair, twisting it into a ponytail and securing it with a white scrunchie. Her clothes were bulky, work gear bought at a resale shop, and hid the toned muscles of her body. She took a slow breath, met her own eyes in the mirror.

You're no longer Belinda Nichols. You're Lila Bannister. You've got a blond dye-job that isn't fooling anyone and two kids at home. You'd rather live in one of these houses than take care of them, rather be a movie star than a cleaning lady, but if wishes were horses, someone would need to muck out the stables. Your ex-husband is long gone, but your boyfriend is a decent man, has a job with the phone company. Saturday nights the two of you drink margaritas on your porch. During good-money months you put aside a little for a rainy day, but minor squalls seem to hit frequently: dental bills, repairs on the Dodge, Mom's nursing home. Still, you have each other, and work, and these days that's a blessing. Life is all right.

Lila Bannister turned the ignition, holding it as the van cranked, cranked, cranked, and caught. She went past the house, then around the block, one last check. All calm. Then she turned back onto Wandermere, drove past the lawn crew she'd seen earlier, and pulled up to Daniel Hayes's house.

There was a security gate blocking the front, and a stanchion with a call button and a keypad. Lila rolled down her window, warm Malibu air flowing in, and leaned out to punch the code. There was the sound of a chain drawing tight, and the gate slid aside. She pulled through and followed the curve of the drive to the house. Her palms were sweaty, and she wiped them on her pants, then killed the engine.

Lila hopped out of the van, the door squealing as she pushed it open. It was November, and though the flowers were gone, the air still smelled sweet. She opened the back and took out a watering can and a duffel bag. Humming softly to herself, she walked up the porch steps to the front door. She knew no one was home, but a house-keeper would ring the bell before walking in, so she did the same. Stood on the porch, feeling the sun on her back, the tension in her calves. After fifteen or twenty seconds, she dug in the bag, came out with a key ring, and slotted one in. The door opened, and Lila walked inside, closing the door behind her.

The moment the door closed, Belinda Nichols dropped the duffel bag of cleaning products and the watering can. She took a quick lap of the first floor, just being cau-tious, doing what Bennett would have done. Someone had been drinking; the kitchen counter had a couple of bottles of whiskey in various stages of emptiness. The trash stank, and there were dishes in the sink. Belinda took it all in, then went back to the foyer and climbed the stairs to the second floor.

The master bedroom was flooded with sunlight and the bed was neatly made, but there was an air of lingering sadness. Belinda shook her head, then walked to the nightstand and pulled open the drawer.

The gun that was supposed to be there wasn't.

She stared for a moment, cataloging what she saw. Lip balm, lambskin condoms, a dish filled with coins, a Gregg Hurwitz novel. No gun. She lifted the book, just in case the gun was beneath it. It wasn't, but something else was. A shiny steel ring. She picked it up, holding it between thumb and forefinger. It was light, and the inside was worn smooth.

What the hell? Why was Daniel Hayes's wedding ring in the drawer instead of the pistol she'd come for?

What kind of game was he playing?

Belinda slid the ring into the front pocket of her work pants, then closed the drawer and headed for the office. Hayes's desk was neither neat nor cluttered. A laptop sat in the center. She opened a drawer — papers, scissors, stamps, rubber bands, a package of blank DVDs — and there, in the back, found what she was looking for.

She looked at them. The squat little revolver would be easy to hide. But it didn't look as effective as the other, which was black with a chrome slide and the words SIG SAUER embossed on the textured grip. It had a sort of sportily efficient look to it, the kind of gun James Bond might carry if he decided he wanted variety. Belinda reached for it, then stopped, hand hovering and skin crawling. She hated guns.

Bennett's voice rang in her mind. "Everybody sins, sister. To own them, all you have to do is see it." A point he'd proven rather elegantly with her. Twice.

You really don't have any choice.

Belinda took the gun, feeling the heft of it, the way it fit her hand. Something squirmed in her stomach, but she pushed it away. Slid the gun into the other pocket of her pants. Daniel Hayes's wedding ring in one pocket; his pistol in the other. There was a strange, ugly sort of symmetry there.

Time to go.

Downstairs, Belinda threw her shoulders back, hoisted the cleaning supplies, and opened the door. Then Lila Bannister stepped out into the light of a gorgeous afternoon. She paused to lock the front door. Tossed her supplies in the back of the van, thinking about the rest of her day, how she had two more houses to do before making dinner for her family. She had a new *Cooking Light* recipe for fish tacos she was looking forward to trying. Chat with the kids about school, watch an hour or two of the tube, maybe a bath, and off to bed.

The gate swung open on an automatic sensor, and the white van with the dented side pulled out, wound down to the PCH, and vanished among the eastbound traffic.

It started in the desert.

Daniel was ragged, worn thin by lonely miles. The last days were blurs of scenery and sunlight, his belly sour from fast food and caffeine. Last night at some ungodly dark hour, he'd pulled the car off on a Utah side road, really just a path of dusty stone and sharp-edged plants. Before he'd gone to sleep, he'd shut off the headlights and stepped out of the car to stare upward. Stars spilled vertiginously across the night sky, a lavish abundance, white and sharp in the desert air. Farther than he could conceive and closer than he could bear. For a moment, all his fear dropped away. He just stared upward, lost in that holy sea, and lifted by it.

Then he shoveled junk off the backseat of the car and collapsed. In his dream, Emily Sweet danced for him, her feet bare, singing something he couldn't make out.

Later that morning he blew through Vegas: the Stratosphere, Caesars, the Riviera looming like monuments to lurid gods. There was a reason the tourist shots always showed Vegas at night, glowing like fireworks. By the bright light of early morning, the glitter seemed surreal and cheap. A hangover after a night of bad decisions.

And far quicker than a hangover, it vanished. But somewhere in the desert beyond Vegas, the feeling started.

Excitement.

With every numbingly dull mile he knocked down, it grew. A palpable feeling in his chest, a joyous bubbling warmth. He was almost home. The answer to every question was only a few hours away. He didn't know what he would find, but at least it would be *something*.

Shortly before noon, he merged from I-15 to the 10. Smooth, wide lanes bordered by concrete under an electric blue sky. It didn't look that different from a lot of the country he'd covered in the last days: car dealerships and strip malls and chain hotels. But it felt right. The streets and towns had names he could taste like ice cream flavors — Covina, Pomona, Alhambra. Each more familiar than the last.

Half an hour later, when the Los Angeles

108

skyline rose in the distance, the mirrored towers bearing the names of banks and insurance companies, the concrete basin of the river shining with shallow puddles, he felt his heart swell against his ribs. Traffic had slowed, and on his right was a convertible driven by a blonde whose hair stirred like a dream of summer; to his left, a guy yelled into a cell phone as he steered his Hummer. The Hollywood sign was just visible through a nicotine-yellow haze. Radio stations came and went like transmissions from the moon; billboards proclaimed that dieting sucked, suggested he get the lap band. It was November, and seventy degrees.

Los Angeles. Home.

He forced his attention back to the situation. The insurance card address was in Malibu, not L.A. proper. But the *Candy Girls* house was in Venice.

No, asshole, it's not. It's in a studio somewhere. The walls are façades and the sky is a light grid. Emily Sweet doesn't exist. She's just a symbol your messed-up brain designed to get you back to Los Angeles.

Well, bravo, two points for the subconscious. But no need to get ridiculous.

He flashed on an image, a dream, maybe? Emily Sweet standing in front of a window, wrapped in sunlight, gauzy with it, her dark hair shining. Her lips were pink and parted as if she were about to say something. She wore fitted jeans and a black bra, and he could see the humming softness of her stomach, the curve of her shoulder, a hint of nipple through lace.

Of course, Venice is more or less on the way to Malibu. What's an hour or two?

In his mind's eye, Emily Sweet's lips twisted into a molasses smile, a promise she'd meet him there.

The show wasn't specific on where the house was supposed to be, but there were frequent intercut shots of local landmarks. The faded letters V E N I C E above Windward Avenue. Jim Morrison looking down from a mural. The boardwalk, Rollerbladers and jugglers and homeless. When he'd seen those on television, he'd recognized them, though the recognition came without any context, the same way he could visualize the Statue of Liberty but had no idea if he had ever actually seen it.

But now that he was here, he did feel a charge, a sense that he had been here. He had driven these streets, eaten in these restaurants. It was jarring in a good way, a pleasant sort of déjà vu, and he found himself growing increasingly excited. Every time he turned a corner, the feeling that he knew this place grew, and around each he expected to see . . .

What? Emily Sweet leaning over a porch railing, waving at you?

Well, yeah. Kind of. And so he drove slow, taking in every stylish boutique, every yoga studio, every tattoo parlor. Lawn-mowered the BMW up and down wide boulevards and narrow streets, looking for the one that held the *Candy Girls* house, and if not Emily, then at least some answers.

Three hours later, he had a headache, a sick feeling, and the dubious claim of having driven every block of Venice.

The house wasn't there.

Of course it's not. You knew that when you started.

Still, it hurt. A surprising amount, actually. Maybe it was just wishful thinking, but during the drive she had become a symbol for him, a sign that all of this had some larger purpose. She was Home and Mother and Lover rolled into one, the temptress with a crooked smile and all the answers.

Get it through your head. There is no Emily Sweet.

By the way, there's no Han Solo either, and no Santa Claus. Sorry, kid.

Daniel found a place to park, stomped to

a restaurant, and ordered a Cuban sandwich and two beers. He sat at a wobbly sidewalk table, chewed numbly, and watched people go about their lives.

It didn't matter. He hadn't come here for that. He wasn't crazy. Confused, yes; scared, certainly. But not crazy. Whacked-out dreams of her may have pursued him across the country, but he'd made the drive based on tangible evidence. The address on the insurance card. That was why he was here.

Sure, it would have been nice to have this strange and glorious symbol guiding him. It would have exempted him from the things he'd done, and it would have given him faith that there was an order, a purpose to things. But wanting didn't make it so.

Maybe an address on an insurance card is a lousy, prosaic way to stake a claim on your life. But it's what you have. Deal with it.

He wiped grease from his fingers, downed the last of the beer, and walked back to his car. Time to hit the PCH, see what Malibu had to offer.

Twenty miles and forty minutes later, Daniel discovered he was wrong.

Turned out he was crazy after all.

■ ■ ■ ■

ACT TWO,
PART ONE

■ ■ ■ ■

"In L.A., you think you're making something up, but it's making you up."
— Steve Erickson, *Amnesiascope*

A blurry week ago he had woken on one coast. It had been cold and gray and lonely, beautiful in a desolate sort of way. It had nearly killed him, and maybe he had wanted it to.

Then the dreams, and the police.

The midnight cities in blurs of light.

The Midwest, flat and pale.

The endless fields of grain.

The gaudy playland of Las Vegas.

The heat shimmer of the desert.

The bright bustle of Los Angeles.

The Pacific Coast Highway, a ribbon winding between knuckled ridges of rock and the blue promise of the Pacific Ocean.

And finally Malibu, nestled like a jewel in the warm bosom of the other coast. More beautiful than anyplace had a right to be. Golden sunlight, salt tang in the air, bungalows in faded shades of mint and turquoise next to multimillion-dollar wonders of glass and stone, waves rolling surfers to shore in long, slow breaks. Twenty-seven miles of beach and canyon, of palm trees and skies that promised never to cloud — except from wildfire smoke or mudslide rain. Celebrities huddled behind security gates while homeless philosophers dispensed wisdom outside organic cafés. Daniel hadn't needed to read the license plate frame on the car ahead of him to know that it said, MALIBU: A WAY OF LIFE. He hadn't needed his map, either. He knew his way around.

It wasn't that he remembered the shocking green swath of lawn fronting Pepperdine, or the white houses clinging to the cliffs. It wasn't that he looked at the Pavilions grocery store and remembered shopping there, or saw the broad span of Point Dume and could picture swimming off it. It was a physical thing. Muscle memory, force of habit, his body knowing when to turn and which direction.

So he'd rolled with it, just followed that instinct until it led him right to Wandermere Road. The same address on the insurance card.

And now, as he looked out at the house, a two-story California contemporary with lots of glass and a wraparound porch, he realized that somewhere along the line he'd gone crazy. Only a matter of time before he started seeing talking cats and mad queens. That was the only explanation.

Because he was looking at the *Candy Girls* house.

"Down the rabbit hole," he said. He tried to laugh, but the sound died.

There was a wall that they had never showed on TV, and a tall security gate guarding the driveway. But what he could see of the house itself was the same: faded peach walls like early sunset, the porch Emily Sweet had stood on while her sister talked to her, the wood-spindle railing. He'd seen it all before on television, and in dreams he'd spoken to the woman who lived in it, a character from a cheap melodrama, a *woman who did not exist,* and besides which, it was supposed to be in Venice, not here, but here it was, standing between a bungalow and a Greek revival, right out the goddamn car window —

The honk of a horn shook him out of his trance. He glanced in the rearview, saw a VW Beetle behind him. He started to move before he remembered that Emily Sweet drove a Beetle.

No way.

The angle of the sun off the glass made it impossible to see clearly, but that profile, it could be . . . He pulled the parking brake and leapt out. Each step brought her into focus — her silhouette, the fine features of her face, fingers on the steering wheel, and then he'd reached her car, the angle better now. The driver was an Indian woman with wide, frightened eyes. He froze, and the woman who wasn't Emily fumbled for the transmission, threw it in reverse. The VW shot ten yards backward with a whine.

"Wait," he said, his hands out and low. "I'm sorry, I didn't mean to —"

He had to flatten himself against the BMW as she blew past. The last of her he saw was her middle finger as she turned the corner, leaving him alone in front of a house that couldn't exist.

Right. Right.

Get it together.

Daniel climbed hurriedly into his car. No sense having made it this far to flip out in the middle of the street. Play it smart. Better to park the BMW out of sight, walk back here, ring the bell.

Then flip out.

When he hiked back up from the beach parking lot, he expected to find the house transformed. It had been a figment of stress and lack of sleep and loneliness. His mind, already strained — to say the least — had gotten confused. He repeated it like a mantra, timing it to his steps, *I'm just, confused, I'm just, confused.*

But when he reached the address, there it was, as large as life. Larger than. A California contemporary with lots of glass and a wraparound porch.

Okay. Well. Be that way.

The gate was metal, about eight feet high, with a section that would slide aside to allow access to the driveway. A metal post held a small panel at car height. There was a keypad and a call button, which he pushed. It made a buzzing sound that he assumed was mirrored in the house. He waited a long moment, then pushed it again. No answer.

Guess I'm not home.

He must once have known the keypad combination that would open the gate, but that was gone with everything else. Daniel glanced up and down the block. It wasn't the most opulent section of Malibu he'd seen, but it was still pretty damn nice; most houses guarded by a fence, Mexicans doing lawn work, probably private security rolling around. Best he could tell, no one was looking at him, but who knew.

Daniel stood on tiptoes, stretched up to

119

grasp the lip of the gate. He jumped and pulled, managed to get his chin up to the edge and hung there, something below his stomach tingling. He twisted his grip to plant his hands like he was getting out of a pool. His feet kicked at the metal with a loud *bong,* giving him just enough purchase to get a knee up and throw one sneaker over. For a second his tailbone rocked against the sun-warmed metal, and then he pulled the other leg over and dropped clumsily to the driveway, the impact ringing through his knees and ankles.

That had been harder than it seemed like it should have been. He straightened, dusted off his palms and his jeans.

Now that he had an unobstructed view, he could see more differences between the house in front of him and the one on the show. Flower beds flanked the walkway here, though the flowers were embattled by weeds and grass. There was a porch swing, and although it wasn't on TV, it seemed right to him. Expected.

The thought sent a chill through him. The whole place did. He was sweatier than the late afternoon sun could account for, and his head felt light. He had a powerful urge to turn around and head back the way he had come. Hop over the fence again, get in the car, and . . .

What?

Daniel straightened his back, wiped his hands, and walked to the house. He started up the steps to the porch, then stopped a few shy of the top. He had the strongest feeling that the next step would squeak. What did it mean if it did? If it didn't? Which made him sane, which made him crazy?

It squeaked.

I know this place. I don't know how that's possible, what it means, but I knew how to get here and I know the sound of the trees rustling in the wind and that porch swing, I know I've sat on it before, and, god help me, I feel like I sat beside —

Emily Sweet.

His sneakers made soft *suss* sounds. He trailed his fingers along the railing, the wood smooth with salt air and paint and touch. At the first window, he cupped his hands to see inside.

The lights were off, but beams of sun spilled in. It looked nothing like the show. The furniture was low and Scandinavian, light colors and graceful curves resting on a rug that looked expensive. The room radiated emptiness, a sixth-sense feeling that no one was home. But someone lived here.

Scratch that. *He* lived here.

He walked to the front door. Through cut glass insets he could see an end table, a marble floor, framed photographs on the wall. He reached for the handle. Locked.

Daniel reached into his pocket and pulled out the ring of keys. The BMW alarm fob, one small key he'd mangled unscrewing license plates, and three others. The second one slid into the deadbolt, snapped it back with oiled ease. He put a hand on the handle, fingers sweaty.

I am Daniel Hayes. This is my house.

So why am I terrified?

He twisted the handle. The door swung open without a sound. With one last backward glance, he stepped inside.

Nothing happened. No trumpets or explosions or gaping holes in reality. He took one step and then another, sneakers squeaking on the marble. The air tasted stale.

The hallway was bright and broad, with an archway leading to the living room and another at the end of the hall. A staircase of polished wood supported by metal framework rose so that each step seemed to hang in the air. There was a faint patina of dust on the end table by the door, and a beaten copper bowl that held loose change, a receipt, sunglasses. He had an urge to pull out his keys and money and drop them there. "Hello?"

He closed the door — *click* — walked to the wall with the photographs. There were three of them, black-and-white shots, professionally matted and framed.

All Emily Sweet.

It looked like they had been shot at the same time. All three showed her in a white tee against a white wall, shirt blending so that her features and hair and the skin of her arms seemed summoned forth from light. In the first she was turned to the side, dark hair draped soft over her features, arm pulling the shirt up enough to show the curve of her breast; in another she faced forward but looked away, the barest hint of a smile teasing her lips. The third, the most sensual, had her pressed face-first to the wall, one hand up, her head tipped slightly back, as though caught in a daydream. They were beautiful but not quite professional, the contrast not perfect, the lighting a little off, as though they had been taken by a journeyman photographer. But the look on her face, the trust in the poses, they gave the images power. These photos had been taken by someone who loved her.

Is this what it feels like to go mad?

But he didn't believe it. Somehow he knew better, knew from that part of himself that had vanished. Knew, even as he walked through the arch into the cluttered living room, that there would be other photographs.

There were. And not just of her.

A collection of frames sat on the mantel. Emily and a man in ski wear squinting into the camera against the intense light of an alpine slope. Emily and a man dancing, her caught in the middle of a laugh, his hand in the small of her back. Another taken at arm's length, Emily and a man in a restaurant, the two of them leaning against each other in the booth, cheeks touching, both smiling a luminous, careless smile. Emily and a man sprawled across the hood of a gray BMW, holding up the title papers.

A gray BMW like the one he had driven here.

And a man who looked just like him.

Daniel floated. The real him was a balloon tethered three feet up and back from his head. He could see himself moving around the living room. His living room. See himself leaning in to look at the photos more closely. Emily arms-deep in a pumpkin, newspapers spread out to catch seeds and orange goop. In one photo a man who looked just like a younger version of him had a cigarette in one hand, and with the other gave the camera the finger. There was Emily in a makeup chair, graceful shoulders bare, someone fiddling with her hair. And here was a man who looked just like him wearing a tuxedo, standing in the ocean with her, the water up to his knees but not quite reaching her white gown.

Daniel reached for the picture. His hands were shaking, and he knocked it backward, managed to grab it before it hit. He lifted it closer, unsteady hands making their wedding photograph tremble.

Jesus Christ.

Their wedding photo.

He could hear his heart, actually hear it, the whooshing thump of the pulse in his neck, his ears. The woman in the photograph, that was his wife. Emily Sweet.

No, you stupid son of a bitch. Don't you dare. The ice you're on is too thin to play.

Not Emily Sweet. Laney Thayer. The actress. And that beach, he knew it. It was lonely and desolate and rocky. He'd woken there, naked and half-dead, just days ago.

So then . . .

His obsession with the TV show, with her, it had been about the woman he loved. The real-life woman, not the character from the show. He was married to Laney Thayer. That explained why he knew what time her show was on, why he'd been so eager to catch it. He'd been desperate to see her. His brain had been trying to guide him back home after all. More literally than he realized.

Okay, he thought. *Breathe. Just breathe. And concentrate.*

He took the picture to the couch, shoved aside a throw pillow. Now that he was home, now that he knew the truth, everything should resolve itself.

There was a date calligraphied in the corner of the mat, 05/23/03. The couple in the photograph looked like the American Dream. Young, beautiful, successful, and lit by love. The kind of people who got married on a beach and then walked into the surf, laughing, and screw their formal wear. It was all there — everything everyone wanted.

So why —

He took a breath, closed his eyes, opened them again.

why can't I —

Easy, he had to go easy. It would come, it would come, it would come.

remember?

He jammed his eyes shut as hard as he

could, ground his fists into them until he could see stars and comets, until the jelly shifted under his knuckles. He felt like screaming, like throwing the picture across the room, like grabbing a chair and hurling it through the window in a sparkling rain of glass. He felt . . . he felt so . . . so . . .

Helpless.

Relax. Relax. It will come back. You can feel it, all of it, so close. Just stay loose. Be calm. Get a drink.

Daniel opened his eyes. Stood up, set the picture back on the mantel. Walked through the living room, the dining room — a showpiece table surrounded by antique chairs, all looking very expensive — to the kitchen. The air changed as he did, a sweet smell of rot.

The kitchen was a cook's dream. Six-burner Viking stove, butcher block counter-tops, a window on the back wall to an avocado tree in an enclosed yard. There were dishes in the sink with food crusted on them. The lid of a stainless steel trash can was propped open, the garbage explaining the smell. There were liquor bottles on the counter, mostly bourbon, some Irish whiskey. The way they were arranged, the level of booze in them, he could tell that someone had been doing some serious drinking.

Binge drinking. Lose-yourself-in-an-amber-sea drinking. And he had a feeling it had been him.

The bottle of Blanton's still had a couple of inches left in it. He opened a cabinet — knew just which one — and took out a rocks glass. The smell was melting caramel; the taste was melting gold. He closed his eyes and felt the familiar, lovely burn. Better. Better.

Okay. What do you know?

Well, first, this was his house, and he was Daniel Hayes. Those two facts were now solid. Which meant the BMW was his car, and that for some reason, he had driven it cross-country to that lonely Maine beach. The same beach, it appeared, where he'd gotten married to Laney Thayer.

So where was she?

No way to tell exactly how long he'd been gone, but at least a week. And what, four days since he woke up without his memory? Four days was a long time for someone to be missing. She must have gone crazy. Been calling the police, the hospitals. Maybe she was running the cops ragged right this second. That would explain the dishes in the sink, the housekeeping.

If that's true, she might have called to see if you were back. You should check the —

He found the answering machine on the other side of the counter. The cords were frayed, and the plastic body was shattered like someone had jumped up and down on it.

Right. No messages, then.

Daniel refilled his glass, then returned to the front hall. Like everything else in the house, the staircase was striking without being gaudy, wooden steps rising from polished marble with airy grace. Whatever worries they might have had, money wasn't one of them. At the top of the stairs, arbitrarily, he chose left.

The master bedroom. Holding the glass like a totem, he stepped in.

The room took up half the second floor. Windows on three sides gave way to sweeping sunny vistas, the backyard, trees. There were more photographs, but he didn't think he could handle more pictures right now. The bed was a full-size, smaller than he'd expected. A size that belonged to couples who chose to touch when they slept. The covers were neat. His end table held an alarm clock, a lamp. He opened the drawer: lip balm, lambskin condoms, a dish filled with coins, a Gregg Hurwitz novel. It felt like something was missing, but he couldn't have said what.

Laney's side table had a pile of scripts a foot high. She'd been looking for her next project, wanting to cash in the *Candy Girls* cred for a meaty role in a serious film. It had always made him smile, the look on her face while she read scripts. Totally unaware of the outside world as she leaned against the headboard, pages held in both hands. Her lips moving and face trying on the emotions of the characters. Sometimes he'd put down whatever he was reading and watch her, catch an advance screening.

The memory took his legs away. His hands shook as he raised the glass to his lips. He took a long swallow, then coughed.

More. There had to be more.

He forced himself up, a little wobbly. Walked into the bathroom: sunken tub, enclosed shower, the lighting an actress would demand. A window looking out onto the avocado tree in the backyard, the leaves so green they looked wet. Daniel moved to the counter, picked up a small container of moisturizer. When he opened the top, a sweet lemony smell rose, like the best dessert in the world, like a night in a Caribbean hammock, like lying down beside Laney, the smell of the stuff mingling with the smell of her, the way she turned on her side and made soft noises and reached back, fumbling, to grab his arm and pull it around her, draping him across her like a favorite blanket. God, they had fit well together, their bodies were made for it, and even after all the years, the feel of her skin against his set him to tingling. As luxuriously comforting as a hot shower.

The bathroom had gone bleary and wet. Daniel wiped at his eyes with the back of his hand. He set the skin cream on the counter, went back down the hall.

The next door opened into what looked like a guest room. Tasteful, but as emotionally resonant as a hotel suite. He didn't bother, just closed the door and went into his office.

It was a third bedroom they'd converted, ripping up the carpet and putting in shelves. Three walls were covered floor to ceiling with books and bound scripts. A pale wood desk sat in front of a window looking out to trees and the street. The desk had a photo of Laney looking dynamite in an evening gown, a stack of unopened mail, a crystal statue, and a closed Dell laptop.

The statue was the one from the photo downstairs, the one he'd been holding while he stood at a podium. An abstract curve of sweeping glass. At the bottom there was a small plaque, which read:

Huh.

Huh.

On second thought, maybe it wasn't a lurid melodrama aimed at teenage girls.

Well, that explained some things. The way he kept jumping into stories — making up tales for the people around him on the highway, the pleasure he'd felt writing in his journal, his "script" at the MRI clinic. He set the award back on the desk, pulled out the chair, and sat down.

It felt . . . like home.

For the first time he could remember, he felt at home. No, he didn't have all the answers yet, but they were coming, each one triggering the next. Just sitting here they were coming. Looking at the wall-to-wall bookcases, he remembered putting them in, doing the work himself. Years ago, sweating in the heat, Drive-By Truckers singing about Daddy playing poker in the woods they say, back in his younger days. The smell of sawdust and the whine of the circular saw. They'd had the money to hire a professional, but he wanted to do it. There had been a time when carpentry had paid his rent, before sitting at a desk started to become more profitable than building one.

This was where he belonged. This chair, this desk, this computer, those windows with their view of paradise, the ocean just visible over the swaying trees, the broad, quiet street, with the work trucks of gardeners and the sheriff's department squad car —

Fuck!

The cruiser was parked two houses up pointing in this direction. The lights were off, but he could make out the shape of a cop inside.

Daniel leapt from the chair and shot to the other window. A pale blue sedan that screamed "unmarked police car" sat at the security gate. As he watched, the window rolled down and an arm reached out to the call box. A bell chimed.

Someone must have seem him climb the fence. Did it matter? He knew who he was now. He was a television writer, and this was his house, and Laney was his wife, and he may as well face things, deal with the police. There would doubtless be consequences for running from them, but he could explain . . .

What? You still don't know why they're after you.

Maybe Laney, petrified with worry, had called the police, and they had tracked him . . . no. The cop in Maine had his gun out. *Hell, he* shot *at me.* This was no missing person case. They were after him. They thought he'd done something, something terrible.

The bell sounded again, longer this time, the cop losing patience. *Decision time. Think carefully.*

Well, he'd already run from the police once. How much worse would it really make it to run twice? And there was so much he still needed to know. Things he couldn't find out from a jail cell.

Besides. Easier to ask forgiveness than permission.

Daniel tore open drawers. Pens, notebooks, a Slinky, a digital camera, rubber bands, stamps, DVD-Rs. The bottom drawer was file folders neatly tabbed: RANDOM IDEAS, DIALOGUE, REJECTIONS, MEMBERSHIPS, SHORT STORIES. A gold mine, but too much of it. He flipped to the back, where the tabs were more prosaic: UTILITIES, DR., CAR STUFF, RECEIPTS, BANK STATEMENTS.

What are you looking for, a folder marked, "In case of sudden amnesia"? How much of your life would be in a file cabinet?

"Mr. Hayes, this is Detective Waters. We know you're there. Open the gate." An intercom somewhere. There must be a button on the call box that let you speak. This was Malibu, home to the wealthy and liberal, and Waters would want to avoid a scene. But that didn't mean his patience was infinite. They'd climb the fence soon.

The laptop! It would have his e-mail, scripts, calendar, contacts. It probably held more clues than anything else in the house. Daniel yanked the power cord from the wall and wrapped it around the computer.

Time to go. The cops were at the front, so the back seemed like his best option. He was halfway down the steps when he thought of one more thing. He froze, cursed. The odds that the house was being surrounded went up second by second. The smart move was to get out right now, to just sprint out the back door —

"Mr. Hayes," the detective's voice echoing closer now; the speaker must be downstairs. "I know you're scared, but running from us is the wrong thing to do. Open the gate."

Daniel turned, raced up the stairs, swung into the master bedroom. Hustled past the bed, into the bathroom, and grabbed the lemon moisturizer, the one that had brought Laney to him so powerfully.

Now he could leave.

The bathroom window was in the back of the house, facing the yard with the avocado tree. He could see the street beyond, but no sign of a cop car. He had the window half-open when he heard banging on the front door.

"Police! Open up!"

He was pleased that he didn't panic, didn't freeze. Just forced the window the rest of the way, then unlatched the screen and yanked it aside. Leaf-carved sunlight spilled across his hands. The avocado tree was densely branched, most of them small, none of them easily reachable. Clusters of dark fruit swung, and he remembered that when they fell the backyard smelled like a Mexican restaurant.

Daniel jerked a bath towel from a hook and wrapped it around the computer, then leaned out the window to drop it to the grass. It landed with a thump, and he winced, partly for the computer and partly for himself, then tossed the moisturizer, put one foot on the ledge, and ducked through the window frame. Behind him he heard the yelling grow suddenly louder, and then pounding footsteps, the horse-hoof sound of men running. *Well, this should be fun.*

He leapt into the tree.

Vertigo only had him for a moment before he felt the leaves slapping at him, the thin branches whipping his face and hands. He squinted as much as he could, kept his arms out and swinging. The air that rushed by was cool and sweet. He could smell the ocean, taste the bitter leaves. Then his hand hit something, and he grabbed, got it, slowed himself, lost it. Tilted back, arms wobbling and flinging wild, panic hitting as his forward vector gave way to gravity, and down he fell, ripping through in a maelstrom of green leaves and blue sky and blinding sun. The ground met him hard, right on his ass.

The suddenness of the pain, the sheer physicality of it brought tears to his eyes, little kid tears for a little kid injury, but he didn't have time. He snatched up the computer and the moisturizer and limped along the wall of the house, ducking beneath the windows.

As he hauled himself over the fence, he could hear the cops inside the house, yelling to one another that a room was clear. His breath was shallow and his heart was racing and pain ran up and down his spine in pulses as he snuck away from his own home like a thief.

For all that, he wanted to laugh, wanted

to yell and dance. Through the looking glass? Down the rabbit hole?

Oh, *hell* yes.

"What are we doing today?" The woman — she'd said her name was Sherri — hid bad skin under a thick layer of makeup. Her hair was elaborately fried.

"I want a change." Daniel met her eyes in the mirror.

"Big or little?"

"Go nuts."

The stylist smiled and led him to the shampoo bowl.

After he'd made it back to his car, the urge to go through the laptop right there had been damn near irresistible. But the police would be after him, and he had to deal with that.

Apparently you're a writer. Television, but still. Used to figuring out the intricacies of plot, of anticipating your characters' next moves. So what would your move be if you were making this up?

Which was how he'd ended up in this hair

salon in Santa Monica, sitting still for damn near two hours. Thinking, *I'm married. My name is Daniel Hayes and I'm a successful writer married to a gorgeous actress and we're in love and have a house in Malibu and a perfect life.*

And: *If that's true, why are the police chasing you from one end of the country to the other? Why did you try to kill yourself in Maine? Why on the beach where you got married? Where's your wedding ring? Hell, where's your wife?*

Meanwhile, Sherri went at his hair like it had stolen her parking spot. She scissored and razor-cut and twisted foils and dabbed coloring. Under her ministrations, his affable, longish brown hair vanished, replaced by a rakish faux-hawk, sandy with blond highlights, gelled and twisted and pointed different directions. He didn't look like a movie star, but his hair sure did.

"What do you think?"

"I don't recognize myself."

"That was the point, right?"

Down the block the smell of tomato sauce from a restaurant tightened his stomach, but he walked past to the tanning salon on the other side. A bell on the door jingled as he stepped in. "Do you guys have that spray stuff?"

They did.

Next was clothing. A squirrel-cheeked girl told him they'd be closing in fifteen minutes, and he browsed quickly, then got a fitting room and pulled the curtain. Time for new clothes anyway. Scrubbing his shirt in a rest-stop sink had stopped doing much seven states back. He slid on a pair of canvas cargo pants, a black tee, and a Hawaiian shirt with blue and green parrots on it. Bug-eyed sunglasses and a canvas messenger bag completed the outfit.

Daniel looked in the mirror. *Well, it's official. You're a douche bag.*

The man staring back had a dark tan, trying-too-hard hair, and sunglasses that obscured half his face. Not so over-the-top that he would be noticeable, but he certainly didn't look familiar to himself.

Of course, that and four dollars will get you a cup of coffee.

"You look familiar," the clerk said as she rang him up.

"I get that a lot." He turned away. Let her think he was a B-list star who wanted privacy. Out on the street, he transferred the bank statements, computer, and Laney's moisturizer into the bag, then bundled up his old clothes and tossed them in a trash bin on the way to the Third Street Promenade.

It was dark outside, and the sunglasses made it darker, but he didn't want to risk taking them off. Luckily, he was in Los Angeles. If a second head had sprouted from his belly and begun pitching a spec script, it wouldn't have drawn more than a glance.

Okay. That takes care of Step One. Now, Step Two.

The café had tall bookshelves and a varied clientele, a few chatting, most lost in their laptops. There were fancy juices and a dozen kinds of tea and complicated coffee apparatus. Most important, there was a sign offering free wireless. He got coffee and a bran muffin and took a table in the back, away from the window.

A person's computer could reveal more about his life than his mother. Especially a writer's computer. There would be e-mail, years' worth. Addresses and phone numbers. Scripts and stories. Pictures and financial statements and maybe even a journal. Plus he could get on the Internet, log back into the world. Google himself and his wife. Do a little research on amnesia, see what the hell he was suffering from exactly, and what could be done about it —

The screen welcomed him to Windows XP by name, and then asked for his password.

Daniel rubbed at his face with both hands. What were passwords? Birthdays. The name of a girlfriend or a dog. The things that people never forgot, that they could count on being able to remember dead drunk or a year after they'd last entered it. The exact kind of thing that he was lacking.

He typed "Laney," hit enter.

Did you forget your password? You can click the "?" button to see your password hint.

When he clicked the button, a dialogue box appeared with the words "Life Begins." Huh. Life begins. Probably just the thing to prompt him if he forgot — unless he forgot everything, in which case it was just cryptic. He tried again.

"Life Begins"
Did you forget your password?
"LaneyThayer"
Did you forget your password?
"CandyGirls"
Did you forget your password?
"EmilySweet"
Did you forget your password?

"Malibu"
Did you forget your password?
"BMW"
Did you forget your password?
"FuckYouYouPieceOfCrap"
Did you forget your password?

This was pointless. He could type random words for the rest of his life and never get it right. It would have been funny if it weren't so tragic. Survive a suicide attempt, drive three thousand miles, break into his own house, flee the police, and then end up stymied because he couldn't remember the name of his favorite movie. Awesome.

Daniel stowed the laptop. It was still a treasure trove; he just didn't have the key yet. There had to be a way to break the security. Or he would remember, the same way little bits of his past kept leaking into his consciousness. Maybe he'd have a dream where the cast of *Candy Girls* broke into a musical number about his password.

As he was choking down the rest of his muffin, he spotted a lonely terminal on a small desk in the back of the room. He stood, brushed the crumbs off his shirt. "How much to rent the computer?"

"A buck for ten minutes, five an hour, ten for three."

Daniel passed the man a ten, got a slip of paper with a temporary log-in. The chair creaked as he sat down; the computer damn near creaked as he fired it up.

He opened Firefox, waited for it to load, then went to Google and started to type. He'd gotten as far as "Laney Th" when it popped up suggestions: Laney Thayer, Laney Thayer Candy Girls, Laney Thayer Naked, Laney Thayer Accident, Laney Thayer Murder.

The world throbbed out of focus.

Everything blurring but the words "accident" and, worse, "murder." The letters not making sense. The vicious serifs of the "M," the complicit wriggle of the "r." The stone in his stomach twisted, revealing edges that snagged and tore.

Laney Thayer Murder.

Oh god.

He hovered over it. Stared. Foolish, foolish man. It wasn't a rabbit hole he was falling down. It was an abyss.

CNN.com, November 2, 2009

ACTRESS IN FATAL ACCIDENT

LOS ANGELES (CNN) — Los Angeles Sheriffs responded to an automobile ac-

145

cident resulting in the apparent death of actress Laney Thayer earlier this afternoon.

Thayer, 30, lost control of her vehicle during a hairpin turn on the Pacific Coast Highway. The 2007 Volkswagen Beetle slid through a barricade and over the edge, falling more than 100 feet before landing upside-down in the water. Preliminary evidence suggests that Thayer was going approximately 75 miles an hour, 30 mph faster than the posted speed limit.

Sheriffs responded quickly, cordoning off the road and calling on the Coast Guard for support. Tidal conditions and the severe slope prohibited officers from reaching the car for nearly an hour.

"At this point, Ms. Thayer's body has not been recovered," said Sheriff's spokesman Parto Barkhordari. "However, given the condition of the vehicle, and the riptides at this time of year, that isn't surprising."

Asked whether Thayer could have survived the accident, Barkhordari said, "We're making every effort to find her. But I don't see how she could have gone over that cliff and lived."

The actress starred in the popular tele-vision melodrama *Candy Girls.* Her hus-band, screenwriter Daniel Hayes, was unavailable for comment.

The Pacific Coast Highway is known as one of the most scenic but dangerous routes in California —

E! Online, November 3, 2009

CANDY GIRL ACCIDENT
NO PIECE OF CAKE

Laney Thayer's story was just getting started . . . until it ended tragically in a car crash that could have been pulled from her hit show.

But now it's turning out there may be more to her story than anyone guessed.

While sheriffs are close-lipped about the crash, the focus of the investigation is shifting from accidental death to something more ominous.

Murder.

Sources within the LASD have revealed that according to skid marks found on the Pacific Coast Highway, Laney may have been forced off the road.

Husband Daniel Hayes has yet to make a statement — or even appear in public.

Meanwhile, what is it about the PCH and celebrities? Let us count the ways those two don't mix: Mel Gibson, Nick Nolte, Robert Downey Jr., Bridget Fonda, Shannen Doherty . . .

**Star, News and Gossip,
November 4, 2009**

**LANEY THAYER MOURNED BY
HOLLYWOOD, CAST**

Since the tragic accident on Monday, outpourings of sympathy have come from every direction.

"Laney was a beautiful woman with a beautiful soul," said co-star Robert Cameron. "Everyone adored her. Me? I loved her."

"It's a total tragedy," co-star Janine Wilson said. "She was totally like a sister to me."

Thayer had recently made news with her decision to leave the FX show *Candy Girls* in the midst of contract disputes. The show, which was a surprise success, has run for four years —

PerezHilton.com, November 4, 2009

WHERE IS DANIEL HAYES?

By now everyone knows about Laney Thayer's ~~murder~~ accident.

Car chases, rumors of affairs with co-stars, sheriff's investigations, oh my!

But where is hubby Daniel Hayes in all this? Why can no one seem to find him?

Maybe he's too busy mourning the loss of his ~~cash cow~~ wife?

Or maybe he had something to do with it?

149

LANEY THAYER HUSBAND SOUGHT

LOS ANGELES (CNN) — Los Angeles Sheriff's Department spokesperson Parto Barkhordari today acknowledged that police sought Daniel Hayes, husband of actress Laney Thayer, in connection with her death on November 2.

The case, originally believed an accident, has come under investigation as a possible homicide based on forensic evidence as well as "financial irregularities."

The officer leading the investigation, Detective Roger Waters, stopped short of specifically naming Hayes a suspect. However, he did note that in cases of this nature, family members were "the first people we look at."

Investigators have confirmed that blood traces found on the airbag matched Laney Thayer's blood type. Analysis of the stretch of highway leading up to the fatal spot bears evidence of a high-speed chase involving another vehicle. Neither Waters nor Barkhordari would go into detail regarding the financial evidence, though both noted that it could constitute a motive . . .

**People.com, Star Tracks,
November 6, 2009**

HAPPY COUPLE?

Laney Thayer and husband Daniel Hayes look awfully cozy in this behind-the-scenes snap from *Candy Girls*. But sources on the set say that their relationship was "anything but simple."

Click for a slide show of Laney's career, from her modeling days to strolls down the red carpet to beach frolics with hunky co-star Robert Cameron!

TMZ.com, November 7, 2009

DANIEL HAYES = SCOTT PETERSON

A murdered wife. A body in the ocean. A vanished husband. A supposedly happy couple with more going on.

Does anybody else notice that Daniel Hayes, husband of *Candy Girl* Laney Thayer, is starting to look an awful lot like Scott Peterson?

True, Laney wasn't pregnant — that we know of — but otherwise, things look grim for the writer.

Especially since he disappeared. Sources within the Los Angeles Sheriff's Department have told TMZ that Hayes isn't just laying low — he appears to have fled.

"We've got credit card information tracking him across the country," says our man in the LASD.

Daniel, if you're out there, remember, Scotty tried to run too . . .

Sponsored Links

- Secret to Sexy Stomach
- Make $5200/Mo. Part-Time
- Trick for White Teeth

Reader Comments

1. First!

Posted at 3:50PM on November 7, 2009 by newsjunx

2. She's rich AND hot but he kills her? Talk about a d-bag play.
   Posted at 3:52PM on November 7, 2009 by hisnameisrobertpaulson

3. 1st.
   Posted at 3:52PM on November 7, 2009 by K

4. Just cause she's dead doesn't mean I wouldn't tap her . . .
   Posted at 3:54PM on November 7, 2009 by PinkLVR

Enough! Jesus Christ, enough.

He closed the browser window, bile on his tongue. November 7, that last article was dated. Today.

This had been going on around him all the while he drove west, oblivious. He could have had half the answers to his questions just by reading a tabloid. All the time he wondered what was wrong, all the time he felt this massive, crushing guilt —

No. That can't be true.

Daniel's stomach was crawling things. He lurched to his feet. Behind him, a voice said, "Hey, dude, you've got like ninety minutes —" The slamming door cut off the clerk's words.

What the fuck is happening to you?
Who are you?

He turned left at random, stalked down the street, everything spinning. A happy couple parted to make space for him. A homeless woman yelled at an ATM. Coffeehouse, clothing boutique, coffeehouse, restaurant, coffeehouse. Fucking Santa Monica and its fucking 340 days of sunshine and its fucking coffee. Last things he needed were sunshine and coffee.

How could all of this happen to one person? It was too much — the memory, the lonely terror of the last week, making it home to find he had a beautiful life, and then scant hours later learning that that life had been ripped from him. Learning that everyone believed he was to blame.

That can't be true. You couldn't have done what they say you did.

Please. Oh god, please. Better to have died on the beach in Maine.

Please let me not be that man.

Belinda Nichols drove her battered white van through the desert.

She'd thought about buying what she needed in one of the towns outlying Los Angeles. The rules in the city were strict, but once you got a couple of miles out, things were simple. Show a driver's license, pay in cash, and you were good to go.

But she didn't really want to show her driver's license. The odds it would lead to her getting caught were slim, but any trail, any trail at all, could be a problem. She'd never killed someone before, and while she wasn't excited about doing it, she was even less excited about the prospect of getting caught.

So she'd gone a safer route. It had taken five hours to make the drive, two of them fighting L.A. traffic. Once she'd cleared city limits and was rolling north on 15, things had thinned out. Just her and the rocky sprawl of the desert and the wide white sky.

She made it to the outskirts of Vegas a little after one. Belinda always felt naked outside of a city. All these wide lanes and huge parking lots, all these car washes and cluttered signs. The Walmart was on a street called East Serene, which she could relate to, being east of serenity. Sort of how she felt since Bennett had come back into her life.

It was the brilliant heart of the afternoon as she parked. She killed the engine, listened to it tick as she flipped down the visor to look in the mirror. The port wine stain shadowed her eye and cheek.

You're no longer Belinda Nichols. You're Barb Schroeder. You've got charm to spare and a laugh that makes other people happy. You grew up in the South, and though you lived most of your life in the Midwest — Wisconsin — you never completely lost the accent. Two years ago you said, "Okay, winter, you win," and packed it in for Las Vegas, fastest growing city in the country. No better place to be in real estate, at least it was, until about the time you got here. But what the hell, it's warm, the sky is blue, and tomorrow is a long way away.

She checked her outfit, jeans a couple of years out of date but snug and flattering, and a fitted white button-down she'd found at Target. Not bad. She undid the top button, then another, so that the lace edge of her bra was visible. Better.

The store was an airplane hangar, the grid of lights running into the horizon. Bored clerks rang up endless lines. Barb Schroeder took it in, then followed the signs to sporting goods.

It had always amused her that these stores had everything, everything, you could ever need. Groceries, clothes, toys, electronics, housewares . . . ammunition.

"Can I help you, ma'am?" The voice came from behind.

Barb turned, smiling, looking him in the face, and watched him take in her port wine stain, the dark red blotch that had defined her whole life. His eyes did the usual dance — the stain, the floor, her face, but not up to the mark.

"I hope so," she said, and threw just the tiniest hint of twang into her voice. Kentucky, not Alabama. "I need to buy bullets."

"Rounds," he said. He was nice-looking in a cowboy sort of way, probably late forties. Perfect. "We call them rounds."

"Sorry." A little giggle and a cock of her hips. "My boyfriend got me this gun, a Sig Sauer something, said if I won't move in with him, I need to have it. He's a cop, says until they get rid of all the bad guys with guns, we all need them too."

"You know which model?"

"A pretty one. Silver and black."

"Well —"

"I'm kidding, hon. I need .45 ACP."

He grinned, then took a key ring from his belt, opened a glass display case. "Got a preference as far as brand?"

"It matter?"

"Not really. Winchesters are good, Blazer is a little cheaper."

"Winchester is fine."

"They come a hundred to a box."

"I'll take . . . three, I guess? Need to practice some."

The clerk nodded, took out three boxes. "Anything else?"

"Targets?"

He showed her a selection, paper targets with bull's-eyes and silhouettes of deer and people. She picked the ones shaped like a man.

"I can ring you up over here." He led her up the aisle to a small register, scanned the ammunition. The register beeped, and he gave her a sly look. "You over twenty-one?"

She laughed. "Hon, I weren't already seeing a man with a gun, I might just marry you for that."

He smiled, put her stuff in a bag. "Eighty-seven forty."

"Easy come, huh?" She counted out the bills, made sure to touch his fingers when she passed them to him. "Thanks for the help."

"No problem."

Barb Schroeder picked up the bag, surprised at the weight, then started for the front.

Now it was almost four, and Belinda Nichols was on the 15 again, heading back through the desert, about ten miles outside of Barstow. A sign told her exit 194 was coming up; she took it, found herself on the kind of dusty two-lane you saw in modern westerns, a long straight run to the sky. A few minutes later a dirt road branched off, and she took that, followed it for fifteen minutes until she was in a low canyon, all brown earth and scrub weeds. Pulled the van over and sat at the side of the road. Nothing happened. No cars, no trucks, nothing.

Belinda picked up the bag of ammunition, the paper targets, and the Sig Sauer she had taken from Daniel Hayes's house and walked into the hills.

She found a twisted tree and hung the

target on it, poking a branch through the paper. Then she walked back ten feet. The sun beat down on her as she held the pistol, found the lever to unlock the magazine. She opened one of the boxes of ammunition and loaded it carefully. Belinda hated the feeling of it, the way it was so clean and smooth and appealing; the machined precision of the gun, the perfect cylinder of each round. Hated the slickness of the whole thing, the fact that for all the flawless appeal on one side, the end result was messy and evil.

Get over it. You don't have a choice. Until you do this, Bennett owns you. When it's done, you'll be free.

She blew out a breath, held the gun up in both hands. It was heavy, and as she stared down the barrel, the thing wavered back and forth across the target. Her hands were sweaty.

When Belinda pulled the trigger, the crack was so loud the rest of the world seemed to buzz.

A neat hole had appeared in the target. It wasn't in the bull's-eye, but it was inside the rings. Not bad.

Not good enough. You can't screw this up. It won't be a target you're shooting at. It will be a man, and you can't miss.

She wiped her hands on her jeans, one

then the other, and then raised the gun again.

And again.

And again.

The building was a rent-a-room in Studio City, a two-story reclaimed from an old dance hall and divided into offices. Nice enough place, the façade intact, and the original floors, the boards battered and wide. Bennett had scoped it, walking into the lobby with a pizza box in one hand. Marking the security camera mounted in the ceiling. Nothing fancy, your standard closed-circuit, likely feeding to a digital recording system, a stack-burner for DVD-RWs. There was a wall board with the list of tenants, and he counted seconds while examining it. Mostly small production companies — who in this town *wasn't* a producer? — as well as a number of writers, a low-rent agent or two, a dentist. He found the name he was looking for, suite 106, then scanned quick for the occupant of 105. He was up to twenty-two seconds before a dude in a blue monkey suit stepped out of an unmarked office door, asked if he could be of service.

"Yeah, I've got a delivery for" — he faked looking at the ticket — "the Council for

Colombian Imports?" He smiled. "That's just *got* to be a joke, right?"

The security guard had grinned, said, "Suite 105. Down the hall, take a right, just past the bathrooms."

"Thanks, brother."

"No prob."

He'd sauntered down the hall, taken the right, walked past the bathrooms, whistling. There was another camera at the corner, but just one to cover the whole hall. The doors were out of an old-time private eye movie, wooden frames with frosted glass panels, the occupant names lettered in gold. Suite 105, THE COUNCIL FOR COLOMBIAN IMPORTS. Suite 106, DANIEL HAYES. Bennett knocked on 105. A minute later, a cute little thing maybe five feet tall, all curls and dark eyes, opened the door. "Yes?"

"Afternoon, ma'am. I'm with Salami Jim's; we've just opened, and to introduce ourselves, we're sending free pizzas to our new neighbors." He thrust the box at her, and she took it, as he knew she would. Predictable, people.

"I — thank you."

"Hope you enjoy. Remember, Salami Jim has the sausage you love to swallow." He started away.

"Wait."

162

Bennett turned, and the cute little thing said, "Can I tip you?"

He smiled as he took the two crumpled bucks she pulled out. Why did women carry bills like they were notes passed in class, something they needed to stuff away quickly?

That was earlier. Now, after ten, he was parked in his truck across the street. The window for the Council for Colombian Imports had gone dark a couple of hours back. Daniel Hayes's hadn't ever been bright, but that was no surprise. Bennett pulled on a pair of driving gloves, slid the Colt in the back of his belt where his leather jacket would cover it, and got out of the truck.

The office building had a parking lot, and in the time he'd sat across the street, he'd seen a security guard — a different one this time, fat and sporting a mustache — stroll through it exactly once. Keeping his gait easy, Bennett crossed Ventura, walked into the lot. Despite the hour, there were half a dozen cars parked. A mixed bag, but the winner was a Mustang, an LED blinking red on the dashboard. He walked past the Dumpsters to a weed-covered ridge that ran along the side of the building. Counted windows, *uno, dos, tres, cuatro,* the Council for Colombian Imports', and then Daniel Hayes's. It was double-paned and fixed, no sensors in the corner, aimed more at numbing street noise than security. Perfect.

In the dark, it took him five minutes to find a few decent-sized rocks. His first throw went long, overshot the Mustang by a couple of feet. Bennett wound up, lobbed another, this one denting the side of a Civic just shy of the Mustang. For Christ's sake. He took a breath, shook out his arm, and tried again.

The rock smacked into the Mustang's windshield. The alarm started, headlights flashing and horn honking, the sound and light seeming to carry the rock as it bounced away.

Wayne Reynolds had his feet up on the desk, sitting sideways to the computer, browser open to Apartments.com. It had a color-coded map of the city, overlays that tinted it gray and orange and purple.

Should just tint it shades of green.

The east side, or in the valley, there were places he could afford. But Marta wanted to leave their cookie-cutter two-bedroom in Crenshaw and head for the beach. Maybe Santa Monica, she'd said, like there was a chance of that. Like all you needed to live there was a taste for ocean breezes.

He clicked to the search, filled the maximum rent field with what they paid now. The results were . . . uninspiring.

"Garden apartment." Code for "subterranean."

"Efficiency" really meant "you like shitting and cooking in the same room?"

And "loft" in this case should have read "windowless bunker."

Wayne sighed, reached for his sandwich — tuna with fat-free mayo and sprouts, Marta trying to help him on the diet — and took a joyless bite. Here was something, a one-bedroom in Tarzana that didn't look bad —

A horn started honking, once, twice, three times, steady. He glanced at the security monitor, saw that it was one of his. Jerry Logue's Mustang. Damn. Wayne couldn't see anyone in the lot. Probably just set off by the vibrations of a passing truck.

That's the problem, Wayne, honey, you never take any initiative. *If you want to get ahead . . .* Marta's voice from their fight last week.

He sighed, shrugged, stood up. Checked the Taser on his belt, grabbed the flashlight, walked out of the office. The lobby was quiet, the track lighting low, casting dra-

165

matic highlights and shadows. Wayne shouldered open the door, the ring of keys on his belt jingling. The night was cool, the sky above a wash of purple clouds.

The Mustang was blaring away, lights flashing. He put one hand in his pocket against the chill and swept the big Maglite around with the other. No one took off running. He reached the car, stood there for a second. *Now what? Dust for prints?*

No one in the lot that he could see. Traffic on Ventura was light. In the drugstore next door, a guy standing next to an Explorer was looking over, apparently drawn by the alarm. When he saw Wayne, the guy nodded, turned back to his truck.

Wayne bent down, shined the light underneath the Mustang. No one leapt out. He shrugged, kicked at the tire. The moment his foot touched it, the alarm shut off.

I am Magical! Wonder Wayne to the rescue. He turned off the flashlight and headed back inside, wondering about that place in Tarzana. Not exactly Santa Monica, but it would be a change at least, and that was probably what she really wanted. And with the economy the way it was, he might be able to bargain the price down.

It felt good to step back into the warmth of the lobby. He glanced at his watch. The next scheduled rounds weren't for another twenty minutes. Still, may as well do them now; he was up, and dinner wasn't much enticement.

Wayne looked down the hall, decided to hit the second floor first. He started for the elevator, heard Marta's voice reminding him he could use the exercise, and took the stairs instead.

From the parking lot of the CVS next door, Bennett watched the fat guard approach the Mustang. The man saw him looking, and Bennett nodded, then turned, started digging in his pocket like he was looking for keys. After a moment, the alarm stopped, and the guard strolled back inside. High security.

Bennett smiled, waited a few more seconds, then left the parking lot and headed back to Hayes's window. He'd thrown the rock through as soon as the Mustang's alarm had started, and even standing right next to it, the crash had been largely drowned out. Careful not to cut himself, he pulled out some of the larger chunks of glass at the bottom, dropped them in the weeds, and let himself in.

The office was simple but appealing. A desk with a couch opposite. A small conference table. A mini-fridge, and on top of it, three bottles of whiskey. He poured himself a couple of inches of the best, sipped at it. Nice.

Okay. Time to work.

He pulled the blinds to cover the glow from his penlight and started with the desk, taking it one drawer at a time. It didn't take long; there wasn't much in it. He'd wondered why Daniel kept this office, what with the lovely room Bennett had discovered in the guy's Malibu home. Apparently, the reason didn't have much to do with writing. Meetings, maybe. Bennett had never been big on meetings, but this looked like a nice place to have one.

He checked behind the framed *Memento* poster for a safe; no joy. Same with the posters for *Solaris* and *The Fountain.* He took down and opened the books on the shelf, titles like *Save the Cat* and *The Writer's Journey,* but again, nada.

Bennett stood in the center of the room, looked around. He traced a ridged scar on his bicep, a deep cut from a knife in Detroit.

Where next?

He didn't really expect to find anything here; it was a little obvious, even for Daniel. Still, the guy had hidden Bennett's payment somewhere. And until Hayes reappeared, it was worth the effort to look. A half-million dollars was worth a whole lot of effort.

Methodically, then. He took another sip of whiskey, set down the glass, and, using the desk as the starting point, began to work his way around the room. If there was something to be found, he'd find it.

Wayne walked a circuit of the second floor, the keys percussion to his tuneless humming. The light was on in Jerry Logue's office, and he knocked. May as well score brownie points. The door opened, and Logue's beak popped out. "Yes?"

"Mr. Logue, it's Wayne, with security," he said, as if the guy couldn't have told from the uniform, as if the dick hadn't walked past him a hundred times.

"Yes?"

"Just wanted to let you know your car alarm went off."

The guy cocked an eyebrow.

"I checked it out, but everything seems fine."

"Great."

"Thought you'd want to know."

"Great." The man shut the door in his face.

You're welcome, asshole.

The rest of the floor was quiet, and he

went back down the stairs, taking each of them, the way they said you got the most exercise. Back in the lobby, he turned right, headed down the hall. Everything was quiet, most of the tenants gone for the night. He turned the corner, past the Council for Colombian Imports — that just *had* to be a joke — realized he needed to take a leak. Unlocked the head, the fluorescents flickering on as he walked in. He stepped up to the urinal, unzipped, rocked back and forth on his heels. Corporate bathrooms always gave him the willies. Something about the weird, impersonal cleanliness of the things. And the no-touch faucets and hand dryers. His other superpower, besides stopping car alarms, was invisibility to sensors. He spent twenty seconds trying to get the sink to admit he existed. *Now to decide whether to use my powers for good or evil.* He didn't bother with the hand dryer, just wiped on his pants and stepped out.

There was a light in suite 106.

Wayne froze. Stared at the frosted glass of the door. He stood still, concentrating. Was that a scrape he heard from inside?

So someone is in the office. That's kind of the point.

Sure. But 106 was Mr. Hayes's. The guy had always been pleasant to him, seemed like a nice guy, but then, that's what every-body said about people who turned out to be killers. "Oh, that Theodore Bundy, he seemed like such a nice boy."

That's the problem, Wayne, honey, you never take any initiative. *If you want to get ahead . . .*

Wayne took a step forward. His keys rattled, and he froze. Slowly, he unclipped them from his belt, held them in one sweaty palm. He tiptoed, feeling ridiculous, too big to be tiptoeing, but what the hell, it was working, and besides, there was no one to see.

A sound like a drawer opening and clos-ing came from inside, and, dimly, another quick glow of light.

Wayne's heart kicked into gear. *What now, Wonder Wayne?*

As quietly as he could, he found the master key on the ring and eased it into the door. Drew his Taser, the grip strange in his hand. He hadn't fired the thing since the training course two years ago. Still, it took about as much skill as a remote control. If he could change the channel, he figured he could Tase one screenwriter.

Okay. Do it smooth. Seeing the headlines already, HERO SECURITY GUARD CAPTURES WIFE-KILLER, he twisted the key, threw open the door, then raised the flashlight and thumbed it on as he stepped inside. Saw Daniel kneeling at a filing cabinet half a dozen feet away, jerked the beam onto him, yelling, "Mr. Hayes, freeze!"

The man froze. But it wasn't Daniel Hayes.

Wayne didn't recognize him, an average-looking guy in a black leather jacket, a penlight in his mouth to leave his hands free as he looked at the files. A dozen thoughts came from a dozen directions, colliding in the center of his brain, leaving no clear winner.

"Whoa," the guy said, and stood up, blinking. "Jesus. You scared the shit out of me."

Wayne said the only thing that came to mind. "You're not Mr. Hayes."

"Right you are."

"I thought —"

"Let me guess." The man at ease. "You thought I was my partner."

"Your partner?"

"Daniel. He's my writing partner."

Which meant that Wayne had just barged into a locked office without permission. *Shit, shit, shit.* But then, wait a second, his thoughts racing, that didn't make a lot of sense. If the two were partners, how come he'd never seen the guy? And what about the flashlight? "What are you doing here?"

"My old lady and me got in a fight. Dan let me crash here till she comes round." The dude smiled at him, lowered his hands, put one to his heart. "She-it, you scared me." He squinted at Wayne, said, "You mind getting that thing out of my eyes, chief?"

"How'd you get in here?"

"I broke the window." The guy gestured over his shoulder. "How do you think? The front door."

"I haven't seen you."

"Been here all day. Now, seriously, get that light out of my eyes."

Something wasn't right, but he was so calm. And it wasn't really Wayne's business, not without an evident disturbance. He lowered the light to splash at their feet, the reflection bright enough still to see by. "You have some ID?"

"At home." The guy looked sheepish, scratched at his head. "Left in kind of a hurry, you know? My wife was throwing plates, and she's got a wicked arm."

Marta wasn't a plate thrower, but Wayne could relate to the desire to get out quick when a fight started. He'd never liked conflict. Something Marta often pointed out when she suggested he might want to get another job, something with a bigger future.

Then his mind processed something he'd seen but not really noticed. "Wait."

"Yeah?"

"Why are you wearing gloves?"

Well, shit.

Bennett laughed, ducked his head sheepishly, his left hand moving up to scratch at his temple again, hoping the first time had gotten the guard used to it. He said, "Funny story," then, while the guard watched his left hand, he snaked his right behind his back, jerked the Colt, and brought it to bear. "That would be so I don't leave fingerprints."

The man stared at him, lips slightly parted. There was a crumb of something in his mustache and sweat on his forehead.

"Here's the story, chief." Bennett kept up the affable tone. "You've got a Taser, security issue — what is that, the C2? — so not even one of the bad boys the cops carry. And me, I've got a Colt Defender. There's three ways this plays out. Number one, I shoot first. A .45 hollow-point is designed to expand on impact and shred internal organs like a blender. Not so good for you. Option two, maybe we both shoot at the same time. This distance, you can't miss, but neither can I. So I get shocked for thirty seconds, no fun, but you get shot, so again, worse for you." He paused, working the theater. "Option three, and this one's the real doozy, maybe you're faster than you look. You get me before I can pull the trigger. Thing is, you know what happens then? All that electricity slams through my system, and wham, my muscles start contracting — including my index finger, which means, yep, you guessed it. You get shot."

The guard hesitated, ran a tongue along his lips. Bennett could see a vein jumping just above the fat man's eye. "Basically, you're outgunned, friend. Bad luck, but that's life."

"Put your weapon down and step over to the desk." The guy's voice squeaky.

"I've got a better idea. I don't really want to shoot you. So here's what I propose. You lower that thing. I'll lower mine. Then we each go out the way we came. Five minutes after I'm gone, you can come in here, find the broken window, maybe you get to be a hero after all."

A long pause, the guy thinking over everything he'd said. "How do I know — how do I know you won't shoot me?"

"Why would I shoot you? Get homicide detectives looking for me? No thank you. I just want to walk out." He held the moment, then said, "Look, it's up to you. Be a hero or a corpse. But if you lower your toy there, I promise, I won't hurt you."

The air in the room was cool, the broken window letting in a November breeze. Bennett held his aim steady, the gun at waist level but square at the man's fat chest. He could see the man thinking it over, could practically read his thoughts: the twelve dollars an hour he made, the dinner waiting at his desk, the way he desperately needed to take a piss. Saw the decision come over his face, a simple weighing of options, and then the guard lowered his weapon.

Bennett cracked him in the face with the butt of the Colt.

The man made a squealing sound, the Taser falling from his fingers as reflex brought his hands to his face. Blood rushed between his knuckles, and his eyes went wobbly. He staggered backward, tripped over his own feet, and fell.

Bennett picked up the Taser, tossed it aside. The guard was panting and keening.

"Funny thing," Bennett said. "I've never understood it. Promise something, people tend to believe it. Even if the guy saying it has a gun pointed at them." He reached for his whiskey, knocked it back. With the heightened senses that came of action, every taste bud glowed.

The guard scrabbled at the floor, pulling himself on his elbows. Bennett wiped the rim of the whiskey glass clean, then set it down and went behind the desk. Found the rock he'd thrown through earlier.

Fatso had a name tag, read Wayne Reynolds. Bennett sighed, then dropped down to straddle the man, pinning the guy's arms down.

"No," Wayne said, the sounds coming out *boh* through his broken nose. His eyes were wild. "Don't."

"Sorry. No choice."

"Wait. No. I don't know who you are. You don't have to —"

"Unfortunately, once I'm gone, you'll get brave again. You'll call the cops, and they'll look through the security tapes, and you, wanting to be a hero, you'll point me out. And then they'll see that I wasn't wearing gloves when I came in earlier, and they might pull a print. And that, my friend, I cannot have."

"*I bohn't.* I won't tell them anything."

"Can't risk it."

"Please —"

"I am sorry about having to do it this way. Nothing personal. But this has to look amateurish." Bennett raised his arm.

Wayne screamed, "Marta!" as Bennett brought the rock down.

The guy stopped yelling right away. But it took more hits than Bennett expected before he stopped breathing.

INT. HALL OF JUDGMENT —
AFTERNOON
A square room made of heavy
blocks of stone. Torches
flicker on the walls, smoke
rises to the ceiling.
There is a faint, solemn sound
like waves in the distance.
DANIEL HAYES sits in a chair,
elbows on knees. There's something dark on his hands. He
starts to touch one with the
other, hesitates.

JUDGE 1 (O.S.)
Blood.

Daniel looks up, startled.
There is a table in front of
him. Behind it sit three

hooded figures. The JUDGES are tall and skeletally thin, and he cannot make out their features.

                    DANIEL
Where am I?
          JUDGES 2 & 3
   (in sync)
Guilty.
               JUDGE 1
Blood on your hands.

The judge's speech is deep, sonorous, a voice from the bottom of a well.
Daniel looks down, sees that dark liquid now covers his fingers. He jerks, holds them out. A drop falls to the floor, and then another.

                    DANIEL
I didn't do anything!
          JUDGES 2 & 3
Guilty.
               JUDGE 1
If you didn't do anything, why are you here?
                    DANIEL

I . . . I don't know.
                    JUDGE 1
Then how do you know you don't
belong here?
                    DANIEL
I'm dreaming. This is a dream.
                    JUDGE 1
The rest was a dream. This is
real.
                    DANIEL
No. No, that can't be —
                    JUDGES 2 & 3
Guilty.
                    JUDGE 1
Blood on your hands. Blood on
your soul.
                    DANIEL
I don't believe you. I don't
believe this.
   (clenches his fists)
I'm not a monster.
                    JUDGES 2 & 3
Guilty.
                    DANIEL
No!

He lurches up from the chair.
The judges sit as still as
buildings, the hollow of their
cowled hoods perfect black.

Daniel turns, starts to run. Trips over the chair, pulls himself up.
There is a heavy wooden door on the wall behind him. He grabs the handle, pulls, the door grinding an inch at a time.

                    JUDGES 2 & 3 (O.S.)
Guilty!

INT. DANIEL & LANEY'S MALIBU HOUSE — CONTINUOUS
The medieval room, the robed judges, the torches, they're gone.
  Daniel stands in his kitchen. Shadows cast through the window stain the floor, the walls, the counters. The sound of the ocean is louder.

                    FEMALE VOICE (O.S.)
What did you <u>do</u>?

The sound is coming from the other room. Daniel starts in that direction.
A door slams.

Daniel begins to run.
He leaves the kitchen, breaks
into the living room.

                FEMALE VOICE (O.S.)
What did you <u>do</u>?

Daniel runs faster. He bolts
out the side of the living
room.
He is back in the kitchen.

                DANIEL
Laney?

He runs the other way, into
the hall, gets to the front
door, rips it open, steps
through.
He is back in the kitchen.
Daniel runs again. The house
is a nightmare maze. Doors
that never existed open onto
impossible hallways.
A voice begins to sing. It's a
woman's voice, but strange,
stretched out somehow.

                FEMALE VOICE (O.S.)

*Hawrk the herald ang-gels
siing-*
  (the voice stops, changes to
  a laughing tone.)
You know, with their heads
thrown back and mouths all
wide —
  (singing again)
*Glo-ree to, the new bowrn
king.*
  (talking)
Remember?

Daniel continues to run,
faster and faster. His hands
leave blood smudges on everything he touches.

            FEMALE VOICE (O.S.)
Remember?
                DANIEL
Laney, I didn't do anything, I
didn't, I know I didn't! Help
me, please, help —

Daniel slows as the familiar
door approaches.

            FEMALE VOICE (O.S.)
  (no sign she's heard)

And then they dance.
  (she sings a soundtrack)
da-na-na-nanana-na-nah, da-na-na-nah . . . da-na-na-nanana-na-nah, da-dada, da-dada. . . .

Daniel opens the door, steps through . . .

          FEMALE VOICE (O.S.)
Bah-dah-dah-dah! Doink-iddie doink-iddie, doink-iddie, Bah-dah-dah-dah! Doink-iddie doink-iddie —

He is back in the kitchen.

          DANIEL
I'm trying! Help me!

The woman's voice dissolves into beautiful, bubbly laughter.
Daniel sinks to the floor.

          DANIEL
You have to help me.
  (fading)
I need help.

(staring at bloody hands)
Please.

Something smacked his feet, and Daniel jerked awake, heart thudding and stomach a tight, hard ball, a blinding white light in his eyes. He raised a hand, squinted through his fingertips. "What —"

"Get up." The voice stern. Used to being obeyed. A breaker slammed into the beach, the impact tremor riding through his back. Daniel scrambled for thought, for context. Where was he? What was going on?

Last night. He'd read those articles, those foul, vile articles. The woman he loved gone, gone forever, and the whole world sure that he had done it, that he was the kind of man who murdered his wife. He'd left the café and stalked the streets. Hating everything and everyone. Hating Los Angeles most of all. He'd finally made it, only to realize he didn't want to be here. It was glitter and vigor up front, all to leave you unprepared for how deep the sorrow ran when things went wrong. A driving city with lousy parking. Yoga during the day, cocaine at night. You can live the dream life with your dream girl, but you don't get to remember it, and when the bill comes, it's a fucking doozy.

He'd finally found a liquor store, where a

Sikh sold him bourbon. Perfect.

Then walking, drinking, more walking. Finally coming onto the beach in Venice. The bottle mostly gone. The surf rolling steady, like it had all the time in the world. Like nothing was worthy of notice. He'd lain down, the world spinning below him, the universe whirling above, and remembered, just before falling asleep, the sensation that instead of looking up he was looking down, that he was clinging to the earth above a terrible and endless night —

"I said get *up.*" The last word punctuated with another kick at his feet.

"Hey, man, easy." Daniel sat up, rubbed at his eyes. "I just fell asleep is all." Thinking, *a cop, a cop, a cop.* He kept his face tilted down, hoping the guy hadn't really studied him, that his new look was disguise enough. The flashlight had reduced the world to inches.

"No sleeping on the beach." The light trailed down to the brown paper bag of bourbon. "No drinking, either."

Part of him wanted to panic, to run wild, but to his surprise, his mind was calmly putting things together. Not cornered, not caught. The man wasn't looking for him. He was just rousting a drunk. Still, if he asked for ID, or wanted to give him a ticket . . .

"I'm sorry, Officer. I'm not a bum or anything. I just . . . me and my girl." He hesitated, found emotion easy to summon. "I lost her." Almost choked the words out. "I lost her."

The flashlight hovered on him for a long moment. Daniel could almost hear the cop thinking, taking in the clothing, the expensive haircut. Calculating the hassle of running in a regular civilian with a broken heart and a buzz, the civilian whining and crying and maybe even puking.

"Just move along, all right? You can't stay here."

Daniel nodded. "Sure. Sorry." He brushed sand off the messenger bag and struggled to his feet.

"And take that with you." The beam dodged to the bottle. Daniel bent to pick it up, then started away before the cop had a chance to change his mind. The flashlight sent his shadow sprawling ahead. Sand slipped beneath his feet. The sky was the burgundy wine of very early morning. Yet another night of barely sleeping, and a hangover to boot. He shivered. That dream. The blood on his hands, and that strange singing voice.

No wonder you're conjuring up judges in

*your dreams. You killed your wife. You drove
her off that cliff, and when you saw what you'd
done, you couldn't deal. So you ran. You got
in your car and fled the monster you had
become. You drove for two straight days,
propped up on booze and pills, the world a
blur of gas stations and highways, and when
you got to the beach where you'd married
Laney, it still wasn't far enough. So you tried
one last route. A cold, brutal swim into
oblivion.*

No.

*No? Because you don't believe it? Or be-
cause you don't want to believe it?*

His stomach rolled, thick and sour. His
mouth was a desert, his head a vise. He
staggered up the sidewalk, the sky growing
lighter with every step. Venice slumbered
behind shackled doors. Laney had always
loved it here, loved the contradictions.
Million-dollar homes on the boardwalk,
needles on the beach. He remembered a
long-ago afternoon, the two of them lying
in the heat of an August day. She'd smelled
of sunscreen and sweat. They'd lounged and
talked about the future, about someday
leaving the business. About having children
and going to soccer games and hosting
cookouts. Afterward they'd gone home to
make slow heat-stoned love as breezes

189

tossed the curtains.

Before. Back when she was alive, when he hadn't —

Wait.

He dropped the bottle in a trash can, took a seat on a nearby bench. Slapped at his cheeks, ran his hands through his hair, the gel in it gritty with sand. A panel truck with pictures of dancing tortillas rolled by. He took a breath, deep, and held it.

This didn't make sense.

He was the first to admit that his memory was suspect. But it had been coming back, and increasingly rapidly. Whatever had happened to his mind, it seemed to be temporary. Brought on by exhaustion and substances and shock and physical strain, it was passing. Not as fast he might like, but steadily. That memory of the beach, for example, it was real. He could remember her crawling on top of him, her hair making a sun-stained cave of their faces. She had smiled at him, and said that she liked it like this, just the two of them in the whole world, and when he'd pointed out that they were on a crowded beach, she'd said, "I don't see anyone else."

That was real. That had happened.

And the pictures in their house. The two of them in love, the two of them getting married, the two of them playing at Halloween and Christmas, the two of them skiing. No pictures of anyone else, just the two of them.

He took the lemon skin lotion from his bag, spun the top off, inhaled deeply.

Hell, when he had been lost completely, when he couldn't remember his own name, she had smiled at him from the television and guided him home. They had been happy. Successful. And blessed with the kind of love that made rom-coms into box office smashes.

The tabloids had it wrong. He'd always hated them. Hated that they not only aired dirty laundry, but hung the clean stuff and tried to tell you it was filthy. All those lurid hints of fights and affairs, implications half-excused by the use of the word "allegedly." Laney had always had more patience for them than he had, and thank god, since she was the one they liked to write about. Sexy actresses trumped writers every time; he'd seen ten thousand magazines talking about Angelina but had yet to see Joss Whedon on the cover of the *Star*.

But it wasn't just tabloids you read. It was CNN too, and a dozen others.

Besides, there was the guilt. The guilt he'd felt since the moment he'd awakened. The guilt that played out in dreams, that had chased him on his ride back west, nipping at his soul in every quiet moment.

It could be nothing. Maybe it was just loss, and sadness, and a feeling that he hadn't been able to protect her. But maybe not.

Daniel sighed, rubbed at his eyes. Everything was fluid. Everything was possible.

He needed more answers. And the only way he could think of to get them was one hell of a risk.

"I think I'm going to write a book," Peter McShane said, gesturing with half a bagel. "Practical tips for aspiring bad guys."

Detective Roger Waters raised an eyebrow, flipped a page in the folder. *Chicken Soup for the Criminal's Soul?*"

"Chapter One. When committing a crime, remember to plan your escape. While Jet Skis and hang gliders offer some amusement, the discerning bad guy opts for a car. When choosing a car for your escape, or 'getaway vehicle,' " McShane said, making air quotes, "you are advised not to use your parents' Audi. Should you fail to observe this basic precaution, you waive the right to look surprised when we show up at your home."

Waters laughed. "You serious?"

"Yep. The white boys snatched that girl out of Torrance, took her to a burnout, had her chained to the pipes? Used Mommy's car. Boo-ya, two masterminds down." Specks of bagel fell on his shirt. "How about you? Anything on Luscious Laney? Still like the husband?"

"Yup." Waters tossed the folder on his desk, leaned back with his fingers laced behind his head. "You know the T-shirt at their house?"

"The bloody one."

"Got the preliminary lab work back. A-positive, same as my victim. Husband is B-pos. It's not his. We won't know DNA until the lab gets around to it next decade, but now in addition to a runner with a half-million-dollar motive, I've got a man's shirt, same size as my suspect, found in his closet, covered in blood that matches the victim's type."

"So, how's it play? They have a fight, he stabs her —"

"Shoots her. Husband has three guns. But she manages to get away in her sporty VW —"

"Except he chases her down, runs her off the PCH."

"And you know the best thing? He's back in town."

"You're kidding."

"Nope. According to his credit cards, Hayes made it all the way to Maine. So I sent a telex, not expecting anything, but some kid from the Washington County Sheriffs spotted the car, tried to arrest him. Botched it. Asshole fired on my suspect too, you believe that?" Down the hall, the lieutenant was guiding a well-dressed woman into his office. She tried to smile but didn't quite pull it off, too much concern on her face. A missing child, maybe. Parents usually had that panicked expression. "Hayes flees. And yesterday a neighbor spots him climbing the fence to his house in Malibu."

"No shit?"

"No shit. We rolled up, but he was gone by the time we got there."

"Why climb the fence?"

"How should I know." Waters picked up a pen, spun it between his fingers. A phone rang, and he heard someone answer *LosAngelesSheriffsMajorCrimesMetroDetail*. "Gets weirder. Other day, LAPD gets a call from a woman named Sophie Zeigler. Someone broke in, came at her in the shower, held her at gunpoint. You know what he's asking? Where my suspect is. And Sophie Zeigler? She's Hayes's attorney."

"He lawyered up?"

"No, she's a Hollywood player, negotiations, that sort of thing. But who's the guy that broke in?"

McShane finished the bagel, wiped his hands. "Accomplice."

"That's what I'm thinking. The husband hired this guy to help, then welched on paying before he skipped town."

"Ah, the humanity." McShane stood up. "What a piece of work is man. How noble in . . . something or other."

"You might want to polish that up for the final draft of your book."

The other cop gave him the finger, and Waters grinned, turned back to his desk. Opened the folder, flipped to the photos of her car. Familiar by now, but still, Christ, what a mess. The Volkswagen upside down, half-submerged, the surf smacking against it in ropes of spray. The top opened like a can of soup. All the glass broken out, the sides crumpled. The next photo was of the barricade, the metal scarred with paint from where the Bug had hit, the bent section stretching outward as if pointing the way to the sea. Then the cliff itself, a hundred feet if it was ten, and steep. A ribbon of ripped up earth and torn vegetation marked the car's route —

"Detective?"

Waters looked up. A patrolwoman in sheriff's beige, tie tucked neatly. "Yes?"

"Got a call for you. Another Daniel Hayes."

Waters sighed. He'd been talking to four, five a day, all calling to confess to killing Laney Thayer. Some of them were pretty entertaining, spinning soft-core fantasies they'd obviously put some time into. None of them had passed the bullshit test. He glanced at his watch. "All right."

She nodded, rounded the corner of the cubicles. He heard her say, "Just one moment," and then his phone rang. He collected the photos, rapped them against the edge of the desk, then picked up the handset and tucked it between his shoulder and chin. "This is Waters."

"Hi. Umm. This is." A pause, then, "This is Daniel Hayes."

Waters slid the pictures back into the folder. "Uh-huh?"

"You're handling the . . . Laney? Her investigation?"

"That's right." He set the folder in his in-box, opened a drawer, swept pens and Post-its inside.

"Was that you at my house yesterday?"

The world snapped into focus. Waters sat up straight, looked around. Was this a cop prank?

"That was you, wasn't it? On the intercom?"

Waters switched the phone to his other ear, said, "Yes, that was me, Mr. Hayes. Why did you run away?"

"I didn't have anything to do with it." There was a ragged indrawn breath, the sound of a man trying for conviction, and in the next sentence he had it. "I did not kill my wife."

Waters was wishing this was a movie, that he could signal for someone to trace the call. "I believe you, Daniel."

"You do?"

"Yeah, I do." Waters pitched his voice earnest. "I've spoken to a lot of people. Your friends and coworkers. Daniel, they all say that you and Laney were very much in love."

There was a choked sound. "If you believe that, then why are you chasing me?"

"Daniel, you have to understand my position. *I* believe you. But my bosses? They're riding me. In a case like this, the husband is the first person we look at. So when you disappeared on us, you didn't leave us any choice."

"How do you even know that someone else —"

"Come on. Don't insult my intelligence. We found skid marks for miles before that barricade."

"Maybe she was driving fast —"

"The marks weren't just hers, Daniel. She was running from someone. You say it wasn't you, I believe you." He projected calm, kept his speech slow and even. "I know that there must be an explanation. But I need your help to find it. For both our sakes." He held a beat. "Come talk to me, Daniel. Let's figure this thing out together."

There was a long pause, then a chuckle. "You said my name four, five times. That's, what, a technique to establish a bond? Make me believe we're friends?"

Heat bloomed across Waters's forehead. He rocked a pen back and forth between his index and middle finger, whapping alternate ends against the desk. "You're right. That's what I was doing. But you do need to come in."

"Why?"

"Because you're in trouble. You've got a lot to answer for. You left the state just after your wife was murdered. You fled deputies in Maine, then led them on a high-speed chase. You ran from us at your house."

"Those skid marks. You can tell what kind of car it was from them, right?"

"We can tell a lot from them."

"So what kind was it?"

Waters leaned back, wondered what the guy was playing at. "We can't get a make and model from tire marks."

"You said —"

"But it was a truck. An SUV."

"I drive a BMW, an M5. Not an SUV."

Then I guess you're innocent. "You see? That's exactly the kind of thing that will help us clear you." There was a long pause. Waters forced himself not to speak, just sat there thinking, *Come on, fish, bite.*

"If I come in, you'll arrest me."

"I'm not going to lie to you. That's possible. But if you don't come in, it's a guarantee. Don't you get it? You're the bad guy now. Even if you didn't have anything to do with her death." He switched tacks. "Besides. If you didn't do it, then someone else did."

"Maybe she just lost control." A little desperate.

"No chance. Someone was chasing her, someone who wanted to kill her. You want to see photos of the skid marks? Want to look at the barricade, the way it's torn up? Want to touch the air bag sample we cut out, her blood on it?" He let it sink in, then continued a little softer. "Now, if someone had done that to my wife, I would do anything, *anything,* to get them. Get her the justice she deserves. You do want whoever did this caught, don't you?

"Have you . . . Have you looked at other suspects?"

"We're looking at everything, Daniel." Noticing the guy called himself a suspect. "With a celebrity, there's always the possibility of a stalker. But I'll be honest with you. Nine times out of ten, when a wife is murdered, the husband is involved. And then there's . . ." He trailed off, waited for the guy to prompt him.

"What?"

"Well, the day she died, she bought a five-hundred-thousand-dollar necklace."

"What?"

"Monday, November 2, just before noon, at Harry Winston. I didn't even know necklaces could cost that much, but apparently they can, because she bought one. Damn near emptied your bank account. Now, why would she do that, Daniel?"

"I don't know."

"She ever do anything like that before?"

"I . . ."

"See, there are a lot of ways to interpret that, but none good. Maybe she was scared, and wanted that for running money. Or maybe you two were getting divorced, and she figured that was a safe way to make sure that she had possession of the cash. Or maybe you forced her to do it, threatened her somehow."

"Why would I —"

"I don't know." Bulldozing the guy, not wanting to let him think. "I don't know. But that's just one of the questions bugging me. Another is, you know someone broke into your lawyer's house?"

There was a pause, and then Daniel asked, "What do you mean?" There was something strange in his voice, like he was choosing his words carefully.

"It's true. Held her at gunpoint."

"Is . . . is she okay?"

"She's fine. My question is, who is he?"

"How should I know?"

"He was asking about you."

Silence.

"Come on, Daniel. Help me. Help yourself. Who is this guy?"

"I don't know."

Uh-huh. Waters bit back his instincts. If they were doing this the right way, in an interview room, home court advantage, marks from the cuffs still on Hayes's wrists, this would be the moment. You saw a crack like that, you hammered hard.

So bring him in. "There's another reason I

202

need you, Daniel." He sighed. "I'm sorry to ask this. But we need you to identify her body."

A choking sound. "I thought —"

"We found Laney yesterday. The currents took her body south —" He paused, said, "Do you want to hear this?"

"I. Yes."

"Your wife wasn't wearing her seat belt. Between the blood on the air bag and the way the windshield was shattered, our guess is that she was killed going through the glass. At that velocity, she would have died instantly." He opened the folder, flipped through to a map of tidal speed and direction in that area. "Given the height, her body was probably flung thirty to fifty feet farther than the car. Based on the currents, we expected it to drift south-southwest. Yesterday we got a call from a fishing crew down the coast. Her body had tangled in their net —"

"Stop." The man sounding weak. "Stop."

"I'm sorry, Daniel. I really am."

"Oh god. I had. I thought, maybe."

"I understand." He stopped talking, just listened to Hayes's breathing. In the background there were voices, music. The guy was in a public place, maybe using a pay phone. "I'm sorry to have to ask you this. I know how hard it must be. But don't let her wait in the morgue. Whatever happened between you, she doesn't deserve that."

"I didn't do this." His voice soft, wavering. Like he wasn't sure, wanted to be convinced. "I couldn't. We loved each other."

"I know."

"It must have been someone else. Someone forced her to buy that necklace."

Waters rolled with it. "That makes sense."

"It does?" Suspicious.

"Sure. A celebrity like that, she would be a target. Lots of people might come after her. They might even have threatened you. Maybe she felt she had to do it."

"Yes. Wait" — hitting on something — "that guy! The one who threatened my lawyer."

"I thought the same thing," Waters said. "As soon as I heard about it."

"So why aren't you looking for him?"

"Who?"

"What do you mean who? The guy that —"

"I know, but who is he? We didn't get any fingerprints, any physical evidence at all. We have Sophie's description, but that's not enough. I don't even know where to start."

"But — I mean —"

"You might, though. Help me, and help Laney. Because I'll be honest with you. As long as you're running, I can't spend time chasing things that are only possible."

"Are you kidding me?"

"Mr. Hayes —"

"My wife is dead, the guy who killed her is breaking into houses, holding my friends at gunpoint, and you tell me you're not going to look into it?"

Shit. "That's not what I'm saying. What I'm saying is that —"

"Yeah, I get it. You're saying you want this simple. Nine times out of ten, right? So why even look at the tenth."

"That's not it at all —"

"I didn't kill my wife. I have to believe that."

Have to believe that? What the hell does that mean? "So come talk to me, Daniel. Give your wife peace, and justice. Let's work together to get the guy who did."

The silence on the line stretched. It was shit or get off the pot, and they both knew it.

Finally, Hayes spoke. "You know what, *Roger*? I don't think so."

There was a fumbling sound, and the line went dead.

Waters hung up hard enough that the

handset bounced out of the cradle. God-damnit. For a moment he'd really thought he might be able to talk Hayes in. Hayes was a Hollywood guy, a writer, used to living in his own fantasies, to thinking the world around him was stories. It sounded like he was well on the way to believing his own version of events. The way he'd pretended to be thrown by the jewelry purchase, some of his phrasing, his hesitations. Daniel Hayes most definitely did not pass the bullshit test.

So now what?

He could always use the media. Change Hayes's status from suspect to wanted man. Put his photo everywhere, maybe even call him armed and dangerous; man did have permits for three guns. It was a crude tool, but it would make it hard to hide.

His phone rang and he picked it up. "Major Crimes, Waters."

"This is Detective Nancy Palmisano, LAPD. Is this Detective Waters?"

"Yeah."

"You're working that TV actress? The one with the husband?"

"Laney Thayer and Daniel Hayes, yeah. What can I do for you, Detective?"

"One sec." There was another voice, someone asking about prints, and Palmisano said, *yeah, check the outside of the window too,* then came back on. "Sorry. I'm on a scene. Guy broke into a building in Studio City, killed a security guard."

"Okay . . ."

"Reason I'm calling — guess whose office we found the body in?"

He had something to live for.

Daniel scooped up another forkful of eggs, chewed mechanically. Stared out the Denny's window to Sepulveda. From a huge billboard, a surly black dude pointed a gun at him, an ad for an upcoming movie called *Die Today*. The guy's name was Too G. Mom and Pop G must be so proud.

"More coffee?"

He nodded, pushed his mug forward.

"You're going to vibrate out of here."

"Huh?"

"From all the coffee." The waitress was a Latina with a pretty smile. Daniel gave her a nod, and she moved on.

At first, he'd been furious with the detective, the asshole gaming him. Trying to lure him in, like he was a moron, like he didn't know that the first moment he set foot in a police station was the last moment he'd have a choice in the matter. But he'd let the guy think he was scripting the conversation, and played for information.

He hadn't expected to hear about Laney, though. His beautiful girl, drifting in the cold currents of the Pacific. Dark hair waving like seaweed, body tumbling slow — *stop.*

But now he had something to live for. Someone had killed his wife.

There was a lot he still didn't understand, but one thing he knew for certain — hell, the cop had all but told him — was that the police weren't investigating. The sheriffs were so sure they had their man that they were letting everything else slip through the cracks. Well, he could do something about that.

The waitress set his check on the edge of the table, "For whenever," and breezed away. Daniel slurped his coffee, finished his bacon. He collected his new cell phone — a prepaid he'd bought at a gas station — and hit the bathroom. Splashed cold water on his face and finger-combed his hair, used paper towels to sponge-bathe his armpits. Then he walked out into a bright blue morning, Los Angeles sick with sunlight, same as ever. He unlocked the BMW, got in.

Nine times out of ten, when a wife is mur-

dered, the husband is involved.

Okay. So what about that tenth time? What then?

Think like a writer. Why do people kill?

Love and money, the old song went. It seemed like money was some sort of factor, given the jewelry Laney had bought. But that didn't help him much, or at least wouldn't until his memory returned.

Which left love. And on that one, he did have a thought.

He started the car and headed north. Navigating on autopilot, innately knowing how the streets connected, which were the fastest routes. Some of the places he passed seemed familiar — a bar he might have haunted, a café with a patio that he could almost remember the view from. He could feel the pressure of his memories, the way they surged and throbbed behind the levee his unconscious had erected to protect him from himself. Maybe the levee would give on its own; maybe he needed more information. Maybe he needed to find the person who had done this.

A lot of maybes. But that was the way things were for now. And he was tired of reacting. It was time to get proactive.

Then he turned the corner, and saw Laney looking at him.

The studio wall was thirty feet high, not tall enough to hide the enormous sound-stages beyond. But it did serve nicely to display enormous billboards of the major FOX shows: *American Idol, The Simpsons, . . .* and *Candy Girls.* The shot was of Laney with her "sisters," the redhead smiling and innocent, the blonde with a scheming seductive look, and Laney smiling that head-cocked Emily Sweet Special.

Daniel stared up at his dead wife. Wasn't there a point where life couldn't get more surreal?

Apparently not. As he watched, a guy in a spacesuit drove a battered Tercel up to security and rolled down his window, passing something to the guard. A moment later, the gate went up and the spaceman drove through. The guard wiped his brow, hitched his belt, and trundled back to his booth.

Daniel sucked air through his teeth, stared across the street. Cars came and went, pausing at the gate in both directions. He thought of the tabloid lines he'd read last night, all that dirty laundry.

"Laney was a beautiful woman with a beautiful soul. Everyone adored her. Me? I loved her."

Robert Cameron. Her "hunky costar." The one that fuck Perez Hilton had said she was rumored to be having an affair with, that *People* magazine had shown pictures of with Laney, the two of them shot in a nightclub, dancing one of those sexy Latin dances.

He didn't want to believe that she might have strayed. But if nine times out of ten the husband was to blame, maybe on the tenth, it was the lover. It was the kind of obvious angle the cops should have followed up on, but apparently hadn't, because they were certain Daniel was to blame.

"Laney was a beautiful woman with a beautiful soul. Everyone adored her. Me? I loved her."

"I bet you did," Daniel said. The light changed, and he pulled away. His wife's eyes hung in his rearview mirror.

But how to get to Cameron? The man's phone number and address would be unlisted. No way Daniel could stake out the studio and watch for him to leave. For one thing, security would notice; for another, the lot was *big.* Who knew how many entrances it had, which one Cameron used, or what he drove. So what then, Star Maps?

Well, he couldn't risk being himself. Fine. Then he had to be somebody else. He could show up at a cattle call, try to land a part as an extra. The studios always needed bodies. But that could take a long time. Besides, he had to imagine those people were thoroughly handled — no one wanted aspiring writers tracking down Al Pacino to thrust a script into his hand.

No, he needed to have reasonably free access. Who came and went on the lot? Who didn't work there but wouldn't draw attention? Who did they let in, then not look at?

Got it.

Daniel gunned the car.

The uniform supply place was at the south end of downtown, and from the outside looked like a warehouse, blank walls and loading docks. The place was in the shadow of the 10. Traffic was a steady roar, and the air was exhaust.

The showroom took up only a portion of the whole, but even so, it was startling. Racks and racks and racks of outfits, the kind he'd never really thought about. Cops had to get the uniforms somewhere, he supposed. And firemen, and chefs, and maids . . .

He fingered a police uniform, thought about maybe changing his plan. The uniform was incomplete, of course; it didn't have the flashing or the insignia. But what average citizen would think to look for those things?

No. People look at policemen. He wanted to be invisible.

In a section toward the back, he found a pair of shiny gray slacks. Polyester to avoid ironing, cut in a distinctly unfashionable style, and with a vertical stripe of shiny blue running up the leg. They were hideous. He grabbed them.

Next was a short-sleeve polo: diamond knit, the texture of paper towel, bright yellow with blue stripes ringing the collar and the sleeves. Perfect. He paid, then went looking for a screen-printing shop.

Timing was key.

He'd gotten everything he needed by eleven, so he killed an hour at a communal table in a Coffee Beanery, between an actor reviewing headshot possibilities and a well-dressed woman sipping a latte and reading a Robert Ludlum novel. Daniel spent the time trying passwords on the laptop, but none worked.

Shortly before noon, he pulled up to the studio gate. The lunch rush had cars going in both directions, and it took a couple of minutes before he reached the security booth.

He left his sunglasses on, rolled down the window. "Hey man. Delivery for," he

214

paused, grabbed the clipboard from the seat beside him. "Robert Cameron."

"Name?"

"Cameron, C-A-M —"

"No, your name."

"Oh, my name's Jay Dobry, but it should be under Arrow Couriers." He pointed to the logo on his bright yellow polo shirt. The guy at the screen-printing shop had done nice work with it, put the words in italics with little speed trails following them.

The guard hoisted his own clipboard, scanned it, shook his head. "I don't see —"

"Yeah, it was expedited. They'd have called down."

"Let me check." He stepped back into the booth. Daniel fiddled with the radio, trying to look bored. A moment later, the guard returned. "No, no badge for Arrow. You're going to need to —"

"Look, man, my boss called me, said it was absolutely urgent I pick this up" — he hoisted a plastic bag with the logo of a vitamin store on it — "and rush it down before lunch. Something about Mr. Cameron's agent threatening to pull him if he didn't get this?"

"What is it?"

Daniel laughed, pulled the bottle from the bag and read aloud. "A natural probiotic supplement of papaya and garlic from the Colombian Andes that helps metabolize protein, remove toxins, and reduce bloat." He passed it over, and the man looked at it.

"So what's the rush?"

"I just drive, man."

The guard hesitated, and Daniel shrugged. "You want to call my boss, he can call the agent, you guys can figure it out, but I'm going to need you to sign to prove that I was here on time. Cameron's agent paid for the Urgent Response Package, which means within an hour, and it's at" — he looked at the dashboard clock "— fifty-seven minutes now, dude, and so if you want to hold it, that's up to you, but I'm not getting caught in the middle, you know?"

Someone honked, and the guard looked up, made a conciliatory gesture to a Porsche. Then he sighed, passed the diet pills back to Daniel. "Stage sixteen. You know where you're going?"

"Dude, I'm here all the time."

"All right. Next time, make sure they call first, okay?" He reached into the guard-house, pulled out a purple parking pass. Daniel tossed it on his dash, then drove through the open gate, smiling to himself. A courier in a BMW rush-delivering diet pills. Hollywood.

The studio lot unfolded in broad avenues and vast, cream-colored soundstages with art deco façades and an air of competent activity. Crews dressed hipster-chic and flannel-grunge carried lights and cables while suits buzzed about in golf carts. Rows of white trailers lined up like racehorses in front of a hundred-foot-tall mural of Marilyn Monroe lounging against some guy. He passed through a section of suburban America, complete with broad grass lawns, a church, and a bandstand in a small park. Looking in one direction, he half expected to see kids playing tag; in the other, massive windowless warehouses like the Manhattan Project.

He had the same muscle-memory pull of directions, and it took only moments to find the correct stage. Apart from the number at the top, it looked just like the others, a colossal block plunked down from space. He pulled into a parking garage and killed the engine. The shade cooled the afternoon, brought relief to his scrabbling headache.

Nice work. You're super-fly. Now what?

The engine ticked. He rubbed at his eyes with his thumb and middle finger.

Well, now you get out of the car and ask Robert Cameron if he was sleeping with your wife, and if he killed her.

217

Or if he was sleeping with your wife, and when you found out, you *killed her.*

As an actress, Laney would have been surrounded by ridiculously attractive men. Glamorous guys, millionaire actors. She would have had to kiss them — hell, he'd seen her kissing Robert Cameron as Emily Sweet on *Candy Girls.* Long shooting schedules, press junkets, time on the road together. An affair was hardly out of the question. Hollywood marriages were a running joke.

A wave of black despair rolled over him. Not so much at the thought of a betrayal — or not only at that — but at the larger situation. Whether she'd cheated, whether she hadn't, it didn't change his circumstances. Neither brought her back from the dead. If she and Robert had been sleeping together, that might provide a motive for the man to murder her. Maybe. Which would get the cops off Daniel's ass, and let him return to . . . what?

A house he didn't remember?

A job writing for the show his wife used to star in?

What was his life now? What would he make of it?

On his long trip across the belly of America, he had played a game, inventing possible identities: he was a firefighter with a gambling addiction; he was a homosexual insurance salesman with a passion for soccer; he was a songwriter living off royalties from penning "Macarena." Trying on selves like clothing. If one didn't fit, if it chafed or was cut wrong, he tossed it aside and reached for the next. But now he was closing in on the hard fact that the options weren't limitless. He had been *someone* before. That person had been the result of a lifetime of choices, good and bad. And like it or not, he was drawing closer to that identity now. Not the freedom of infinite variety, but the tyranny of a decision made, a path walked, a life lived.

What if he didn't like the view?

Then you'll deal with it. You'll make changes. You'll take up fucking yoga. Whatever. Right now, stick to the plan. Do what the police won't.

He climbed out of the car, headed for the stairs. *Find out who killed your wife.*

Coming to the studio was a risk. But he quickly discovered that no one really looked at a man carrying a clipboard and wearing gray slacks and a bright yellow shirt. His new haircut and fake tan probably helped, but most people immediately classified him as a member of a different caste, and didn't spare more than a cursory glance. He adopted a blankly busy expression and walked with purpose. It wouldn't fly if he bumped into someone who knew him well, but it was as close to invisible as he could manage.

This section of the lot was all concrete and buildings, none of the carefully maintained greenery of faux-America. Stage 16 had a marked entrance, but he figured there would probably be another round of security. Halfway down the enormous building, he found a tall cargo door rolled open, with a semi backed up to unload. Daniel nodded at a black-clad woman smoking a cigarette, dodged around a costume rack, and stepped out of the street —

— into his front yard.

He stopped.

The set in front of him was the truncated exterior of a house. Not just any house, though. His house. The one in Malibu.

This version ended twelve feet off the ground. Above hung a light grid of black pipe, two dozen glowing lamps flooding the porch with soft sunset colors, a sort of hyper-clarity that made the fantasy house seem more real than the world surrounding it: the cavernous height of the soundstage, the dolly track laid on the floor, the craft services table stocked with sandwich meat and protein bars and vitamin water, the people buzzing about —

the afternoon he and Laney closed on the place in Malibu, they'd driven straight from the lawyer's office and wandered giggling around their new home. The first either had ever owned, and how lovely that it was the one they'd shot B-roll of in the early days. The one Cindi, the art director, claimed had the perfect Candy Girls *energy. Malibu instead of Venice, but who would believe aspiring starlets lived in Malibu, so he'd rewritten reality, as he was paid to. A few taps of his fingers on the keyboard had lifted the house and whirled it south, plunked it down ready for the Sisters Sweet to live in. And now, two years later, paychecks from the show provided the deposit to buy the real thing. Reality in a feedback loop. A writer and a once-aspiring actress buying their home with money from a show that used the house as home for an aspiring actress scripted by that writer —*

He shook his head. The memory had come as strong as a vision, and he wished he were alone, that he could sit and stare at the façade of life and try to peer behind it. But he wasn't, and it was only a matter of time before someone working at the other end of the soundstage recognized him.

Daniel raised his clipboard at an angle that screened his face, as if he were squinting to make out handwriting. Over the top edge, he scanned the people milling around his house. Though he probably knew them all, none of them were cast members. All crew then, setting up for a sequence.

He turned back the way he'd come and walked around the side of the soundstage until he reached the end, where a handful of trailers were parked. The third one had ROBERT CAMERON stenciled on the door. He took a breath, rocked his shoulders back, and knocked. "Arrow Courier. I have a package for you."

"It's open."

With a glance over his shoulder — no one around — Daniel opened the door and stepped inside. The trailer was nicely outfitted: leather couches, a side bar with scotch and glasses, a Bowflex nestled in the corner. Robert Cameron sat at the table, script pages in front of him. He had a stone jaw and dark hair, wore expensive jeans and a thin cashmere sweater. "Need me to sign —" Trailing off as their eyes met. *Daniel?*

Daniel closed the door behind him, took in the room, the actor. The guy was preposterously handsome, his features even, a hint of stubble, the kind of eyes you noticed the color of. Daniel imagined him kissing Laney, her rising up on tiptoes, pressing against his muscled body, and the thoughts were bitter.

"My god." Something washed across the man's face, a surge of emotion it was hard to read. Surprise? Guilt? Fear? Hard to say. The first character every actor learned to play was himself. The expression was quickly supplanted by a wide grin. "I'm so glad to see you. Where have you been? Everyone has been looking for you."

"It's complicated," Daniel said.

"I bet." Robert rose, looked him up and down. "What are you wearing?"

"Yeah, I . . ." He gestured at his courier outfit. Daniel tried on a smile, said, "Sorry about this. I needed to talk to you, but I didn't want anyone to know."

"You could have called. My god, ever since the accident, everyone thinks — I mean . . ."

"I didn't have anything to do with it."

"Of *course* you didn't."

Something in Daniel loosened. To hear it from someone else felt wonderful.

"I was just about to order lunch." The man walking over to a desk. "Let me get you something, you can tell me all about it. Sushi okay?"

"Umm. Fine." He glanced around, unsure what to do next. The actor picked up the phone, began to dial, his fingers shaking. In Daniel's fantasies, the man had come at him fists flying, or else had cowered, guilt in his eyes. The last thing he had expected was this affable conversation, an offer of lunch —

Daniel lunged forward, knocking over a chair, and jammed down the button to hang up the phone. Robert looked up, the mask of camaraderie gone.

"Calling security?"

"I . . . Of course not." The words falling lame. "Just ordering —"

"You thought you'd play nice, keep me busy while they came to get me."

Slowly, the man hung up. "What do you want?"

"I want to hear about you and Laney."

"What are you —"

"You've been telling the tabloids that you loved her. Tell me." He knew that the actor wasn't going to come out and admit to her murder. But Daniel wasn't a cop. He didn't need that. He just needed the man to slip, to let out one careless confirmation of impropriety, one hint of an affair. Bluffing was his best option. "I want to hear how much you loved my wife."

Robert seemed perplexed. "She was my best friend."

Uh-huh. "Your costar."

"Yes."

"Long hours. Lousy shooting schedule. All that time together. Must have been nice to have such a good friend to help pass the time."

"What are you getting at?"

"I know about the two of you." *Blink. Wince the tiniest bit. I'm watching.* "Laney told me before she died."

"Told you what?"

"About the affair."

"The affair?"

"You and her." He stared at the man's eyes, watching for anything, any hint of hesitation, any sideways dart.

What he didn't expect was for Robert Cameron to break out laughing. "How much have you had to drink today?"

"Don't you lie to me, mother —"

"Is this a joke?" Robert shook his head. "I knew you were an asshole, but I never thought you were that kind of asshole."

"What kind is that, *Bob?*"

"The redneck kind who thinks sexuality is multiple choice. I mean, really. I know you're from cow country, but this is beneath you."

"What are you — what?"

Robert sighed, reached for a frame on the desk, handed it to him. "Remember Alan?" The photo showed the actor and a blond guy with surfer hair, his arm slipped around Robert's lower back, the tips of his fingers resting on the curve of a hip.

Daniel felt a flush come into his face. "You're saying —"

"Oh for god's sake. It's not something to try on a Saturday night. I don't just browse a little man-on-man porn to spice up my private time. I'm not gay when the wife isn't looking." Robert took the picture back, glanced at it before setting it down. "Yes, I loved your wife. Laney was funny and smart and way out of your league. But of *course* I wasn't sleeping with her, you homophobe."

It should have been a relief. And on one level, it was. Sure, it assuaged his ego, but more than that, he didn't want to believe that she had been unhappy. That he had bored her, or hurt her, or driven her away. That the life he'd seen in their house was a lie. He had little enough to believe in. If he couldn't believe in them, he was done.

So he was glad that she hadn't been sleeping with Robert. But now the problem was that once again he had no idea what to do. Ever since he'd decided Robert Cameron might have been responsible for Laney's death, he'd had a purpose, and a reason to believe in his own innocence. Now that was gone.

"I'm sorry. It's not that at all, I promise. I just . . ." He didn't know how to finish the sentence.

"You know I'm gay. You used to tease Laney about being a fag hag. You planning to just forget that inconvenient fact so you can write an ending in your head that makes things easier on you? She's dead, so she must have been cheating on you, because that would make her loss easier to bear?" Robert shook his head. "I'm sorry, Daniel, I really am, but you're not the only one who's sad. I loved her too. And I won't let you mess up her memory just to make yourself feel better."

"Look, it's not that. I really didn't remember. I've got — I know this is hard to understand, but I'm . . . I'm . . ." Daniel found he couldn't say the words. He didn't want to tell Robert about his amnesia. Maybe it wouldn't matter, but that secret was all that he had, and he was reluctant to give it up. Plus there was a trace of shame in it too. Shame at not knowing who he was, and at the way he'd come off, as a small-minded homophobe revising history. "Never mind."

Robert snorted. "Of course."

"What?"

"You were about to tell me something, right? And then you decided to hide. That's you all over."

Embarrassment and confusion were burning in his belly, but the actor's words stoked them into something else. A cinder that was the beginning of anger. It felt better than shame. "Excuse me?"

"You heard me."

"What do you know about me?" Thinking, *Asshole, you don't have the first clue what I'm going through.*

Robert laughed mirthlessly. "Plenty."

"Yeah? Try me."

"I don't think so, Daniel. I don't really see the point." He straightened, brushed his hands. "Now, I have work to do. Why don't you show yourself out."

"No. I want to hear what you have to say."

Robert sighed. "You really want to do this?"

"Yes."

"Fine. She's gone, so we don't have to make nice anymore, do we? You want the truth, here it is. I never understood what she saw in you."

Daniel made himself smile, a thin thing that felt false. "Go on."

"You're a nice enough guy. But who are you, really? A mediocre writer in a town thick with them. Not particularly talented, not particularly smart, not particularly brave. The top of the middle of the bell curve."

Daniel stared him down. "Well, I certainly wasn't the star of *Candy Girls.*"

"And all the ways you hurt her," Robert continued. "Exorcizing your relationship demons on national television. Laney playing Emily playing Laney, with you as the puppet master, and who cared if maybe these things were private, she didn't want them out; this was art! Your drinking. Your distance. All of it."

The smoldering in his belly caught fire. "Bullshit."

"Oh, I know you were in love once. A long time ago, Laney told me that your wedding was the day her life began. But you know what I think? I think she outgrew you."

Daniel's fingers were curled into fists, the nails biting his palms. He didn't reply, didn't trust himself to speak. *It's not true. None of it is true. You loved her and she loved you. When she died, you tried to* kill yourself, *for Christ's sake.*

"I think that she was getting tired of all the things I always saw in you," Robert continued. "I think that scared you, because you knew those things too. I think that's what all those fights were really about."

"What fights?"

"Sure, revise again. Just forget about all the yelling, erase that whole week before someone drove her off the PCH."

He never liked you, he admitted it. So you can't trust what he says. You and Laney loved each other.

"My god. You killed her, didn't you?" Robert asked in a low voice. "I didn't. I hadn't believed it before, but. You did it, didn't you?"

"No." *I'm not that man. She loved me. If I can't believe that, I may as well not have made it off that beach. She loved me.*

"You killed her. She didn't love you anymore, so you —"

Daniel rocked forward and punched the actor's perfect nose. His hand and wrist exploded, but it felt distant somehow, something to deal with later, and he swung again, sunk a fist in the man's gut. Robert's eyes went wide in shock and pain, and he staggered into the trailer wall. Daniel followed, arm cocked back, looking the actor right in his fucking movie star eyes —

— and saw the terror in them.

The anger blew out of Daniel in an instant, and in the void, a terrible sick feeling crept in. What had he done? He reeled back. The room spun. Where had that rage come from? And what had he — he had almost . . . He bumped into the desk, knocking over the framed photo.

"I — Robert, I'm." He rubbed at his forehead, feeling the pulse throbbing. Think. He had to think. "I'm sorry. I'm so sorry."

The man wiped at his bloody nose with a shaking hand. "You broke my nose." The magisterial tone replaced by a stunned trembling that filled Daniel with shame.

Get out of here. This is not you. You have to get away.

He looked toward the door. If he left now, the man would have every security station locked down. Guards watching. Police on the way.

The sick feeling in his gut grew as he glanced around the room. His eyes stopped on the phone, and Daniel unplugged the cord from the base, then yanked the rest out of the wall. It was about eight feet long. He walked back to Robert, who stiffened at his approach, simultaneously raising his fists and sliding farther away.

"Get out of here, Daniel."

"I need to tie you."

"Get *out!*"

"I'm sorry. I just — I couldn't — the things you were saying, I couldn't." He sighed. "I can honestly say that I've never felt worse about something than I do about hitting you. But I still need to tie you."

"No —"

Daniel grabbed one of the man's arms, yanked it ineffectually. The actor was far stronger than he was, and Daniel doubted he would have had a chance in a fair fight. "Look," he said. "I'm not going to hit you again unless I have to. But I need to tie you. So put your hands *out.*"

For a moment, it looked like Robert might resist. Then he held his arms forward, wrists together. Daniel lashed the cord around and around, threaded the rest around the leg of the desk, then tied a couple of clumsy knots. It wouldn't hold for long, but it would do.

"I'm." He sighed. "I really am sorry, Robert. I . . ." What was the point of explaining? It wouldn't undo the damage. Daniel walked to the door, opened it, then turned back and said, one more time, "I'm sorry."

Outside, it was a perfect day, but laid atop the bustling lot and the beautiful people and the bright sky, Daniel could see Robert Cameron's eyes. See the way they had stared as he closed in. The wet panic in them, the animal fear. Daniel walked for the parking deck as fast as he dared.

Thinking, *It wasn't the punches. He wasn't scared of me as a fighter.*

He was scared because he believes I'm a killer.

And as he remembered the blind red fury that had taken him, Daniel wondered if it might be true.

For a lawyer, Sophie Zeigler had remarkably little experience with cops. She was a negotiator, a contract maven, a frontwoman, the person who said *no comment.* A hired fountain pen. On the occasions her clients got themselves arrested — DUIs, scenes in nightclubs, drugs — she held their hand, listened to the sob story, and then referred them to a criminal lawyer.

But in the last two weeks, she'd learned an awful lot about the police. Especially about Detective Roger Waters — *I know,* he'd said with a shrug, *go ahead with a David Gilmour joke if you like* — who had called her pretty much every day, asking the same questions. Where was Daniel? Why had he fled? Did he understand the serious nature of the charges? Did she?

She'd put up a stone wall. But it was getting harder to ignore the cracks. The worst thing Daniel could have done was vanish.

And there was that phone call, just before he took to the road, his strange, guilty apology for a sin he wouldn't explain. *He was confused,* she thought for the hundredth time. *Drunk and hurting and confused.*

And worst of all, there was the man who broke into her home. Asking questions about Daniel and smiling, always smiling, his face as bland and banal as a supermarket manager's even when he talked about torturing her.

It was getting to be a bit much. And perhaps sensing that, Waters surprised her at her office that morning. A shortish, intense-looking guy with just-so hair and a blocky suit made blockier by the shoulder holster. Seeing the gun prompted a quick flash to the intruder pulling the pistol from his belt, asking if she watched movies. She fought to keep her face straight. "Good morning, Detective."

"Good morning, Ms. Zeigler." His handshake was dry and professional. "I heard about what happened, wanted to make sure you were all right."

"I'm fine."

"You must have been terrified."

Gee, do you think? The police who had responded had been very polite. They had listened and taken notes and wandered around shining flashlights in the locks. But their expressions had been easy to read. They weren't going to catch the guy. The whole process had taken about an hour, and then the police had left, promising to send extra patrols down her Palisades block, suggesting that she get a dog if she was still nervous. "I'm fine. Thanks for your concern."

"What can you tell me about him?"

"I already told —"

"That was LAPD. I'm with the sheriff's department. Sometimes communication isn't as good as you'd like. We butt heads, you know." He smiled. "We both have pretty big heads, tell the truth."

She ignored the attempt to disarm her, said, "It's not your jurisdiction, right?"

"No, ma'am. But your intruder was asking about Daniel Hayes."

Sophie leaned back in her chair, studied the man. Most people who walked into her office, those who weren't in the business, they had a surreptitious voyeurism thing going. They took in the leather couch, the framed poster of *Accelerant* that Phil Hoffman and Parker Posey had signed to her, the picture of Bobby De Niro kissing her cheek, and you could see them wondering if there was a portal to Oz somewhere. Nonindustry folks didn't realize that making movies wasn't the same as watching them, that a hundred minutes of fantasy took three years of mundane, even boring work to produce.

Waters, though, seemed not to care. Maybe he was a book guy. Regardless, he'd taken in her office at a glance, and his eyes hadn't left hers since.

"As I've told you before, I have no information about Daniel Hayes's whereabouts, nor have I had any direct communication with him since —"

"I know." The detective held out his hands. "But what I'm wondering, maybe this guy was involved in what happened to Laney."

Sophie met the man's eyes, couldn't read them. She pressed the intercom button. "Mark, could you bring me a cup of coffee?" Pointedly didn't offer one to Waters. The tiniest crinkle around his eyes told her he'd caught the move, but otherwise he gave nothing away. "He was average height. In shape. He had on slacks and a black —"

"I read the report. I meant, what was he like?"

She hesitated. "Calm."

"Calm?"

"Like it was no big deal. Like this was a

regular thing to him."

"He surprised you in the bathroom?"

She crossed her arms. "As I was getting out of the shower. He was standing there."

"Anyone have keys to your house, codes for the alarm?"

"My housekeeper. A few friends. The man I'm seeing."

"Could one of them —"

"No."

"Can you remember what he said to you? Specifically?"

Do me a favor and don't scream, okay, sister?

Sophie said, "He asked me about Daniel, where Daniel was. He threatened me, told me that he wouldn't enjoy it, but that he would hurt me." Her voice mechanical.

"Did he say anything about Maine?"

She stiffened before she could catch herself. Looking up at Waters, she could tell that he had caught it. *Sloppy, sweetie. Very sloppy.* Well, no point bluffing now. "He asked why Daniel was in Maine. If he knew anybody there."

"And you said?"

"I said I didn't know that he was in Maine."

Waters nodded. "I did."

This time she controlled her reaction. "Oh?"

"In a town called Cherryfield. A little place way up north."

"I see." Her mind racing. So much to put in order. Daniel would need a first-rate criminal attorney, stat. The media had already crucified him in absentia; now that he'd been arrested, the whole cycle would start again. God, it was going to be the trial of the year, had all the elements: sex, violence, money, celebrity. "When will he be transferred back here?"

"He won't."

"He's entitled to a —"

"Daniel isn't in custody, Ms. Zeigler."

"I'm sorry?"

"A sheriff's deputy responding to a Teletype spotted his car and tried to arrest him."

Tried? What does that mean?

"Your client, you know what he did?" Waters knuckle-leaned into her desk, looking down at her. "He assaulted the officer, then drove his BMW through a hotel sign and led the deputy in a high speed chase. More than a hundred miles an hour." Waters paused, let his words sink in. "The officer fired on him."

There was a tentative knock on the door, and her assistant Mark poked his head in, coffee cup in hand, "Here you —"

"Not now," she snapped. Mark looked wounded, but she ignored him, spoke to Waters. "Did he — Is Daniel all right?"

Waters paused, straightened. He shot his cuffs. "We don't know."

Sophie leaned back, put her fingertips to her temples. Flashed on a Thanksgiving years ago, one of her Hollywood Orphan dinner parties for those who couldn't, or wouldn't, go home for the holidays. Someone telling a joke and Daniel laughing at it, laughing that particular way he did, starting with a hand clap like he was marking the scene. He'd laughed that way as far back as she'd known him. It was a gesture that stayed the same while his body aged around it, while both their lives changed, while time plodded forward. She thought about how seeing that clap and hearing his laughter had given her a glow in her chest that was neither exactly lustful nor precisely maternal, but somewhere in between; a desire to help and protect him and relish the pleasure of his progress.

"Another thing," the sheriff continuing, relentless. "Daniel had an office, right?"

"In Studio City. He didn't use it much."

"Last night someone broke in —"

She rolled her eyes. "You're kidding. Wait,

let me guess. You're thinking Daniel did it, right?"

"— and when he was surprised by the security guard, beat the man to death with a rock."

Sophie's mouth dropped open. The retort withered on her tongue.

"Got your attention now? I understand that he's your client, and your friend. I do. But this is the second murder he's tangled up in. So please. Help me."

"What." Her voice came out a croak. "Why do you think —"

"The guard was in Daniel's office. The rock had been used to break the window. Daniel's fingerprints were all over."

"It was his office."

"I know. But it still places him there." The sheriff sighed. "Look, I'm sure he didn't want to kill the guy. Probably didn't even mean to. But you know Daniel has a temper. Everyone he worked with said so. Said he was the nicest guy in the world, but that he could pop, go off."

It can't be true. Daniel wouldn't — he couldn't — Oh, sweet boy, tell me this isn't true. "He yells. He never hurts anyone."

"He never hurt anyone *before*. But now he's scared. Desperate."

"Wait. I told the LAPD officers that the

241

man who broke into my house was asking about a necklace. You know that Laney bought a necklace, an expensive one, the day she died. He's who you should be looking for."

The sheriff nodded. "I agree."

"You do?"

"Absolutely. And we are. But you need to understand. The way Daniel is acting, he's not giving us any choice. Even if this other guy is involved, right now it looks like Daniel was working with him. Until he talks to us, he's going to look guilty."

His words triggered a memory, one she'd tried a hundred times to ignore. The middle-of-the-night panic of a ringing phone. Daniel, his words running together, slurring drunk. Far past crying. Sobbing, the wet and choking sound of raw misery. Of a person torn in half. And barely audible between the shuddering gasps, his voice saying, *I'm sorry. I'm so sorry. It's my fault.*

She kept her mask in place. *He was drunk. It doesn't mean what this cop would think it means.* She looked at the detective, calm in his suit, eyes sharp and hard, mind already made up. And she couldn't blame him. Everything he said, it made sense.

"Sophie. Please. Is there anything else you can tell me?"

But Daniel was still her boy.

"It's Ms. Zeigler. And I have no information about Daniel Hayes's whereabouts, nor have I had any —"

"Fine," he said, going rigid. "As you like. But, Ms. Zeigler, you might remember this. You know when people are most likely to get hurt by the police?" He paused, then spoke with careful enunciation. "When they run from us."

She opened her mouth, closed it.

"I'll see myself out. But if you really want to protect Hayes, you'll help me."

Belinda Nichols was getting tired of bars.

She'd been working her way down Sunset, focusing on the dives, the tiki joints, the art bars with films projected on the wall and board games in a corner. Left on Silver Lake, the neighborhood Hispanics, homosexuals, and hipsters, a great combination for nightlife. But her head was pounding and she could smell a stale funk on herself — sleeping in the back of the van wasn't doing much for her hygiene — and the gun tucked in the back of her waist was driving her crazy, digging in when she leaned back, feeling loose enough to slip when she didn't. And through it all, the two thoughts spinning and colliding, dusting themselves off, and then spinning up again.

You're going to point a pistol at a living, breathing person and pull the trigger.

And *Where is Daniel Hayes?*

It was only seven and a Monday night, so she found a place to park easily enough. As she walked past the side of the van, she stroked the four-foot wound in the side, felt the paint flake against her fingers.

You're no longer Belinda Nichols. You're Niki Boivin. You find people. You wanted to be a private-eye-slash-nurse who knew kung fu, like something out of a seventies action show, but really you work for lawyers and creditors. Most of the time that means you sit behind a computer and dial the phone, but sometimes you have to do it old-school, and those are the nights you like best. The happiest moment of your day is jogging through morning mists with your dog, a mutt whose pit bull/dachshund heritage just had to include rape.

She'd been Niki Boivin most of the day, and slipped her on like old jeans.

A squat gray bunker abutting an auto repair shop and marked with only a small marquee, Spaceland looked like a roadhouse on some sad stretch of Southern highway instead of one of L.A.'s best music venues. Niki stepped in, blinking. The silver-blue curtain that framed the stage was bathed in light, but the band hadn't started. She pushed over to the bar, ordered a beer she didn't want from a pretty emo girl, all dyed hair and sadness. When it arrived, she pulled out a twenty, told the girl to keep the change.

Niki leaned back with her elbows on the bar. The place wasn't crowded yet, maybe fifty people milling about. Friends of the band, probably. Monday was for up-and-coming acts hoping to share the success of others who had strutted the same stage. As she watched, a skinny kid with nerd glasses walked on, picked up a bass, and began tuning it, the notes ringing low and slow.

Daniel Hayes wasn't here.

She sighed, took a swig of beer. The headache was getting worse; the bassist might as well as have been strumming her raw optic nerves. When the bartendress came back, Niki gave her a finger wag.

"Whatcha need?"

"Actually, I'm looking for someone."

"Somebody who works here?"

"No." She pulled the photo of Hayes from her pocket, the print a little crinkled. "This guy."

"Whoa, this is so film noir." The bartendress leaned in to stare at the photo. She was wearing citrus perfume, clean-smelling and nicer than Niki expected. "Wait, wait. I know my line." She straightened, tipped her head, hardened her eyes. "You a cop?"

Niki laughed. The girl wasn't bad. "Nope."

"Bounty hunter?"

If she wants to play, let's play. "Something like that."

"What do you want him for?"

"What's it to you?"

"What are you going to do to him if you find him?"

"Well . . ." Niki stuck her pause. "I'll probably shoot him in the head."

The bass player ran through a quick little riff, a handful of notes cut off in the middle as he stopped to tighten the strings.

"I don't want no trouble."

"You don't want trouble, you better tell me what I'm after."

The emo girl smiled, said, "This is fun, but I got customers."

"So —"

"Sure I've seen him. On the news. That's the guy killed his wife."

"But in here?"

"I think he's been in before. But I haven't seen him in a while."

"All right. Thanks." Niki folded the picture, took another sip of beer, then started away.

"Wait."

"What?"

"You forgot. You're supposed to pull out a business card and say" — she dropped her voice an octave — " 'If you remember anything, anything at all, you give me a call.' "

Niki paused. The gun bit into her back. She stared at the girl. Read her whole life. Born in the Midwest, Michigan or Ohio. Acting classes twice a week. A spec script she'd had "almost finished" for two, three years. Been an extra on a handful of films, landed a role on a sitcom that died in development. Probably blown a rock star or two in the stockroom; had offers to do porn, but so far turned them down. Twenty-four years old. But L.A. years were dog years, and she didn't have many left.

"I told you," she said, and turned away. "I'm not a cop."

It was time to get more botulism pumped into his face.

Jerry D'Agostino squinted in the mirror, swiveling his head to the left and right. Crow's-feet. No question. And were those lines on his forehead? *Lines?* Jesus Christ, cats and dogs living together. He'd have to schedule another Botox session. After Tuesday's shoot, maybe, as a little reward.

He opened the medicine cabinet, took out the face cream — fifty bucks an ounce, you ought to be able to chop it up and snort it — and squeezed a pea-sized dollop on each index finger. Patted it in, careful not to rub.

He walked down the stairs, past the framed posters of *The Last Taboo* and *A is for . . .* and *Mommy's Nasty Secret*. In the kitchen he pulled out a bag of carrots and began peeling them with long steady strokes, neat strips falling to the sink. When he was done, he chopped them and tossed the pieces in the juicer. A thick trickle of orange liquid filled a pint glass. He mixed in fish oil, green tea extract, a packet of vitamins, stirred the brackish liquid, and took a sip.

Uugh.

He coughed, took another slug, then tightened the belt of his robe and walked through the house to his office. Stood at the window watching the San Fernando Valley flicker like ten thousand candles. The 405 was a glowing ribbon. Planes coming in to Burbank rose and fell like sparks. Up in the hills, though, the bright spots were fewer, jewels in the night. In dazzling, cramped Los Angeles, darkness was a luxury.

Can it really have been thirty years?

He'd come here after Watts but before

Rodney King, the big bad eighties, when Arnold Schwarzenegger was dropping one-liners in action movies instead of speeches on the news, and Simi Valley was one of those jokes that wrote itself. Back then, he'd thought he was going to change the town, make it his. Thing about L.A., though, even though nothing stayed the same, it never really changed. But no matter how fortunes rolled and shifted, there were no slums in the Hills. If he hadn't changed the world, at least he'd improved his address.

He moved to the couch, pulled out his laptop. The Dago Productions logo flashed onscreen, the "o" of it the male symbol, a big proud cock of an arrow straining ever upward. It was strange, looking at it now. He felt, what was the word, conflicted. He owed everything he had to cocks straining ever upward. But still. Thirty years in the business, four-hundred-plus films, a dozen Woodys lined up on his mantel. But what did it all mean?

Stop, he corrected. *Clouds do not have to bring rain. You are of the sun. Feel the rays of empowerment, and let them change you.*

He opened the script, scrolled to the last page.

INT. HOLLYWOOD APARTMENT —
NIGHT
It is a small room. JENNA ST.
JOHN SIMONE, a beautiful woman
with a pure heart who has come
to Los Angeles to become a
STAR, sits on her bed. She is
wearing a beautiful white
dress symbolizing her PURITY.

                    JENNA
I know that you are out there.

Jenna bites her lip. She is
sad.

No, better than sad. He highlighted the
word, looked at the synonyms.

Jenna bites her lip. She is
wistful.

                    JENNA
Where are you? The man who
will see that I am more than
just a beautiful woman. Who
will love me for my heart.

Jerry sighed, rubbed at his eyes. It was
good, but what now? The books all said that

a screenplay was about 110 pages, but he was on page 68, and so far, Jenna St. John Simone hadn't had any luck either becoming a star or finding the man she knew was waiting for her.

Don't lose faith. You are of the sun —

Someone moved on his patio.

Jerry came upright so fast the computer slipped off his lap and hit the carpet. He killed the light, stepped closer to the window. Squinted. A man's shape was framed against the railing, barely visible in the glow of his pool lights.

A boyfriend. About once a year some brokenhearted hick from Kansas tried this. They all had visions of rescuing their girlfriends, like D'Ago the Dago was some kind of fairy-tale monster who had enslaved them, instead of a businessman who knew talent when he saw it. Though none of the boyfriends had been dumb enough to sneak onto his fucking property.

Well, this one was going to get a lesson in business. He slid open his desk drawer, pulled out his pistol, and racked it. Then he tightened his bathrobe and padded through the house. Squaring his shoulders, he yanked open the patio door.

"Asshole, you're trespassing."

The guy didn't move, didn't turn around.

What the hell?

Jerry stepped forward. "Hey! I can see you. Turn the fuck around."

Bennett turned, leaning back against the railing with his elbows propped up. The wavering illumination of the pool lit D'Agostino from below, splashing a pallid yellow over his tan and glinting off the gun in his right hand. "Hell of a view you got here, Jerry."

"Bennett? Jesus." The producer heaved a sigh, lowered the pistol. He had that slightly pickled motivational speaker vibe: skin too tight, teeth too white, spray-tan too thick. Still, for a man who used to boast that breakfast was best served on a mirror, he looked damn good. "Didn't know you were back in town. What are you doing here?"

"Calling in a marker."

"Whose?"

"Yours."

"Hey, whoa. You said we were even. After I did the thing."

"I lied."

"You promised."

"I lied." He nodded at the gun. "And if you don't put that away, I might decide you're being inhospitable."

The producer paled and quickly tucked

the pistol into the pocket of his robe. "Sorry."

Bennett said nothing, just let the silence deepen. Every second was weighing on the other man, he could see that. Poor Jerry had always been a nervous boy.

"So. What do you —"

"I'm going to be staying here for a while."

"Great. Let's plan dinner, some drinks. I'll have a couple of girls join us —"

"You don't understand. I'll be staying here."

"Here? In my house? I mean," the guy tripping over himself, "we go back a long way, you know I'm glad to see you, but come on. I can't —"

"Jerry."

Just saying his name was enough. The trick was always in breaking them the first time. They would never forget. After that, it rarely took more than a hint. Didn't matter if you were talking about a hard guy or a TV starlet or a porn producer.

Back in '81, Jerry D'Agostino had convinced his girlfriend to let him shoot video, fantasy stuff — the secretary who gave her all for the company, the cheerleader raising team spirit — promising that it would be just for them. That was back in the dawn of porn's golden day, when every home suddenly had a VCR and every video store had a back room obscured by a bead curtain. The girlfriend hadn't lasted, but Dago Productions' first film had done quite well, and hundreds had followed.

Bennett had heard rumors, did his due diligence, and found out that the Dago kept two sets of books. A dangerous move, since the men he was skimming had ties to Vegas and New York and a habit of leaving bodies in the desert. He'd come at Jerry sideways, offering a business proposition, a little sideline using some of D'Agostino's "stars" to run a honeypot scam.

Dago had tried to pass. But in the end he'd come around to Bennett's way of thinking.

"So. Um. You just need a place to crash?"

"Something like that."

"Okay, yeah, sure. I'll ah, I'll make up the guest room."

"Sorry, Jerry, I wasn't clear. I need peace and quiet." He put on his affable smile.

"I don't —"

"You're going on vacation."

"What?"

"Tonight."

"No, I can't, I've got a shoot this week. This new girl, she's dynamite. Eighteen and tits like artillery shells. Plus she'll do it

254

rough, doesn't mind choking, spitting. She'll throat-job and moan like it's the highlight of her day. Shit's hot now, near-rape fantasies. They eat it up in the Midwest."

Bennett said nothing. Just smelled the night air, listened to the murmur of distant traffic and the burble of the pool filter. His thigh ached a little in the cold, where the bone had been broken a dozen years ago. Complications on a job in . . . Dallas, had it been?

"B., really, I can't." The man talking faster, angling and wheedling. "How about this, how about I take a room at a hotel? You can have the house, you know, my pleasure, I want you to have it."

Ripples in the pool's surface cast streaks across the producer's face. Far away, a car honked, loud and long. There was really no need to drive Dago out of town — Bennett mostly didn't want the guy near him, talking too much and thinking too little — but he also didn't want Jerry to think that they were negotiating. So he just slowly let his smile fade.

"I." D'Agostino staring at his bare feet. "I'll get packed."

Bennett nodded, turned back to the view. A police helicopter swung back and forth in circles somewhere over Van Nuys, the searchlight glowing. He heard the sound of Dago's footsteps, waited till the man was almost at the door, then said, "Jerry?"

"Yeah?"

"The gun."

A pause, and then the sound of the guy walking back. He came alongside Bennett, reached into his pocket, pulled out the pistol. Bennett took it, held it loose, not quite aiming at the man. "And your car keys."

"What? How do I get to the airport?"

"Call a cab."

Later Bennett explored his new house. It really was a nice place, the décor a little tacky, but the views spectacular. He set up his laptop in Jerry's office, at a desk facing the window, so that he could look out at the city spread wide below him.

Shortly after Laney's death, Bennett had broken into their house and left a few things. Life had gotten so much easier these days. God bless the Internet. Used to be difficult to get surveillance equipment, never mind streaming video, broadband wireless, scriptable file transfer protocols.

He'd placed three cameras. The first appeared to be a carbon monoxide detector and plugged into the wall in the entryway, with a clear view of the door. The second, secreted in a book, had gone on a shelf in Hayes's home office. The final camera, his personal favorite, was in a Kleenex box, one of those decorative types that rich people liked, so that even their tissues matched their color palette. That one he'd put in their bedroom, on Laney's nightstand. All three were high-res, worked in near darkness, and best of all, were motion-activated. They broadcast right over Hayes's wireless router, dumping everything they recorded to an anonymous file server.

Not so many years ago, Bennett would have had to sit on his ass and watch the house himself. Now he just logged in.

All three cameras showed multiple files. Busy busy. He opened the most recent first, starting with the hallway. The video began with the front door flying open, men rushing in, cops with their guns out. Moving fast and splitting up, yelling, *Clear!*

Interesting.

The office and bedroom cams showed the police — scratch that, sheriffs — coming in equally hard. Then, once it became clear that whoever they were looking for wasn't there, they relaxed, wandered about. Opened drawers, glanced in closets. The audio was a little muffled, but he could hear them talking about an intruder, and saying

Hayes's name.

So his boy was back in town.

He was about to switch to earlier files when he saw one of the deputies glance around, then quickly open one of the dresser drawers, pull out a pair of white lace panties, and jam them in his front pocket. Bennett chuckled. He took a screen cap into Photoshop, upped the image size, and tinkered with the unsharp mask settings until he could read the cop's nameplate. "Deputy Wasserman. You nasty celebrity crotch sniffer." Bennett saved the file, made a note of the sheriff's info. Never knew, might come in handy.

The next video clip was the man who vanished. Daniel Hayes in living color, walking into his front hall.

Gotcha.

The man looked exhausted. No surprise, given the distance he'd covered. Bennett had a woman at American Express who'd rather her boss didn't know about her "recreational" freebase habit, and based on the charges on Hayes's card, he'd sprinted east like his ass was aflame. Then vanished once he reached Maine.

What brings you back, Dan?

On the screen, the man stared at photographs, a shell-shocked expression on his face. Up in the bedroom he moved slow, a glass of whiskey in his hand, going through his own drawers like he was looking for clues. He looked over at Laney's side of the bed, right at the goddamn camera, and for a second Bennett wondered whether he'd been burned. But no; something else had obviously affected him, the guy slipping to his knees, shaking and crying.

In the next scene, the writer walked into his office like he'd never been there. Looked at his shiny award, chuckled. Then sat down at the desk, gazed out the window, and saw something that spooked him. He was on his feet, tearing through cabinets, snatching his computer. The audio caught something, a voice, but too far and too garbled. Based on the time stamp, that would be the sheriffs. Hayes sprinted out of his den, then into the bedroom, and then, nothing. Must have gone out a window.

Bennett leaned back, tapped a finger against his teeth. *What did you just see?*

There had been something off in Hayes's behavior. Grief? Partly, sure, but there was more. Exhaustion? The guy had driven back and forth across the country in near record time. He had to be ragged as hell.

You know what ragged looks like. This is something else. He couldn't put his finger on it, but the guy seemed . . . well, off.

Bennett watched the video again. There it was. In the office, when Daniel picked up his award. He had smiled. It was a small thing, but it was out of place. Exhaustion and sorrow made sense. He'd lost the love of his life, and it didn't look like he'd slept since.

So would a writing award cheer him up? Even briefly?

Bennett set the video to loop and watched until he was certain. Something else was going on. He didn't know what, but something.

Regardless, he'd gotten what he really needed. Daniel Hayes was back in town. Bennett was about to close the video when he noticed there were earlier files. Someone else had been in the house. The police again?

He fired up the camera in the hallway. The front door opened, and a woman walked in, a bag on her shoulder.

Bennett froze the image. Stared at it.

You have got to be kidding me.

It was risky to be out in public, but Daniel couldn't make himself care. Too many hours in the car, in shitty hotel rooms, in his own head. He needed space and a view and a place to think. So he'd parked the BMW at the north end of Fuller, put on his ridiculous shades, and started up Runyon Canyon.

The drooping sun painted the sky a smudgy orange. A lot of people were hiking the path, dogs running orbits around them, but things thinned out when he veered off to the harder route, a stern uphill that was more dirt and sand than pavement. His quads and calves and lungs were burning in minutes. It felt good, the pain, and he made himself go hard, jogging where he could. Punishing himself. As though half an hour of exercise could make up for his behavior with Robert Cameron.

You're not cruel. You don't have to be.

But he remembered that cinder in his belly, the way it had flared up and made him snap. Remembered the fear in the actor's eyes as Daniel tied him. Whether or not Cameron had believed it before, in that moment, he certainly thought that Daniel had killed his wife.

But I didn't. I know I —

Yeah yeah.

He hit a hard stretch near the top, a narrow, steep incline that had him panting. Sweat soaked the armpits of his silk shirt. But the exercise drove out thought.

The top of the canyon came on almost as a surprise, a leveling off as he rejoined the main path. The sun was below the horizon now, though the sky was still bright. A woman in a sports bra jogged by. Two guys walking the other way paused in their conversation to watch her pass, then shook their heads at each other and grinned. Daniel felt a pang of envy at the exchange, the easy camaraderie of friends.

The trail paused at an overlook point with a tall bench and a stunning view of the L.A. Basin: Hollywood, Beverly Hills, Westwood in the distance. A million tiny Christmas lights shimmering, god knew how many people out there living their lives. Daniel mopped his forehead, walked to the edge.

The hills spread out on either side, mansions with unimaginable price tags, architectural wonders with blue-green pools on broad concrete decks. For a moment he stared, breathing hard but moved by the beauty of it all.

What had happened in the actor's trailer? Daniel honestly hadn't realized that he had a temper like that. That there was something inside of him that could explode not just into violence, but into an enjoyment of it. When he moved in on the actor, he had been excited about the thought of hurting him, of messing up his perfect movie star looks.

Yes. But you also thought that your wife had betrayed you with him. That maybe he even had something to do with her murder. Your reaction could belong to anyone.

Daniel flexed his fingers, squeezed his right wrist with his left hand. It was sore as hell. Turned out punching someone hurt quite a lot.

And the things he was saying. That you weren't good enough for her. What does he know about that?

It was like the tabloids. They painted one picture, a squalid, hateful image. But everything else he had seen of the life they had lived painted another.

Still. The guilt. That dream about his bloody hands, the faceless judges looming like towers. Was it possible that he and Laney had some sort of fight? He could have lost that same terrible temper with her.

And then, what? Chased her out of your house, borrowed an SUV, and ran her off the road? It's fine to question. Crucial. But don't stop thinking.

No, though he wasn't proud of what he'd done to Robert, it didn't erase the facts. Too many things didn't fit. Like the diamond necklace. If Laney was going to run out on him, she wouldn't have needed to empty the bank account. He was just a writer; she was a star. Their money would have come from her. A weird feeling, but what the hell. It wasn't like he'd been eating bonbons on the couch. Wasn't his fault that the industry valued actors more than writers.

But what the hell are you? A mediocre writer in a town thick with them. Not particularly talented, not particularly smart, not particularly brave. The top of the middle of the bell curve. Robert Cameron's words in his ears.

On second thought, decking the guy maybe wasn't *that* much of a sin. Asshole. He'd claimed to be Laney's best friend, but he'd been feeding her poison about her husband? Not the friendliest move in the playbook. Especially since he'd said, directly, that Laney had loved him. "Laney told me that your wedding was the day her life began."

That was something. He was right to feel the certainty he did. Laney had loved him, and he had loved her, and he hadn't had anything to do with her —

Holy shit.

Daniel froze, mouth hanging open. Then he turned and sprinted down the hill.

He didn't dare drive down his block. If cops were watching, that's where they'd be parked. Instead, Daniel left the BMW by the beach and walked back up. He made himself go slow, just a neighbor taking a stroll. When a gray security vehicle slowed, he gave them a nod and kept walking. The driver waved and moved on.

Life begins. The password clue for his laptop. And Robert Cameron had said that Laney had referred to their wedding as the day life began.

Daniel knew, he *knew*, that the password was their wedding date. How many answers must be on that computer, hidden behind that simple code? A date he'd seen inked on the mat of a photograph of him and Laney standing in the water in Maine, her dress hiked up, both of them laughing.

Which was great. Except he couldn't remember what the date had been. *Funny. Can't even blame this one on the amnesia. You just can't recall.*

Yeah. Funny. Sometimes irony was so funny you wanted to shoot yourself in the head.

It took Daniel ten minutes to make it to the block that backed up to theirs. The house he picked looked unassuming from the street, the security fence almost festive with the Christmas lights strung on it. No way to tell if someone was looking out a window, but at least the street was quiet.

He took a deep breath, shook out his arm, and launched into a run. He put on as much speed as he could, leaping at the last second to plant a foot against the wall. His momentum carried him far enough that he could grab the top and pull his legs up and over before dropping to the grass beyond.

God*damn,* but that felt good.

The yard was broad and brightly lit, floodlights spilling up the undersides of trees. He stayed low and moved to the perimeter. One nice thing about conspicuous wealth, it made for enough space to be inconspicuous. No one with a house in

Malibu wanted to acknowledge that anyone else lived there, and there was a thick tree line between this house and its nearest neighbor. Daniel kept to it. A dog barked from inside the house and his heart jumped, but he kept moving until he reached another fence, this one oriented more to privacy than to security.

Ten seconds later, he was in his backyard.

A gust of wind tugged at the avocado tree, the leaves whispering against one another. Broken branches were scattered on the grass where he'd tried his hand at flying. He smiled ruefully, then went to the back door. The third key on his ring unlocked it.

He started to fumble for the light switch, caught himself. *Idiot.* He took a moment to catch his breath and let his eyes adjust. Then he crept through the kitchen into the living room.

In the dark, the house was at once familiar and strange, a long-lost friend whose face had been weathered and changed by time. He moved slowly, the faint light through the windows silvering everything. The frames on the mantel were black shapes, but he was pretty sure which one he wanted. He picked it up, walked to the front window, tilted it to catch the light.

There they were, frolicking in the surf,

again, forever. The date was written in the bottom corner. May 23, 2003. Right. Good thing to remember.

Brilliant white light spilled in the window.

Daniel collapsed like he'd been shot.

That wasn't the offhand bounce of headlights. It was a spotlight. Like the kind police had mounted on their cars.

No, no, no! Not now. Run, you have to run, if you hurry you can —

He took a deep breath. Exhaled slow. He had to think, not panic. On elbows and knees he army-crawled back from the window. The light wobbled and moved, sweeping like an accusing finger, white and sharp and unforgiving. It vanished from the window, spilled in the glass on either side of the front door. Paused, and then panned back to the window.

It's a patrol car. Waters probably has them swinging by the house just in case. That's all it is. If they were really coming for you, it wouldn't be like this. It would be men with flashlights and guns coming in the front and the back.

It was one thing to think. Another to act on that. But he made himself hold steady, just lie on the ground, the wedding photo in his hand.

Ten heartbeats later, the light shut off. He

heard the sound of a car engine revving.

Daniel let himself breathe.

Back on the streets, the hard part was walking slow. Running would attract attention, but running was what he desperately wanted to do. Partly for fear the police might return, but the greater portion by far was the certainty of answers.

It took a long, long time to make it back to the car.

The moment he was safe inside, he pulled the laptop from his bag. Waited, fingers tapping, while the thing loaded. When the welcome screen came up, he typed "052303."

Incorrect Password.

You've got to be fucking kidding me.
He stared. Thought. Then he typed "05232003" and pressed enter. The loading screen vanished. There was a rising sound and a string of piano notes from the computer speakers, and the desktop appeared. The wallpaper was a picture of a nun giving him the finger. There were program icons on the left side: Word, Final Draft, Outlook, iTunes, Firefox, Quicken, Steam, Mine Sweeper. The right side had folders: My

Documents, Scripts, Photos, My Music, Video.

Daniel stared. Ran his finger along the touchpad like it was a holy artifact. When the mouse responded, he double-clicked Outlook. There was a pause, and then the e-mail program popped open, displaying dozens of folders in one pane, and his inbox — 1,128 items — in the other. Subject headers ranging from "Notes on Episode 97" to "All Natural Penis Enlargement!!" Names, names, names.

Including Laney's. He opened one of her messages at random.

From: Laney Thayer (malibubarbie27@gmail.com)
To: Daniel Hayes (DHayes@comcast.net)
Sent: 10/29/08, 11:18 AM
Subject: Urgent News

Psst — they're bringing in cupcakes for Kelly's birthday! The good kind, with the sour cream frosting. Here's the plan.

You get two, tell them one is for me. Then I'll get two and say one is for you.

Meet you behind my trailer. I'll be wearing a gray trench coat. The password is "yum."

This message will self-destruct in 5, 4, 3 . . .

Daniel read the message again. Then he shut the laptop and threw the car into gear.

The girl at the counter took in her port wine stain, popped her gum, and assigned Belinda Nichols a computer.

For days Belinda had been looking for Daniel Hayes, tracking him through the bars he frequented, following friends and acquaintances. So far, nothing. It was time to try a different approach. She walked through the too-bright Internet café, found her system, logged on. Daniel had spent most of his life in front of a computer screen; maybe he still did. She started with Facebook, searched for his name, found his fan page — 2,314 fans. The wall had posts from many of them:

Florian Maas Daniel, I know you didn't do it!
3 hours ago

Brandee Crisp Where are you, Daniel? You can come hide at my house if you want. I'll help you forget Laney.
8 hours ago

Kelly Hager I'm so, so sorry for your loss. This too shall pass.
Sunday November 8th at 9:08pm

The "In a relationship with" link read Laney Thayer. For kicks, Belinda clicked on the name — 153,289 fans. Funny world. Laney's wall had posts too:

Keith Henneman Only the good die young. R.I.P., Laney
about 2 minutes ago

Steve Medallin U were a ray of light 2 so many people. RIP, baby. Sorry to your husband.
about 5 minutes ago

Sara Varys i think it sucks that so many of you joined only cause she died. i've been a fan since 6,000. Laney we miss U!
about an hour ago

Bob Egan Such an ugly thing to happen to someone so beautiful. My condolences to your husband and family and friends.
2 hours ago

Kilburn Hall Umm, hello? You all know

that her husband killed her, right?
2 hours ago

Friendship requests over computers. Kids texting instead of passing notes. Digital persona that had more vitality, more animus, than the real people. Celebrities famous for being famous celebrities. Homepages for the murdered; fan groups that swelled after a tragedy; condolences from total strangers. All of it virtual, part of a floating domain no one could ever visit. Facebook For The Dead. *What a weird thing we've made of the world.*

Belinda shook her head, went back to Daniel's page, scrolled quickly. Nothing from him, no posts to fans or police, no status updates saying he was okay. She wasn't surprised, but it had been worth a try.

Let's get a little deeper.

She typed in the address for his Internet service provider. When she clicked on the portion that opened webmail access, it presented her with fields asking for e-mail address and password. The e-mail she had. The password . . .

What are passwords? Birthdays. The name of a wife or a pet. Things people never forget.

Hmm. She tried the obvious ones first:

CandyGirls. His birthday. His wedding anniversary. On the last, it opened right up. Bennett was right. People really were predictable.

There were more than a thousand messages. Belinda started at the top.

He found a hotel off Sixth Avenue, in what used to be called Skid Row, down near the Greyhound station. A narrow storefront of chipped brick with dead neon declaring it THE AMBASSADOR. Daniel was fairly sure it wasn't a favorite of the diplomatic corps; the lobby was parquet and piss, the counter was sealed behind an inch of Plexiglas. The clerk looked like she had rollers in her hair, but didn't. Her eyes were locked on a twelve-inch television.

"I need a room."

The woman just held up a finger for silence. On the TV screen, a square-jawed man in a doctor's coat stared into the middle distance as the music swelled.

"Hey." Daniel rapped on the Plexi. "Aunt Bee."

She looked over. "Ex*cuse* me?"

He pressed a wad of twenties against the glass. "I need a room."

The walls might once have been white, but were now a palimpsest of stains he didn't care to look closely at. His neighbor had an affinity for game shows and a gargling cough like drowning. A radiator hissing in one corner heated the room to sweltering. Daniel opened the single window, then plugged in the laptop. He entered the password, and once again programs teased their familiarity, folders beckoned with secrets, and a nun flipped him off.

He took a deep breath, put his fingers on the keyboard. Suddenly nervous. There would be so many answers, so many details. The record of his life in minutiae. But it was minutiae that made things real. What if he didn't like what he found? What if it turned out that he was a violent man, that Laney was frightened of him, that their marriage was a sham, that she was unhappy . . .

Moment of truth, my friend. Time to face the life you built. It's something most people never have to do. How many, given the chance to be something different, to start fresh and be whatever they wanted, how many would take it? How many marriages survive out of habit, how many lives are lived in quiet desperation?

What if yours was one?

He looked out the window. Purple clouds moved in Mark Rothko gradients. A packed bus rumbled by, not one white face on it. In the distance, police sirens.

On the other hand, that does beat a life of noisy terror.

Daniel smiled and dove in.

There was so very much of it. Thousands of e-mails in scores of folders, and a thousand more that hadn't been sorted. Long threads discussing the best way to handle a casting situation on the show. Short exchanges with people he apparently had known well, planning lunches, drinks, parties. Notes to his agents, the producers, the studio execs, his lawyer. Catch-up rambles with people he hadn't seen in years. And Laney. So many e-mails with Laney, ranging from . . .

From: Laney Thayer (malibubarbie27@gmail.com)
To: Daniel Hayes (DHayes@comcast.net)
Sent: 07/23/08, 7:54 PM
Subject: Pavilions

Grab toilet paper on your way home?

. . . to . . .

From: Laney Thayer (malibubarbie27@gmail.com)
To: Daniel Hayes (DHayes@comcast.net)

Sent: 9/10/08, 9:23 AM
Subject: Saturday . . .

Can we please lock the doors and turn off the phone and spend all day under the covers watching Battlestar Galactica?

From: Daniel Hayes (DHayes@comcast .net)
To: Laney Thayer (malibubarbie27@gmail .com)
Sent: 9/10/08, 9:25 AM
Subject: RE: Saturday

Can I pretend I'm in bed with Starbuck? ;)

From: Laney Thayer (malibubarbie27@ gmail.com)
To: Daniel Hayes (DHayes@comcast.net)
Sent: 9/10/08, 9:27 AM
Subject: RE: RE: Saturday

Why not? I'm planning to.

Love letters and bill reminders. Jokes and forwarded baby pictures. Links to articles on politics and bitchy rants about colleagues. He read for hours, his eyes sore and dry, words starting to wobble. It was like trying to navigate a forest by turning a random direction every time he came to a clearing. There was simply too much information, and not enough context.

He moved on to the pictures. There were tons of them, he and Laney on vacation, on the set, in the car, in their house. An early morning shot of him with his hair pulled into a wacky tangle. Laney holding someone's baby, making the little girl wave at the camera. Shots of dinner parties and Christmas trees and friends. But by and large, the photos were of the two of them, individually or together.

A world of two.

It was surreal. He had the queer sensation of eavesdropping on his own life. And that was before he discovered the videos.

INT. DANIEL & LANEY'S KITCHEN — EVENING
A cook's dream — a six-burner Viking stove, butcher block countertops, a window on the back wall to an avocado tree in a small enclosed yard. Two bottles of wine, one empty, one half, and a couple of glasses.
LANEY THAYER, casual in jeans

and a pink tee worn over a black long-sleeve shirt, stands at the counter. Strands of hair slip from her pony-tail, and she is caught mid-giggle.

> DANIEL (O.S.)
> Okay.

Laughter bubbles through his voice, and it sets Laney off again. The video is grainy and wobbly, obviously shot with a simple digital camera.

> DANIEL (O.S.)
> All right. Okay. Okay. So.
>   (collecting himself, then
>   adopting a theatrical voice)
> And now, Laney Thayer, star of television's hit series *Candy Girls,* performing her rendi-tion of *The Peanuts Christmas Movie.*

Laney sets down her glass of red, turns to face the camera. Her smile could power a city. It is nothing at all like her

signature *Candy Girls* pout.
She launches into song.

                    LANEY
*Hawrk the herald ang-gels
siing-*
  (she stops, changes to a
  laughing tone.)
You know, with their heads
thrown back and mouths all
wide —

She opens her mouth hugely,
uses her hands to mark an
imaginary Pac-Man maw.

              LANEY (CONT'D)
  (singing again)
*Glo-ree to, the new bowrn
king.*
  (talking)
Remember? Remember?

Daniel's answer is a laugh
that shakes the camera.

              LANEY (CONT'D)
And then they dance.
  (she sings the soundtrack)
da-na-na-nanana-na-nah, da-

na-na-nah . . . da-na-na-nanana-na-nah, da-dada, da-dada . . .

Her dance is silly, a jig of hopping from foot to foot, arms behind her, head thrown back as she sings her own soundtrack.

LANEY (CONT'D)
Bah-dah-dah-dah! Doink-iddie doink-iddie, doink-iddie, Bah-dah-dah-dah! Doink-iddie doink-iddie —

Her voice dissolves into champagne bubble laughter. She poses for a moment, then sweeps out a deep, showman's bow.

LANEY (CONT'D)
Yup. That's it. That's how they do it.

The video goes wonky, twisting sideways, then upside down. There is a clear flash of her shoulder, then a blur of

hardwood floor, then something fuzzy and dark, perhaps a sweater.
The cameraman appears to be neglecting his duties in order to cop a hug.

> DANIEL (O.S.)
> (a melting tone)
> You. Ahh, you.
> (a beat)
> You are one foxy chick.

Laney giggles again, and then the video freezes.

Daniel's mouth stretched in a smile wide enough to hurt, but his body was tense and rigid. He felt like a man gut-shot in the middle of a joke.

That was all? How could that be all? He stabbed the button to play it again.

Their kitchen sprang to life, not the morbid drunkard's cave he'd seen, but the heart of a warm home. Red wine glowed. Laney, his Laney, laughed and sang and danced for him. Her ponytail bobbed from side to side, her feet tapped out that goofy Riverdance, her hips swayed lithe and graceful. A silly, private moment, not the kind of thing epic love poems were written about. But the kind of thing they *should* be written about. Not love as stormy skies and sweeping passion, gathered armies and pounding seas. Real love. Love that had to pick up the dry cleaning, and worked too late, and could swim in a moment's laughter. Love that could fit into a life.

He set it on loop.

Again and again and again she danced for him. Joyful and unself-conscious and free. Daniel didn't realize he was crying until he felt the slick trickle of a tear paving a route down his cheek. He didn't stop himself. Just sat and watched her dance and bawled like a child.

Oh baby, my baby, where did you go? How could you leave me alone here?

He paused the video to check the date stamp. It had been recorded on October 18th. Laney had been murdered on November 3rd.

Just two weeks separated the woman dancing in fluffy socks from the broken body spinning in cold ocean currents.

Nausea twisted his guts like a handful of rope. He staggered to his feet, stumbled to the bathroom, collapsed in front of the toilet, barely making it before everything exploded out, sick and hot. His fingers clutched the dirty porcelain. Shoulders shaking with fever. The pain tore through him like lightning, flashes that left him blind and weak.

It was all gone. The life he had led. The thousand intimacies they'd shared. The victories and struggles and banal moments. Cooking dinner or watching television or sitting with his feet in her lap, it was gone forever.

Nothing was supposed to be this bad.

No wonder. No wonder I got in my car and took off. The only amazing thing is that I made it all the way there.

And all he had to look forward to was remembering it all again. Like a slow drip of acid, each memory would leave a wound. Each would be a reminder of what would never be again.

Daniel huddled on the cracked floor of the flophouse bathroom and wept.

He couldn't say how long he lay there. But eventually, he forced himself to his feet. Flushed the toilet, then spun the cold water tap all the way and jammed his head beneath it, ribbons of icy water splitting his hair, rivulets pouring down his neck, into his ears. The cold was shocking after the dozy heat of the room. The sink's porcelain was a network of hairline cracks intricate as a spider's web. There were no towels, and he took off his shirt, used it to dry himself.

Before, he had wondered if it was possible, all the things that they had said about him. His temper and the money issues and the rumors of an affair and the unbearable possibility that he had had something to do with her death.

No matter what else he might learn, he would never again doubt that they had loved each other, that he would have done anything for her. That he would have torn the whirling world to shreds before he laid an angry hand on her.

The past was an origami puzzle, planes and edges touching here, spreading there. There would be answers somewhere about how this had happened, who had done it. But right now, even the thought of those answers was meaningless. By Christ, yes, he would find who did this, and they would pay.

But really, who cared? Not even him. The question wasn't *Who killed my wife?*

It was *How could this happen to us?*

And, *God, please,* please, *can you take it back?*

Daniel had jerked awake with a sick wet snort like a drowning man frantically kicking for the surface. He'd been in a concrete canyon, but woke in the hotel, dripping sweat, head throbbing. Clean sunlight through the dirty window. Laney still dancing for him from the laptop propped on the pillow, the volume off. He'd fallen asleep staring at the image of her, hoping that there would be a moment haunting the borderlands of consciousness when he might see her and not remember that she was gone. Might, for even a second, be whole again.

For a moment he'd lain still. The hollow in his chest almost enough to crush him. Then he sighed, pulled himself up, staggered to the bathroom.

Now, as he cruised in morning sunlight through the Palisades, the headache had settled to a steady thrum, the loss to an ache like a cracked tooth.

You're not done grieving. You've only just begun.

But you had your time-out, your moment to pretend nothing else mattered. To howl to God and beg for a change.

Now you have to make one.

After the worst of his tears had passed last night, he'd paused the video, gone back through his e-mail. Not the ones from Laney this time, but the others, especially the recent ones. Notes from friends asking if he was okay, messages from reporters looking for a quote, dozens of Google Alerts with his name in them.

And seven, count them, seven, e-mails from a woman named Sophie Zeigler.

The messages had varied in length and tone, but basically came down to a plea for him to call, to get in contact, to stop running. A stern reminder that his grief didn't end the world, and that by vanishing he was incriminating himself in the eyes of both the media and the police. He'd checked her name in his contacts, discovered that she was his lawyer, found an address for an office in Beverly Hills and a house in Pacific Palisades.

Revealing himself to anyone was a risk. But he needed help. And his lawyer had to be about the safest place he could look for

287

it. So he'd cleaned himself up as best he could and remounted the BMW, his faithful steed.

He'd been wondering if her house would be one of the palaces nestled on the cliff face, but it turned out to be in a more accessible residential area, a neighborhood section north of Sunset, block after beautifully maintained block of broad, leafy trees and gingerbread houses. Hers was a funky Frank Lloyd Wright knockoff with elaborate flower beds and a cobblestone driveway. Paving stones placed with Zen precision led to the porch. A lacquered bench that would have been at home in a museum sat beside the door. He rang the bell and heard faint musical tones. Daniel rocked on his toes, glanced over his shoulder, rang again.

Okay. Be prepared. Detective Waters said that someone broke into her house and held her at gunpoint. That's going to strain things. Plus, you vanished, not something that's going to make a lawyer happy. She might be nervous, maybe even a little bit cold.

The door opened until the chain stopped it, revealing three inches of a woman's face. An attractive woman in her late forties, he'd guess, maybe a little bit older. Her eyes widened when she saw him.

"Ms. Zeigler," he said, "I know this —"

The door slammed shut.

Okay. Maybe cold was an understatement. He looked behind him again. Best to get —

There was the rattle of the chain, and then the door jerked open and the woman threw herself at him, arms wide, yanking him into a hug. He stood rooted and rigid as she squeezed, feeling the warmth of her body, the hard good pressure of her arms, the feel of her hair against his cheek, all of it so sudden and surprising and strange. It was the first time anyone had touched him since he'd woken on the beach.

It felt amazing.

"Daniel, oh honey." She squeezed him harder. "I can't believe — is it really you?"

"I —"

Sophie released him, stepped back, eyes flashing. "Where the *hell* have you been?"

"I —"

"Are you okay?"

"Well, I —"

"I could kill you, if I wasn't so happy to see you." Her smile brought laugh lines and delicate crow's-feet. Then she looked past him, to the street, and a shadow crossed her face. "Are you — do the police —"

"I'm alone."

"Come inside."

"Are you sure?"

"No, Daniel. I want to talk to America's Most Wanted on my porch."

He laughed, mind still a whirl, body still feeling her hug, the intoxication of human contact. She held the door and he stepped in.

Polished maple floors and colorful art on the walls. Sophie closed the door, chained it, and then started down the hall, saying over her shoulder, "I can't believe you're here. Where have you been?"

"That's . . . complicated. But I didn't mean to scare you."

"Well, you did. And not just me. The whole world's been looking for you. The sheriff's called me twice a day."

"Yeah, that's what he said." They stepped into an airy kitchen. A sunny window, a breakfast nook with the *New York Times* spread out, a coffeepot burbling.

"What?" She whirled. "What who said?"

"I —"

"Please don't tell me. You *haven't* talked to them." Her tone sharp. "Tell me you haven't talked to the police without your attorney."

"No. I mean, well, yes. I spoke to a detective. But on the phone."

"Are you *kidding* me?"

"No, look, I had —"

"Why would you do that? Don't you get how serious this is?"

"Yeah, but —"

"Never, never, *never* talk to the police without a lawyer. Especially on something like this. Why didn't you call me first?"

"I —"

"When did you talk to them?"

"Yesterday."

"On the phone?"

"Yes." Softly, like a scolded child. It felt oddly good.

"Detective Waters?"

"Yes. He said —"

"And where have you been?"

"I —"

"I mean, you just *vanished.* You call me late at night, drunk, and then you disappear? How do you think that looks?" She banged in a cupboard, brought out two coffee mugs, gestured with them wildly. "You realize what a hash you've made of this?"

"Sophie, I —"

"*Where* have you *been?*"

Daniel stepped forward, took her forearms in his hands. "It's complicated. I need to explain —"

"So explain already —"

"Which means," he said, "I need you to shut up for a couple minutes." He cocked

291

his head, said, "Pretty please?"

She snorted a laugh. "Same old Daniel." Sophie pulled her arms from his, poured the coffee, handed him a mug. "Okay, kiddo. Explain."

"Is this a joke?"

Daniel sipped at his coffee. It had taken half an hour to fill her in, starting with the beach and running all the way through to last night. Sophie had listened with quiet, focused attention. There had been something cleansing in confessing, and he'd left nothing out. "No joke."

"You have amnesia."

"Or something like it. You know those weird news stories you hear about? A guy on a train wakes up and can't remember who he was, a girl goes jogging and vanishes for weeks, she doesn't recall anything? A fugue state. I think it's something like that."

"What's the difference?"

"Hell if I know. I'm just telling you how it feels. I remember how to drive, I can talk, write. It's just the personal stuff that's gone."

"Completely?"

He shook his head. "It's coming back. Sometimes in small bits, sometimes more. Sometimes I won't even notice until later.

When I went home, that brought a lot back. And my dreams. I don't think it's really amnesia. More some sort of . . . blackout. Temporary shock."

"Shock wouldn't last this long."

"Well, maybe not just shock. I think it was a combination of things. Laney's . . . Laney, then driving all the way across the country. I think I did it in one run, amped on caffeine and speed. Booze too. And then when I got there, I —" He hesitated, realizing what he was about to say, how it sounded. "I tried to kill myself."

"Kill yourself."

"Maybe I just wanted the pain to stop. But maybe once it came down to it, some part of me didn't want to die. I came damn close, though. I think the memory loss was my subconscious mind's way of protecting me. Keep me from trying again."

Sophie picked up her mug, held it in both hands, elbows on the table. "And you don't remember me."

Daniel hesitated. He'd come here expecting a professional meeting at best, and wouldn't have been surprised if he'd had to flee again. Instead he'd found someone who loved him. "I'm sorry. It's not personal. I don't even remember Laney well. I mean," he said, trying a laugh that came out sick, "when I first woke up, I thought she *was* Emily Sweet."

Sophie's gaze was cool, a card player's stare. "From a legal standpoint, you know what this looks like? A premeditated defense. The timing is too convenient."

"Says you. From where I'm sitting, it couldn't be less convenient."

"What do you mean?"

Daniel stared at her. "I had to lose my wife all over again."

Sophie paused. "I'm sorry." She looked away, fingers tapping on the table.

"So what do you think?"

"What's the best part about sex with twenty-seven-year-olds?"

"Huh?"

"It's a joke. What's the best part about sex with twenty-seven-year-olds?"

"I don't . . . care, Sophie. I'm not in the mood for jokes."

She stared at him with an intensity that made him uncomfortable. "Your memory really is gone, isn't it? You're not kidding."

"No. I'm not."

"And you don't remember me at all."

"No."

"There's twenty of them."

"What?"

"The best thing about sex with twenty"

— a beat — "seven-year-olds. There's twenty of them."

To his surprise, he felt his lips curl in a smile. "That's awful."

"That's what I said every time you told that joke. Which was about once a month."

Sunlight bounced through a crystal in her window to paint the walls in dancing spectrums of color. After a long moment, Daniel said, "We were friends, weren't we?"

"Down here on Planet Earth, we still are."

"Yeah, I mean, of course. I just."

"Don't remember."

He nodded. "It's so strange. Without context, everything is equal. I don't even remember who I am. Take Laney. I *know* I loved her. I can feel it, physically feel it. When I realized that she was gone, it just — I mean, I wanted to die all over again. And that will only get worse as I remember more. Everything that comes back will change love from a feeling to an action, a verb, something that happened. The moments when we loved each other. We were together for years, right?"

"Six or seven."

"Seven *years*. Of emotions and decisions and moments. But with her dead and my memory gone, what do they mean? What is love without history? Like Alzheimer's. A husband and wife live their whole lives together, make love, buy a house, raise kids. Then one of them gets sick and can't remember the other. Are they still married? Are they still in love? Did the time they had mean anything on its own, or is everything just . . . temporary?"

"Life is a raindrop."

"What?"

Sophie smiled. "Something my grandmother used to say. 'Life is a raindrop.' It never made sense to me when I was young, but the older I get, the more it means."

"Life is a raindrop. Whoa." The line was so simple, and yet so beautiful it tugged at his chest. It felt like there was a truth at the center of it, that, like a Zen koan, you could meditate on it forever and still find fresh meaning. "Life is a raindrop."

Through the walls there was the roar of a car engine, something coming fast. Daniel stiffened. The car grew louder, then quieter as it passed. He glanced over to Sophie, ready to explain himself, and saw that she had tensed as much as he.

Why? What's she scared of? It took a moment to click. "The sheriff told me that someone broke into your house."

She nodded, shoulders knotted under her light top.

"Someone asking about me."

"That's right." Sophie stood, took her coffee to the sink.

"I — Did he hurt you?" The heat in his belly was back.

"I'm fine." She dumped her mug, began to scrub it.

"Can you tell me about him?"

"Why? Not like you'll remember anyway."

Ouch. Daniel eased out of the breakfast nook. She didn't turn around, just kept washing dishes. "Soph."

There was a tiny hitch in her movement. Then, over her shoulder, "Funny. That's what you always called me. Do you remember, or is it just there?"

"Soph, I'm sorry."

"What are you sorry for?"

I'm sorry some sick fuck came into your house. I'm sorry he did it looking for me. I'm sorry that as strong as you obviously are, it shook, maybe even broke, something in you. He sighed. "Everything, I guess."

"Don't be an idiot." She shut off the faucet and turned around. "He didn't hurt me. Scared me, is all." She picked up a towel and began to dry her hands, her voice slow. "He was so calm. Smiling, always smiling. That was the worst part. I think he could have done anything to me, and then gone on about his day. Not felt a thing about it."

He opened his mouth, closed it. Didn't know what to reply. Finally he said, "I hope you told him everything."

"I didn't know very much."

"This guy. He must have been the one who . . ." *Say it. You have to face it.* "He must have killed Laney."

"Do you think so?" Her tone flat.

"Someone comes and threatens you with a gun right after she's been driven off the road?"

"But he wasn't asking about her. He was asking about you."

"Yeah, but. You don't think I had anything to do with it?" She didn't answer, and he sighed. "Look, I understand. I wondered myself. In fact, I was even starting to believe it. But I know now. I know it's not true."

"Then what did you mean —" She tossed the dish towel on the counter, shook her head.

"What?"

"Never mind."

"Sophie."

She sighed. "You called me. Very drunk. You kept saying you were sorry. When I asked what for, you wouldn't tell me. You just kept saying you were sorry, and . . ."

"What?"

"That it was your fault."

"My fault?" He braced a hand on the counter. "I can't . . . I didn't."

"What were you talking about, Daniel? What were you sorry for?"

"I don't know." He closed his eyes. Tried to remember. Let the words float in front of him, and when that didn't work, tried to force it. Nothing came. "I don't know. But I know I didn't kill her. Damn it, Soph, I spent all last night looking at video of the two of us. There are pictures from two weeks ago that would break your heart, we look so happy. Why would I kill her?"

"I don't know."

"No." He shook his head. "I'm not going down this road again. Whatever I said that night, I *know* I didn't kill Laney. We were happy, goddamnit. Everything was perfect. You know that. You *remember* that. Right?"

"Perfect?" She raised an eyebrow.

"Well, okay, but the point is, we were in love, and there's no way —"

"Christ, Daniel, it was a marriage, not a fairy tale. It wasn't perfect. And don't get it in your head that it was just because she's gone. Relationships don't work like that."

He took a breath, made himself pause. "We fought?"

"Of course you fought."

"Over what?"

"The things people fight over. Money, sex, children, who did the dishes last."

"But like you said, people do that." He saw her expression. "What? We were bad?"

"Laney was an *actress,* hon. They're all crazy. And you" — a snort — "you've got a temper. When the two of you went at each other, you went for blood. You'd scream yourselves hoarse. The last time, she spent the weekend in a hotel, and you spent it at the bottom of a bottle."

He had a sick feeling, a primal, caught-jerking-off shame. The same way he'd felt in Robert Cameron's trailer the morning prior, listening to the actor describe the way he'd seen Daniel: *A mediocre writer in a town thick with them. Not particularly talented, not particularly smart, not particularly brave. The top of the middle of the bell curve.* It killed him. Why couldn't the past be perfect? If he couldn't have it anyway, couldn't he at least have that certainty? "Did it happen a lot?"

"What's a lot? My marriage didn't work out, so who am I to judge?" Sophie sighed. "You fought, and your fights blew the roof off. But you always made up. And when you did, you shook the walls down. That's just the way the two of you were. It was a

300

tempestuous relationship. When you were happy you were giddy. When you fought, you fought hard. My point is just that you're not doing yourself any favors believing it was perfect."

Daniel nodded, the queasiness not any better. He grabbed his mug from the table, poured a cup of coffee he didn't want. His mind a whirl, too many things to keep track of, too many pieces that didn't fit. "You didn't answer my question."

"What question?"

"Do you think I had something to do with this?"

It was her turn to stare. Her fingers knotted one over the other. He realized that he was hanging on her answer. This woman, this friend, knew him in a way he didn't know himself anymore. If she thought he had done it . . .

"I don't know what happened. I don't know what you meant with that phone call. I don't know who this guy is, or why he's after you, or what the necklace he was asking about has to do with anything," she said.

"I don't —"

"Hold on. The police believe you did it. And there's more. Someone was killed in your office."

"What?"

301

"A security guard. The cops think you did that too."

"When was this?"

"Night before last."

"It wasn't me. That much I can remember."

"Okay, good. But the other questions, I don't know the answer to them. Do you?"

"No. But that's not what I'm asking."

"You're asking if I think you killed Laney. Or wanted her dead."

"Do you?"

"Not in a million years."

Daniel's chest swelled, and his eyes were wet. He put a hand to his mouth, breathed into it. It was as though a giant hand had been pushing him down. At her words, it vanished. He inhaled deep, exhaled slow. "Thank you."

"Don't thank me. You're still screwed."

Despite himself, he laughed. "Like a Texas cheerleader."

"Do you trust me?"

"You're the only person I know," he said. "If I don't trust you, I may as well throw myself back in the ocean."

"Good. Because here's what you're going to do. You're going to turn yourself in."

"What?"

"Your turn to shut up, kiddo." She pointed

at him, mock stern. "You're going to get a lawyer. A *criminal* lawyer. I'll call my friend Jen Forbus. She makes Johnnie Cochran look like Mr. Bean."

"Soph, I know you're trying to help, but —"

"Shut up. Jen will call the sheriff, and she'll broker the deal. You'll turn yourself in on our terms. No media circus, no questioning without her. Plus we'll explain your condition, and make sure that access to medical care is part of the deal."

"I don't need a doctor, I had an MRI —"

"Shut up. We don't know what caused your memory loss. Maybe you were drugged. Maybe you have a rare disease. We need to know."

"What do you —"

"Shut up. A specialist — a team of them, probably — will be crucial to your defense. Right now, the only evidence they have linking you to either murder is circumstantial. Hell, I could get it knocked down. But you resisted arrest in Maine, and again back here. They'll use that. The medical diagnosis is going to help us there."

"Soph —"

"I'm not going to lie. It's going to cost a lot. And you might have to do a little prison time. But don't worry, it'll be minimum security, you won't need to explore alternative lifestyles while you're there. Probably won't be more than a couple of months. Meanwhile, once you turn yourself in, I'll go to work with the press, get them applying pressure to the sheriff's department, see if Waters wouldn't maybe like to get off his ass and find the man who killed my friend's wife."

Daniel stared at her, smiling from the inside out. What a woman. Whoever Daniel had been before, whatever character flaws he may have had, he had been a man Sophie Zeigler had found worthy of friendship. "Can I talk now?"

"Who said you couldn't talk? You wanna talk, talk."

While Sophie called her lawyer friend, Daniel wandered. Coffee cup in one hand, at a friend's house, he felt whole in a way he hadn't before. Just a guy. With some problems, yeah, but with a plan to fix them.

Her house had a long hallway from the entrance to the kitchen, and the run of it was decorated with neatly framed photographs hung in a perfect horizontal, like a museum. Her life in snapshots. A twenty-something version of her at an outdoor concert, wearing a flowered dress and holding a Bob Marley joint, eyes closed as she danced. Her with a handsome Mafioso type, his hair slicked back and a lazy smile, his arm draped proprietarily over her shoulders. Photos of her with actors and musicians. Halfway down the row there was a black-and-white shot of a long banquet table, a dozen smiling people surrounding it. The guy second from the end was him, in a badly fitting blazer, raising a turkey drumstick in a toast. He looked himself in the eye.

Hello, self. Guess what? You have no idea what's ahead of you.

The thought made him grin. He took another sip of coffee, then turned at the sound of her bare feet on the hardwood floor. "When was this?"

She glanced at it. "Nineteen ninety . . . six? Around there. Hollywood Orphans."

"Huh?"

"I keep forgetting that you don't remember. Every Thanksgiving I host dinner for Hollywood Orphans. Friends who don't go home for the holiday."

"Where *is* home?"

"You were born in Little Rock. But home was always here."

"I don't have family?"

"Depends what you mean."

305

He nodded. "So I've lived here a long time."

"You used to say that one of the things you loved about Los Angeles was that it had no memory. Kind of ironic now, huh?"

"Yeah." He leaned in. "So's that haircut."

"Not your finest hour, on a fashion level. But then, like you always say. Fuck 'em if they can't take a joke."

"I say that?"

"All the time, sweetie. That and 'It's easier to ask forgiveness than permission.' The twin pillars of the Daniel Hayes Philosophy of Life." Sophie straightened and said, "I got hold of Jen. She was going into a deposition, only had a minute. But she's in. She says that from what I told her, you'll be fine."

"Really?"

"Her exact words were 'By the time I'm done, that sheriff will be wondering if there's a god in heaven.'"

He shook his head. "I can't thank you enough."

"It's what we do. Anyway, Jen is going to come over as soon as she's out of court. Probably won't be until six or so. She said that meanwhile you should just stay put."

"Not a chance."

"Huh?"

He turned to her, put his hands on her arms. "I was thinking about it while you were on the phone. You're a lawyer."

"This took thinking?"

"What I mean is, I can't stay here. I'm a fugitive. You're harboring a fugitive. I didn't go to law school, but I'm guessing that won't go over so well."

"It's not —"

"You've already given me more than I ever dreamed. I'm not going to do anything that could get you in trouble. Hell, you could probably get disbarred for this."

She hesitated.

"Right?"

"I doubt it. Besides, no one needs to know."

"I'm not going to risk your career over this. I'm just not."

"So what —"

"Don't worry. I'm not going all Charles Bronson. I've got a room at a shithole hotel downtown. I'll pick up some Thai takeout, lock the door, and wait for your call."

She paused, that professional mask back up, the one that meant she was weighing the arguments. Finally, she said, "You'll stay there?"

"Cross my heart." He smiled at her. "Anyway, I've got the laptop, there's a lot still to go through. Maybe I'll find some-thing that can help us."

She nodded slowly. "All right. That makes sense. I've got work to do anyway."

"A studio to squeeze?"

"A party to manage. Too G."

"Huh?"

"The rap star, Too G. The premiere of his movie is tomorrow night, and he's throwing a big press party at a club called Lux. It's a pain in the ass. He's 'gangsta' " — making air quotes — "so the whole thing has to look tough. We're hiring security, setting up metal detectors at the door, hiring limos with bulletproof glass, all to maintain the il-lusion that Tudy Wadell is a dangerous man."

"Gotta love Los Angeles."

"It's a company town, what can you do. Anyway, how do I reach you?"

"I bought a cell phone last night." He gave her the number. "One more thing." He bit his lip.

"What?"

"I — this sounds weird, but would you mind. Could I — would you —"

"Spit it out, kiddo."

"Could I hug you again?" He shrugged, embarrassed. "It's just, it's been —"

To his relief, she didn't say anything. She

just smiled up at him and opened her arms. He stepped into the warmth and safety of them, squeezed her hard. God, but it felt good to have someone love him.

When he stepped back a moment later, he said, "You be careful."

"You're the fugitive."

"Yeah, but — Just do, okay?" He opened the door, stepped out, then turned. "And thanks again. For everything. Most people would have let me hang."

"Hey," she said. "Fuck 'em if they can't take a joke."

Daniel smiled at her, then stepped outside, walked to his car. As he cranked it up, he glanced back, saw her framed in the door. The expression on her face was hard to read, a complicated blend of emotions, happy and sad all mixed together.

It was a gift.

He waved to her, then pulled away. The sun poured down, and Daniel rolled the windows open and turned on the radio. He hadn't had much use for it in the past few days, but now he wanted music, loud rock and roll filled with joy. He flipped around until he found something with a pounding guitar and crisp snare, a singer yelling about being only seventeen and holding back his screams, about him and his girlfriend burning the sheets down to the seams. He cranked the volume, banged out the beat on the steering wheel as he merged onto the 10.

For the first time he could remember, he felt okay. Better than. The questions that had been clawing at his brain would have answers. No more running. No more fear. He would finally be able to face things. The relief was tremendous. All that sprinting and hiding and shadowy panic, it had been like a straitjacket that tightened every time he squirmed. He glanced in the rearview — traffic light behind him, a couple of imports, a big white van — and pressed down on the accelerator. The road open before him, a good song, and a plan. He sang along, surprised to find that he knew the lyrics: *Your memory bla-zes through me, burning everything, like gasoline, like gasoline, like gasoline.*

The song ended, and a DJ came on. Daniel turned the volume down, then realized he was doing almost ninety. Whoa there. He braked to a steady sixty.

Okay. So.

Back to the Ambassador. Get settled. Take a shower, make sure he looked sane for Sophie's lawyer. Then spend the afternoon reviewing the laptop. He'd barely scratched the surface. There might be some sort of clue, an e-mail from Laney maybe, that would help them figure out what the deal was. Whatever had happened, it had the elements of a classic conspiracy plot — shadowy men with guns, a missing diamond necklace worth more than a house — and as a storyteller, he knew those things came with a backstory.

The radio settled on an old Cracker tune, *Being with you girl, like being low, hey hey hey like being stoned.* He turned the volume back up, but watched his speed this time, glanced in the mirror as he signaled.

It was only after he had moved into the next lane that he realized the white van was still behind him.

So what? Where else would it be?

But then, he'd been going pretty fast for a couple of minutes. The van had kept pace. And when he had slowed down, so had it. Daniel kept his eyes flickering between the road in front and the mirror. Couldn't make out much; it was a big panel van, the kind landscapers and cleaning crews favored, not unlike a million others. There was a long and vicious dent in the side, evidence of some past collision. The distance kept him from making out the driver's features, but he wore a baseball cap and sunglasses.

Let's see. Daniel signaled right again, then took the next exit, north on Fairfax. The van followed. Daniel snapped the radio off, turned right on Venice. The van stayed with him.

His happy mood vanished like fog. Someone was following him. Not the police. Even if the van was the world's lousiest undercover vehicle, they would have had plenty of time to box him with squad cars. Who, then?

He was so calm. That was the worst part. I think he could have done anything to me, and then gone on about his day. Not felt a thing about it.

Daniel's fingers clenched the wheel, his palms wet. The man who had broken into Sophie's house and held her at gunpoint. The one who had been searching for him, asking about a diamond necklace.

The man who had killed his wife.

The light at Hauser was red, and he slowed, then pulled into the left turn lane. Again, the van followed.

Okay. Simple. Wait for a break in traffic, then instead of going left, floor it. Race across the intersection. Other cars will block the van in. By the time the light changes, you'll be long gone.

How could the guy have found him? Los Angeles was huge. The chances that they'd randomly bumped into one another were incalculably small. Daniel's spine felt like an ice cube had been run down it. This asshole must have picked him up at Sophie's. Which meant he'd go back there if Daniel lost him. And this time, he wouldn't just scare her.

I think he could have done anything to me, and then gone on about his day. Not felt a thing about it.

No. No chance.

The light turned green, and Daniel moved forward. Two cars between him and the van. *You need a plan. You cannot, cannot, let any harm come to Sophie. Besides, this man murdered your wife. Wouldn't you rather chase him than run from him? So think. You're the writer.*

Write something.

Belinda was smiling.

Staking out Sophie's house had been a calculated guess. The lawyer had sent Daniel a pile of messages, telling him to come see her, to do it soon. But even Belinda hadn't imagined it would happen that fast. Hell, she and Daniel Hayes might both have been reading his e-mail at the same time.

She stayed a few cars behind Daniel's BMW, kept her speed steady as he wound up Hauser, then turned left on Third. He signaled again almost immediately, then pulled into the parking lot of the old Farmers Market. Against the blue of the sky, the white clapboard clock tower looked ridiculously picturesque, more appropriate for rural Maine than the outskirts of Beverly Hills. It was early yet, and the parking lot was only half-full. She let Hayes get ahead of her, chose a spot near the entrance. She took the gun from behind her back, set it on her lap. Through the windshield, she saw Daniel get out of his car and saunter toward the entrance, bright Hawaiian shirt easy to track. He moved like a man without a care.

Go after him here? Not ideal. There were too many people about, too many prying eyes. Probably some security cameras inside too. Belinda killed the engine and leaned back. Daniel wasn't going anywhere without his car. She'd wait, then follow him somewhere she could approach him alone. She eyed the people walking in and out: a mother with a kid, a couple of teenage girls, a well-dressed man moving lightly. Belinda squinted. Was that —

She snatched up the gun and threw open the door of the van.

Bennett walked quickly, but not so quickly

anyone noticed. The gate to the Farmers Market was open, throngs of people inside, and Daniel Hayes had strolled in like he didn't have a care in the world.

Asshole. Every cop in the state looking for him, and here he was in a populated place. If someone recognized him, it was game over.

Ah well. The soul of tactics was flexibility in your approach to a goal. The best chess players saw the whole board fresh every move, and reacted accordingly. Which was why he'd figured that even if Sophie wasn't lying to him, she was still worth watching, and that had paid out. He'd just have to adapt again. Follow the guy, lure him out of sight — the man didn't know what he looked like, after all — and take him.

Then go somewhere quiet and convince Daniel to give him what he wanted.

He stepped inside, past a toy store, a T-shirt place, a churrascaria. Bennett slipped through the crowd, looking for his man.

Daniel's palms were wet, but he made himself move slowly, not turn around. This would only work if the guy didn't think he'd been spotted. Daniel was willing to bet that he wouldn't last long in a fair fight.

So don't fight fair.

He took a quick lap around the market. Rich smells came from every direction, dizzying in their variety, salsa verde overlapping chocolate; caramel corn battling roasting beef. The sun slipped through gaps in the canvas tents. At a nearby bar, a group of men exploded in laughter.

There was a place that sold sunglasses and jewelry, and he stopped, pulled a pair of shades off a display, tipped them way down his nose, and looked in the tiny mirror. Over his shoulder, men and women of all ages moved through the aisles. A lot of them wore baseball hats. Damn. He put the sunglasses back on the rack, kept moving. He needed a quiet place, somewhere away from all these crowds.

He started working his way to the outskirts. Glancing at every man he passed, wondering which one was the killer. The Mexican with the tattoos? The dude in the suit? A short, ripped guy wearing a Dodgers cap? It could be any of them. *Be cool. He won't make a move on you in this crowd.*

He hoped that was true.

Belinda had sprinted across the parking lot, going for a gate a little farther down. No point coming in right behind Bennett.

"Excuse me," she said, nearly knocking over an aproned man with porkchop jowls. She stopped at the corner of a barbeque place on the east patio. Plastic tables and chairs, the sweet smell of garbage, the closed-in feeling of tent shadows. No sign of Daniel, but she saw Bennett moving west, and mirrored him one aisle over. The gun tucked in the belt of her jeans chafed her belly.

A deli, a candle store, an aromatherapy place. It was crowded, and she couldn't see Bennett. Was she reading him wrong? Maybe he was just following Daniel, making sure the man didn't vanish.

No. Bennett had always said that the trick was to be very careful until it was time to act boldly. Coming in wasn't careful. Which meant —

Daniel Hayes crossed her row, all the way at the end, the bright print on his shirt slipping between the tables of diners.

Belinda glanced around. No sign of Bennett. She'd have to move anyway. She touched the pistol through her shirt, then started forward as fast as she dared.

After the crowded halls of the food court, the maintenance hall was a stark change. Painted institutional gray and lit by fluorescents, it screamed "employees only." Daniel

317

stepped into it and around the corner. The hall ran thirty yards before turning the corner. There were a couple of doors near the end, closets maybe?

Halfway down, two men leaned against opposite walls, talking in Spanish. They glanced up at Daniel, then went back to their conversation. Damn. The place was perfect, other than these two.

So get rid of them. He walked over, said, "What, you guys don't have jobs to do?"

A guilty look flashed across one of their faces, but the other said, "We're on break. Who are you?"

"Excuse me?" Daniel raised an eyebrow. "You think this place manages itself?"

"You're not my boss —"

"Believe me, I am. This is a working market, boys. You're on break, fine. But don't be cluttering up my hallways."

For a moment he thought the man might push him, but then the old power dynamic took over. White man with attitude trumps Hispanic in an apron. A shitty fact of life, maybe, but he'd worry about moral righteousness later. The guilty one said, "Sure, sure, no problem." They began down the hall, one of them muttering in Spanish, *"¿Quien se cree? Mamón presumido."*

"Y cuidate lo que dices, pendejo," Daniel

replied over his shoulder, then did a double take. *Huh. I know Spanish. Cool.*

Focus. There wasn't much time. Before heading into the hallway, he'd walked a couple of circuits of the market, wanting to make sure that the killer was able to follow him. It had been incredibly hard not to look back, knowing that his wife's murderer was behind. *Soon enough, you'll get a look at the fucker. A look and more.*

He raced to the end of the hall, tried the left-hand door. A janitor's closet, mops and pails and brooms. The door on the other side opened into a small employee bathroom, the tile dingy, a roll of paper towels sitting on the sink.

Make a stand here, or go back out and see what's around the corner?

Daniel opened the janitor's closet again. A dark, private place. So long as he didn't dawdle, he could do anything he wanted here. All he had to do was lure the man in.

He smiled and set to work.

Belinda lost Daniel, then, as she rounded the end of the row, saw him vanishing down an employee's hallway. She took a moment, scanned the crowd. Hundreds of people, the static noise of overlapping conversations, of forks grinding plates and chairs scraping concrete. But no sign of Bennett. Maybe he hadn't seen Daniel head down this way.

It doesn't matter. You're Belinda Nichols. You're a dangerous woman with a loaded gun. And the man you've been looking for just went into an empty hallway.

She took a breath, started forward. A couple of Hispanic guys walked out of the hallway, one of them pissed about something, the other trying to make a joke. Belinda let them pass, then started down the hall.

The floor was tile, the lighting bright. About thirty yards away, the hall turned another corner, maybe out to the trash? Perhaps this whole thing had been a game. Maybe Daniel had known he was being followed, wanted to lose them in the crowd. He could be doubling back right now, heading for his car.

She hurried down the hallway, her sneakers squeaking on the floor. When she was almost to the end, she noticed that the door on the left wall was open a crack. She slowed, glanced behind her, nerves popping like firecrackers. The light inside the door was out, and she couldn't see much but shadows and shapes . . . and a green and blue pattern. One a lot like the shirt Daniel had worn.

He's hiding in the closet.

Belinda hurried forward, reached for the handle, and yanked the door open.

Daniel had never known his heart could beat so loud. He half worried the killer would hear it. He squeezed his eyes closed, took a deep breath. *You get one shot at this.*

The mop handle felt right in his hands, the wood smooth, the finish worn off by a thousand nights of cleaning. He listened, knowing the man was coming, wanting him to, but scared too, the fear a taste in his mouth.

Footsteps, and a squeak like tennis shoes.

He held his breath, choked up on the stick. *Come on, come on.*

The footsteps paused. Then suddenly they were hurrying, and he heard the sound of the door opening.

Now.

With his left hand he ripped open the door to the bathroom and lunged out, the make-shift bat cocked back, ready to take the killer's head half off, to beat the man help-less. He swung as he stepped out, taking aim at the temple of the —

It was a woman. Lithe, slim, and wearing a baseball cap.

Belinda yanked open the door of the janitor's closet, the light flickering on as she did, so that she could see brooms and mops and a sink with a slow drip, a drop of water trembling at the faucet. A bucket stood just inside the door, the broken handle of a mop sticking straight up, a black Hawaiian shirt with blue and green parrots draped over the top, the whole thing like an anemic scarecrow. *What the —*

There was a noise behind her, the scrape of a door, and she whirled, one hand flying to her belt, fumbling against the gun as Daniel Hayes surged at her, a mop handle in one fist. She flinched back, watching that arc of wood whistling toward her with more than enough force to bat her arm aside. She could imagine the snapping sharp pain that would numb her hand, then the smack as it hit her head, stars and comets and the world hopping.

Only the blow never landed. At the last second Daniel pulled it, twisting awkwardly to bring the club whistling over her head. Momentum kept him going, following through like a batter at a pitch, and he stopped, arms up in an awkward backhand pose. He froze. His fingers opened, and the stick clattered to the floor.

Belinda lowered her hands. Daniel stared at her. It looked like he was trying to speak but had forgotten the muscles. He blinked, gaped, blinked. Managed to twist his lips into motion. *"You?"* His voice dry and thin. "But. You're —"

"Dead. I know. I'm so, so sorry, Daniel."

And then Laney Thayer stepped forward and threw her arms around her husband.

■ ■ ■ ■

ACT TWO, PART TWO

■ ■ ■ ■

"People always think something's *all* true."
— J. D. Salinger, *The Catcher in the Rye*

Someone had hooked electrodes up to either ear and slammed waves of electricity through his skull. His brain was static and noise. Questions surged on that buzzing sea, thoughts tumbled and spun. The mop handle slipped from his fingers and hit the floor with a hollow clatter.

His wife was alive.

Dressed in a plain T-shirt and jeans, her hair now blond and pulled through the back of her baseball cap, a splotchy mark like a bruise running up her cheek and across one eye, but all of that no more concealing to his eyes than tissue paper. There were the high cheekbones, the pale pink lips he'd kissed a hundred thousand times, the long graceful neck, and the eyes, the eyes, bright and alive.

The connection between body and mind strained. He felt like a marionette with half the strings cut, a jerky, drunken thing. Was he going mad, really mad? Had all of this been some crazy dream? How could she possibly . . .

He blinked, swallowed, made his lips move. "You? But. You're —"

"Dead. I know. I'm so, so sorry, Daniel." Emily Sweet's voice, the one he'd followed home from the edge of death. And then Laney threw herself at him, her arms ringing his sides and squeezing, her body fitting tight, the smell of her, that old familiar smell of home.

His wife was alive. Alive, and in his arms.

The wife whose loss had driven him to suicide. The woman he had fallen back in love with only to realize she was gone. Somehow she had crawled out of the underworld to stand in his arms.

A choking sound wrenched from his chest, and he pulled her tighter. She responded, crying and laughing against him, her skin warm, and the charge running through his body was like a swim in ancient waters, like finishing a screenplay, like over-proof bourbon and an expensive cigar, like making love for the first time. He could flex his arms and knock down the world.

"I thought you were. My god, how — Are you okay?"

"I'm sorry, baby, I'm so sorry." Her words

tumbling against his chest. "I wanted to find you, but you were gone, and I couldn't go to the police, he had to think I was dead, it was the only way."

"The only way to — What do you mean?"

"We have to go." Laney pushed back from him, glanced down the hall. "Bennett's here."

"What's a Bennett?" His fingers tasted the softness of her arms.

She cocked her head, said, "Huh?"

"I don't know what —"

"Bennett, Bennett, the guy who." She stopped. "Are you okay?"

"Well . . ."

Someone laughed out in the common area, and the echo of the sound made her jump. "Later. Let's go. You have to trust me." Laney's eyes entreated. "Can you trust me?"

Nothing made sense. His wife back from the dead. Scared. Someone named Bennett was here. That must be the killer. The one he had been trying to trap. Only it had been Laney. And she wasn't dead, so there wasn't a killer. But then, someone had come after Sophie. And Laney was saying — He blinked, said, "Of course."

"Hurry." She grabbed his hand, their fingers lacing with easy habit; he could remember the way they slid together, but there was no time to savor it as she tugged him down the hall. The fluorescent lights a blur, his heart singing. They rounded the corner, stepped back into the market proper.

And directly in front of a man with a gun.

"Hello, kids," the man said. "Miss me?"

Laney's fingers tightened on his, hard enough that he could feel the fear humming in her skin.

"You look good for a dead woman, sister. You made a hell of a cleaning lady too." The guy seemed relaxed, like he was chancing on old friends. His black shirt and pressed slacks, his neat hair and bland expression juxtaposed against the pistol to create a shattering dissonance. What had Sophie said? *He was so calm. Smiling, always smiling. I think he could have done anything to me, and then gone on about his day. Not felt a thing about it.*

"Bennett?" Daniel asked, knowing the answer.

"The one and only." The man had his back to the patio area, gun held low and out of sight, and none of the hundreds of people behind him seemed to have a clue what he was doing. "Let me guess, I look different than you expected. Taller, and with a bigger cock." He smiled, turned back to

330

Laney. "Speaking of my cock, it's nice to see you again, sister."

"I'll scream," Laney said.

Bennett shrugged. "Go for it."

She opened her mouth, hesitated.

"Thought not. You scream, maybe the man who comes to rescue you is a cop. And you don't want to be talking to any police, do you?"

Daniel turned from one to the other. He felt like he was lagging behind the conversation. By the time he'd processed one set of words, the next had come and gone. It had to be a blackmail thing, he'd put that much together, but the way this guy was goading Laney, it seemed like he knew her personally. And what was she doing? Why not scream? "Why don't we want to be talking to the police?"

Bennett laughed. "I love it. Why do you think, Dan?"

"I have no idea."

"Sure you do —"

"No, I fucking don't. But if you don't stop pointing a gun at my wife, I'm going to . . ."

"What? You're going to what? Kill me?"

"Stop it," Laney said. "You can't shoot us. If you do, you don't get the necklace."

"I don't have to shoot both of you, sweetheart. For your next role, how about life as a widow?" The pistol swung half a degree to center on Daniel's chest.

She stiffened. "No."

Daniel wanted to act, to *do* something, but he didn't know what. It had felt right to threaten Bennett, but jumping him would be suicide. The man may have been all smiles and ease, but the pistol was steady, and his finger was inside the trigger guard.

"I want what I'm owed, sister. Then we can all get on with our lives. I promise."

"I remember what your word is worth."

"Oh, snap," Bennett said. "Ouch. I'm cut to the quick." His smile could have curdled milk. "Let's go. Back down the hallway."

"I don't think so." Laney's right hand blurred to her shirt and came out with a gun of her own.

What the *fuck?*

Bennett snickered. "You can't shoot me, Laney. Any more than you could go to the police."

"I'm not going to shoot you," she said. "I'm going to put you in the spotlight." Then his wife pointed the pistol skyward and pulled the trigger three times fast.

The crack of gunfire was unbelievably loud, setting his ears ringing. For a moment, nothing happened, just silence and the slipping smile on Bennett's face.

Then the screaming began. Chaos hit as if God had flipped a switch, everyone lunging into motion at the same time. People threw themselves to their feet, upended tables, sent chairs clattering. Everyone went in different directions, tangling with one another as they searched for an exit or looked for the source of the gunfire. Dropped glasses shattered on the concrete, and somewhere someone shrieked, a high-pitched sound like steel on his teeth.

Laney's hand grabbed his and yanked. "Run!" He caught a split-second look at Bennett's face, fury and calculation mingling, the gun hand coming up, and then the pull of Laney's momentum snapped him into motion. He started after her into the maelstrom, people shoving and shouting. Laney's slim frame was no match for the chaos. He shook his hand free of hers and took the lead, lowering his shoulder and tightening his arm, bull-rushing a hole for them, adrenaline and panic powering their flight.

But even as he ran, his mind was racing faster. *What the* hell *is going on?*

Fuck, fuck, *fuck.* Bennett spun on his heel, took in the scene, mob mentality at its worst. Most people were trying to escape, but some would be coming this way, wannabe heroes and security guards, maybe even cops. Laney and Daniel took off, and instinct brought his pistol up, tracking their retreating backs. Ten feet, child's play. One shot, two shot, red shot, blue shot.

Only morons play a losing hand. Killing them wouldn't get him paid. But it might get him caught. He tucked the gun away. Laney and Daniel disappeared into the crowd, bobbing heads in a sea of frightened humanity.

You've gotten smarter, little girl. You're not the wide-eyed kid I remember.

He turned and sprinted down the maintenance hallway.

They'd fought their way to the edge of the market, one of the gates in sight, the river of people now moving mostly in one direction. A woman fell, and Daniel bent to haul her to her feet before she was trampled. A man behind him shoved past, his knee connecting with Daniel's shoulder as he rose, almost sending him tumbling. Daniel shoved him, then fought forward.

"This way!" Laney slid past, quicksilvering through the crowd. He followed, and then they were through the gate and into the western parking lot, a lane of cars backing onto Fairfax.

Laney turned to make sure he'd made it. The neck of her shirt was torn, and she'd lost the ball cap. She still held the gun in one hand, like she'd forgotten it was there.

"Put that away," he said, and she looked startled, then hid it under her shirt.

"Let's go." She turned toward the north lot.

He grabbed her arm. "No. This way."

"What? Why?"

"Just trust me."

For a moment he thought she would argue, but she nodded again. They ran south, away from their cars, the space opening as people spread out. Hit Third at a sprint, the street a mess, cars spun the wrong direction, a collision in the center lane, running people scrambling over hoods and between bumpers, horns screaming. They darted across, came to a black wrought iron fence on the other side. "Come on," he said, and cupped his hands for her. She stepped into them, grabbed the top, then jumped over. He followed, the metal digging into his stomach as he balanced and dropped.

They were in a huge apartment complex. It seemed strangely familiar, tall towers surrounded by town houses, the whole thing landscaped and organized. Curious children stared from the playground at the corner.

Laney was running again. The streets angled in spokes from the towers, every intersection looking the same, but she seemed to know her way, and he followed, panting now, his shoulder throbbing where he'd been kicked. After they had gone maybe half a mile, Laney slowed to a jog, then a walk. She didn't even seem to be breathing hard. "I left my car back there," she said.

"I know" — gasp — "me too."

"So why did we come this way?"

He stopped, laced his fingers over his head. "Bennett wasn't in the spotlight anymore."

Laney narrowed her eyes. "He went for our cars."

"That's what a smart bad guy would do."

She stepped forward, put her hands on his cheeks. "That's my brilliant writer husband." Then she kissed him, and everything else — the horns in the distance, the police sirens drawing closer, the crack of gunfire, the sun in the sky, and the ground below — went away.

A long moment later, when he could breathe again, he said, "I'm so glad you're not dead."

"Me too. You, I mean. I thought Bennett — When I couldn't find you, I thought maybe he had."

Daniel shook his head. "No. I wasn't in L.A."

"Huh? Where were you?"

"That's . . . a long story." He was about to explain when a thought struck him. "Oh, shit." He dug for his disposable cell phone. "Sophie."

Laney's eyes widened. "You think —"

"I've got to warn her." He powered up the phone. "Shit."

"What?"

"Her number. I don't have it."

"You don't have —" She gave him a strange look. "You've been friends for fifteen years."

"It's complicated. I'll explain later." It was on his laptop, but that was in the BMW. Four-one-one, maybe? But Sophie was a high-powered entertainment lawyer. Her home number would be unlisted. Well, maybe they could call a cab, race over there, hope to beat him. Or better yet, call the police —

"310-274-6611," Laney said, reading the number off her own cell phone.

Daniel looked up. Felt a lightness run through him. Such a little thing, her having the answer to a question, but somehow it was almost as good as finding out she was alive. He wasn't alone anymore. He had a partner.

Sophie answered on the third ring. "Yes?"

"It's me, you have to —"

"Are you okay? I don't have anything new from Jen yet —"

"Sophie, listen to me. You have to get out of there."

"What?"

"You have to get out of your house. He's on his way over."

"Who is?"

"Bennett. The guy who broke in before. He's coming to your house right now."

"What?"

"There's no time. You have to get out right now. Go somewhere safe, a friend, or a hotel. Don't go into work, he'll look for you there."

"You're serious?"

"I swear."

The sound that came over the line was almost a whimper. It was the last thing he wanted to hear from this woman, this strong, capable woman. "Listen, you don't have a lot of time, but you should have enough. He's coming from the Farmers Market, it will take him a little while. But seriously, right now, get going." Silence. "Sophie!"

"What?"

"You can't freeze up right now —"

"Who froze? I'm packing."

He smiled. "That's my girl. Don't bother with much. Just grab your purse and get the hell out."

"Are you okay?"

"Yeah," he said, staring into Laney's eyes, seeing them staring back at him. He didn't even want to blink. "Yeah, I'm fine. Better than."

"Where are you?"

"Don't worry about it," he said. "Things have changed. For one thing I found —"

Laney shook her head, put a finger to her lips. She didn't want Sophie to know she was alive? Why?

It didn't matter. He trusted her. "I, ah, I found the guy who did this. That will help us."

"How do you know he's coming —"

"No time. Are you out?"

"I'm locking the door. Hold on." There was the sound of keys, then heavier breathing as she walked.

"Get in your car, drive around the neighborhood a couple of times. Keep your eyes on your rearview mirror. If any cars follow you, any at all, you go straight to a police station. If they don't, go somewhere safe."

"All right. How do I —"

"I'm about to learn more. I'll call you when I can."

"All right."

"I love you, Soph. Be careful."

"You too. But once this is over, I'm going to kick your ass."

"Fair enough." He hung up the phone, took a deep breath.

"She's okay?" Laney asked.

"Yeah."

"You're sure?"

"It would take him, what, twenty, twenty-five minutes to make the drive? It can't have been more than ten."

"So Sophie's safe," Laney said, stepping closer, her eyes locked on his.

"Yeah."

"And you're okay."

"More or less. And you're alive."

"More or less," she said, inching closer still, her gaze lasered onto his.

"What happened to your eye?"

She smiled, licked the tip of her finger, dragged it across the purple splotch, smearing it down her cheek. "For a while I was a blonde named Belinda Nichols. She had a port wine stain. Amazing how no one looks at anything else."

"But now you're you."

"Yes."

"And Bennett doesn't know where we are."

"No."

"Well, then." He swallowed hard. "Would it be okay if I kissed you?"

"No," she said, the syllable barely floating on breath. "Not unless you want to make love on the swing set. Next time I kiss you, I don't intend to stop."

"Ever?"

"Not for a long time."

His body responded to that, to her. "Where?"

"A hotel downtown? One of those cheap ones that won't need ID?"

He thought of the Ambassador: stained walls, piss smell in the lobby, bedding home to whole civilizations of crawling things. No. "I thought you were dead. And I very nearly was. I'm not having our reunion at a flophouse."

"What do you have in mind?"

The façade was gray stone carved in intricate patterns, framing an archway thirty feet high. Lavish flower arrangements spilled out of concrete planters. The flags above the arch whispered and popped in the breeze. A uniformed doorman stood at attention. "Welcome to the Beverly Wilshire."

"Thank you," Daniel said, and gestured Laney through the open door, ignoring her are-you-crazy? look. The lobby was echoing marble and graceful curves. A chandelier of shimmering crystal hung in the center of the room. Daniel took a deep breath: clean air, faintly scented with lemon. Behind the reception desk, a smart-suited man nodded to him.

"What are you doing?" Laney asked under her breath. She had her sunglasses on, one hand up to obscure her face.

"First, I'm going to get us a room. Then I'm going to do terrible things to you in it."

Still looking down, she smiled, but said, "This very romantic, but we can't take the risk. Bennett has people everywhere; he'll know if you use your credit card."

"How much cash do you have?"

"About five thousand dollars."

"Five *thousand* dollars? What are you doing with — It doesn't matter. That's plenty."

"But they won't let you —"

"Relax," he said, feeling better than he had in weeks. "I'm a writer." He winked and turned away, strode over to the desk. The man behind the counter flashed a bright smile, said, "Good morning, sir."

Daniel straightened his posture, glad he'd left the gaudy Hawaiian shirt back at the Farmers Market. Great thing about L.A., anyone in a black T-shirt might be a producer. "Morning. Are you the manager, by any chance?"

"Yes, sir." The man's suit had never had a wrinkle. "How may I help you?"

"I'd like a suite."

"We have several Beverly suites available."

"The rooms are nice?"

"They're lovely, sir. King-size bed, Italian marble soaking tubs, balconies offering stunning city views. For how many nights will this be?"

"Just one."

"Yes sir." The man clicked on a hidden keyboard. "All I'll need —"

"Here's the thing — I'm sorry, what was your name?"

"Thomas River."

"Here's the thing, Thomas. I'd like to be discreet about it." He gave the tiniest motion with his head to indicate Laney behind him. "I'm sure you understand."

"Certainly, sir. We just need a credit card to book the room, but we don't charge it, and you can pay however you like." The ready answer of a man experienced at accommodating cheating husbands.

"I appreciate that, Thomas, I do. But my credit card bills go to my house. And while I'm sure *you* would be careful, I can't chance one of your employees making a mistake, maybe charging room service. I'm afraid I need a little more discretion than that."

"I see. Well —"

"So what I'd like to do, if I may, is give you cash, up front, for the room. And of course for your trouble."

"Sir, I —"

"How about . . ." He pulled the money from his pocket, all that remained from pawning his Rolex a week ago. "Two thousand, one hundred and . . . eighty-seven dollars. I'd leave it to you to determine how that money broke down, of course."

The manager's smile widened by a scant degree, and then he nodded his head with military polish. "Welcome to the Beverly Wilshire, sir. I hope you enjoy your stay."

"I will." He took the key cards the man handed him, nodded again, and turned back to the lobby.

Laney had settled in a tall white throne screened from the entrance by a broad pillar. She sat with legs to the side, knees together, one hand at her chin. Her hair was blond instead of the dark brown he remembered, and she was smaller than she looked on TV. The oversize sunglasses could have landed on the diva side of the scale if it weren't for the slow smile that bloomed as she saw him coming toward her. With calculated languor, she brought her hands up to tangle through her hair, arms framing her face.

Daniel shook his head. "Jesus."

"Did you miss me?"

"Come upstairs and I'll show you." He held out a hand, and she took it. Their footsteps echoed through the lobby. The elevator seemed to take a long time, and he studied her as they waited. This was his wife. The woman he had married. They had lived together, loved each other intensely and as best they could. They had made dinner and cleaned the house and woken on Christmas morning. They had fought and been ill and overworked and stressed.

And you still don't remember it.

Suddenly he felt like a fraud. Who was he to be taking this woman to a suite, to be planning to make love to her? The adrenaline from the escape had worn off, and the reality that remained was complicated. He may have been her husband on paper, but without his memory, this felt like a violation. Like he was pretending to things he didn't deserve.

With a gentle tone, the elevator arrived. They stepped aboard and Daniel hit the button for fourteen. He said, "Listen. There's something I should tell you."

"What?"

"I. Things." He stopped. "Have you ever felt like you didn't quite know who you were? No, that's not. I mean, I know who I am. It's just that —"

"What?" she asked softly, stepping forward. He could smell her sweat, and see the downy hairs on her neck. "You haven't forgotten where everything goes, have you?"

He laughed. "No. But I have forgotten — well, not completely, but . . ."

"Daniel." She stepped closer.

"I —"

"We just escaped from a psychopath. We're alone in an elevator. Can't you think of something better to do?"

"I just, I don't want to take advantage —"

She put a finger to his lips, and he felt that solar plexus kick. Desire, but also recognition, and something even more elemental. *On the other hand . . .* She stepped forward, her head tilted up, eyes on his, lips slightly parted —

The tone sounded again, and the door

346

opened. Laney held the gaze for a second, then glanced down at his hand, snatched the key card, and bounded out of the elevator, giggling. For a moment, he stared at her retreating body, conflicted.

Fuck it.

He ran after her.

Laney had barely opened the door by the time he caught up, and he grabbed her, pulled her inside. The suite was wide and spacious and there was a king-size bed, and that was all he saw of the room. She didn't so much touch as envelop him, her whole body against his, making a clumsy two-step across the room without breaking the kiss, his blood pounding as he tugged at her shirt, yanked it up over her head, the neck getting caught, her giggling again, skin creamy and glowing, and then they both went sideways over the bed, and the giggle became a throaty laugh. He pulled the shirt the rest of the way off, fumbled at his own, both of them rolling now, flesh to electric flesh, every nerve ending singing. She reached behind her back to unsnap her bra, tossed it, breasts falling free, his lips kissing down her neck, teasing a nipple into his mouth, his cock straining in his pants, throbbing against her as she ground into him, her head going back in a moan, god, he knew that sound, knew it on some base level deeper than thought. He hooked one foot behind the other, kicked off his shoes as she straightened above him, ran her hands through her hair, shook it free, then bent back down so that it enclosed them, the world narrowed down to a whimpering prayer and a dance of touch. Somehow she had her jeans off, and he could feel the heat of her through the thin lace of her panties as she rocked forward to undo the buttons of his pants. He arched his hips and reached down, got his jeans and briefs down to his thighs in one motion as she pulled the panties aside and slid herself over the length of him, wet and warm and welcoming, and then she used her hand to guide him inside, and there was nothing but sensation, her head back, a cry from her lips as he pushed all the way into her, yes, yes, *yes*.

Home.

Sweat, and the smells of sex, earthy and rich.

The tangle of limbs, the awkward weight of flesh.

The sweetness of the curve of the inside of her thighs.

A rhythm feverish then measured then greedy again.

The spill of her hair across luxurious white sheets.

Her voice, begging, urging, pleading, cajoling, teasing, ordering.

The cold of her bare toes — they were always cold, he remembered that — the feeling as familiar and intimate a knowledge as her most secret wetness.

That sense of reaching for something shimmering and just out of reach as he thrust into her.

The way her whole body tightened as she came, every muscle straining. His own orgasm a release, the bars of a cage flying open, a soundless howl, a taking and a giving.

And then he collapsed on top of her, both of them panting, skin slick and sticky. So close he couldn't tell where he ended and she began. Their breath fell into sync, the rise of her back matched to his exhale. He buried his face in her hair, his eyes closed, nose filled with the smell of her. They lay together, floating in a world beyond words.

Finally, she cleared her throat. "Wow. You did miss me."

"You have no idea."

She blew a breath, shifted slightly, and he moved to lie behind her, spooning. Sunlight spilled across their bodies. "I don't know," she said. "Maybe we ought to fake my death every so often, just to spice things up."

His laughter was almost as good as the orgasm.

When he could move again, they untangled themselves. She sat up, yawned. Stretched her arms wide, then sat cross-legged, every inch of her body exposed. She had always been completely unselfconscious about nudity. He'd loved that, loved that it was only for him, that she had always refused to do it for the screen, to share her body with the hungry eyes of strangers.

"I hate to spoil the mood," he said, "but can we talk?"

"Where do you want to start?"

"How about the part *where you're alive*."

Laney reached for a pillow, dumped it in her lap, lay her hands on top of it. Her expression was hard to read, the traces of satiation mingling with something else, fear maybe, or regret. He flipped onto his back, put his arms behind his head, content to wait her out.

Finally, she began to speak.

EXT. DANIEL & LANEY'S MALIBU HOUSE — AFTERNOON
LANEY THAYER digs keys from

her bag, unlocks a powder blue
VOLKSWAGEN BEETLE. She slings
the bag into the passenger
seat, cranks the engine, and
opens the security gate.
Her fingers open and close
nervously on the steering
wheel.

                LANEY
It's okay. He's not here. It's
okay.

She takes a deep breath and
pulls out.

EXT. MALIBU STREETS —
CONTINUOUS
Laney drives fast. Her eyes
dart from mirror to mirror.
She turns without signaling.
Pulls through parking lots,
does a loop, comes out going
the opposite way. Circles the
block several times.
Eventually, she gets on
the . . .

PACIFIC COAST HIGHWAY —
CONTINUOUS

Laney blows past hotels and surf shops, past Pepperdine, past the houses of the uber-rich perched on rocky cliffs. Traffic is light and she's making good time. Malibu is well behind, L.A. approaching.

A light goes from yellow to red. She reluctantly brakes.

A car noses out of a canyon behind her. Sunlight off the windshield hides the driver's features.

The car turns in her direction.

Laney bites her lip.

The car draws closer.

> LANEY
> (to the traffic signal)
> Come on.
> (glancing in the mirror)
> Come on, come on . . .

The car comes closer. Closer still.

Laney is about to gun the Beetle through the light — and a stream of turning cars — when the car behind her rolls

under a tree.
The shadow reveals the driver
to be a middle-aged woman with
a bad haircut.
Laney laughs.

                    LANEY
Twitch much?

A horn sounds a quick beep-
beep.
Slowly, she turns her head.
From the driver's seat of the
NISSAN XTERRA next to hers,
BENNETT waves.

                    LANEY
No.

She jams on the gas.
Horns squeal as she tears
across the intersection. She
dodges between cars.
Laney risks a glance at the
rearview. Her sudden accelera-
tion caught Bennett off guard,
but the Xterra is following —
and gaining.

                    LANEY

Shit.

Her fingers dig divots in the steering wheel.
Laney reaches for her bag with one hand, begins to rummage through it.

                    LANEY
Come on, come on.

She finds her cell phone. Glances in the mirror, pales to see Bennett right behind her. He wags a finger reproach-fully.

                    LANEY
Screw you.

She flips open the phone. Her hands shake as she tries to dial.
Laney glances down at the phone, sees that she has punched in 8-1-1. She gri-maces, clears the number, begins to dial again.
The Xterra honks twice.
Laney jerks her head up.

A large DELIVERY TRUCK is right in front of her.

LANEY

Shit!

She drops the phone, grabs the wheel with both hands, yanks to one side.
The front of her car barely clears the bumper of the delivery truck.
But now she is in the wrong lane, facing oncoming traffic.
She gasps, starts to turn back to her lane, realizes she'll collide, and instead puts the accelerator to the floor. The Volkswagen is moving past the delivery truck, but slowly.
And in front of her, a battered OLD PICKUP is approaching fast. It holds down the horn.

LANEY

I see you.

She continues racing forward, playing chicken at reckless

speeds.

Bennett has followed her into the wrong lane. She is now hemmed in, death on all sides. The pickup is incredibly close.

Laney grits her teeth, glances at the delivery truck beside her. Almost there.

The pickup brakes hard, rear tires smoking and slewing sideways.

At the last possible second, Laney throws the wheel to the right, shooting in front of the delivery truck.

Squealing tires and angry horns fill the afternoon air as the pickup loses control. Its rear end slides too far, and suddenly it is sideways in the road.

The delivery truck reacts, jerking aside to try to avoid the collision. Too late. The pickup broadsides the truck, and both spin out of control.

But Laney is past.

And better still, as the two trucks drift to a stop, she

sees that they have blocked off the PCH.

Bennett's Xterra is trapped behind them.

Laney yells, laughs, punches the roof of the car.

But she's going a hundred miles an hour on one of the most dangerous roads in America. And there's a curve coming up, a ruthless twist with nothing but empty air and a long drop to the ocean below.

She brakes hard. The car jumps and swerves. She wrestles with the wheel to fight the fishtail. Her car sideswipes the barrier rail. Metal screams and sparks fly.

The world spins as she loses control. Out the windshield: sky, tree, canyon wall, sky.

Laney fights back and manages to stop the spin. But the Beetle is now heading directly into the barrier.

LANEY

No!

She screams as she slams into the metal.

Her body is thrown against the seat belt. The air bag explodes.

The world is chaos and breaking glass and smoke.

And then, suddenly, it's over.

Laney groans. She reaches up with fumbling hands, touches her face. Her lip is split, and there's a smear of blood on the air bag. But she's alive.

Out the cracked windshield, she can see only sky and water. The Volkswagen's engine coughs and shudders.

LANEY

Oh god.

She throws the vehicle into park, struggles with her seat belt, panic setting in. She gets it on her third try.

On the passenger seat, her bag has fallen open. Makeup, wallet, sunglasses, and pepper spray spill across the seat.

As do five neat bundles of twenty-dollar bills.

Laney hesitates for a fraction of a second, then stuffs the money back in the bag, retrieves her cell phone and wallet, and leaps out.

Wobbly on her feet, she looks around. The VW has broken through the barrier. The front tires are inches from the cliff's edge.

But she's alive.

Laney looks behind her. The accident is out of sight around the curve and has temporarily blocked traffic from that direction. There are cars coming the other way, but they are far off. No one can help her.

And Bennett will be here in seconds.

An idea occurs, and she is in sudden motion. She climbs halfway into the Beetle, presses the brake, and shifts the engine to drive.

Then she guns the gas as she leaps out of the car, landing

in a clumsy heap.

The VW lunges forward. Momentum carries it over the cliff. It slams down the rock face like a dumbbell down stairs, every impact stunningly loud, and then there is a splash, and the sound of waves.

She edges to the cliff, looks over. Her little car is upside down in the surf, and sinking. One tire spins lazily.

From behind, the roar of an engine.

Laney rushes across the PCH and into the low scrub brush on the other side. She flattens herself in the ditch, wriggling beneath the thin cover of dry brush.

The engine is near.

The Xterra brakes, coming to a stop near the mangled barrier. The door opens, and Bennett hops out.

Laney holds her breath. If he looks on this side, he'll find her.

Bennett hurries to the cliff edge. He leans over.

BENNETT

Oh, fuck me.

He rubs his forehead.
Then he turns and hurries back
to his truck. The Xterra races
away.
Laney waits only seconds before she climbs out and begins
limping in the other direction, bag slung over her
shoulder.

LANEY

Jesus. Jesus.
  (beat)
You should be dead.

A steep path winds up the side
of the cliff a hundred yards
away, and she aims for it.

LANEY

You <u>are</u> dead. Laney Thayer is
dead.
You're no longer Laney Thayer.
  (beat)
You're . . . Belinda. Belinda
Nichols.

> As she begins to climb the hill, sirens sound in the distance.

"At first," Laney said, "I was only thinking of getting away from Bennett. But then I realized that if he thought I was dead, he might back off. Of course, for that to work, everyone had to think so. Even you."

"Why —"

"You know how smart Bennett is. He would have been watching the house. Maybe even tapped the phones. He liked to do that, plant microphones and cameras. And if he realized I was alive, he'd come after you."

"So your plan was, what, lay low forever? That doesn't make any sense."

She shrugged. "You're the writer. You plan things. I was improvising."

"Improvising."

"It's what actresses do, love."

"So you were just going to let me think —"

"Only until I could find a safe way to get in touch with you. A day or two at the most. I knew it would be terrible for you, I just didn't see any choice. But then you were gone. And I figured, well, if Bennett thinks I'm dead, maybe that's useful. Maybe it will give me a chance to get close to him. So I dressed as a cleaning lady, became a woman named Lila Bannister, and went to the house for one of your guns. Then I started looking for him. And for you."

Daniel stared at the ceiling. His mind screening footage of the car chase, of her limping away. "I see how you're alive, but why was Bennett chasing you in the first place? Who is he? How do you know him?"

Laney laughed humorlessly. "Yeah, right."

"I mean it."

"I don't want to go through it all again, okay? I don't want to fight. It was a long time ago."

Daniel stiffened, stomach going sick. *What was a long time ago?* Every time he got one answer, two new questions popped up.

Then he realized. He had known all of this. He must have. It's just that it was gone, along with the rest of his memories.

"Besides, it's not like you don't have things in your past," Laney continued, voice rising. "What was the name of that skank you used to sleep with? The one who got pregnant and told you and *four* other guys that they were the father, asked for money. What was her name, huh?"

"I don't know," Daniel said. He rubbed at his eyes.

"Yeah, I bet. So don't you —"

"Laney."

"I never thought he'd come back into our lives. I thought that was behind —"

"I need to tell you something." He took her hands. *How are you going to explain this? It's one thing to tell Sophie you don't remember her. But this is your wife.* "You know that woman you asked about?"

Laney's shoulders tightened. "What about —"

"I don't remember her name. I don't actually remember her at all. In fact" — he tried to laugh, but the sound was wrong — "I don't remember most of my life."

"What? What are you — are you being philosophical again? Because now isn't the time to go all Sartre on me."

"No. Literally. I don't remember. I have some kind of amnesia."

She stared at him. He met her gaze. After a long moment, she said, "What are you talking about?"

"I'm still figuring it out myself. Things are coming back, a lot of them. But most of my past, it's . . . I can't remember it." Haltingly, he took her through the last week of his life. Waking in panic and pain, half-dead on the wrong side of the country. The pursuit, the endless drive, the loneliness, the dreams. The revelations about their life

364

— okay, yeah, he downplayed the complete shock to discover they were married — and the discovery that she was dead. His grief and anger and attempts at revenge.

Laney listened, her face neutral. She seemed to be consciously withholding judgment, as if someone were telling a joke that might be offensive and she was waiting for the punch line to see which way it landed. Her reserve made him talk faster, wedging words between words, embroidering his statements, spinning the tale as best he knew how, trying to paint for her the state of his life, the edge of madness he'd haunted, the constant uncertainty.

Finally she broke in. "You don't remember anything."

"Like I said, it's coming back. Some of it. And I'm hoping that now that we're together . . ." He broke off, realizing how lame that sounded.

"You're not joking."

"No."

"This isn't some weird game."

"No."

"Last Christmas, when I roasted a chicken and we lay in the backyard looking at the stars. You don't remember."

"No."

"Our wedding day, on the beach in

365

Maine."

Slowly, he shook his head.

"The day we met."

"I'm — I'm sorry. It's not something I chose, believe me."

She turned away. "Do you remember me at all?"

"I . . ." He took a deep breath. Guilt and shame had been constant companions for the past week, but now they found new ways to twist within him. "I know that I love you. I have certain things, images, little . . . vignettes, I guess, that come to me. I don't control them. But I can tell how precious you are to me."

She made a sound that might have been intended as a laugh.

"I realize how that . . . especially . . . I mean, you know." He gestured at the twisted bedding.

"That's what you were trying to say in the elevator."

"Laney, I'm so sorry. If I could turn this off, get rid of it, I would. It's been tearing me apart ever since I woke up on that beach and realized I didn't know how I got there." He reached out to touch her, stopped before his fingers made contact. Held them there for a moment, and then lowered his hand. "I know this much," he said quietly. "Even when I didn't remember anything at all, I knew you were out there. I knew that I had to get back to you. I followed a television show, a fantasy, across the country. I chased you before I knew your *name*. I was trying to get home. And home is you."

She knit her fingers together, palms up — *this is the church, this is the steeple, open it up, see all the people* — and spoke to them. "You need a doctor. It could be a brain tumor, or an aneurism —"

"No," he said. He told her about the MRI clinic, the radiology tech shrugging, saying, *Man, you want to see a doc, up to you, but this is your brain, and there ain't nothing wrong with it. Physically, at least.*

"It could be something else. Something that doesn't show up on an MRI."

"I don't think so."

"What do you know about medicine? I mean, if it's not physical, then how did this happen?"

"I'm only guessing."

"Okay."

"I think maybe my brain was trying to protect itself."

"From what?"

"From . . . dying."

"Dying? What do you mean?" She turned suddenly, her eyes gas-burner blue.

He looked away.

"Daniel?"

"I don't know for sure. I think maybe I was." He sighed. "Maybe I was trying to kill myself."

"*What?*"

"I don't know —"

"Trying to *kill yourself?* What are you talking about?"

"Well, I mean, it's . . ." He tried for a sheepish grin, failed miserably, turned away again. "It's my best guess of how this all started. My amnesia. I thought you were dead, and so I tried to kill myself."

"What?"

"I don't know, all right? I don't *remember*. All I know is that I thought you were dead, and next thing I can put together, I woke up on the beach where we got married. So I figure that I was . . ." He shrugged. "Lost. Miserable. And I ran from L.A., and kept running until I made it to the beach. I had a gun with me, and I'm guessing maybe I planned to use it on myself, but then decided to swim into the ocean instead. That seemed more fitting, somehow, and —"

"Asshole!"

Daniel blinked. "What?"

"Was that supposed to be romantic, all Romeo and Juliet? Did you stop to think for half a second what that would do to me? Did you?"

"Well, I don't remember. But seeing as how you were dead at the time, I'm going to guess not."

Laney looked like she wanted to keep yelling, but his words threw her. She shook her head. Laughed emptily. "Yeah."

"I've been feeling this terrible guilt, I mean, just unbearable guilt and shame. Ever since I woke up. And these dreams. One in particular that keeps coming back, where I'm standing in front of this dark tunnel, and there's something horrible about it, something I can't take back. Which would make sense if I tried to kill myself, wouldn't it?"

"A tunnel?" Something flickered across her face.

"Yeah. Somewhere made out of concrete, and there's a tunnel."

"And that's all you remember?"

"Of the dream? Yeah."

She nodded slowly. "So you don't remember anything about Bennett."

"No."

"Nothing from the last couple of weeks?"

"No."

"Nothing? At all?"

369

He cocked his head. "Is there something —"

"No, I'm just getting used to this." Laney looked like she might continue, but then she closed her mouth, gave him an empathetic wince. "It must be scary."

He nodded. They sat for a moment. Daniel said, "So who is he?"

"He's . . . a nightmare. My nightmare."

"What does that mean?"

She stared at her hands again. It took an effort of will not to fire questions at her, to just wait for her to be ready.

"I started modeling when I was fourteen. Small stuff, local. Ads for the kids' clothing store in the mall, that kind of thing. But when I was seventeen I went to this casting call for Abercrombie. There were a couple of hundred girls there, and that was just in Chicago. Somehow they picked me. It was a national campaign, in all their stores. Suddenly I was a capital-M Model. I got an agent, and she got a lot of calls. My dad didn't know what to do about it, but I was almost eighteen, and he knew he could only put it off for a couple of months, so he gave in. I spent that year flying all over the place. Making ridiculous money. Seventeen, and I made more for a week's work than Dad brought home in a year at the garage. I thought life was one big adventure. Beautiful clothes, famous people, fabulous parties. And at one of them, I met this guy."

"Bennett."

"He wasn't like anyone else. The world was a game to him. He had an angle on everything. He knew things about people, funny things, embarrassing things."

"He's a con man?"

She laughed humorlessly. "And Michelangelo did some painting. Bennett destroys people. He cons, he blackmails, he toys with them. Finds out their secrets. He always said, 'Everybody sins. I'm just there to see it.' "

"What was your sin?"

"Stupidity." A loose curl of hair had fallen across her face, and she brushed it back. "I was seventeen. Seventeen-year-old girls are stupid. They like boys who ride motorcycles. He was mysterious. Charming. Smart."

"So what . . ." His words stalled. Did he want the answer to this question? "What happened?"

"You have to understand, my life had gone surreal. Other girls were trying on prom dresses, going to football games. I was posing for ads in *Vanity Fair* and *Esquire*. At the time I thought it was great, but I look back now, and I think, *Oh, you stupid, stupid child.*

I mean, those ads. Boobs forward, head tilted, lips open, tongue on teeth" — she struck the pose — "the point is sex. That's what the industry is about. Models don't sell clothes, they sell the fantasy of sex. And so the fact that I was still a virgin seemed, I don't know. Immature. False. I thought of my virginity as something I wanted to get rid of. I knew it wasn't love, but it felt glamorous. Most girls lose it in the back of a car; for me it was the penthouse at the Four Seasons."

Daniel's skin crawled. *You evil, evil fucker. You let her give something she couldn't get back, just for fun. I already wanted you for what you did to Sophie, to our lives. Now . . .*

"And the next day." She paused. "The very next day, Bennett tells me about this guy running for Congress. A man with family money. He says the guy likes" — she made air quotes — " 'young pussy,' and that I was going to help blackmail him."

Daniel's thoughts were sewage, stinking and black.

"He'd hidden cameras in the hotel. Pictures of me naked, of us . . . doing things. He said he'd send them to my father, my brother, post them in my high school." She shook her head. "Now, I think, *Who cares?* My dad wouldn't have liked it, but teenagers have sex, and the world still turns. It wouldn't have killed him. It wouldn't even have killed my career. But that's now. Imagine being seventeen. Everyone pointing. Imagine trying to go to church with your family, and everyone in the congregation glancing sideways, all of them picturing you naked, and not just naked, but . . ." She stopped. "Stupid. Vanity. But that's how Bennett works."

Daniel moved to wrap his arms around her from behind. "So you did it."

"Yes. I . . ." A shiver ran beneath her skin. "I did. I felt like throwing up, but I did it. Bennett got what he wanted, and I got free. I left Chicago and came to Los Angeles, the best place in the world to reinvent yourself. I came here and I said, 'You're no longer Elaine Sedlacek, model and victim and Stupid Girl. You're Laney Thayer. You're an aspiring actress with a reason to make it. You're going to become a star, and eventually you're going to meet a real man and fall in love, and you never need to think about Bennett again.' "

He closed his eyes. Her back was hot against his chest, and the smell of her was in his nostrils. "When did he come back?"

"Two weeks ago. In a way, I'm surprised he waited this long. He already knew my

sins, after all. Maybe he saw me as an invest-
ment, waited for the money to get bigger.
Anyway, when he did come back, it was the
tape of seventeen-year-old me and the married congressman."

"He said he'd release it."

"Maybe my career would have weathered
it — maybe — but maybe not. For every
Drew Barrymore the public forgives, there
are a hundred women whose names no one
remembers. Plus, he'd blackmailed the
politician, and there was no way to prove
that I hadn't been in on that. But really, it
wasn't those things. It was you. I didn't
want to put you through that. The embarrassment of it. Of people watching your
wife . . ." She spun the ring on her finger.
"And all he wanted was money."

"So you bought the necklace to pay him
off." It burned him to think of rewarding
this fucker who had taken so much from
her. Maybe it was the simplest way to
handle things, but Bennett deserved to be
hit with a car, not paid off.

"He wanted that one specifically. And ten
grand in cash." She paused, looked at him
quizzically. "I don't know why he didn't just
want the whole thing in cash."

"Taking out that much draws a lot of attention. Most banks don't have half a mil-

lion just sitting in the back room. Plus, with that much, it's easy to include a bunch of sequential serial numbers, which the FBI might be able to track — What?" She had an odd look on her face.

"That's almost exactly what you said before."

"Before?" He caught on. "You asked me that before." She nodded, and he said, "So what was that? A test?"

"I'm just getting used to it. It's kind of interesting, though, don't you think? That you would answer almost exactly the same way? I remember because when you said that about half a million in the back room, I flashed to the image, you know, fluorescent lights, a big metal door, stacks of cash on shelves. It's like those words were in you. Waiting."

"Yeah. My head is a wondrous place," he said. A silence fell. The glass door to the balcony was open, and a breeze rippled the sheer curtains. "Can I ask you something?"

"Anything."

"Did you tell me? About Bennett?"

"Of *course.*" She turned to face him. Her eyes were steady and close. "I told you years ago. All of it."

"How did . . ." He realized he was frightened of the answer, but had to ask the question anyway. "How did I react?"

"You asked me to marry you."

"I did?"

"That's how we ended up getting married on a beach in Maine. We'd been dating about a year then, but that was our first real trip together. You'd been busy, writing for *Brothers Blue* —" She caught herself, explained, "it was a cop drama, great show but misunderstood, got canceled halfway through the first season — and we were in this place on the coast. Lying in bed, talking, you could hear the waves in the background, and I felt . . . safe. So I told you. And when I was done, you asked me to marry you, and I said yes, and you said you meant right away." Her eyes in a happy distance. "So we paid a Unitarian minister five hundred dollars to marry us on the beach the next afternoon. You gave him your camera to take a couple of pictures, and then you said, 'Thanks, we appreciate it, now get the hell out of here so I can do my wife.' "

Daniel was a writer, but he would have been hard-pressed to name the feeling that rolled through him. The warmth and love and trust, the sense of coming home and loving the view, all mingled with relief — after a week of shame and the very real suspicion he had done something terrible, to realize that of this, at least, he was innocent, that was hard to roll into one word.

But maybe "bliss."

Bennett waited for three minutes. Not a lot of time. About what it took to nuke a can of soup. Not a lot of time, but time enough; when neither Laney nor Daniel had returned to their cars by then, he knew they weren't coming.

Ah well.

He climbed out of Jerry D'Agostino's Jaguar and started across the parking lot. The screaming had stopped, and the running. But in typical herd fashion, now that the immediate danger was over, fear had been replaced by curiosity. There had to be two hundred people milling around the Farmers Market parking lot, circling at a distance. People were so predictable. He watched as a police cruiser pulled up, lights flashing. They burped the sirens a couple of times to clear a path; then two cops got out and hustled inside. Everyone stared after them. No one noticed him open his flick knife and cut the tires on Daniel's BMW and Laney's piece-of-shit van. If nothing else, at least he'd limit their mobility for a while.

It took him half an hour to make the drive back to Sophie Zeigler's neighborhood. Bennett rolled with his windows down, arm on the door frame, wind pouring in. The Palisades were all peace and prosperity. Sunlight showered through the canopy, a woman pushed a stroller down the broad lane. He parked the Jag in front of her house and drummed his index finger against his lips.

This was a mess.

For two decades, he'd beaten the system by being careful. Keeping a distance. Made sure that no one who knew much about him stayed alive. His techniques had been honed over time, based on mistakes he saw others making. Again and again, people fell into patterns. Even the criminals got careless. Got too close. Let it become personal.

Is this personal?

He considered that. If it was, he needed to walk away. Start to care, and it all went to shit. The world was a game board. You couldn't win if you valued your pieces too much. They were just means to an end.

For years he'd followed Laney's career.

She was his tech stock — he'd bought her cheap, and her value just kept rising. Another couple of years, she might have been doing features, raking in the big money, and he could have come after her for a lot more. Which made the mess he was dealing with salt in his payday wound. Plus, sure, it was annoying that they'd outplayed him at the mall.

But did he *care?* Not the way other people meant the word.

So it wasn't personal. But it was still a risky situation. And there were always other opportunities.

But then, the clock was a factor. Homeland Security, the FBI. All those smart boys with expensive toys looking for him after that FUBAR in Chicago. It was time to move operations. Somewhere warm, with a nice corrupt government. Mexico, maybe. A lot of money flowing through those cartels. It would be easy for a careful, well-funded man to siphon off a fortune.

Unfortunately, you're only one of those things right now.

Bennett pulled on gloves and strolled up the driveway of Sophie's house. It took less than a minute to pop the locks on her front door.

The house was cool, air-conditioning running steady. He sauntered down the hall, glancing at the photos. Sophie in fragments, slivers of a life framed and hung like butterflies on a board.

Her bed was made, that neat way only women seemed able to manage, the duvet smooth, pillows spilling from the headboard. But her closet door was open, the light on. Bennett looked from one to the other, shook his head. Damn.

He went into the master bathroom to confirm it. The towels hung from the rack, and he remembered Sophie's expression as he had held one out to her, the way she had known what he was doing. She'd stared, naked and dripping — she had a killer body for someone her age — and then taken what he gave her.

Bennett opened the medicine cabinet. Lotions and potions and creams and powders. Four kinds of hair chemicals, but organic deodorant. Bikini Zone and tweezers and a couple of prescription bottles, Lunesta and Prilosec and Allegra. Vitamin supplements. Expensive hand cream. Advil.

No toothbrush. No toothpaste. She'd run.

He left the bathroom, walked into the kitchen. Coffee mugs in the sink. The pot was still on. How much had he missed her by?

There was a phone on the wall, and he picked it up, dialed *69. A pause, and then a recorded voice. "We're sorry, but directory information is unavailable for that number." A payphone or a disposable cell. The happy couple had thought to warn her.

She hadn't just run; she was hiding.

Her office was off the back, a small space splashed with sunlight. There was a slim retro desk of pale blond wood, a filing cabinet, a shelf full of books. Not law volumes, he noticed, actual books, novels. He skimmed the titles; her tastes ran to National Book Award winners.

Like everything else in the house, the desk was clean and neat. An in-box held bills and a couple of issues of *Variety*. There was a rice-paper lamp, a jar of pens, a stapler. A fax machine, but no computer; she would have taken that. He opened the file cabinet, thumbed through the neat tabs until he found her bank statements.

Huh. Should have been an entertainment lawyer.

Bennett placed the latest in the fax machine, pressed copy. He added recent bills from the three credit card accounts he found. Her auto insurance policy and cell phone bill. Last year's tax return. By the time he was done, the stack was a quarter-inch thick. It would take the machine a few minutes.

He walked back to the kitchen, opened the fridge. Half a six-pack of Red Hook sat on the top shelf, and he pulled one of them, found an opener in the drawer by the sink, popped the top. Took a long, cold swallow.

Would they go to the police?

When he'd first approached Laney, he'd played it carefully, presenting her with a cocktail of lousy fates. Humiliation, yes, but also damage to her career, legal consequences, and the real motivator, the way she could expect her husband to look at her. The timing had been key, of course. He smiled to remember her expression when he'd sauntered into the spa. There was the fabulous Laney Thayer, celebrated legs spread wide so a woman could dab hot wax on her pussy. The — what did you call a waxer? Vaginal Design Specialist? — had started to yell, and he'd shushed her, said, "We're old friends."

The look on Laney's face had been priceless, but she'd known enough to calm the woman, ask for a moment alone. Then tried to keep her dignity as wax cooled on her naked pubes.

After that, it had been a simple matter. Part of the art of breaking someone was offering what looked like a way out. Laney could afford to pay; she couldn't afford to risk the police.

Would the scene at the Farmers Market change that? He didn't think so, but both Daniel and Laney had been more erratic than he liked. Probably should clarify things for them.

The fax machine beeped, and he walked back to the office, rapped the stack of papers to even them, then replaced the originals in the file cabinet. He went down the hall and out the front door, papers in one hand, bottle in the other. The day was shaping up hot, and the cold beer tasted wonderful.

Back in his truck, he took out his cell phone and dialed.

The water scalded her calves and thighs, brought a gasp at her belly and breasts. But by the time Laney Thayer was submerged in the bathwater to her neck, the heat had already started to enter her, and she could feel her muscles relaxing, that leaning back *ahhh* moment. She'd poured complimentary bath salts under the running tap, and the water smelled of citrus and sage. The marble caught the heat of the water, bounced it back, and quickly she couldn't feel where her skin ended and the bath began.

She closed her eyes and leaned her head back. *You're no longer Belinda Nichols. You're Laney Thayer. And wow is it good to be home.*

It wasn't that simple, she knew. But it felt wonderful anyway. Ever since the moment Bennett walked back into her life, it had been one misery piled on another. The fear, the shame, the fights, Daniel's terrible reaction, the panic of flight, her faked death and assumed lives, her half-baked plan to hunt Bennett down and kill him. Each had been worse than the last, and it was nice to call a time-out.

It was nice to be Laney Thayer again too. Being other people had been both a comfort and a strain. Every moment spent as Belinda Nichols or Barb Schroeder or Niki Boivin was time that she didn't need to face the loss of her life, didn't need to worry about her beautiful husband. But it had also worn heavy; something of each of those roles came into her, made murky the facts of her personality.

Now that was over. She and Daniel were back together. That part of this ordeal was done with. Now they just had to deal with Bennett. And with Daniel's amnesia.

She imagined him on that beach, lost in every way. What a terrible, lonely experience. To remember everything you needed to live, and yet nothing of your life. To wake in pain and fear, like a wounded animal.

Yet in a strange way, how freeing it was. Daniel could choose to be anyone he wanted. He was unconstrained by the facts of his past, by ugly truths or terrible mistakes. Maybe that would all come back to him, eventually; but maybe not. Maybe all he would remember was the things he wanted to. Memories excavated like dinosaur bones. Unearthed gently, cleaned and polished until they shone. And the ugly ones, the things better forgotten, those could stay buried forever. She could help him, guide him toward some and away from others.

It could be a blessing.

Laney peeled the paper off a bar of moisturizing soap. A week sleeping in a van and washing in the bathrooms of gas stations had left her funky, and sex had added the fecund smells of sweat and spit and semen. She had that good ache, the sweet one that she knew she'd get twinges of when she walked, and those twinges would remind her of them in the bed. After they'd talked they'd made love a second time, slower, gentler, and during the whole of it she had forgotten all of their problems, all of the things that pursued them, and gotten happily lost in the moment. That was the best part about sex, really; not the orgasm, but the forgetting that led up to it.

The water had cooled, and she drained off a couple of inches, spun the tap to hot, refilled it. She stretched out one leg, scrubbed slowly and thoroughly, wishing she had a loofah or some exfoliant, then laughing at herself. *Low maintenance, much?*

Her best friend spoke from her purse.

Laney started at the sound, the motion sending a tsunami across the bathwater. She could see a faint tracing of green light at the lip of her purse, and then heard Robert's voice again, muffled but clear. "Ring, sweetie." A year ago, waiting for the grips to finish lighting a scene, he'd started playing with her cell phone. He'd been delighted to discover how to record a ring tone, and ever since then, every time someone called, Robert's voice echoed from her purse or her pocket, saying, "Ring, sweetie."

All of which was fine, except that she liked her privacy, a lot, and so besides Daniel, the only people who had the number to her cell phone were her agent, her director, her dad, her brother, and a handful of trusted friends like Robert. All of whom thought she was dead. So who would be —

There's another name on that list.

Laney's body slid on the marble as she grabbed at the edge of the tub and hauled herself out. Water ran off in sheets, soaking the thick white bath mat. She dried her hands quickly — "Ring, sweetie" — and fumbled through her bag, pushing aside the pistol, the keys to the van, the remaining bundles of cash. Glancing over her shoulder to be sure the door was closed, she pressed the talk button.

"Guess who."

No, no, no, no no no . . .

"Funny thing, if I knew you were alive, I'd've called earlier. Could have saved some time."

"Whatdoyou —" She made herself slow down. Looked at the door to the bedroom, lowered her voice to just above a whisper. "What do you want?"

"Here's a fun fact. If you don't want to be found, you should be sure to take the battery out of your cell phone. Even switched off, it's basically like carrying a tracking device. Someone can triangulate on that signal, find you easy as pie."

Her chest rose up her throat and cut off the air. *The gun.* She opened the purse, slid her hand inside, distaste for the weapon outvoted by panic. If he could triangulate on her, he could be, where? The lobby? Could he be as accurate as the hallway —

Over the phone, Bennett broke into laughter. "Ahh, I'm just playing. I don't know how to do any of that stuff."

Laney didn't let go of the gun. "What do you want?"

"I know I'm supposed to insert a little witticism here, like, 'world peace,' or 'a glass of hot fat and the head of Alfredo Garcia,' but instead, how about we just go with the classic 'what you owe me.'"

Laney was about to retort when she heard footsteps approaching the bathroom door. Her heart went crazy. She dropped the cell phone on the counter, jerked the pistol up as the door swung open, her hands shaking, the door seeming to take forever —

"Whoa!" Daniel staggered back, raised both his hands.

She realized she was holding her breath, let it out in a rush. "Jesus." She lowered the gun quickly.

"What the *fuck?*"

"I'm sorry, baby. I'm, umm." She glanced away, and her eyes fell on the cell phone. In her haste, she hadn't hung up. *Shit.* No way to reach it without making it obvious. She looked away, set the pistol on the counter. Praying Bennett wouldn't speak, wouldn't draw Daniel's attention to the phone. "I'm just jumpy."

Daniel gave that single laugh sound he made, touched his fingertips to his temples. "Well, *that* woke me up."

"I'm sorry."

"It's okay. Just, you know, don't shoot me."

She worked practiced muscles to conjure a smile. The mirror bounced it back to her. It looked natural enough. "No promises."

He laughed. "I was going to call room service. You want anything?"

"A salad? Whatever looks good."

"You got it." He started to close the door. "Be careful, okay, Hopalong?"

"I will." The moment the door was closed, she stepped over to it and eased the lock button in. Then she picked up the cell phone.

"You know," Bennett said, "secrets are the death of trust."

"What do you know about trust?"

"Elaine, that's a topic I know thoroughly. That and love. The poets don't have a thing on me when it comes to love and trust. Neither do the divorce lawyers. Without love and trust, I'd be out of work. So tell me, why don't you want your loving, trusting husband to know you're on the line with me?"

She couldn't think of an answer, kept her mouth shut.

"Let's try another. What's up with Daniel? He seemed a little off at the market. Of course, until then he didn't know what I really look like, did he?"

Her skin goose-bumped despite the steam in the air.

"Still," he continued, "funny that he would ask about the police."

"We're going to go to them."

"Of course you're not," Bennett said. "You're going to pay me and get on with your lives."

"I don't have the necklace."

"Don't try to tell me it went over the cliff with your cute little car. I know better."

"No," she admitted.

"So where is it, cupcake?"

"Listen," she said. "I understand how this sounds. But it's the truth. Daniel is . . ." She took a breath. "He's having memory problems."

"What, has he got amnesia?"

"Yes."

There was a pause. "You're kidding."

"I'm not."

"Amnesia."

"Yes. Or something like it. A blackout. His memories are coming back, but not . . . He won't know where the necklace is."

"Huh." Bennett's voice was oddly thoughtful. She'd expected mockery, incredulity, even threats. But quietly taking it in? Maybe even believing? She hadn't dared to hope.

"So the thing is, we can't pay you. I would, I really would. I just want this over. But I used most of our cash to buy that necklace. We can't sell the house or anything, not right now, not while I'm —"

"Dead. Sure. I understand."

"You — you do?"

"You know what else? I even believe you."

Could this be? "I'm telling the truth."

"I just don't give a damn."

The fragile hope collapsed. "But —"

"You're going to pay me. I've still got your star performance, and I'm still happy to let it out there. Maybe I'll make a Web site. WatchLaneyThayerGobbleCock.com. What do you think?"

"I —"

"But you know what? That's not the real reason you're going to pay, sister. It's not for your career, or to avoid criminal charges, or even the way you'd humiliate your husband. Not anymore. Now you're going to

392

pay because you don't want Daniel to find out the truth all over again."

Her stomach twisted. "You evil —"

"Yeah, yeah, my karma's rotten, I know. But Dan didn't handle it well the first time, did he? I bet he was hugging the toilet and retching his guts out."

It took all her effort, but she made herself speak. "I told you. I don't know where it is."

"Find it. Fast."

And then he was gone, and she stood naked, shivering, holding a dead phone to her ear.

Dressed only in his underwear, Daniel leaned on the balcony railing. Below, Beverly Hills spread out in a dream of shiny afflu-ence. Angelenos moved down the sidewalks, shopping bags in hand. A soft breeze tugged at the trees. Somewhere a horn honked.

He smiled and stretched. His body was warm with sunlight and sex. They'd made love again, slower this time, sweeter, their eyes locked, the whole experience filled with a glowing charge. He had lost everything, and then discovered that it wasn't gone, only hidden. And now that he had found his way back to his life, he would never lose it again. His memory would return in time.

His beautiful girl would stand with him, help him through. He wasn't alone anymore.

Daniel wandered back into the suite, left the door open so the wind could tug at the curtain. Through the bathroom door he could hear the whir of the hair dryer. The room was gorgeous, tastefully modern and sumptuous in every detail. It beat the crap out of the Ambassador.

A soft knock at the door made him jump. "Yes?"

"Room service."

He snagged a robe from the closet, tied the belt as he walked to the door. A glance through the peephole showed a server holding a heavy tray at shoulder height. Daniel opened the door, and the man walked in. "Good afternoon, sir."

"You too. Just put it over there?"

The man nodded, carried the tray to the bed. When Daniel pulled out cash, the server shook his head. "The manager, Mr. River, took care of it, sir."

After the man left, Daniel rapped on the bathroom door, told Laney the food had arrived. He lifted the heavy silver cover off her salad and his own meal, steak sandwich with blue cheese and caramelized onions. He used the bottle opener to pop one of the

Sierra Nevadas and took a long, lovely swallow.

Laney walked out of the bathroom on a cloud of steam. Her robe was open, and her skin was bright pink. She caught him looking, smiled, and went to the tray. "Man, that sandwich looks great. Why did I order a salad?"

"I'll share."

"I love my husband." She sat on the bed with one leg curled beneath her, and lifted half the sandwich, leaning over the tray to take a bite.

Daniel sat on the bed against the headboard. The steak was tender and bloody and dripping juice.

"So I got a call," Laney said, "while I was in the bath."

"You have your phone?"

"Even bought a car charger for it in case you called."

He shook his head. "All this time."

"Yeah. Anyway, it's good news." She took a bite, chewed a moment before continuing. "It was a girl I knew a little bit, back in Chicago. I've been trying to reach her all week. She knew Bennett too."

"Really?"

Laney nodded. "I saw her at one of those parties in the hills a couple of years ago.

Back then neither of us wanted anything to do with the past, so we didn't talk. But I got to thinking, maybe she knows something that could help us."

"Like what?"

"I don't know. Maybe she has a picture. Or maybe he forced her to do something too, something that we could use."

"Is it safe to talk to her? You're supposed to be dead, and you said Bennett will be watching everyone."

"I don't think he knows she's here."

"Why don't we just go to the police?"

"No," she said.

"Why not?"

"They'll arrest you."

"For what? You're alive."

"But you ran from them."

"Big deal. I don't really care at this point."

"Okay, but what happens if they arrest you? Bennett will still be out there. And I'll be alone."

The thought brought him up cold.

"Look," she said. "I'm not saying let's not go to the police. I'm just saying, let's not go to them yet. Let's keep our options open."

"Okay," he said. "Fair enough. I'll call down for a cab for us."

"No," she said. "I have to go alone."

"No chance."

"Daniel, she's freaked out. The only way she'll help is if it's just me."

"So I won't go in with you —"

"Yeah, because a strange man in a cab at the end of her driveway is going to be re-assuring."

"Laney —"

"I have to do this alone."

He drummed his fingers together. He'd just found her again, and nothing in him wanted to be parted for even a minute. On the other hand, Laney wasn't some useless woman in a horror film. She'd been alone for the last week. *And let's not forget that she's not the one with a broken brain.* "How long will it take?"

"An hour. Maybe two."

"You'll be really careful?"

"Of course."

"If anything at all seems suspicious — If someone follows you, or the girl seems like maybe she's hiding something —"

"Trust me. I'm not going to take any risks."

Daniel set his sandwich down, grabbed his beer, walked to the window. Stared out at the city beyond.

"I think this is the right thing to do," Laney said from behind him. "But if you really don't want me to, I won't."

It's a big city. Bennett can't watch all of it. And she's right — if you go to the police, there's a good chance that she'll be truly on her own. Not for an hour or two, but for days, maybe weeks.

None of it did much for the fear in his belly. He raised the bottle to his lips, realized it was empty.

"Take the gun," he said.

Before she left, Laney called Robert. It took her two minutes to convince him it was really her, and another five to calm him down. Finally, she cut in. "Robert, I promise, I'll tell you everything, everything, but later, okay? Right now I need your help."

"Of course, sorry. I'm just so . . . god, I don't even know what the word is. What can I do?"

"Lend me your car?" Neither she nor Daniel knew how long the police would be at the Farmers Market, but it hardly seemed worth the risk. And she trusted Robert to keep quiet.

"Sweetie, you can *have* my car."

Laney smiled. "Can you do me a favor and bring it to me?"

"Where are you?"

"The Beverly Wilshire."

"Wonderful place to be dead. We're be-

398

tween takes, but I'll play the diva card."

"No, no need. Just bring it when you're done." She gave him their room number. "Leave it with the valet?"

"Wait, what? I want to see you."

"I know. Me too. But I can't risk it."

"Why not?"

"We have to stay out of sight —"

"We?"

"Daniel and I."

"Daniel." Robert might have been saying "hemorrhoids."

"Yes. My husband?" She knew that he and Daniel had some friction. Male territorialism, heightened by the fact that the three of them worked together. "Listen, now's not the time. I just need your help. Will you help me?"

"Of course. But why the secrecy? Can you at least tell me that?"

"I'm sorry. I can't, not right now."

There was a long pause. "Are you all right, Laney?"

"No," she said. "But we're working on it."

By the soft lighting of the bathroom, she reapplied her port wine stain, steadily painting on a false face. Afterward, she showed Daniel the full charge on her cell phone, the almost-full magazine of the Sig Sauer. She rose up on tiptoes to kiss her husband.

Then she walked out of the suite and down the hall and took the elevator to the lobby and stepped out into the cheery sunlight of another perfect Los Angeles afternoon.

All without letting one hint of the lie show on her features.

You're no longer Laney Thayer. You're Elaine Hayes. The first name was your mother's; the last is your husband's. You're the private side of a public person, the one who would rather spend Saturday night playing Scrabble and splitting a bottle of red than playing starlet and strutting a red carpet. You stand straight and look people in the eye, but you don't pose or preen. Your sunglasses are regular size.

She'd repeated it to herself as she walked the streets of Beverly Hills, headed not for a taxi and an imaginary girl in West Hollywood, but here, this bland institution, this lobby with its fake plants and fluorescent lights and insipid carpeting. What was it about a bank that made everyone so quiet? Any other situation where people stood in line, they chatted and joked and answered cell phones. But in the implied presence of money, everything went quiet, the only sounds the shuffle of paper. An occasional cough, or the rustle of a sleeve as someone glanced at a watch.

There are cameras and security guards and yours is a famous face. If someone recognizes you . . .

"Can I help you?" The greeter looked fresh-scrubbed, his suit nice but not stylish, his cheeks pink.

"Yes," she said. "I have a safe deposit box?" Letting her voice go higher at the end to emphasize that it didn't hold false passports and unregistered weapons, but the kind of documents regular people might store there, and that thus it was something not often visited. That this was a small novelty, but not worth noting.

"Yes, ma'am," the man said. "Come with me, Ms. . . ."

"Hayes."

"Ms. Hayes." He led her to an empty desk — why were there always empty desks at banks? — and sliding behind it, "May I see your driver's license?"

She nodded, dug her wallet from her purse, slid out her ID. The picture was a few years old, taken around the time *Candy Girls* first aired, and showed her with her real hair, dark brown and shoulder length, layered to frame her face. It was a dead ringer for the image on a hundred billboards and magazine ads, and no port wine stain marked her cheek. She held it for a second,

401

not wanting to pass it over. What if this guy recognized her? Would he think to ask a question? Would he say she looked like that actress? The name on the ID was her real name, Elaine Hayes, not Laney Thayer, but still, the leap was small.

Find it. Fast. Bennett's voice ringing in her ears.

Elaine Hayes passed the card across the desk and made herself smile.

The man punched a few keys, his eyes on the computer monitor. He glanced at the license, punched a few more keys. Finally he said, "Here we are. Box 152?"

"Yes."

"Okay." He typed some more. "Did you hear the news?"

"What's that?"

"There was a shooting at the Farmers Market."

"Really?"

"Just this morning." He looked across the desk at her. "Can you believe it?"

"Wow. No. My husband and I go there all the time."

"Scary, isn't it? You think you're safe, that that sort of thing only happens somewhere else, but." He shook his head. "Right this way, Ms. Hayes."

She followed him, keeping her head down,

feeling the cameras pointed like accusing eyes. He led her to a side door, typed a quick code on a number pad. An LED went from red to green, and he opened the door, then gestured her through.

The room was just as she remembered. A wall of numbered boxes with metal doors, gray carpet on the floor, and a clean, powdery smell. A closed-circuit camera stared from the corner.

"Here you are," he said. "You can use this for privacy." He gestured to a desk framed with a curtain. "When you're done, just put the box back. The door will lock behind you."

"Thanks," she said, and waited for him to leave. Then she took out her key chain and used the smallest one to open the lock, pulled out the box, and took it to the desk, closing the curtain behind.

She said a little prayer to the universe: *Let it be here, please, let it be here and I'll finish this quietly. Daniel will never need to know.*

Elaine flipped up the lid of the box. Inside were papers in manila folders, contracts and tax statements. Two passports, hers and his. An envelope with a dozen photographs. She'd forgotten about those, the pictures she'd let Daniel take of her; he'd called them "erotic," she'd called them "porno," but posing for them had been fun, given her a glow, knowing that in fifty years they would have these shots, the two of them young and lusty and naked. Once the show hit, they moved them here, not wanting some ambitious faux-friend to ransack their drawers and sell the pictures to paparazzi. There was a brooch that had belonged to her mother, and seeing it gave her a flash of memory, golden sunlight and hair that smelled like honey and the necklace dangling down as her mom leaned over her.

What was not there, what was conspicuously absent, was a diamond necklace worth half a million dollars.

She wanted to turn the box upside down and shake it. She wanted to punch the table and scream.

Be calm. If you want to keep your secret, you have to be calm.

Elaine closed the box. Slid it back in the frame. Walked out the door. The same man wished her a good afternoon as she passed, but she just kept her head down until she stepped back out onto Wilshire.

Somehow things had gotten worse instead of better. Laney Thayer raised a hand to her forehead, squeezed her temples. It had been a long shot, she supposed. But where else would Daniel have put the necklace? This was the safest place. Though now that she thought about it, she couldn't imagine him driving in from Malibu to tuck it safely away before he went on his cross-country suicide run. That was the problem with improvising; you just had to hope that you were going in the right direction. If it had paid out, and the necklace had been here, she could have called Bennett —

"Hey, is that Laney Thayer?"

She whirled.

Bennett smiled at her. He wore the same nondescript clothes as before, the same bland expression, but in one hand he held an ice cream cone, a scoop of pink perched atop one of white.

"How — what are you —"

"Last time I was in your house I went through your bank records. Terrible habit of mine. I saw you had a safe deposit box, and thought you might have stowed my necklace there." He bit a chunk out of the ice cream.

"No." Her skin was cold despite the sunlight. The gun bit into her belly. "I thought Daniel might have. But it's not."

"Want a lick?" Bennett held the cone out to her. When she just stared at him, he shrugged, pursed his lips around it, rounding and smoothing the portion he'd bitten.

"I need more time," she said.

"We all need more time, sister."

"I'm trying. But I don't know where it is."

"Daniel does."

"Look, his memory, I told you —"

"And I told you," Bennett wiped a drip of pink off his chin, "I don't care. Daniel knows. Go to work on our boy." He took another bite of the ice cream, then tossed the cone sideways. It landed in the street with a splat. He brushed his hands off. "Or I will."

Bennett turned and walked away. She stared at him, his back to her. It would be so simple. Pull the pistol from her belt. Aim carefully, the way she had practiced. Squeeze the trigger —

Yeah. Shoot him in broad daylight in front of a bank on Wilshire Boulevard. Excellent plan.

She gritted her teeth until her jaw ached.

Then she started walking.

"Los Angeles Sheriff's Department."

"Hello hello. Did you miss me, brother?"

"Damn it" — a rustling sound over the receiver, and the voice dropped — "I told you never to call me again."

"You did. That's true."

"So what the —"

"I need another favor."

"No. No more."

Five, four, three, two . . .

"What is it?"

"I need an address."

"Whose?"

"I don't know. I have a phone number, need you to run a reverse lookup."

"What am I, your computer guy? Use the damn Internet."

"It's unlisted."

"Then call one of your connections."

"That's what I'm doing." A pause to let that sink in. "You don't have to like me, brother. I can stand the rejection. But do you really want me to share what I know, just to avoid pressing a few keys on your fancy cop software?"

"I'm not going to let you do this forever. Be careful you don't push too far. People disappear all the time."

"Wow. That was scary. Seriously, I've got chills."

"Listen, you cockroach —"

"No, you listen. I vanish, a whole lot of secrets get revealed. Including yours. Do you really want that?" A pause. "One of the things you learn, my line of work, is the real weight of a debt. I still have credit left on this one, and you know it. So stop wasting time and run the reverse for me."

A sigh. "What's the phone number?"

Daniel was in a concrete canyon.

Again. Back in a concrete canyon.

Water trickled. The bleeding sun stained everything crimson. Ahead, a tunnel, tall and broad. The mouth of it was a perfect black shadow, but he knew that something waited in that darkness. Waited and watched.

Something terrible.

It was clearer this time, the dream. There were buildings beyond the canyon, a skyline of mute towers framed black against the red sky, windows glowing like eyes. In the fading light of day, the buildings loomed like hooded figures of judgment.

His hand was heavy.

From the darkness of the tunnel, a faint rasping. A movement sound, but indistinct and wrong, snakes squirming across one another in dark pits, the slow inhale of some huge beast. His fear was childlike in its perfection. It seized him completely. He wanted to run.

What's there?

Why am I here?

He took a step forward, dread lighting up his spine. He had the vague and drifting feeling of being near the edge of waking. He couldn't control the action, but he could nudge it, could float suggestions, and yet he knew it was a dream. Familiar, though, and maybe not just from having dreamed it before. And yet what was a dream but a mash-up of memory and imagination and worry?

The mouth of the tunnel was perfect black. Preternatural darkness. Light died when it crossed that boundary.

In that blackness, something waited. Watching him. Staring.

Judging.

As much as fear, there was guilt, that overwhelming sense of horror and shame.

A dusty breeze tugged at his clothing.

His hand was heavy.

He took a step forward. And another. He was almost to the tunnel —

"Daniel?"

Eyes snapping open, he jerked his head back, cracked it against the wooden headboard. He grunted, blinked. "Wha? I'm here."

The tunnel was gone, replaced by the hotel room. How had he fallen asleep? After Laney left, he'd stood on the balcony and watched the street. Paced ruts in the carpet. Finally, he'd decided to distract himself with the news. When it had gone to a commercial, the braying of the sales voice had bothered him, and he'd muted it, leaned back, closed his burning eyes just for a second . . .

Laney said, "Are you okay?"

"Yeah." Grimacing, he rubbed at the back of his skull, then swung his legs off the bed, leaned on his knees. He had never been a napper. It sounded nice in principle, but he always woke up wooden and confused, feeling worse than when he lay down. "Sorry. I guess I drifted off." There'd been no real sleep in a week, not since he woke on the beach. He blinked, then looked up at her. "How about you? You okay?"

She nodded, pulled a chair from the desk, flopped into it.

"How'd your thing go?" His thoughts returning to him slowly. "The woman you were meeting."

"What? Oh." She shook her head. "No. It was a waste of time."

"She won't help us?"

"She didn't know anything." Laney ran her hands through her hair, bundled it up behind her head, then let it drop. "What if we just pay him?"

"Huh?"

"That's what we were going to do, before. It's just that he startled me showing up like that on the PCH, and I ran, and after that, everything got complicated. But why not pay him?"

He shook his head. "After all he did to you?"

"It's only money. It's not our life." She ticked at her teeth with her fingernail. "Where's the necklace?"

"Pardon?"

"The necklace."

"I thought — Don't you have it?"

"No."

Daniel laughed. "Well, that's a bitch."

"You don't know?"

"Maybe I did. I don't remember. Hell, I don't remember our wedding day." A look of real sadness and disappointment swept across her face. *Asshole.* He spoke quickly. "I'm sorry. I don't mean to be casual. I just — laughing about it is the only way I've been able to keep myself together."

She twisted a length of hair between her fingers.

"I did have an idea, though." Daniel stood, stretched. "I was thinking about it after you left. You went to see this woman — what's her name?"

"Huh? Oh. Lisa."

"Lisa, you went to see her hoping she might have something to help us, right? Even a picture? And it wasn't until you were gone that it occurred to me to think, what difference would a picture make? But you were right. It's actually kind of brilliant."

She raised an eyebrow.

"See, the thing is, if we go to the police now —"

"Daniel, no —"

"Hear me out. If we go to them now, all we have is a description, right? Sophie could come as well, and she'd back up our story, and of course you're alive, so there's that. But we don't really have anything on Bennett. Nothing that they could use to catch him, and no way to make sure he doesn't come after you if I'm locked up."

"Okay," she said, in a tone he remembered. It was the way she used to respond when he was talking out plot twists to her. He had a flash of another room, filled with sunlight — his office at home, maybe — and her leaning back, a little smile on her lips, saying, *Okay,* as he led her up to a cliff-hanger. It was a good memory, and a good feeling, and he went with it, pitched his idea like a script.

"So what if we did get something on him?" He paused, held the moment. "What if, for a change, *we* had something *Bennett* didn't want released?"

Late afternoon, and already the streets of Westwood Village had started to clog, UCLA students heading north to the Valley or south to Mar Vista. Bennett rolled up Broxton, past a falafel joint, a movie theater, a mystery bookstore. He got a kick out of the fact that it called itself a "village," like somewhere there were huts and friendly peasants.

"K-Earth 101, the greatest hits on Earth!" the radio proclaimed, and then Diana Ross came on, singing about how you can't hurry love, no, you just have to wait. Bennett turned up the volume, whistled along. Diana in her day, that was a woman.

His cell phone rang, a slow pinging sound like sonar. Bennett switched the wheel to his left hand, held the phone in his right, glanced at the display. "Hi, Laney." Turning west. "That was fast."

"If we give you the necklace, will you leave us alone?"

"Cross my heart," he said.

A long pause, and then she said, "We're going to do it somewhere we feel safe."

"And where would that be?"

"The Santa Monica Pier."

"Kind of cliché, don't you think?" He turned down a quiet neighborhood block a bit west of campus. "I mean, why not just do it at the foot of the Hollywood sign, go the distance?"

"Will you meet us or not?"

"When?"

"Sunset."

"Romantic."

"We'll pay you. After that, we never want to see you again." She hung up.

He tossed the cell phone onto the passenger seat, glanced at the sky. He had an hour, maybe more.

The houses were large and well maintained, fronted by flowers and lawns. Though it was a short walk to campus, living here would be out of the budget of most professors, let alone students. The address he was looking for turned out to be a one-story with Spanish influences and tall trees spilling shade over the corner lot. A hammock was slung between two trunks. Ben-

415

nett went past, parking on the opposite side of the street a block down.

One thing led to another. He'd gotten the phone number by looking at call records, highlighting the five that appeared most, and then choosing the one dialed on weekends and late at night. That gave him digits; his cop friend had translated that into an address and a name.

With a little convincing, of course.

Bennett's leverage with the man stemmed from a police cover-up a decade old, and truth be told, it was getting thin. Of course, what the man hadn't realized was that by supplying the address, he was tying himself to Bennett forever.

One thing led to another. Flirting with seventeen-year-old Laney led to pictures of his cock in her, which led to the perfect bait for an aspiring congressman, which led to a nice fat payday, which in turn led to leverage on Laney all over again. That was the way it worked.

The house belonged to a guy with the unlikely name of Charles Charlemagne, Esq. A little digging revealed that Chuck was a lawyer before he was a professor, and was still titular partner in a small but profitable firm, hence the digs.

Esquire. What a dick.

416

Bennett climbed out, walked down the block, whistling Diana Ross. He didn't bother with the front, just hiked up the driveway of the place next door, then cut around the side yard and into the back, where Chuck had set up a vegetable garden and a nice little patio with an elaborate grill. French doors opened into what looked like a kitchen.

He slid on a pair of gloves, then pulled his sleeve over his fist and popped one of the panes of glass inward. It hit the tile and broke. Before the sound had died, he'd reached inside to unlock the door.

There was a double beep. Alarm.

Bennett sprinted down the hall. He could hear the sounds of panic, someone else in the house. Racing for the front door, because that was what people predictably did. He rounded the corner just as the deadbolt unsnapped. The woman heard him coming, spun, hands up and eyes wide.

"Hi." Bennett smiled. "Let's start with the alarm code."

The sun had slipped beneath the horizon as Daniel paced the Santa Monica Pier, and the sky was fading fast, gory reds and brutal yellows slowly washing purple. He checked the clock on his cell phone.

Waves rolled in slow breaks up the beach, foam trimming lace and pewter. Surf kids bobbed and floated, calling across to one another, occasionally paddling to catch a swell, riding in halfway before dropping off. A handful of photographers with cameras mounted on tripods pointed long zoom lenses out to sea, hoping for the perfect stock photo, a dream of a summer evening to sell to all the landlocked in Wichita.

After Laney had made the call to Bennett, they'd left the hotel. Robert Cameron had been as good as his word, leaving his silver PT Cruiser with the valet, along with a note:

L:
I hope you know what you're doing. Please be careful. I love you.

— R

"You drive," Laney had said. "I'll get my phone set up."

He nodded, took the wheel. The car was nice, but he missed his BMW. The thing had become home base for him.

"Okay," Laney said. "Try it."

He pulled out his disposable phone, dialed. Robert Cameron's voice said, "Ring, sweetie."

"That's your ring tone?"

418

"Just test it, okay?"

Daniel tucked his phone into his shirt pocket, still on. Said, "Lady, your husband is one sexy mofo."

Laney hung up, pressed a button. The speaker on her phone was small and tinny, and the sound was muffled. But his voice came through clear enough, saying, *Lady, your husband is one sexy mofo.*

"I don't know," she said, frowning.

"What do you mean? Worked fine."

"Yeah, but it's quieter here."

"It will do."

"I'd rather just pay him."

"With what?" Daniel shrugged. "This will work. We'll have pictures of him *and* a recording of him threatening us. That should give us enough."

"I don't like you out there alone."

"Has to be that way. If you're there, then there's no reason he can't take us. But grabbing just me does no good." He leaned over, touched her hand. "You said Bennett is careful, that he survives by people not knowing anything about him. There's no way he'll want us going to the police with this."

Laney didn't reply. The setting sun filled the air with gold.

Daniel flexed his fingers, tapped a beat on

the steering wheel. His exhaustion was making him manic. The couple of minutes of sleep in the hotel had only managed to remind him how very tired he was. "It's funny, kind of. Using a recording against Bennett."

"Ironic."

"Yeah. A lot of that lately. You know, if it hadn't been so terrifying, this whole experience would be kind of interesting."

"Interesting?" She cocked an eyebrow. "Are you kidding me?"

"It's changed the way I think about things. About what's real. You convince yourself that you know who you are, what your life means. You remember the things that have happened to you. But really, that's not true, is it? Memories are just stories we tell ourselves to explain how we got where we are. There's no absolute to them. It's all subjective."

"My memories aren't subjective."

"Sure they are. You're just comfortable with the order they're in. But you chose which to keep and which to dump. Maybe not consciously, but still."

"We don't choose our memories."

"You know we do. Same way you chose to be somebody else. When you were all those other women, you gave them memories, and you used those memories to make them real."

"That's different."

"How?"

"Because . . ." She made an exasperated sound. "Because it is. When I become someone else, I don't really become them. I still know who I am."

"But see, I don't. And it's made me realize that it's always up for grabs." He swiveled in his seat to face her. "Like that tape. The one Bennett has of you."

Laney glanced over, her eyes narrowed. "What about it?"

"It's you, right? Doing things you're not happy about, that you wish you could take back. Having sex with a man to —" He cut himself off. "But the thing is, there's also video of you in our kitchen, singing the *Peanuts* Christmas song and dancing."

She smiled. "I remember."

"So both exist. Is one more real than the other? Do we have to weigh them the same? They're in the past. Frozen moments that will never come again. You've changed since both of them." The world outside rolled by, smooth and removed, cars and billboards and other people. "Over the last week, if there's anything I've learned, it's that you're only who you choose to be. Every moment.

The past is gone. Memories are no more solid than dreams. The only real thing, the only true thing, is the present. That's it."

"So the things we've done don't count?"

"Of course they do. But we can decide how much. And we can decide what we want the present to be like. We can live it however we want. Own every minute. Be the person we want to be."

Laney was silent for a long moment. Finally, she said, "I think there are things that can change who we are. Things we can't forget. Or get over." She spoke to the windshield, her tone even and measured.

Gentle. You're poking at a wound. "Look, I don't care what you did ten years ago. That's my point. I want to be with you. The video I'm going to remember is the one of you singing and dancing."

Laney didn't respond, and he let it drop. Traffic was slow. As the sky started to shade with color, he found himself remembering a concrete canyon and a tunnel of perfect black. The buildings looming like judges. "I had that dream again."

"Which one?"

"The same one I've been having since I woke up. It's weird. I feel so guilty in it. Like I've done something terrible. Before I found you —"

422

"I found you."

"— before I found you," he continued, smiling, "I was starting to wonder if maybe that was my subconscious. If I was telling myself that I'd killed you."

"So much for your subconscious."

"I know, right?" He laughed. "I wonder what it means, though. Since you're alive, shouldn't it have gone away? What do I have to feel so guilty about?"

Laney shrugged. "It's probably a guy thing."

"What do you mean?"

"Well, you thought I was dead. And guys want to solve things. Hunt the woolly mammoth and protect their women. But you couldn't, and I died."

"Huh." *Maybe.*

Ten minutes later, he got off the freeway in Santa Monica, looped around, and pulled into a wide parking lot beside the pier. On a Saturday afternoon, the lot might have been packed, but now it was barely a quarter full. The kiddie roller coaster on the pier swung around a turn, its rattling rumble wafting on cool ocean breezes. He slowed to a stop. For a moment they stared out the window.

"Time to hunt mammoth."

Laney looked over, tension drawing taut the lines of her face. "Daniel . . ."

He waited, but she didn't say anything else. "It's going to be okay."

"I love you."

"I love you too." He reached for the door handle.

"Hey," she said. "You forgot something."

He turned, saw her smile, and realized what he'd forgotten. He took his time collecting it.

When he got to the end of the pier, Daniel found half a dozen photographers leaned against their tripods, long lenses pointed out to sea, snapping pictures of surfers and the fading sunset and the bright lights of the pier winking on against the coming dark. He chose one slightly apart from the rest.

At first the photographer didn't understand what Daniel wanted. "Is this, like, for a movie?"

"Something like that. Listen, just take as many pictures as you can of the guy who comes to talk to me. Get close-ups of his face, get us both together, get any details you can."

"Five hundred bucks?"

"Five hundred bucks."

"I'm your man, dude."

And now here Daniel was, standing on the pier beneath the fading sky with its gory red and brutal yellows, its pewter foam and bobbing surf kids. The handful of photographers tried for the perfect stock photo, and from this distance there was no way to tell that one of them had the lens pointed at him.

In theory, the idea was straightforward. He just had to keep cool long enough for Bennett to expose himself. Then he would turn it around on the guy, tell him what they had done, and offer a simple quid pro quo: If Bennett went away, they wouldn't pass the audio or photographs to the police. He'd keep his anonymity, and they'd keep their lives.

Let's just hope your theory is sound.

The wind off the ocean was cold, and Daniel fought a shiver. A tourist family was taking snaps of themselves on one railing; on another, a couple sat holding hands.

Daniel checked his cell phone. Time, now. No sign. He continued pacing, moving from one weathered wooden plank to another, trying not to step on the rusted metal bolts. Making a game of it. Anything to distract him from how very exposed he felt out here.

What if Bennett decides just to kill you, and go after Laney alone?

What if he puts a gun to your back and makes you call out to her?

What if Bennett doesn't care about the money anymore, and just wants to tie up loose —

"Are you Hayes?"

She was slight, the woman who asked, a hundred pounds with her clothes on. Her face was pretty but so angular it looked like it might cut a hand that touched it. Blond bobbed hair framed jumpy eyes.

"I . . ." *Your picture has been in the news. It was only a matter of time before someone recognized you. And all she has to do is yell and the whole world will come crashing down, and your neat shiny plan with it.* "Umm."

The woman glanced around quickly, then pulled a pack of cigarettes from her pocket, tugged one out with uneasy fingers. "I'm supposed to ask you for the package."

"What?"

"He said to ask you for the package." She struck at a match, then again, cupping her hands around it. "Hope you don't mind if I smoke. I'm nervous."

What does she mean? What pack—

Oh, shit.

Daniel's mouth fell open. He had been so focused on making sure he was safe, picking a location that Bennett couldn't attack him. And instead, the man had outflanked them.

Daniel rose up on his toes, looked up and

down the beach. No sign of Bennett. The photographer he'd paid was busily clicking away, taking pictures that would be no use at all.

She had the cigarette going now, took a deep hard drag. He could see her relax as the smoke hit her lungs. "So? Do you have it?"

"Where is he?"

"He said not to chitchat, just to get the —"

He stepped forward, grabbed her wrist. "Where is he!"

She tried to pull away, but he gripped harder. "Ow! Let me go!"

The father of the happy tourist family caught her tone, looked Daniel's way. He gritted his teeth, opened his fingers, and she snatched her arm back, massaged it with her other hand. "Asshole."

"Listen," he said, wanting to grab her tiny body and dangle her over the railing until she gave him what he needed. "I don't know what Bennett told you. But he's coming after my family. My wife. He's trying to kill us."

The woman's eyes darted. "I don't know anything about that. He just — I owed him, and he told me to come get this bag. He said you were trying to play him, and he was going to take care of something while I talked to you."

What does that mean? "I'm sorry about before. I am. But please, I'm begging you. Tell me where he is." *Take care of something while she talked to me . . .*

"Look, I told you, he just —"

. . . while she kept me busy.

Oh, fuck!

Daniel turned on his heel and sprinted down the pier, left the woman yelling after him. His sneakers pounded on the dry wood, a childhood sound. He threw himself forward, arms flying, breath coming fast. Visions of horror splashing across the back of his retina. Of finding their borrowed car empty. Worse. Finding her in it. Really dead this time, eyes empty and staring.

"Move!" Daniel shoved through a row of giggling high school girls, knocked an ice cream cone flying. Behind him curses rose in two languages. He dodged around a bicycle, then ran for the edge of the pier. Grabbed the railing and vaulted it, dropping the ten feet to sandy beach. Hit with a ring of distant pain in his ankles and his shins, but he didn't fall, just leaned into his run, pushing for the parking lot where they'd agreed to meet. The parking lot where Laney had been left alone, where

Bennett could have come at her from any direction. Jesus, how had he been so stupid, how had he let this guy outthink and out-plan him, and then his feet hit concrete, and he pushed for the far end, where he saw Robert's silver PT Cruiser parked, the sunlight off the windshield hiding any-thing —

The driver's side door opened, and Laney stepped out. She squinted into the sun, held one hand over her eyes.

Daniel covered the distance between them in seconds, threw his arms around her, crushed her to his chest, feeling the sun-warmed heat of her body, her hair against his nose, the bird lattice of her rib cage.

"Are you okay?" she asked into his chest.

"It was someone else. Bastard sent some-one else."

"I know, I heard. Then it was all static, and I saw you running . . ."

Daniel laughed a syllable's worth at him-self. "The phone. I didn't even think of it. I was so scared, I just had to get here." He pulled it from his pocket, hung up the call. "I screwed it all up, baby."

"It's not your fault. He's very good."

Her tone irked him. "Is there a fan club?"

"Don't be an idiot."

Before he could reply, Daniel's cell phone

rang. He glanced at the display and picked up. "Sophie, now isn't a —"

"You know why television is so predictable?"

The voice wasn't Sophie's. The world slipped and spun, palm trees going sideways as his knees went weak.

"Television is predictable because it's written by guys like you."

"I swear to god," Daniel blurted, "if you —"

" '— hurt her, I'll kill you.' See what I mean? I don't even need you for this conversation. I may as well be talking to myself. In fact, I think I will. 'Gosh, self. Do you think it's a wise idea to fuck around?' 'You know what, self? I don't think that's smart at all. I think I should just pay the man. Otherwise, who knows *what* he'll do.' "

"Bennett —"

"Seems you still don't get the point. So let me underscore it. Denslow and Levering."

"What? I don't —"

"Be talking at you."

"No, wait, Bennett, please, I'm sorry, we'll —"

The line went dead. Daniel stood in the parking lot under the darkening sky, his mouth open, a silent phone to his ear. From the pier he could hear the sound of laughter. The air smelled like corn dogs and exhaust.

"Honey?" Laney looked across the Cruiser at him, her eyes wide. She rocked back and forth like a wobbling doll. "What happened?"

Daniel lowered the phone. Made himself swallow. His throat like sandpaper. A snatch of music came from somewhere. "Sophie," he said. "He found Sophie."

"How?"

"I don't know."

"What did — Did you talk to her? Is she . . ." Laney trailed off.

He shook his head. His mind whizzed and whirled in conflicting directions. He had to help Sophie. He had to call the police. It was a trap. It didn't matter. She was dead. She might need help. "Denslow and Levering. He said Denslow and Levering. I don't know where that is. Do you?"

Laney paled. "By UCLA. It's where Charles lives."

"Who?"

"Charles. The man Sophie's seeing. He's a law professor. We went over there for dinner a month ago."

Of course. It made sense. Where would Sophie go on a moment's notice? Somewhere that seemed safe. Not her office, not a hotel. Her boyfriend's house.

And somehow Bennett had found out where he lived. "We have to go."

"Wait. What if Bennett is —"

"I don't care." He circled the car, held out his hand. "I'll drive."

"This could be a trap."

"You think I don't know that?" His face felt rubbery, his hands wooden. "We can't just leave her."

For a moment, he thought Laney was going to argue. Then she dropped the keys in his hand. "Let's go."

The two-mile drive took forever. He avoided the highway, kept to back streets, Laney throwing out directions when he wasn't certain. Rush hour, and the streets were snarled with L.A.'s famous traffic. A sea of brake lights in every direction. The ride was a nightmare of stop and go. He cut through parking lots, sped around cars, ran yellows and soft reds. Horns shrieked and lights flashed and he didn't give a damn.

This is your fault.

He'd underestimated Bennett. Even after everything Laney had told him, Daniel had forgotten that the man stayed in the shadows, that he preferred end runs to charges down the middle. That he would never just walk into a situation someone else controlled. He would redirect it. Find leverage.

Blood on your hands, Daniel. Blood on your soul.

It was twilight by the time they made it. On the surface, the neighborhood seemed idyllic. Beautiful homes, beautiful trees, beautiful people walking beautiful dogs. They made it to Levering first, followed the winding curves up to the intersection.

"That one." Laney gestured to a Spanish-style house set back from the corner. She looked around. "It doesn't look like anything's happened."

"Maybe he was bluffing."

She bit her lip, didn't respond.

"I know what you're thinking," he said. "I'm thinking it too. But if she's in there, and she needs help . . ."

"What do you want to do?"

He looked over. "Your gun."

"Your gun." She pulled it out. "Here."

It had been three thousand miles and another life since the Glock he'd found in the glove box. But it felt just as good, just as right, to take the Sig Sauer in his hand. He ejected the round from the chamber, popped the magazine, reinserted the round, racked the slide, switched the safety off.

Look at you. But then, you probably learned

for your writing. Probably fired off hundreds of rounds — at paper targets.

"Okay. Wait here."

"What?"

"If there's any problem, call the police."

She shook her head. "No way. This is not a woolly mammoth situation."

"Laney —"

She pushed open the passenger door and started down the sidewalk. Grimacing, he followed. The thrum of traffic sounded from the 405 to the west. Somewhere, someone started a leaf blower. His heart banged two beats for every footstep.

Laney started up the front path. He thought of arguing, couldn't see a better way. If Bennett was here, there would be no safe or secret way in. And no time to waste.

Daniel reached for the front, twisted the handle. Unlocked. Holding his gun low and out, he pushed open the door.

The hallway was dark. He didn't wait for his eyes to adjust, just went in before Laney could, the gun held in front of him. Trying to remember every maneuver he'd ever seen on a cop show. *Stay calm. Don't shoot just because something moves.*

His breath sounded loud. Laney stepped in behind him, shut the door. The click of the latch made him jump. He took a step, and then another. The place seemed familiar, though he couldn't remember how.

A clatter came from down the hall.

Daniel was running before he realized it, charging past the staircase, through the living room, gun up and sweeping, vision blurring. Light fell through an archway. The room beyond had a tile floor, and he saw a baker's rack with an array of pans. There was another sound, something he couldn't place, and he spun around the corner, staying low, praying for he didn't know what, that she would be okay, that Bennett would appear in his sights, that —

The first thing he saw was the cat. It was tubby and mottled orange and sitting on the counter. A container of cooking tools had been knocked over beside it, and the cat was swatting at a spatula.

The second thing he saw was Sophie. On her back on the kitchen table. Her arms hung on either side. Her empty eyes were open.

"No." His hands started to shake. With the quiet, mechanical processing of shock, he saw the neat round hole in her forehead, and the gore spattered on the table. "No."

Laney came up behind him. She gasped, hands flying to her face.

A man sat at the head of the table. His

hair was gray, his face weathered. Duct tape lashed him to the chair. Deep cuts on his arms split the skin in red tears. Muscle and fat bulged through like fabric from an over-stuffed cushion.

Laney whimpered. "Oh god."

Daniel stared. The writer in him put the scene together. Bennett making Sophie watch as he tortured her lover. Asking questions. Telling her that it would all end if she told him what he wanted to know. If she told him where a half-million-dollar neck-lace was hidden.

Asking questions she didn't know the answer to.

Laney came up behind him, buried her face in his back. He could feel her warmth, and the hectic beat of her heart. The vibrating ring of his cell phone hit like electric shock. He scrabbled back, slapping at his pocket with one hand, pulled the cell phone free. "Motherfucker. You evil motherfucker."

"This is on you, Daniel."

Bile spilled up his throat. "I swear to god —"

"Oh, stop. All you had to do was pay me."

"I will never fucking give you —"

"Then I'll visit someone else. Maybe Laney's buddy. Robert Cameron. After all, he was nice enough to loan you his car."

Daniel straightened, pushed away from Laney. How did Bennett know —

"A PT Cruiser, interesting choice for an actor. Distinctive, I guess, but a little pedestrian."

Adrenaline dumped into his bloodstream. He shoved Laney back from the archway, sprinted to the living room, phone in one hand, gun in the other. Easing around the edge of the window, Daniel peered out. The porch was empty. So was the lawn and the front walk.

There was a silver Jaguar across the street. As his eyes fell on it, the dome light snapped on. The interior of the car glowed against the purple light of evening. Bennett lounged behind the wheel. He raised one hand. His lips moved, and a fraction of a second later, Daniel heard his voice through the phone. "Hi."

Daniel narrowed his eyes. Took a step back, raised the pistol.

"Tricky one," Bennett said. "Thirty yards with a sidearm through two panes of glass. And you're firing one-handed. Plus . . ." The dome light snapped off, and darkness washed the interior of the Jaguar. "Now you can't even see your target. What do you say, Daniel? Want to try for a lucky shot?"

He stared down the barrel, aimed square

at the place Bennett's head had been. He could do this. He knew he could. His hands were steady, his aim sure.

Do it. Now!

His finger wouldn't move.

"On the other hand, I've got my pistol propped on the seat and aimed with both hands. What do you think, Sundance? Want to bet which of us hits? Want to guess what happens to your lovely bride afterwards?"

A shiver curled inside him as a vision of Laney in Sophie's place flashed into his imagination. The car swam between the sights. Daniel lowered the gun, stepped away from the window. "We don't have the necklace with us. If you kill us, you get nothing."

"I know that. Why do you think I'm not inside?"

A terrible revelation seized him. "You killed her as a lesson."

"That's right. And you've got other friends. This isn't a boxing match. We're not going to fight fair. You try to screw me again and maybe it will be Robert Cameron tied to a chair and whimpering like a Girl Scout. You go to the police, and while they're working on you, I'll be working on Laney. No one can protect you. There is no safe place to hide. Do you understand?"

Daniel closed his eyes. The broken body of his friend stared at him from the darkness behind his lids. "Yes."

"Say it."

"I understand."

"Now, I believe that you don't have the necklace with you. You hid it somewhere. Go get it. Or tomorrow I visit another of your friends." The line went dead. A moment later, an engine revved. Daniel stepped back in front of the window, watched the Jag pull away. He squinted, caught the license plate, 5BBM299. *Of course, it's not his any more than the one on the BMW is yours.*

"Daniel?"

He turned. Laney was framed in the archway, silhouetted by the kitchen light.

"He's gone." *But not far. Never far.* It took him two tries to lock the safety on the Sig Sauer. His fingers were carved out of wood. His legs were heavy. Numb. "He said that we have to get him the necklace. That he would come after Robert if we don't, and others. I should have — there was a second there, where I could have — why didn't I shoot him?"

"Stop." Laney stepped forward, wrapped her arms around him. He stiffened. Didn't want to be touched, didn't want comfort.

Didn't deserve it. A beautiful person, a beautiful friend, gone. Her last moments horror. Because of him.

The sob took him by surprise, seemed to break from somewhere deep inside. Laney reached up to stroke his neck. He struggled. "Let me —"

"Stop, baby." She seemed to be wrapping her whole self around him. "Stop."

He squeezed his eyes closed hard enough to see stars and spots. They almost blurred out the vision of Sophie. His body shook, his chest heaved. The sounds he made weren't quite crying. More like grunting, an animal sound. No tears came. Just ragged heaves of pain.

"Shhh. Shhh." She pressed against him, primal in her comfort.

He didn't know how long they stood like that, while the world outside darkened and the pistol he hadn't fired dug into his belly and Sophie . . .

Finally, he took a deep breath. Patted Laney's back. He pulled away, and this time she let him.

Daniel rolled his shoulders, shook his head. He had a flash of Sophie in her kitchen, washing the coffee mugs, talking over her shoulder. The ease of that moment, the familiarity. She had been the first person to touch him. The hug she had given him this morning — *my god, only this morning?* — had brought him back from the dead.

He took a deep breath, then opened his cell phone.

"Who are you calling?"

"911."

"What?"

Daniel pressed send, raised the phone to his ear, turned to look out the window. *Be calm, but specific. Give them the address. Tell them there's been a murder —*

His hand was yanked away from his ear. He spun, surprised, but Laney had a grip on the phone, managed to tug it free. Immediately she snapped it shut. He stared at her. "What the hell?"

"Let's just think for a minute, okay?"

"Think about what? Sophie's dead. He killed her. Tortured her. We have to call the police."

"And tell them what? That we broke into her house and found her dead? How's that going to look? They already believe you're a killer."

"Yeah, but *I'm not,* remember? And why would either of us hurt Sophie or her boyfriend?"

Laney shook her head, slipped his phone into her pocket. "No police, baby. We can't."

"Why not?"

She didn't answer immediately. Just raised her hands and ran them through her hair. "It won't solve anything."

"What are you talking about?"

"You said he threatened Robert, right?"

"Yeah, but . . ." Daniel spread his hands. "Look, it's different than before. *He killed Sophie.* And her boyfriend. The police will go after him now. And if we tell them everything, there's no reason for him to hurt Robert."

"What if he doesn't need a reason?"

"So we'll have Robert come with us. He'll be safe while we —"

"Listen to me." She stepped forward, took his hands in hers. Her gaze was steady, those hypnotic blue eyes locked on his. "We can't go to the police."

"What do you mean?"

"Just that. I know why you want to call them, I do, and I wish we could, but we can't."

"Why —"

"I know how confusing this must all be. I can't imagine how scared you are. I'm scared, and I *do* remember my life. But we can't go to the police."

He opened his mouth to argue. Yes, things looked bad, but who would really believe they would murder Sophie?

On the other hand, what did going to the police accomplish? There still wasn't much to point them to Bennett. The man was careful, would surely have worn gloves, collected his spent bullet casings. Besides, even if by some miracle the police did catch him, it would lead only to a trial and — maybe — jail. What kind of end was that? A cage wasn't enough. He wanted Bennett dead. Dead for all the things he'd done to Laney before they even met, and for every obscenity he'd wreaked on their lives since, and most especially for Sophie. Daniel was a writer, and he believed in the justice of a story, and the only ending that fit was Bennett's death.

But before he could say a word, before he could argue with Laney or agree with her, a terrible thought flashed across his mind. What if she didn't want him to go to the police, not because of what Bennett would do, but for some other reason?

What if there was more going on here than he knew?

"Please, baby. I love you. And I need you." His wife stared up with eyes wide and soft. Her hands were warm against his. He could smell a hint of citrus, her shampoo, and it smelled wonderful. "Can you trust me?"

I don't know.
God help me.
I don't know.

The plane shook the world.

This close to LAX, every 747 on a west-bound approach was a streak of white he could almost touch. Each started with a subsonic tingle deep in Daniel's belly, then a rumble that became a roar, and out the window the plane would come to ground like a long aluminum duck, landing lights bright, the blur of superheated air through the engines making the moon wobble.

Eleven o'clock in another shitty motel, one of those long-stay places for C-list business-men. The "kitchen" was a microwave atop a mini-fridge. The flowered bedspread wilted. A stink of cigarettes rose from the sofa. Out the window was a parking lot hemmed in by the 405. A steady stream of head- and taillights rolled in each direction, people with places to go, safe warm homes waiting for them. On the other side was a billboard for a movie, *Die Today,* with a glowering actor pointing a gun at him.

He was Sophie's client. Daniel raised the disposable plastic cup, took another swallow of bourbon.

"It's not your fault," Laney said from behind him, as if she could read his mind.

He didn't respond. She had taken his silence as guilt over Sophie, and of course, she was right — *blood on your hands, Daniel; blood on your soul* — but the truth was more complicated. His head was a tangle of contradictory thoughts, of half-formed plans and animal urges. Of white-hot hate for a man he barely knew. Of fear of the police, and of Bennett, and of whatever fresh horror tomorrow might bring.

But worst of all, the terrible question. Could he trust her?

If he couldn't, he was lost. She was the home he had brought himself back to. She was the keeper of their mutual story, the only person in the world who truly knew what they had been to each other. Until his memory came back — if it did — the only truth was the one she told.

Besides, what reason did he have to think he couldn't? Just the fact that she didn't want to go to the police. Even if he didn't fully agree with her thinking, it was a big leap to deceit. To read too deep into her hesitation was like walking into a party just as people started laughing, and assuming the laughter was aimed at him. There was no evidence.

It's more than that, you asshole. She so haunted you that before you knew your name, you knew to look for her. She hates violence, but when she thought you were in danger she grabbed a gun and chased a murderer. Her feet are always cold and your chin snugs perfectly into the curve of her shoulder and she moves her lips when she's reading a script and, in short, you love her.

So stop it. Stop letting exhaustion and fear make you paranoid. You are who you choose to be.

Tired. He was so tired. He took another sip of bourbon.

"Won't you talk to me?"

He turned, leaned against the window. Laney sat on the edge of the bed, hands between her knees. Her face was pale and drawn.

"I'm sorry. It's not you. I'm just thinking." He shook his head. "I still can't remember her. You'd think that would have made it hurt less."

"Why? You loved her. Like I said, there are things we do that we can't change. Love is one of them."

"Is it?" Yes, he realized. It was. What had he said earlier? *Memories are stories we tell ourselves to explain how we got where we are.* "I guess you're right. I just . . . I owe it to her to remember her, and I don't."

Laney was silent for a moment. Then she leaned back on her elbows. "Do you remember Bernie?"

He shook his head.

"A couple of years ago Sophie was working in her garden, and this puppy came up to her. She didn't like dogs. Something had happened to her as a kid, I think. Anyway, she shooed him away. Five minutes later, there he is again. Just sitting there. She chased him off again; five minutes later he's back. That's why she started calling him Bernie — same as her ex-husband, he was hard to get rid of. He was a husky. He was going to be huge, you could just tell, and he had this enormously fluffy white coat. I mean, he was supposed to be pulling sleds in Alaska, you know? And here he was roasting in Los Angeles." Laney shook her head.

"Anyway, Sophie finishes, goes inside, makes herself a sandwich. Only, Bernie just climbs up on her porch and flops down in the shade. And Sophie being Sophie, even though she doesn't like dogs, she goes back out, looks more closely. He doesn't have a collar on. And he's got scars, places where the fur is missing or lopsided. He'd been mistreated, or maybe just had to fight, but she can't let that go. So she opens the door, gives him water and the rest of her sandwich. Lets him fall asleep on her couch."

"She adopted him?"

Laney laughed. "No, she posted signs looking for his owner. Called her neighbors. But nobody knew the story. He's a stray. He could be dangerous. They have children. People tell her to call the pound."

Daniel thought he saw where it was going. "But she won't. She may not like dogs, but she likes strays."

"Uh-huh. She couldn't stand to imagine him rotting in a cage, waiting to be put down. So she puts an ad in the paper. 'Puppy looking for good home.' "

"That's nice."

"I'm not finished. She gets all kinds of calls. But somehow she can't do it, won't go through with it. Something about just passing him off, it bugged her. So she puts another ad in the paper. 'Purebred husky, smart, loyal, four hundred dollars.' "

"She *sold* him?"

"Only after she'd gotten three people interested, played them against each other, and raised the price to six hundred."

In spite of everything, Daniel laughed. "You're kidding me."

"Nope. See, the way Sophie looked at things, if she'd given him away, he would always be a stray. This way he was something special. Plus she used the money to throw a dinner party. BernieFest."

Daniel smiled, rubbed his eyes. His belly ticked with the approach of another plane. He thought of sitting at Sophie's table, sipping coffee. Of the way she wouldn't let him talk. Those photos on the wall, her life in pictures. None of those versions of her earlier self could have imagined what was to come for her. The plane roared overhead.

"Stop it," she said.

"Huh?" He looked up, surprised.

"You're blaming yourself."

"How did you —"

"Because I know you. You're sitting there thinking it's your fault."

"It *is* my fault."

"No, you egotistical ass. It's not. You didn't hurt her. Bennett did. You didn't kill her. Bennett did."

"Yeah, but —"

"And if I really had gone over that cliff, that wouldn't have been your fault either. If anyone is to blame, it's me. Bennett came for me, not you."

"Yeah —"

"But maybe that's not far enough back. Maybe the jerks I was with in high school are to blame, for making me think that was how boys treated girls. Maybe Marlon Brando is to blame, for teaching girls to like guys who ride motorcycles. Maybe my parents are to blame for conceiving me."

"Come on. I came up with that stupid plan that got her killed."

"No. You called her and told her to run. It's not your fault that he found her. And you still don't get Bennett. He was going to kill her regardless. That's how he stays alive. No one knows anything about him. He doesn't trust anyone. It's just Bennett, self-contained and all alone. Sophie knew too much."

"You can't be sure of that."

"How soon after you left the pier did your cell phone ring?"

"I don't know, maybe two minutes —" He caught her line of thinking.

"You see? She was already gone." Laney leaned forward. "You're a good man and a smart guy. But just because you see life as scenes in a story doesn't mean you're responsible for how everything works out. You don't write the goddamn world."

He opened his mouth. Closed it.

She slid back on the bed, patted a space beside her. "Come here."

Daniel set his cup on the windowsill, walked across the room. He kicked off his shoes, then lay down beside her. She leaned back, her head nestling in his chest, her arm across him. His nose was buried in her hair, and he could smell her skin, the clean scent of soap from her bubble bath. She yawned, burrowed closer. They lay still. It should have been wonderful, a sanctuary. Everything he thought he had lost, returned to him. But his brain wouldn't let him enjoy it. When he closed his eyes, he saw Sophie's face. When he opened them again, the bare drop ceiling stared hopelessly back.

Into his chest, she said, "I'm sorry."

"For what?" Daniel stroked her hair, a gesture so familiar he knew he must have done it a thousand times.

"Everything. All of this."

"It's not . . . You didn't know. You were a kid. He's to blame, not you."

"I know. But still." Her head rose and fell with his breath. "What do we do now?"

"I'm not sure."

"If we can figure out where the necklace is —"

"No." He cracked the word. "Maybe you're right. Maybe we can't go to the police. But I'm not paying him. Not after what he did to her."

"But if we don't, he'll keep hurting people."

She was right. They were trapped. Every road led to hell. The only question was how direct a route.

His eyes were dry and raw, and his head throbbed with every beat of his heart. His whole self ached. To have lost and gained and stand poised to lose so much again, all in the space of such a short time. To discover that the distant past could shatter the present. A mistake Laney had made before Daniel had even met her. Before they had started to forge all the memories he had since lost.

Outside the windows, the traffic moved down the freeway, as steady and implacable as waves on a beach. A rap star pretending to be an actor pretending to be a gangster aimed false menace down from a bright billboard, while real evil lurked in the shadows, only attacking where they were weak. His own past played hide-and-seek, while their future raced toward them like an express train off the rails.

It's not about who you were, or what you can remember. It's about who you are. Who you choose to be, and what you decide to do.

"I'm scared," she said, in a voice so soft it tore through him.

"Me too. But sleep now. We'll figure it out."

"How?"

"I don't know," he said. "I don't know."

He stroked her hair until he heard her breath steady and her muscles relax. Then he slipped his arm free, took the gun out. His fingers tapped the grip as he stared at the ceiling.

How did you beat a man who anticipated your every move? Who would never face you directly? A man who survived by being invisible, who had no weaknesses to lean on, and so was free to lean on yours?

And especially, how did an actress and a writer do it? He thought back to Laney's rebuke, telling him that he didn't write the world. The words had been meant as a comfort, but now they stung. If he did, he knew the ending he'd write for that fucker.

They couldn't get help. They couldn't pay him off. They couldn't run and hide.

What does that leave?

■ ■ ■ ■

ACT THREE

■ ■ ■ ■

"I have memories — but only a fool stores his past in the future."

— David Gerrold

"We have to kill him."

Laney heard the words but didn't really process them. Half-awake for a while, she'd been hiding in that hazy dream realm where everything ended before it got too bad. They said you never died in a dream, and she couldn't remember that she had, though often enough she'd been about to when she woke up. "What?"

"We have to kill him."

Apparently she'd heard correctly. She blinked, sat up. The left side of the curtains were closed, submerging her half of the room in murky shadow. The other side was burning with morning sky, silhouetting Daniel. His hair stuck up in wild spiky directions. He had the gun in his hand.

"Did you sleep?"

"Did you hear me?"

"Yes." Her mouth was gluey, her brain and body stiff. "I heard you."

"It's the only way. We can't run, we can't hide, we can't get help. So we have to kill him. Then it all goes away."

"Okay." She pointed her fingers like a gun, sighted out the window. "Pow. He's dead."

"I'm serious."

"I need coffee."

"Would you stop screwing around?" She had been midstretch, but his tone froze her arms. "Would you?"

"I'm not."

"I'm a vegetarian. You work for a show called *Candy Girls.* How are we supposed to kill him? What are you going to do, write him to death?"

"Actually, yeah."

"Apparently you need coffee too." Laney spun, sat on the edge of the bed. The blood running from her head made the world spin.

"Listen. It's simple. All we need to do is get him to come to us. We'll write a scene for him, a play to lure him. He'll think he knows what's going on. But he won't."

"Simple as that."

"Well, not simple. But I did come to it by thinking like a writer. I made Bennett into a bad guy, a character. And I thought, what would you do if this was a script?"

"And what would you do?"

He told her.

When he finished, she stood, moved to the window, opened the other curtain. Stared out at sunlight blinking off the windshields of moving cars. L.A. smog had gotten better in the time she'd lived here, but "better" was a long way from "vanished," and the distance was filtered a nicotine yellow. She stared for a long moment, feeling him waiting on her the way he always did when he'd pitched an idea, with impatient hope. "What if he sends someone else?"

"He won't," Daniel said.

"He did yesterday." *And in a concrete canyon.*

"The difference is, this time we'll have the necklace. Not only that, but he'll know we have it. Not think. *Know.* Bennett is cagey, right? Yesterday he must have suspected we weren't going to play straight. So he limited his exposure. But if he'd known for sure that we were bringing it, he'd have been there."

"Why?"

"Because he doesn't trust anybody. A necklace worth half a million dollars is too much temptation. There's the chance that whoever he sent would run, and then he'd be back where he started."

"What if you're wrong?"

"We have to make sure that I'm not. We have to use the necklace as bait. That, and the sense that he knows what we're going to do."

I'd buy it in a script. But this isn't a script.

"So what do you think?"

I think I'm tired and sore and scared so deep that I can't remember what it was like not to be. I think we're going to lose. She said, "I think I should have given him what he wanted in the first place."

"He would have killed you."

"At least you would have been okay."

"Yeah," Daniel said, and smiled that lopsided grin she liked. "You can see how okay I turned out when I only *thought* I'd lost you." He took her hands. "I know this is scary. But it will only work if we commit all the way. That's the only way we can beat him."

There was something in his expression that reminded her of their first date. It was a couple of years after she'd moved here, midway in her journey from model to actress. She'd dated a predictable string of L.A. boys. Producers and finance guys, eager to impress, hitting the restaurants of the moment, clubs that didn't have signs. But Daniel had taken her to an East L.A. taco joint, the kind with laminated menus and piñatas. He was the first guy she could remember who didn't flaunt or flex. Instead he asked about growing up in Chicago. About her first kiss. Over margaritas he talked about coming from Arkansas — something the others would never have admitted, not in this town where everyone pretended they'd sprung full-formed from the froth of the cold Pacific — and about his regrets over the relationship with his family. Then, just when things were getting a little serious, he told that stupid joke of his, about sex with twenty seven-year-olds, and the way he said it was so gleeful and innocent that she couldn't help laughing, and by the time he drove her home in his Sentra, she'd known that this was what it was supposed to be like, two people connecting, not shiny dangled bait, not motorcycle bad boys, not full-time glamour, but this, two people who talked and listened and laughed.

Plus he was a really good kisser.

She looked at him now, at his earnest expression and goofy hair and burning eyes, and she thought, *So we'll lose. Bennett will take from you the only thing he hasn't yet. At least your secret will stay secret.*

You're an actress. Act.

"I committed all the way years ago." She

held his gaze, matched it. "What do we do next?"

Something happened to his body, his affect — his shoulders relaxed, his eyes warmed, his lips unclenched. It was as though her support was the fuel he needed. "The necklace. I was thinking about it. Do we have a safe deposit box, a storage locker, anything like that?"

Laney felt a tremor rise, killed it before it made it to her face. "No."

"Perfect. Then it has to be at the house."

"Why?"

"It was there the day you died, right?"

"You think you hid it?"

"It was the worst day of my life. Would I have given a damn about a necklace? I probably just threw it in a drawer." He rubbed at his chin with a sandpaper sound. His eyes were red, and he badly needed a shave. "Only thing I don't get . . ."

"What?"

"Well, I knew about Bennett, right? That he was blackmailing us."

"Yes."

"And since I thought you were dead, I must have thought he was responsible. If I believed that, why didn't I grab a gun and go after him? Maybe he'd have killed me, but I wanted to die anyway, and better to do it trying to pay him back. But it doesn't seem like I even tried, and I don't know why."

Laney stared. Desperate to think of an improvisation that would make sense to him. When nothing came, she just said, "I don't know, baby. Maybe you didn't want that on your conscience."

"Come on. I'm sure it's not easy to kill someone, but that fucker?" Daniel scowled. "There had to be a reason. Either that, or I really don't like the guy I was very much."

"I do," she said, and put a hand on his cheek. She smiled, then changed the subject. "So, the necklace."

"First we have to figure something out. This all depends on the location. I was thinking the airport, but it won't work. We'd need tickets to go through security, and we can't show our ID. Can you think of somewhere else that has metal detectors?"

Laney clicked her tongue against her lip. Metal detectors. Hospitals might have them, in the emergency room. Government buildings, but Bennett would never go for that. A school, but then, no way.

She stared out the window at the low sprawl of Los Angeles. The angle of the sun sharpened contrasts. The 405 crawled along. The sky was crisscrossed with contrails. A billboard for *Die Today* faced the window, Too G pointing a gun at them. A lot of people made fun of rappers who tried to become movie stars, but as a model turned actress, her horse wasn't any higher than theirs. And really, it was too bad that other than Will Smith and Mos Def and Queen Latifah, all they got were movies about urban gangsters and slums and drug dealers. In order to get a role, they had to maintain all the trappings of ghetto toughness —

Laney laughed. "Want to go to a party?"

It was like fishing. Not that Bennett had ever been fishing, but he'd read Hemingway. He liked Ernest. The man would have been hard to beat. When it came to his sinning, he was up-front and unabashed. And he was a self-contained dude too. Hence all the wives.

Anyway, from what Ernest had to say about fishing, if you were fighting a big one, you had to let it out some before you pulled it in. You couldn't just yank the whole time, or the line would break.

So he'd given them the night. Let them twist and run and flounder, wear themselves down trying to fight his hook. Let them run the options over and over and over trying to think of a way out.

When his phone rang, he was taking in the sun on Jerry D'Agostino's pool deck, shirtless and pants rolled up so his feet could dangle in the water. He answered without looking at the display. "Morning. You sleep okay?"

"You win." Daniel sounded ragged. "We'll pay your blood money. But there are conditions. First, you stay away from us. Forever."

"You got my word."

"Second, we're going to do it where we choose, not you."

"No."

"Listen to me, you psychopath. You wanted to scare us? It worked. We're scared. And we're not going to meet anywhere you can hurt us."

"Sociopath."

"Huh?"

"I'm really neither, but probably closer to a sociopath. A psychopath is in it for the fun. I don't get off on hurting people. I'm just willing to do it for money." He swung his legs, watching sunlight dance on the bottom of the pool. Were they recording this? It didn't matter. All they'd end up with was a voice on a tape, and a phone number he would walk away from tomorrow. "Anyway, what do you have in mind? What will make you feel safe, brother?"

"There's a party tonight. After a screening. It's at a club downtown, Lux. The cast from the movie has rented out the VIP room. They're rap stars, and they want to look tough, so there are going to be metal detectors at the entrance."

Bennett laughed. "Why, Daniel, that's ingenious. Bravo."

"We're going to get the necklace now. We'll be at the club at nine-thirty."

"Sounds like fun. I'll see you there." He started to hang up, then said, "Hey, what's the movie?"

"What?"

"The screening, what is it?"

A beat. "It's called *Die Today*."

"Yikes. Bad omen, huh?"

Another long pause. "Nine-thirty. After that, you leave us alone." The line went dead.

Bennett smiled. Leaned back on the stone of the pool deck. The sun had cooked the tiles, and the warmth felt nice against his back. He traced the dimpled scar tissue on his stomach, fingers finding the pockmarks of healed bullet holes, one-two-three. Mementos of a deal in Baltimore.

It was possible that Daniel and Laney still believed he'd let them live. But he doubted it. Before, maybe, but now things had gone too far.

No, they'd try to get clever. Maybe have police there undercover. Or a friend, some half-assed tough guy to help. Could even be the rap star.

Most important, they'd be counting on him not having his gun. Taking comfort in the location. Feeling safe because he was unarmed and all those witnesses were about, as if that meant nothing bad could happen to them.

It showed a lack of imagination on their part.

Daniel closed his phone, set it in the cup holder. Squirmed in his seat. The half a bagel and coffee he'd managed to choke down lay heavy in his stomach, and the ride out to Malibu wasn't making it better. Last night he'd treated this like a story, and written an ending for it. But Bennett wasn't a script problem. And no story had just one ending.

"They fixed it already," Laney said.

"What?"

She took a hand off the steering wheel, pointed. He didn't see anything special, just a metal barrier on a wicked curve — oh. "I'm sorry. I wasn't thinking. Are you —"

"I'm fine. It's just strange." She spoke to the windshield. "It's as though nothing ever happened. Already."

"Life is a raindrop."

"What?" She turned to look at him.

"Something Sophie told me. Life is a raindrop."

"It's pretty. What does it mean?"

"I don't know." He paused. "I guess that every life is beautiful and self-contained and unique and yet also short and totally insignificant."

"You really know how to cheer a girl up."

"Sorry."

The traffic on Highway 1 was light. She kept it at the speed limit. The road was as beautiful as ever, the homes as magnificent, the view as lush, but it felt distant, as though seen through thick glass.

"Are you sure the cops won't be there?"

"I don't think so," Daniel said. "They're busy. Having someone parked on our block day after day would add up, especially since they wouldn't guess we're headed there."

"They came when you were there before. Getting our wedding photo."

"Yeah, but it was just a patrol. They probably drive by once an hour. And more at night."

"What if —"

"We don't really have a choice."

She nodded slowly. Her grip on the wheel didn't loosen any.

Half an hour later, they'd made it to their neighborhood. Everything seemed as calm as ever. The PT Cruiser was spotless and shiny and no one should be looking for it. Laney had her makeup back on, the port wine stain painted around her eye, her now-blond hair down. At a glance, they were normal people.

They drove the neighborhood first, avoiding their street, just getting a sense of things. He used the time to review the plan again. Picturing it as a plot outline. Looking at surprises, at twists, at the expected actions of their antagonist. On paper, it looked good.

But she's right. You don't write the world.

His stomach churned, but he kept his face calm. "Looks clear. Let's go."

Three minutes later, they were pulling up to their security gate. It was strange how many different things it meant to him, this California contemporary with a lot of glass. The house he'd seen on television. In his dreams. The one he'd visited when he didn't know who he was, and returned to in order to find out when his life had begun. And now, this final visit, and final incarnation.

The central element in their plan to win back their life — or die trying.

Laney keyed in the code. Their anniversary. Of course. The gate swung open, and she pulled in, then around the circle so the car was out of sight and facing forward.

The keys jingled in her shaking hands as she shut off the motor.

INT. DANIEL & LANEY'S FOYER — NOON
The shot is from a locked-down camera, low and pointing at the front door.
The door opens. LANEY THAYER and DANIEL HAYES enter. He closes the door, then peers out the window beside it.

                    DANIEL
No sign of him.
                    LANEY
Yet.

They walk toward the stairs.

                    DANIEL
We can always go to the police instead —

LANEY

We've been through that.

They pass the camera as they climb. Their voices continue, tension evident, but the words unclear.

INT. MASTER BEDROOM —
CONTINUOUS
The camera seems to be shooting from the nightstand. Laney moves to the dresser and starts opening drawers. Daniel glances longingly at the bed.

LANEY

You really don't have any idea where you put it?
DANIEL

Nope.

He moves to the nightstand, checks it. Drops to his knees, looks under the bed.

LANEY

Anything?
DANIEL

Nope.

He straightens, looks around, obviously frustrated.

                LANEY
Maybe it's not —
                DANIEL
It has to be.
                LANEY
Why?
                DANIEL
Just keep looking.

They continue searching.
Laney straightens, rubs her back. They look at each other. She shakes her head.
They exit.

INT. DANIEL'S OFFICE — CONTINUOUS
The camera angle is high and wide. The couple walk into the room and resume the search.
  Daniel ransacks his desk, tossing the contents on the floor. A rain of paper and pens and junk.

                    LANEY
It's not going to just be ly-
ing in a drawer.
                    DANIEL
Why not?

                    LANEY
Because Bennett would have
already found it.

Daniel yanks a drawer out,
turns it upside down. Everything falls to the floor. He
squats to sort through it.

              LANEY (CONT'D)
If it's here, it'll be hidden.
                    DANIEL
Do we have a safe?

Laney shakes her head. Then a
thought strikes her. She
stands.

                    LANEY
Wait a second.

She walks to the bookcase,
reaches for something near the
camera. Steps back, smiling.
She's holding a thick book,

which she passes to Daniel.

                    DANIEL
Studies in Contract Law, Vol-
ume 2?
                    LANEY
Open it.

He does.
The book is hollow, a hiding
place for small valuables.

              LANEY (CONT'D)
You and your toys. You always
wanted a reason for that
thing.

He dips his hand inside, comes
out with a breathtaking DIA-
MOND NECKLACE. It glitters
like it's lit from within.

                    DANIEL
So that's what half a million
dollars looks like.
  (shakes his head)
This is Sophie's life. A
string of sparkly stones.
                    LANEY
I've been thinking. I want to

pay him.

> DANIEL

No.

> LANEY

He'll go away if we do.

> DANIEL

I don't want him gone away. I want him dead.

> LANEY

You're not a killer.

Daniel tucks the necklace into his pants pocket. He closes the book, tosses it on the desk.

> DANIEL

We just have to focus. Get through tonight.

> LANEY

So you can pretend you're Charles Bronson?

> DANIEL

What do you want, Laney? He almost killed you and he cost me my memory and he murdered my friend.

> LANEY

So you're going to commit suicide?

Daniel shakes his head. He turns to face her.

                    DANIEL
This will work.
                    LANEY
What if it doesn't?

Daniel strides to the door. Laney hesitates a moment, bites her lip, then follows.

                    LANEY (CONT'D)
I'm sorry, but I love you, and I don't want to see you hurt. And Bennett is a killer.

They leave the room.

                    DANIEL (O.S.)
Not tonight.

INT. DANIEL & LANEY'S FOYER — CONTINUOUS
The two of them hurry down the stairs, Daniel in the lead.

                    LANEY
Listen —

Daniel whirls to face the camera. He raises his arms in a what-do-you-want-from-me? gesture. The movement tightens his black T-shirt, revealing a SIG SAUER tucked into his belt.

                    DANIEL
I don't know what to tell you, Laney. I don't have any choice.
                    LANEY
   (softly)
I'm scared. If anything happens to you . . .
                    DANIEL
Look. At the end of the night, I'm going to be holding a loaded gun. And he's not.

Bennett hit pause and leaned back in D'Agostino's ergonomically correct chair. On the laptop, Daniel Hayes was frozen. The pistol butt protruded from his belt. Bennett clicked his tongue against his lip, looked out the window, where the Valley spilled out in all its earth-tone glory. It looked better at night.

He could send someone else. Little Suzie hadn't worked off her debt just by making a run out to the pier. And no way, no *way* would she try ripping him off.

On the other hand, Daniel and Laney probably wouldn't give her the necklace. If they wanted to take their turn trying to kill him, they wouldn't give up the only thing that would bring him there.

He could make an end run on the whole thing. Maybe snatch Laney's actor friend. Call them at the last minute, make the guy whimper into the phone, give them a new venue. But it would mean yet another body, and more police attention. Besides, why bother? He knew what they were up to. A secret plan wasn't much good once the secret was out.

They had the necklace. They were willing to meet.

So meet. But do it your way.

Daniel hadn't slept much.

When was the last time you did, amigo? He rubbed at his eyes, yawned deeply. Lifting his shirt, he pulled out the Sig Sauer, opened the glove box, stowed it inside. Then he put the Smith and Wesson snub-nose he'd taken from his desk drawer beside it.

The two guns looked ominous in the dim light.

Hope we don't get pulled over.

He must have snatched a few hours of sleep toward dawn, because he'd dreamed again. The concrete canyon, the darkness, the guilty terror. And a new dream too, Sophie screaming, but when she opened her mouth, the sound that came out was the roar of jet engines. He'd come to propped in the desk chair, his feet on the windowsill. Stiff and sore and too tired to move, he'd just sat there, let himself drift.

For some reason, he'd been thinking of last Christmas. Some years they flew to Chicago to see her family, but the visits were always glum and awkward times. His father-in-law was a mechanic, a man who fixed broken things. He didn't know what to make of a life spent creating something so ephemeral as entertainment. And her brother had the conversational skill of a watermelon.

So last year they'd decided to stay home. They'd slept late, lounged over coffee and scripts. Her first Christmas gift for him, she'd looked up from the other end of the couch, said, "Want me to be Emily for you, baby?" They'd piled into the bedroom laughing, and she'd stayed in character, made love to him like Emily Sweet, her moves and mannerisms and moans all her but just a little different, and it had been so hot they'd both finished fast and coated in sweat. They spent the afternoon watching movies and reading and cooking an elaborate supper. She was a mostly-vegetarian, but had always wanted to roast a chicken, and it had turned out weirdly picture-perfect, crispy and golden brown. They'd eaten with their hands, fingers shining with grease, pairing it with store-bought eggnog spiked with rum, a combination that had flattened them both, left them food-stoned but warm and happy. Around nine they'd shared a joint in the backyard, sitting beneath the avocado tree he'd strung Christmas lights in, staring up at what stars they could see and holding hands.

He'd found himself caught in a labyrinth of dope thought, one of those Gordian knot moments where he couldn't quite put his finger on what had brought him to this exact spot. The long chain of events, forged one decision at a time, that had led them from the places they were born to the softness of this Malibu evening. He'd tried to explain it to her, what he was thinking, how improbable it was. How impossible. If his mother hadn't married that asshole, or if his high school girlfriend hadn't dumped him, he might have ended up in a suburb of Little Rock. If Laney's car hadn't dropped its muffler in West Hollywood, she would never have pulled over at the Midas where he was having his own changed out, giving them half an hour to chat in the waiting room over terrible coffee, his heart thumping as he tried to work up the nerve to ask her out. How, when viewed mathematically, their coming together was a near impossibility, a miracle of chance.

"It's like tossing a dart," he'd said. "There's nothing amazing about it. You throw and it sticks somewhere. But if you try and backtrack every factor that led there, the force of the throw and the angle and the air resistance, all of it had to be perfect, just exactly right, for it to end up where it did."

She'd rolled her head sideways, smiled, said, "You're funny when you're stoned."

"I'm funny when I'm not stoned too."

"Meh." And she'd laughed, and he'd joined her, and that had been perfect too. It was like those French philosophers' ideas of love and life, the sense that there was nothing real but what you chose. That when most people talked about love they really meant habit, whereas maybe love wasn't about commitment — it was about choice, about choosing to be with the person you were with, and choosing it every moment.

Then he'd realized he was really, *really* hungry, and they'd gone inside and stripped the rest of the flesh from the chicken before collapsing into bed.

It was only after he'd been smiling for a long time that he realized he remembered it. Fully and completely. His past was coming back to him. The thought was enormously comforting for about ten seconds, and then he'd thought of Bennett, and wondered if he would have the chance for the rest of it to trickle in.

And since then, he'd been thinking about the future. About the visit to the house, and about tonight. About killing Bennett and getting away with it, so that there would even be a future.

Enough with the past. Enough with the future. The now is what you have. Focus on it.

He looked over at Laney. She was staring out the window and chewing on a cuticle.

"I'm sorry," he said.

"For what? I got us into this, not you."

"For . . . everything. For all the things I should be sorry for. All the moments I wasted, and the stupid fights, and working too many hours, the drinking that made you worry. All of it."

"Don't be. I'm not sorry for anything that happened between us. Not one minute of it."

"Sucker."

"Yep." She drove with one hand, rubbed at her neck with the other. "Honestly, I just wish this was over. It's the waiting that's killing me. Hours to go, maybe our last, and I can't let myself enjoy them. It's like that first week shooting *Candy Girls*."

He laughed. "You barfed every morning. I thought maybe you were pregnant."

"I barfed in the afternoons too. You carried gum for me. I was so sure they were going to fire me and bring Evangeline Lilly back in. Remember?"

"You know what? I do. I also remember that you nailed it. Nervous or not, you went out there and *killed*."

The word was out of his mouth before he could think about it. Jesus Christ, for a guy good with language, what a boneheaded choice. He spoke fast to cover it up, saying, "Think we can get into Lux now?"

"They'll probably have some staff prepping for the party."

"Then let's go." He gestured at the glove compartment. "Having those two on us is making me nervous." *Plus, it will distract us from the thought we're both having:*

So long to wait. But if this doesn't work, such a short time to live.

From this angle, Daniel and Laney looked like pieces on a chessboard. It was an image that pleased Bennett immensely.

He'd found Lux no problem. The place was anything but subtle. A former warehouse, it took up most of a city block. The exterior had been painted gold — not yellow, gold — and there was a huge cursive "L" hanging above the entrance. The front walk was wide enough to allow for a rope line or even a red carpet. At night, it probably looked opulent, but by the hard light of afternoon, the word was "garish."

He'd arrived a couple of hours ago. After watching the video, he'd packed his gear and loaded the truck; then he'd spent an hour cleaning Jerry D'Agostino's house. Used an entire tube of those premoistened disinfecting wipes, swiping down every hard surface, every spot that might have held a fingerprint. He'd run the dishwasher and vacuumed the whole place. There were no absolute certainties when it came to DNA, but he'd done the best he could. And after tonight it was bye-bye La La Land, hello sunny Mexico.

The building he stood atop was in the process of being converted to a club itself, and it had been the easiest thing in the world to walk in like he was inspecting it, passing Hispanics hanging drywall and Polacks wiring electricity, then climb the rear stairs. The roof afforded a panoramic view. To the north, the mirrored towers of financial companies bounced sunlight. To the east, he could make out the concrete canyon of the Los Angeles River basin, dry at this time of year. South was the 10, followed by a wasteland of industrial buildings.

And due west was Lux, as gaudy as a showgirl, and in front of it, the PT Cruiser that Daniel had just climbed out of. Bennett squatted behind the lip of the roof, a three-foot abutment of brick. The sun warmed his shoulders and heated the tar of the roof to stickiness. Below him, Daniel turned a slow circle, one hand shielding his eyes. Satisfied they were alone, he gestured, and Laney climbed out of the car. The two of them hurried to the entrance.

Bennett took the parabolic mic from his

bag, propped it on the brick, the dish pointed down at the front door. The earpiece crackled as he flipped the thing on, and then scraped with the sounds of their footsteps.

"Locked." Daniel's voice thin in his ear. The man banged on the door. Laney seemed ready to crawl out of her pretty skin. Her blond hair was limp and fried. She looked much better brunette, and without that shit around her eye.

After a moment, the door rattled and then opened a few inches. A burly guy with tattoos down both arms looked out at them. "Help you?"

"Hi," Daniel said, "I'm John Freyer, and this is Belinda Nichols. We're with the publicity team for Too G."

"Uh-huh?"

"The rest of the crew will be here later, but Too wanted us to come by and take a look, make sure things were set up in the VIP room."

"We're not ready yet —"

"I know. But you mind if we just stroll through, take a look? That way we can tell the boss we did."

The tattooed man shrugged, said, "Sure, I guess." He stepped aside, held the door open. "Not really much to see."

"That's okay. I'm sure it will be —" The slamming door cut off the rest of whatever lie Daniel was telling.

Bennett took out the earpiece, glanced at his watch. *What's your plan, kids?*

He had a bet. A couple, actually. Bennett reached into the bag again, pulled out a sandwich wrapped in paper, tore it open, took a bite. Needed salt.

The necklace had looked every bit as spectacular in the video as it had when he'd gone into Harry Winston to pick it. As with a lot of jewelry at that price point, some of the value was in the craftsmanship and the style. But what had sold him on this piece was the number of high-quality stones, all about the same carat. If it felt too risky to sell the necklace as a whole, he could move it a diamond at a time. Even if he had to sell it cut-rate, it would still be worth three, three-fifty. More than enough to get him clean papers, a safe location, and operating expenses for his next move.

He'd just crumpled the paper around the crusts of his sandwich when the front door opened and Daniel and Laney walked out. They headed straight for the car. Bennett didn't bother with the mic, just watched them drive down the block and around the corner. He waited ten minutes, then shouldered his bag and went downstairs. A foreman in a hard hat glanced at him, and Bennett nodded, kept walking.

It only took a couple of seconds of banging for the tattooed guy to open the front door. "Yeah?"

"Hi. Listen, I'm sorry to bug you, but I'm John Freyer's assistant. The guy who was here a few minutes ago? The woman he was with, Belinda, she just called me, said the dumbass thinks he might have left his cell phone. You happen to find it?"

"No."

"Mind if I take a look? Only be a minute."

The guy shrugged. "Yeah, sure." He stepped back, and Bennett followed him in.

The entrance hall was bright with houselights. There was a coat check to one side, and a winding staircase to the other. Double doors led to the main body of the club. An enormous chandelier of dripping crystal had been lowered almost to the ground, and a guy was fiddling with it, replacing lightbulbs. Thick fabric draped the walls. Liquor boxes were stacked five high, two set by the front, where Tattoo must have dropped them to open the door.

"Nice place," Bennett said.

Tattoo grunted. "VIP's upstairs, he probably left it there. There or the can."

"Where's that?"

Tattoo pointed to the bar area. "Halfway down, to the left."

"Thanks. Listen, I don't want to waste your time. Go ahead with what you were doing. I'll just be a minute."

Bennett went up the curling staircase. The VIP room was a balcony overlooking the main floor. Couches and cushions were scattered about. The space was divided by huge black-and-white photos suspended from the ceiling. Steamy stuff, all tangled flesh and fabric tight across thighs and backs. A Hispanic woman maneuvered a vacuum, dodging photos and shoving chairs aside with her hips, headphones in her ears.

Would they hide it here?

He didn't think so. Too many variables. The cleaning woman, the VIP-ers. With Daniel wanted and Laney supposed to be dead, they wouldn't risk running into someone they knew. A costar, a C-lister, a paparazzi. The kind of folks who would hang out here.

Bennett went back downstairs, wandered through the main floor. It was a cavernous room hung with speakers. Bars ran the length of both sides, and Tattoo and another man were moving the liquor boxes behind them. Thousands of crystals hung like stars above the dance floor.

The men's room had marble floors and a drop ceiling painted black. The faucets and towel dispensers and even the trash can were plated gold, or something meant to look like it. He checked the first stall, found nothing. Likewise the second and third.

In the fourth, duct taped behind the toilet tank, Bennett found the gun. He smiled. He did love predictable people.

Careful not to tear the tape, he peeled the edges from the bottom and freed the pistol. A Sig Sauer P250 Compact. A nice weapon: modular, precise, small. He ejected the round, caught it one-handed. Forty-five ACP. Excellent stopping power.

Not a bad little plan, Daniel's. Get here early, plant the gun. Then he could walk through the metal detectors without a worry. When everything went down, Daniel would be armed and Bennett wouldn't.

Unfortunately for them, they weren't the only ones who'd seen *The Godfather.*

He could take the gun, but when they got here and found it missing, they'd panic. Better to keep them calm, let them think they were a step ahead of him.

Bennett slotted the round back into the magazine, then replaced the Sig and smoothed the tape down. Let them have it if it made them feel safe. Now that he knew what they were planning, the pistol wasn't a threat. People who watched a lot of movies tended to equate holding a pistol to winning a fight. He knew better. Besides, he didn't intend to let Daniel keep the gun long.

He stopped to wash his hands, dried them on his pants, and stepped out, whistling.

"You find it?" Tattoo stood behind the bar.

"Yeah," Bennett said. "I found it."

The suit was Armani. Gray, lightweight, single-breasted, 41R. Daniel slung it over his arm, moved to a long row of bins holding oxfords in every imaginable color. They glowed in the shadowless light of the department store. A rainbow of fabric, every shade vibrant. Green like sea glass smoothed by a decade of waves. Blue the color of a nursery ceiling. Yellow of lemon sorbet on the first really hot day of summer.

The world was so beautiful. There was magic everywhere, even in the most mundane bits.

He glanced at his new watch. Five-twenty-seven. Jesus. He must have looked at the thing a hundred and fifty times, and only an hour had passed.

He picked a blue shirt with delicate gray

stripes, took two sizes.

"I think I'm ready." Laney had come up behind him, a handful of dresses draped over her arm.

Chamber music drifted from somewhere. The air bore traces of a hundred perfumes. Glass display cases caught the light and made it dance. He followed Laney, watching the graceful sway of her hips. He could have walked behind her all day, all night, all the rest of his life, considered himself a happy man.

A saleswoman counted their garments, opened two changing rooms for them, hovered long enough to make sure they went into separate ones. Daniel began to undress, pulling off his T-shirt and laying it on the bench. Sliding his pants down his legs. Stepping out of his shoes. Cognizant of every feeling: cool air on his chest, cotton moving across his thighs, the firm weave of the carpet under his socks.

He looked at himself in the mirror. The same way he had in a tiny shithole hotel in Maine not long ago, when he had stared, praying for recognition. When the man in the mirror had seemed a doppelganger, known and unknown at once. The face of a man who had lost everything, even himself. Who had tried to end his own life. Air-conditioning made him shiver. Just days ago he had wanted to die, to throw his life away. And now he was facing that again, and now his desire to live was at an almost cellular level.

People thought about their mortality all the time, made a late-night exercise of it, a philosophical discussion. Tried to grasp the idea that someday they would cease to exist. And, worse, the most painful betrayal of all: the world would continue.

But it was a very different thing to stare in the mirror and realize that the question wasn't someday. It was right now, today, tonight.

Keep it together. She needs you. You have to believe you're going to win.

You have to believe that at the end of the night, you will be holding a loaded gun — and Bennett will not.

Glanced at his watch. Five-twenty-nine. Daniel pulled the pants from the hanger and began to dress.

When he stepped out of the dressing room, an angel of cream and gold stood in front of the mirror. Laney wore silver sandals and a peach dress that looked like it had been cut just for her. It was backless but fell below the knee, and when she spun, the hem whirled out. She caught him catching her legs, and smiled.

"Wow."

She popped a hip, put her hands at her sides. "You like?"

"Wow."

"And you," she said, "look like James Bond."

"Connery?"

"Craig."

He laughed. "You're missing something." From his pocket he took the necklace, stepped behind her. She lifted her hair so he could fasten the clasp.

They stood side by side in the mirror. The two of them staring into it, and the two of them staring out of it. *Such a long time to wait. And such a short time to live.*

"I've got an idea," she said.

"Where are we going?"

"You'll see."

"Laney . . ."

"Turn left."

"We don't have time —"

"Park over there."

"The beach?" After they'd paid, she'd led him out to the car, tossed him the keys. Then she'd steadfastly refused to tell him anything beyond directions. But "over there" was a wide parking lot at the foot of broad expanse of sand; Manhattan Beach, he guessed, not that it much mattered. The western hundred yards of the whole coast was bright sand, one beach blending into the next. He pulled into a parking space. "Now what?"

Laney reached in the backseat for her purse, slung it over one bare shoulder — man, that dress — then opened the door. "Come on."

His first instinct was frustration, the sense that this was a waste of time. Then he remembered how very little time they might have left, and he followed her.

She walked fast, designer sandals flashing on the pavement. The air smelled of salt and sun. The sky was all the colors of autumn. He caught up to her just as she reached the sidewalk fronting the beach.

"Now what?"

Laney bent one knee, reached down to undo the strap of her sandal, then repeated it with the other. What the hell. He unlaced his new shoes, pulled off his socks, and then joined her on the beach. It was cool beneath his feet, and good. He wriggled his toes, took in the sensation of sand moving between them. *The world is so beautiful.*

"Ready?"

"For what?"

She smiled. "Go!"

And then she was sprinting, hair whipping behind, the hem of her dress flapping, one hand up to hold her purse strap to her shoulder.

He leapt after her, a dress shoe in each hand, bare feet digging deep into the beach. Every planted step dug to the cooler sand beneath. The wind pressed against him, constant and sweet. His slacks tightened at his knees, the tie flipped over his shoulder like a tail, and there was something so ridiculous about running on the beach in a new thousand-dollar suit that he found himself laughing without a sound, that inner laugh that was a soul's cry of joy, and he gave himself over to it, leaned into the run. The soles of her feet flashed, and the dress, backlit against the burning sky, clung to the curves of her hips. She looked over her shoulder, mouth wide, eyes sparkling, a moment straight out of an advertisement or a dream. Light like melted butter burnished the air, and the sound of his breathing, and the *scruff-scruff* of the fabric on his legs, and it was perfect, the rest of the world forgotten. Laney was angling for a faded lifeguard stand the color of seafoam, and he pushed harder, not to win but just because it felt so good to throw himself into this moment, to have nothing but this, to hold it full and complete and wondrous and yet as fleeting as a drop of rain.

She beat him to it by a second or so, slapping the wood with one hand, then raising her arms high. "Victory!"

"Oh yeah?" He stepped forward, hoisted her up over his shoulder. She squirmed and laughed, hair whipping around his waist, hands beating on his back and thighs. Ten paces took him to the hard-packed sand and pewter lace of the surf.

"You'll wreck your suit," she warned.

"I don't care." He stepped into the water, the cold of it lovely shocking, running up over his feet, his shins, his knees. The fabric of his trousers swirled in the surf. "In you go." He braced himself.

"No!" Her hands went from batting to grabbing, snatching handfuls of his clothing. "No."

He laughed, then lowered her down gently, feet first. The next wave slapped at his calves, splashing around them. She shrieked and danced back, pulling him with her, until they were only ankle deep. Daniel put his arms around her and kissed her as the Pacific rolled in and out, endless.

Finally, she lay her head against him and spoke to his chest. "You know what this reminds me of?"

"Yes." Sand slid over and under and around his feet. "I just wish I remembered it myself."

"You will. But until you do . . ." Laney pulled back, slid her purse to the crook of one elbow. She dug for something, came out with her hand closed. "Until you do, we'll just have to make new memories."

She opened her fingers. A silver ring glinted. He looked at it, at her.

"Daniel Hayes, will you stay married to me? Even though you don't know who you are, and I'm dead?"

He looked at her, this woman he had lost and found and for whom he was risking losing everything again. Then he took the ring and slid it on his left hand. With its presence he was conscious suddenly of the absence that had been. A piece of himself, returned. He spun it on the finger. "I will." Then he looked up and smiled. "So long as you don't start to smell."

They lingered as long as they could. There were a few others on the beach, but enough sand and distance separated them that they could pretend to be alone. The sun vanished and the sky darkened and the water turned from silver to slate. The wind never let up, and Daniel found himself thinking about how far it had come. All the way across the ocean, just to blow against them.

Finally, he couldn't pretend any longer. "We —"

"I know." She sighed. "Time to go."

He rose, brushed the sand from his pants, held a hand down to her. They walked up the beach together. When they made it to the sidewalk, Laney looked around, said, "I'm gonna run to the bathroom. No point dying with a full bladder. Hold my purse?"

"Sure." He leaned against the low wall separating the parking lot from the beach. It never got truly dark in L.A., but he could see a few stars, and the wind felt so good that it was a pleasure just to sit here. To soak up every sensation.

"Ring, sweetie."

It was a man's voice, and familiar. Daniel whirled, looked behind him. No one.

"Ring, sweetie."

The top edge of her purse was lit from within. Her cell phone. Someone was calling her. The voice was Robert Cameron's. Her ring tone.

Who would be calling?

He reached into her purse and pulled out the phone. The display had no name, just a string of digits. Wrong number? He put a finger on the button to reject the call, then decided to let it ring through to voice mail on its own. The phone vibrated again, Robert Cameron spoke one more time, and then the call dropped, leaving the recent calls list on-screen, this number at the top of it, and below —

The world tilted. Daniel reached down with his other hand to steady himself. The wind knifed through his clothing. His throat tightened.

He looked up. She was still in the bathroom.

There was a roaring in his ears. He looked at the phone again, sure he must have imagined it.

Bennett
310-209-0415
Yesterday, 3:12 pm

Yesterday, 3:12. That would have been . . .
In the hotel.

Shortly after they'd made love. When she was taking her endless bubble bath. The one he'd interrupted.

He'd opened the door, and almost leapt out of his skin to see her aiming the pistol at him. She'd been standing at the sink, still wet, skin flushed with heat. Her purse on the counter —

— and her cell phone beside it.

The screen was lit up. You didn't notice at the time, not really, but some part of you did.

She had been talking to Bennett. And she'd lied to him about it. Lied and smiled and asked him to order her a salad.

That sudden mysterious errand, her "friend" that might be able to help . . .

The way she freaks out at any mention of the police . . .

The tiny hesitation that's flickered in her eyes a dozen times . . .

The way she keeps wanting to pay Bennett off, despite everything . . .

Muted by the cinder-block walls, he heard the institutional roar of a flushing toilet. Daniel closed the call list. Grabbed her purse, stuffed the phone inside. He slid his sweating hands into his pockets. The wind had grown cold and smelled of rotting sea-weed.

Laney came out of the bathroom shaking wet hands. Dynamite in a designer dress and mussed hair and a television smile. "Ready?"

Daniel looked at her. "As I'll ever be."

Spotlights crissed and crossed, searching fingers scraping the low bellies of purple clouds. It was eight-thirty, early by Los Angeles standards, but even so, the parking lot for Lux had a good crowd of cars. Bennett ignored the valet, rolled down the lane, found a spot near the exit, did a quick three-point turn to pull the Jaguar in facing forward. He took a deep breath, rolled his shoulders, cracked his knuckles.

He pulled the Colt from his belt, locked the safety, tucked it beneath the front seat. From the duffel bag on the passenger seat, he took the cheaper of his camera bodies and attached a fixed 500mm lens. Though the shake was bad, it let him read a license plate across the lot. Good. He grabbed the parabolic and a pair of earbuds, and then started for the club.

Lux looked better at night. The gold paint shimmered and sparkled, some sort of metallic flecks in it. Not sophisticated, but it made for a nice backdrop to the red velvet rope line, and the oversized framed posters for the movie.

The line was still manageable at this hour. He stood behind a couple of shiny girls in short dresses, both of them posing and preening, pretending the cold wasn't bothering their bare legs. Every time someone walked into the club, a bite-sized blast of music poured out.

"You press?" The bouncer's chest strained the seams of his suit.

"Freelance."

The bouncer nodded, said, "Can you take off the camera and hand it to him, please? And that thing too. What is it?"

"It's a microphone." Bennett handed both to another bouncer, this one Hispanic but otherwise indistinguishable.

"I've done some work, never seen a mic like that. Raise your arms, please." The bouncer ran a handheld metal detector up Bennett's legs, around his back, down both arms.

"You're an actor?"

"Mostly stunt work so far. I had a part in that last Tobey Maguire film."

"Speaking?"

"Don't you fucking move."

"Huh?"

"That was my line. 'Don't you fucking move.' I was Enforcer number two." The metal detector beeped. "Lift your shirt, tilt out your belt?"

Bennett showed him the belt buckle, his belly behind it. The other bouncer took off the camera's lens cap, peered through the viewfinder.

"Tobey and I hit it off, though. He's going to use me in his next picture."

"I bet he is, dumb fuck."

"Huh?" The guy's eyes narrowed.

"I said I bet he is. Good luck." He smiled blandly. The bouncer shook his head, said, "Give the paparazzi his gear." Bennett slung the camera, moved for the door. From behind, he heard the guy say, "And I better not catch you crashing the VIP. That's invites only."

"Yep." He opened the door. The bass line hit him square in the belly, *thoom-thoom-thoom-thoom.* The chandelier blazed above, the light making the red velvet draping the walls richer. A staggeringly hot blonde asked if he was with the movie party; when he said no, she charged him $25, told him the VIP room was closed for the night.

That's okay, sister. I have different VIPs in mind.

Bennett walked past the staircase and through the broad double doors into the main bar. Several hundred people milled about, scattered between the bars on either side of the room and the café tables placed in clusters. The dance floor had maybe twenty people on it, that usual crew of near-professional dancers who came to be watched. Tight spotlights flashed overhead, sharp stuttering white beams. Every time light struck one of the thousands of crystals, the glass showered down rainbows. The effect made it seem like the air itself was sparkling. The beat came from everywhere, surrounding him, compressing him, ringing through the soles of his feet and the skin of his arms. He didn't recognize the tune, a dance remix of some rap song, probably one of Too G's.

He kept to the side, and found an unclaimed table with a good view. Daniel and Laney had said nine-thirty, an hour from now. He scanned the crowd to be sure — it wasn't yet at the humid, shoulder-to-sweaty-shoulder press that would come by eleven — but didn't see either of them.

Bennett leaned back, drew his anonymity around him like a hood. Just a man at a table. He put the parabolic mic on a chair, ran the earbuds up under his shirt. Entertained himself by aiming the mic up at the VIP lounge, where Too G's movie folks would later be partying.

"— heard his agent got him three for the picture."

"Too made three, huh? Well, good. After all he been through."

"Hard life."

"That's truth."

Bennett smiled, flipped the off switch. He leaned back, eyes moving, sorting, categorizing. Marking the bouncers, the security by the bar. The employee exit that would lead to a storage room, an office maybe, probably an exit. Gauging the crowd, looking for threats.

His body tingled, and he rolled with it, that in-the-moment tingle that let him feel the flow of blood through his veins, sense the shifting weight of each body in the bar, anticipate the flicker of spotlights.

Killing time.

"Are you okay?" Laney had stopped just outside the doors to the main bar, her face marked with concern.

She's lying to you. She has been since the beginning.

The woman you made your home, the wife

you've gambled everything for. She's lying to you.

"I'm fine," he said.

"You were so quiet on the way over."

"Just thinking." *Lying lying lying lying lyin—* "Come on. Let's get ready. He could be here any minute." He stepped into the room before she could argue.

The club wasn't crowded yet, but there were more people than Daniel would have liked. So many faces, a blur of eyes and mouths. *Lying lying lying.*

He took a breath, glanced at his watch. A few minutes to nine. A thousand lifetimes had passed in the past hours.

"Do you think he's here yet?" Laney was radiant. The rainbows that fell from the ceiling bounced off the necklace and lit her skin with fire. *Lying lying ly—*

"I don't know." He stood in the entrance to the club, letting his eyes get used to the dim light. Taking in the surroundings, the same and yet so different from the room he had seen this afternoon. His pulse thudded as loud as the beat but faster, and his armpits were clammy cool. "Get us a space by the bar."

"Daniel."

He turned, and she stepped forward. Took

his hand and stared into his eyes. "I love you."

He made himself smile at her. "Get us a seat." He squeezed her fingers, then fought his way toward the bathroom. Snatches of conversation as he passed.

"— two-picture deal at Paramount, with back end —"

"— should see this place, it's magic. Maybe after we have a drink —"

"— so I said, 'Look, I don't care what role you played in *My Fair Lady*, you're not cut out to —"

"— I mean, this girl was unbelievable. She had these eyes, man, just hypnotized me —"

"— it's *Pretty Woman* meets *Requiem for a Dream* —"

"— get me another, yeah? Ketel, up, clean, dry, blue —"

The door to the men's room was heavy. The space was all marble and gold plating. A Spanish-language tape played over the sound system, a resonant voice saying, *"¿Puedo afilar mi lapis?"* and then, a second later, "Can I sharpen my pencil?" A couple of the stalls were filled, but not his. Given the choice, men generally took stalls at the end over the middle. Daniel stepped inside, fumbled with the lock. The Sig Sauer was still strapped behind the toilet tank. He peeled the tape away. The gun was wonderful and terrible in his hands.

"*Me siento enfermo . . .* I'm feeling sick. *Me siento enfermo . . .* I'm feeling sick."

Daniel dropped onto the toilet. The porcelain was cold through the thin material of his slacks. He buried his head in his hands. The gun pressed hard against his temple.

She's lying to you.

But why?

Was she working with Bennett? Could this be some sort of elaborate scam?

It didn't seem possible. No one could have planned on his vanishing, his amnesia.

So what happened leading up to that?

The parts of his life he could remember, it all glowed. But it was mostly history. Of the week or two leading to her "death" and his dash to suicide, he'd gotten nothing but the briefest of flashes. What he could remember was confusing and painful. There was guilt and shame and sickness, he knew that. Something terrible had happened. He'd assumed that was the arrival of Bennett.

But what if he was wrong? What if it was something else?

What if you discovered something that changed the way you felt about her?

What if she turned out not to be the person

510

you thought?

An urge to retch, cry, and scream tore through him. He clapped his hands against his head, hard, the hit of the gun blunt and painful.

Ever since Maine, he had put his whole trust in Laney. He'd rebuilt his identity, such as it was, around her. Even when he'd thought her dead, he'd defined himself through her.

What if she'd been the problem from the beginning?

He had a powerful impulse to get up, walk out of the bathroom and the club and the city. To just go. Pick a direction and leave all this behind, all these questionable certainties and uncertain questions. To forget figuring it out, and just start again as someone new, somewhere else.

But as who? Where? Why?

You are who you choose to be. But does that mean you can choose again and again and again? Does nothing matter?

No. You've made decisions. Live or die by them. Besides, maybe there's an explanation. Ask. Give her a chance to explain.

And then do whatever you have to. One way or the other, it ends tonight. All of it.

Even if it means the end of everything.

He prepped the Sig, then tucked it in his

waistband and climbed up on the back of the toilet tank.

From his shadowed table, Bennett watched Daniel walk out of the washroom. The man did not look good. Pale and shaky and wound too tight, ready to explode with the slightest touch.

His suit was nice, though. Gray and slim. The jacket buttoned.

Hayes threaded his way through the crowd to the side bar, where Laney waited. She looked great, her dress cut for cleavage but longer at the leg, that balance that kept it from going slutty. The blond hair wasn't really her; skin like that worked better with her natural brown. But there was no denying the sex appeal of the string of diamonds dripping down her neck.

Daniel slid in beside her. She smiled thinly. Her hands fidgeted with the strap of her purse. Hayes took the bag from her, hung it on the back of a chair, then said something to the bartender, who nodded.

Had he put the gun in her purse?

Bennett rested his camera on the edge of the table for stability. The digital display glowed as he focused. The lens magnified the image, brought him as close to Daniel's midriff as if he'd been standing beside the guy.

No. There's the bulge, on the left-hand side. The same place Hayes had tucked his gun before. People were predictable.

He slipped in the earbud and turned on the microphone.

"Chardonnay and a Booker's neat, double." The bartender set them down.

Daniel nodded, laid a couple of twenties on the bar. "Keep the change."

"Thanks."

"For luck?" Laney held her wineglass by the stem.

"Something like that." Daniel raised his heavy rocks glass, took a swallow. The Sig felt strange tucked into the front of his pants, heavy and intimate. The sights dug into his flesh. He leaned back against the bar, glanced around. The place was filling up, and the flashes of glowing light reduced the crowd to anonymity, just teeth and shoulders and hair and sweat.

"Did it —"

"Yes," Daniel said, and nodded to her purse, where he'd hung it over the back of the chair. "Just like we planned."

He tracked her eyes, saw the panic in them. She hated guns. At least, he thought she did. That could be a lie too. "Can I ask you something?"

She looked up at him.

"Is there anything I don't know?"

"What — how do you mean?"

"I have this feeling there's something really important I'm missing. I keep almost getting it, but not quite. You know when you're trying to remember somebody's name, you know it starts with R, and you just keep thinking Robert, Ryan, Rick, Randy, Roger . . . Roger . . . Roger . . . I feel like that."

"Well." She shrugged. "You have amnesia."

"I know," he said. *Come on, baby. Please.* "But I feel like there's something specific."

"You haven't slept in a week. You're exhausted. Your head is probably playing tricks on you."

He was tired. God, was he tired. Could that explain things? Paranoia and exhaustion were a dangerous combination. Daniel took a swallow of bourbon, didn't taste it. *You know what you saw on her phone.* "Bennett will be here soon, and then we're all in. Win and live or lose and die. And I guess I'm just asking if there's anything you think I need to know." He turned to her. "Anything at all."

Laney sipped the Chardonnay, her lipstick leaving kisses on the rim of the glass. "What are you getting at, Daniel?"

"I'm not sure." He stared. *This is it, baby. This is your chance. Our chance.* "I'm hoping you'll tell me."

For the tiniest fraction of a second, she hesitated. He let himself hope. Hope that it wasn't all a lie, that she wasn't tied up with the monster in their lives. That he hadn't saved his life just to learn it was a ruin.

Then she said, "I'm sorry. I don't know what you're talking about."

Daniel stared at her. Kept his face smooth and still, while behind it, everything fell apart.

It was all for nothing.

All of it.

"But I hope you know," Laney continued, "that I love you. More than you can imagine."

"Me too," said a voice from behind him. "I love you both."

There was a reason he worked alone.

Bennett had listened in on their conversation, amused. Poor Daniel, knowing just enough to suspect he was being lied to, and drawing the wrong conclusion. Poor Laney, trying so hard to protect her man. Both of them pure and true and on a collision course. Neither the iceberg nor the *Titanic* had evil intent, but they still made for a hell of a smashup.

It was good TV. But he was on a timeline.

So he'd slipped out the earbud, set the camera on the chair beside the microphone, and given both a quick wipe before walking away from them. The crowd had grown, and he threaded his way between party people, Daniel and Laney now in sight, now out of it. He'd come up just in time to hear Laney's proclamation of love.

"Me too," he said, smiling. "I love you both."

Laney started, took a fast breath in. But Daniel seemed almost calm as he turned, wearing the unsurprised look of a man who'd been expecting the worst. "You're early."

"I'm a go-getter." Bennett glanced at Laney. "Lovely necklace."

"Take it," she said, one hand moving to her throat.

Daniel said, "Not here."

No, you'll want to go somewhere quiet, won't you, brother? "Where?"

"There's an exit over there" — the man gestured across the crowded dance floor — "behind those curtains."

"It might be alarmed."

"It's not. I checked this afternoon."

"Why not just go out the front?" Bennett curious what kind of a lie the man would come up with.

"Too many photographers out that way now. If anyone notices Laney, we're in trouble."

"All of a sudden you don't want the crowd?"

"I know you don't have a gun. That was the point."

Which you think I'll read as an amateur's overconfidence, since of course I don't need a gun to take care of the two of you. So now I'm supposed to feel so pleased about the fact that you're willing to walk into a deserted alley with me that I never stop to wonder if you have a gun yourself. Kinda slim, brother. You should respect your opponent more. Bennett said, "All right. Before we go, I want you to know. It was just business."

"Die screaming."

"I guess that covers the formalities. Shall we?"

"I want your word that you'll leave us alone afterward."

"I promise." Bennett stuck out his hand.

One of the neat things about people: hold out your hand long enough, the person opposite will take it. Daniel stared at him with disgust. But after a long moment he returned the shake.

The moment their hands touched, Bennett clenched down hard, and then with his left hand jerked open Daniel's suit and snatched the Sig Sauer. The gun was his before the button torn from Daniel's jacket hit the floor. He thumbed the safety off and put the barrel to the man's belly.

"You don't mind if I hold this, though, do you?"

Daniel's mouth fell open. The blood rushed from his face.

"There are enough people here that I can shoot you both and walk out while everyone is busy panicking." He kept his face calm, the mask of ease that hid everything. "But I don't want to do that. Okay?"

"What." Daniel coughed. "What do you want?"

"First, I want your beautiful wife to give me my necklace."

Laney had gone pale. As slow as a reluctant bride, she reached up, unclasped the necklace. Held it out to him. "Here."

Bennett didn't let go of Daniel's hand, didn't take his eyes off the man. "Put it in my pocket."

Laney hesitated, then moved up beside

him. He felt her hand steal into his pants, felt the sharpness of the stones. *Hello, Mexico.* With Laney's hand still in his pocket, Bennett winked at Daniel. "Good. Now. Let's all take a stroll."

Laney started to protest. "But you said —"

"Easy, sister. I'm not going to kill either of you. I only want a few more minutes of your time."

Daniel said, "Maybe you should just leave."

"Sorry. I can't trust you not to run to one of the bouncers. No, the three of us are walking out together. Once we're outside, we'll go our separate ways." He released his grip on Daniel's hand, stepped back. "It's almost over. Hold it together for a few more minutes, and then everything will be fine. I promise. Here." Bennett tucked the gun in his belt. "See?"

Maybe it was the words. Maybe it was the action. Maybe it was desperate, animal hope. But Daniel and Laney looked at each other, and then Laney picked up her purse. With what must have been a heroic effort, she turned her back on him and started for the alley door. Daniel followed, and Bennett took up the rear, close enough that neither would bolt, but far enough that they couldn't make a suicide play for the gun.

Every detail was crisp and sharp. The constellation of freckles spilling up the décolletage of a girl raising a martini glass. Each star in the crystalline heavens above the dance floor. The texture of Hayes's suit jacket and the safety pins serving as temporary hems on the cuffs of his pants; the tension in Laney's bare shoulders and the sweat beading her neck. The beat was *thoom-thoom-thoom* and it was the beat of his heart, the strike of his footsteps. Half a million dollars in his pocket and a gun tucked in his belt and the pure sure rush of victory.

If there was another reason to be alive, he couldn't think of it.

Laney's heart hammered a hundred beats a second. Her breath came shallow. The dancers seemed warped and slow, their motions twitchy in the flashing light. She could feel the music but couldn't hear it.

It's going to work. The plan is going to work.

There had been a moment, at the bar, when she had thought everything was coming apart. Daniel obviously suspected her. Had he remembered what had happened? The truth behind what drove him so close to the edge?

She didn't know. But he had been fishing

for something, and the war inside her had raged fierce and brutal. Half of her had desperately wanted to tell him the truth, no matter what it would do to him. The other half remembered how very close the truth had come to destroying him, and argued that every moment spared that pain was a victory. In the end, it had been a pragmatic decision — she couldn't risk him coming undone. Not now. They just had to get through.

Laney glanced over her shoulder. From five feet back, Bennett tapped the gun hidden beneath his shirt. She winced, looked forward. Used the move as a cover for letting one purse strap slip so the bag fell open. She could feel the extra weight, and the hard edges.

She'd been afraid that Bennett might ask about the purse, or even search it. When he'd come up behind them, all he would have had to do was look into the bag and it would all have been over.

Daniel walked half a step behind her. Once they'd made it out the door, she would be in a perfect position to reach into the bag, find the snub-nosed revolver, and pass it back to Daniel. That was the plan.

Only, she had a modification in mind. It was her mess. She was the one who had brought Bennett into their lives. She was the one who should clean it up.

Somehow, her heart managed to beat even faster.

This is right. Daniel has done enough. It's time you did your share.

Fast, too fast, they had crossed the crowded floor. The door was painted black and partly hidden by velvet curtains. Laney glanced over her shoulder again. Daniel wouldn't meet her eye. *He knows you lied to him.*

It doesn't matter. In a few seconds, it will all be over.

She pushed open the door. Night air poured over her sweating skin. The loading dock was broad and bright, a sodium lamp on the building casting remorseless light down on concrete stained and pitted. Two huge Dumpsters ran along the wall, the metal rusty. The air smelled sour.

Let them both get outside. Then finish it.

She took a few extra steps, ears straining. She could sense them behind her by the way they blocked the sound. *Wait until —*

The heavy door banged shut, turning the music down.

Now.

Laney reached into her purse, feeling for the revolver. Her fingers traced the hard,

522

cool edges of the —

— glass?

She jerked her hand out, found herself holding a heavy-bottomed tumbler, a couple of drops of amber liquid still in the bottom.

An image flashed across her eyes. Bennett coming up behind them. Close enough to her purse that all he had to do was look down.

He must have seen the gun and slipped it out of her purse, trading the glass in for weight.

Oh god. Oh god, no.

She turned, wanting to warn Daniel, to tell him to run, but Bennett was right there. His smile was bland and cold. "So, Daniel, you were wrong. At your house today, you said at the end of the night, you'd be holding a gun" — Bennett reached for his waist, drew the pistol, and pointed it at her beautiful husband — "and I wouldn't."

No, it won't work, not now, no —

"Tell me something. You're a writer, you're supposed to understand the human heart, all that stuff. Why is it that when you tell people to trust you, they tend to?"

"We want to believe in each other."

"Simple as that?"

Daniel shrugged. "I wouldn't say simple."

He looked at Laney.

*He's waiting for you to hand him the gun.
And all you have is a glass.*

Her head and heart screamed to move, to try something, to charge Bennett.

"Never made sense to me. Words are just breath with sound. For example, I promised I wouldn't hurt you." Bennett pulled the trigger.

The hammer fell with a click, as she expected.

"Actually," Daniel reached behind his back and pulled out the snub-nosed revolver. With his left hand, he drew out a handful of shells from his pocket. "What I said was, I'd be holding a *loaded* gun, and you wouldn't."

It was like she'd been bound by iron bands and someone had cut them. She could suddenly breathe, smile, even laugh. He'd done it. Somehow, her baby had pulled it off.

Then Daniel turned and pointed the gun at her. "Go stand over there with him."

There was a high-pitched hum ringing through his brain, and he knew it for the howl he wouldn't let himself make.

She lied to you. She and Bennett are in this together. There's no way to win. But that doesn't mean you have to let them.

Better all three of them end up on the concrete.

Laney said, "What?"

Bennett said, "How?"

"I hid two guns in the bathroom. We picked up this one" — he moved it to point at Bennett — "at the house this afternoon, and I hid it in the ceiling. The plan was to put it in Laney's purse in case you searched me. But that was before I knew she was lying to me."

"Daniel, what are you doing?" Her voice frantic. "What are you —"

"I saw your cell phone. You talked to him yesterday. From the hotel."

She looked at Bennett, then back at him. "Yes. But it's not what —"

"I don't want to hear it." His headache was an avalanche, a stampede, a typhoon. "You know, ever since I lost my memory, I've been looking for you. I thought you were the center of my world. But you were the reason I tried to kill myself, weren't you?"

Bennett's mask of cool had slipped, revealing the creature behind it, all angles and cunning. He looked from the gun to Laney to the street beyond the loading dock, then took a half step back.

"Don't move, fucker." Daniel raised the

gun. It felt so right in his hand. *No, wrong, it feels wrong, not right, you don't want to, not ag—* He blinked, tried to steady his hand. At this range, there was no way he could miss. All he had to do was pull the trigger. Swivel his aim a couple of degrees, at Laney, and pull it again. Then, finally, put the barrel in his mouth and finish what he'd started in Maine.

Laney's eyes were pools of wide panic. She stepped toward him.

"Stay there."

"No." She stared at him, the woman who'd been lying to him — *the woman you love* — her face beautiful — *terrible* — a monster — *your life* — "You're not going to do this, Daniel."

"I have to."

"No, you don't. Don't you remember?" She spoke softly. "I know you do. That's why you couldn't shoot him at Sophie's house, and why you keep having that dream —"

"What are you —"

"— about the concrete canyon." She took another step. "Only it's not a canyon, Daniel." Her eyes hypnotizing him. "It's the river basin." He felt dizzy, almost as if he were —

"Where you killed Bennett last time."

526

— falling.

EXT. L.A. RIVER BASIN — EARLY
EVENING
The sky is crimson and gold
above a concrete canyon with a
narrow trickle of water down
the center. The skyline looms.
A silver BMW splashes through
a puddle.

INT. BMW — CONTINUOUS
DANIEL HAYES pulls to a stop
near an overpass. He clenches
and unclenches his hands.
He peers out the windshield.
Beneath the bridge, headlights
blink on and off once.
On the seat beside him, his
cell phone vibrates. The display has a picture of LANEY
THAYER.
He looks at the phone, but
does not pick it up.

                    DANIEL
No, baby.

He opens the glove box, takes

out a paper bag.

                DANIEL (CONT'D)
Not after what he did to you.

EXT. L.A. RIVER BASIN — CON-
TINUOUS
Daniel walks toward the overpass. He holds the bag in his
left hand.
After a dozen steps, he stops
at the edge of the shadow.
Footsteps ring on concrete.
A STRANGER's silhouette appears. His features resolve
as he comes closer. A stocky
man of average height, with a
shaved head and tattoos down
both arms.

                STRANGER
You're late. Where's your
wife?
                DANIEL
It's just me.

The stranger digests this,
then nods at the bag, holds
out his hand.

                    STRANGER
Give it here.
                    DANIEL
I know about you. You're a
cockroach.
                    STRANGER
Wow. Tough guy.

The man's smile is bar fights
and prison time.

                    DANIEL
We're not afraid of you. I'm
giving you one chance, one, to
leave us alone.
                    STRANGER
Or else what? This isn't a TV
show.
                    DANIEL
I'll give you this, but I'm
telling you now. You'll do
better to walk away and leave
us alone.
                    STRANGER
What are you, laying a Bud-
dhist trip on me? Fuck you.
                    DANIEL
No.

He reaches into the bag and

pulls out a GLOCK.

                    STRANGER
Wait —
                    DANIEL
Fuck you.

Daniel pulls the trigger, once, twice, three times.
Each bullet is a hammer blow.
The man stumbles.
Blood spurts from a hole in his neck and spatters Daniel's T-shirt.
A childish look of fear and bafflement crosses the stranger's face.
Then he collapses.
Daniel stares at him. Then at the gun.
The body twitches on the ground. Lips twist in agony.
Blood spills onto the dirty concrete.
Daniel stares. He looks like a man waiting for someone to yell "Cut!"
No one does.
The stranger coughs red, and dies.

Daniel looks around. His face is pale.

The skyline looms, the high-rises leaning like hooded judges.

A sudden convulsion takes Daniel, and he doubles over, claps a hand over his mouth.

Barely holds the vomit down.

Staggers back to the car.

INT. BMW — CONTINUOUS
Daniel collapses into the seat.

The gun in his hand trembles.

He stares out the windshield at the man he murdered.

Then he yanks open the glove box, throws the gun inside, and squeals away.

The drive is a blurry montage of neon and darkness.

Horns squeal out of time.

Daniel's knuckles squeeze the steering wheel.

His face is wan and sticky.

He mutters to himself, word fragments of an argument in his head. Angry and scared and horrified.

                    DANIEL
Had to . . . he would . . .
didn't . . . I didn't . . .
meant to . . . why . . .
fuck . . . oh fuck . . .

The city rages and burns
outside his windows.
The PCH is a guttering candle.
The ocean is cold steel.
The night is slithering hor-
ror.

INT. DANIEL & LANEY'S MALIBU
HOME — MOMENTS LATER
LANEY THAYER sits on the steps
in their foyer.
She speaks into a cell phone.

                    LANEY
Daniel, please, whatever
you're going to do, don't. I
know you're trying to protect
me, but you don't want to do
this.
   (a beat)
Answer your phone, baby.
   (a beat)
Answer your phone!

At the sound of a car engine, Laney jumps. She runs to the front door, yanks it open just as Daniel comes in.
His white T-shirt is stained crimson.

                    LANEY
Oh my god.

He pushes past her.

                    LANEY
Are you okay?

She hurries after him, to the . . .

BATHROOM — CONTINUOUS
where Daniel crouches in front of the toilet. He vomits explosively.

                    LANEY
Talk to me! Are you hurt?

Daniel's chest heaves. He straightens, looks at her.
His eyes belong to a man hanging from a cliff — and slowly

losing his grip.
Laney rushes to him, begins to
pat at his body.

                    LANEY
Where is it coming from?
                    DANIEL
It's not mine.

The words gut punch Laney.
Daniel's fingers clutch porcelain.

                    LANEY
What did you <u>do</u>?
                    DANIEL
I didn't mean to.

He wipes at his mouth with the
back of his hand, and stares
at something far away.

                    DANIEL (CONT'D)
I gave him a chance. Told him
to leave us alone.
  (a beat)
Maybe I did mean to.

Laney paces.

DANIEL (CONT'D)
It feels different than I
thought it would. Worse.
  (a beat)
When I shot him, it was just
like on a set, with squibs and
dye packs. I even, I thought,
wow, this guy is good — he's
playing it well. I almost
believe he's really . . .

Another wave of nausea hits,
and he vomits into the toilet,
coughing and spitting between
heaves.
Laney kneels behind him and
slowly rubs his back.
Daniel finishes. Folds his arms
across the porcelain and lays
his head down on them.

LANEY
It's . . . okay. We'll figure
it out.
  (a beat)
I wish you'd told me. I would
have stopped you.
  (a beat)
Or come with you.

DANIEL

I didn't think it would be like this.

LANEY

Did anyone see you?

Daniel seems not to have heard.

DANIEL

There's no way back from this. Is there? Once you've done this, you're a different person.
  (a beat)
Forever.
  (a beat)
It's too high.

Laney seems like she wants to say something, but doesn't know what that would be.

DANIEL (CONT'D)

After all Bennett did to you, I wanted to. I was so —
  (a beat)
But he didn't kill anyone. I did.

A muffled sound, perhaps a man's voice. Laney digs her cell phone from her pocket, finger already stabbing to shut it off.
But then she sees the name on the display.
She stares.
Uncomprehending.
And then getting it.
Horror.
She watches Daniel as she answers.

                    BENNETT (O.S.)
You know, I always thought that line about not killing the messenger was just a metaphor.

Laney whimpers. Daniel looks up from the floor.

                    BENNETT (O.S.)
How's Dan feeling? He know he shot the wrong guy?
    (a beat)
Think the police will help you now?

— dizzy, almost as if he were falling. Daniel wobbled on his feet, sucked in a breath of cool air. Reeling from the force and abruptness of the memory, from the crystal clarity, from the echoes of nausea and horror.

Laney stared at him. Something in his eyes must have told her that he remembered. "Now you see why I had to lie, baby. Why I've kept us from going to the police, and why I wanted to just give him the necklace, even now. I didn't want you to have to remember this. I didn't want you to face it again."

Oh fuck me.

In the instant the memory had flowed through him, he'd been lost in it, but now he found himself here again. Back in a concrete canyon holding death in his hand. A loading dock instead of a dry river basin, but the decision the same.

Only heartbeats had passed. The snub-nosed revolver was still pointed at Bennett. Through the walls of the club, bass still throbbed. The glaring buzz of the sodium light was unchanged.

But everything was different. He knew what he'd done.

And what it had cost him.

Bennett had his mask back in place, his features collected. He held his hands out

538

and vaguely up. "Easy, brother. Easy. You tried this once, and you didn't like it."

Daniel stared down his arm. Shoulder, biceps, elbow, forearm, hand, pistol. All connected. *A gun is just a tool of your will. You pull the trigger, the man in front of it dies.*

It's not the gun that does the killing.

"Tell you what." Bennett lowered his hand.

"Don't!" Daniel's mouth was dry. His throat closed tight.

"Easy! I was just getting your necklace. Okay?" Very slowly, Bennett slid two fingers into his pocket, pulled the glittering chain out. "Here." He dropped it on the concrete. "See?"

It all comes down to this. Every mile you drove, every memory you chased, every moment you've had of this too-short life. Everything you've learned along the way. All conspired to bring you right back where you started.

Sweat dripped down his forehead, and he wiped it away with his other hand. Laney watched him. His Laney, the woman he loved, and who loved him.

My god. You almost — you were going to —

"I'm so sorry, baby. I didn't know. I didn't —"

"It's okay. I understand. I love you."

"Listen, Daniel." Bennett's voice calm. "We can work something out."

You're here again. Only this time you realize what it means.

When he'd driven to the river basin, the gun in his glove compartment, he had been telling himself that he would give the man a chance to walk away. But he'd known that he didn't really want that. He'd wanted the man to give him a reason to kill. He'd gone there with murder in his heart.

Only you didn't understand. You thought it was just another story you were writing. Didn't understand how taking a life would change you. How part of you would die too. Didn't realize you were living the last days of Daniel Hayes. At least the Daniel Hayes you thought you were.

But pulling a trigger is different from typing words on a keyboard. Different from imagining the story of your life. Different even from writing a real-life scene, the way you scripted the one for Bennett's cameras, and the twist that left you with the loaded gun.

"You're not a killer, Daniel." Bennett spoke calmly. "Let's just all walk away."

"Shut up!" Laney turned to Daniel. "You don't have to."

"What choice is there?"

She held out one hand. "Give me the gun."

"What?"

"I'll do it."

The words tore through him like a fist through a screen door. He could see the fear in her eyes, the dread. See that she remembered what killing had done to him, and knew that the same thing might happen to her. That some part of her would die along with Bennett. And yet she was willing to do it. Not because she wanted to, but to save Daniel from going through it all a second time.

He shook his head. "No. I won't let you." He wanted to lie down somewhere and close his eyes. Somewhere with cool breezes and the smell of flowers. *You are who you choose to be. Make sure you can live with the decisions you make.*

He lowered the gun.

Bennett smiled.

"I'm sorry, baby."

"Don't be," Laney said. "You have nothing to be sorry for."

You are who you choose to be.

"Yes," Daniel said, "I do."

He turned, snapped the gun back up, and pulled the trigger. In the confines of the loading dock, the explosion was enormous.

It left his ears ringing enough that the second shot seemed quiet in comparison. The silence that followed pressed heavy.

Make sure you can live with the decisions you make.

Bennett staggered. His legs went wobbly. He raised one hand, touched his chest. Stared at the blood that soaked his fingers. Eyes wide and stunned. Like he couldn't believe what he was looking at.

Then he collapsed.

Daniel stared. It all flashed through him in that moment. The long journey of the last days. The terror, the confusion, the stakes. The road and the loneliness and the exhaustion and guilt. Laney and the life he'd lost and then found again.

Sophie. Most of all, Sophie.

He looked at the body on the concrete.

I can live with that.

Daniel Hayes put his arms around the woman he loved and drew her to him.

INT. TELEVISION STUDIO — MORN-
ING

A graphics package for THE
TODAY SHOW wipes from the
screen, revealing a desk in
front of huge windows. The
windows look out onto a cold
morning in Manhattan. A crowd
of tourists bundled in snow
gear peer in the windows,
snapping pictures and waving.
Four people sit at the desk:
MEREDITH VIEIRA, a girl-next-
door beauty; AL ROKER, kind-
eyed and smiling; DANIEL
HAYES, looking uncomfortable;
and LANEY THAYER, radiant and
at ease.

MEREDITH
We have the most amazing story
to share with you this morning. You've all heard about
the terrible accident involving our guest Laney Thayer.
And of course we all know
about the media circus that
followed, including a police
investigation and implications of murder. This morning, for the first time, Laney
and her husband, screenwriter
Daniel Hayes, are going to
share what happened to them.
And what a story it is. Laney,
Daniel, thanks for being here.
LANEY
Thanks for having us. We're
big fans.
MEREDITH
We've all heard the official
version. But, Laney, can you
share your personal take on
everything that happened?
LANEY
Sort of.
 (she laughs)
That's the problem with amnesia.

                    AL
Tell us about that.
                  LANEY
Well, it's really called a
dissociative fugue. What happens is that in a traumatic
situation, sometimes your mind
loses track of itself. The
doctors think it's a way of
coping, a last-ditch effort
the mind can make to protect
itself. But it's so rare they
don't know much about it.
                 MEREDITH
And in your case, it was triggered when your car went over
the cliff.
                  LANEY
We think so.

Video feed from a news chopper
is cut in, showing a powder
blue Volkswagen Beetle upside
down in the ocean, the car
crumpled and torn.

              LANEY (V.O.)
All I remember is waking up in
the ocean. I was cold, and
everything hurt, and at first I

was just trying to get to shore. But when I did, I re-alized that I couldn't remem-ber how I had ended up in the ocean in the first place. Or anything else.

The camera cuts back to the desk.

                AL
That must have been terrify-ing.

                LANEY
It was. I was so confused. I could remember how to walk, and drive, and count, but I couldn't remember who I was.

                MEREDITH
What did you do?

                LANEY
Well, this might sound strange, but the doctors say it's normal. I bluffed.
  (she laughs)
I was sure that my memories would come back to me, so in the meantime, I just sort of became this other person.

                AL
A natural thing for an actress

to do.

LANEY

I think that was part of it.
I'm used to pretending to be
other people.

MEREDITH

Why didn't you go to the
police, or the hospital?

LANEY

I was scared. Everything seems
menacing if you can't remember
who you are.

MEREDITH

And of course, Daniel, you
didn't know she was alive.

DANIEL

I did, though. I just knew it.
Part of it was that the police
hadn't found her body. But it
was more than that. Somehow I
knew she was alive, and that
she needed my help.

MEREDITH

But the police were questioning your involvement.

DANIEL

I don't blame them. They were
just doing their job. But all
I cared about was finding

Laney. So I went looking for her.

MEREDITH

And we've all heard about what happened then. Your drive across the country to the beach where you'd gotten married; coming back to Los Angeles; even running from the police.

DANIEL

I know that my behavior might seem wrong to some people. But to me, it was simple. The woman I loved was in trouble, and nothing else mattered.

AL

That sounds like something out of a mystery novel.

DANIEL

It kind of was.

MEREDITH

It's incredible, the way the two of you were looking for each other, that you were connected even in these impossible situations. What did you learn from all of this?

Daniel and Laney look at each

other.

                    LANEY
That life is a raindrop.

Daniel smiles at her, takes
her hand.

                  MEREDITH
Life is a raindrop?
                   DANIEL
Someone I loved once told me
that. Basically, I guess it
means that everything you
think you are is exactly as
real as you choose for it to
be. But that no matter what
you choose, your life can
change in a moment.
                    LANEY
So choose carefully.
                   DANIEL
  (squeezing her hand)
And never let go.

Laney smiles, then leans over
and kisses him.

                  MEREDITH
"Never let go." What an amaz-

ing story — and a wonderful couple.

(she turns to the camera)
And speaking of wonderful, after the break Jamie Oliver will share his secret for making a perfect roast chicken dinner for your family. Stick with us!

Out the windows, Los Angeles, bleary and smudged.

So tired. Sleep hadn't gotten any easier. Some of it was the things they'd been dealing with — the lawyers, the media, their appearance on TV, flying to New York. Doctors and tests. The cold fact that no one could tell him exactly when — or if — his past would return to him.

But mostly, it was the memory of a concrete canyon. The horror of that moment hadn't lessened. Every time he closed his eyes, he found himself back. Every time, he woke in sweat and panic. The dream wouldn't go away.

It never will. Until you pay for it.

Laney was driving again. Probably best given his nerves. Out the windows, Los Angeles, sun-drenched and blurry-bright. Taquerias and Thai joints, day spas and massage parlors, holistic healing centers and high-end boutiques and a thousand places to get a cup of coffee. Cars and cracked sidewalks, billboards and boulevards.

"I still don't like this," Laney said again. "It could be a trick."

"Maybe." His voice raspy. "But he said he had something to tell me, that it was important. We can't hide behind our lawyers forever."

"What if he arrests you?"

"Then call Jen Forbus and tell her to go to work." The criminal lawyer had been dying to strike first, to file suits against the LASD and the media for their portrayal of Daniel as a murderer. *We won't win,* she'd said, *but we can make damn sure it will cost them way more than they're willing to pay.*

"That will only work if he's arresting you for running from him," Laney said. Dappled shadows fell through trees as they wound uphill. "What if he knows about Bennett?"

"Then we'll deal with it." He leaned back against the passenger seat, closed his eyes. "I have to face this. It's something I need to do."

"I just don't want to lose you again."

"Hey." He straightened, turned. "You will never lose me again."

Laney smiled at him. She'd dyed her hair

back to its proper shade, and her eyes burned as bright as the California sky. "What if I start to smell?"

He returned the grin. "I'll buy nose plugs."

Five minutes more and they'd reached the top of Mount Hollywood. By evening the parking lot would be jammed with tourists watching the sunset, but at this hour, she found a parking place easily enough. "At least let me come with you."

"No. He said he wanted to talk to me alone. Besides. Someone has to be able to call our lawyer." *And more important, you might try to stop me. Might even sacrifice yourself. I won't let you do that.* He reached for the door handle.

"Daniel." She leaned over. "Be careful, okay?"

"I will. I love you." He stepped out of the BMW. Ahead of him, the Griffith Park Observatory loomed. A building from an earlier age, it looked like a sultan's palace, white and massive and capped by gray domes. Children scampered back and forth on the lawn while their parents posed for photographs. Daniel followed the path around the side. A stone rail rose to waist height. Beyond it the mountain fell away, yielding a breathtaking view of the city shimmering with heat and smog.

Detective Roger Waters sat on the railing, back to Daniel, feet dangling off the far side.

Daniel took a deep breath. He'd hated having to lie to Laney, but she would never have understood the truth. Never have understood that he had to turn himself in. How could she? No one who hadn't gone through it would.

Killing Bennett he could live with. Bennett was a monster. But the man in the river basin. That had just been some guy Bennett twisted. The same way he'd twisted the two of them. He'd been a victim.

Which made Daniel the monster.

You are who you choose to be. Be sure you can live with the decisions you make. Daniel squared his shoulders. He said, "I don't think you're supposed to sit on the ledge like that."

"Benefits of the badge." Waters didn't turn. "You get to break a few rules." He patted the concrete beside him. "Have a seat."

"I'll stand." He took a breath. "Listen —"

"Beautiful, isn't it?" The man stared out into the distance. "People say Los Angeles is fake, but that's not true. It's just that it's got no memory. Am I right?"

"I —" *What was this?* "I guess. There's something —"

"Reason I asked you out here, I wanted to

tell you a story." The man bulldozed him. "About a guy named Larry Morgan. Larry was born in Reseda, but this story doesn't start till he was nineteen, when he started selling coke. He wasn't very good at it. LAPD busted him, he went up for five years. Inside he joined the Brotherhood — you know the Aryan Brotherhood? — probably mostly to stay alive."

Daniel leaned against the railing. Was this some sort of scare tactic, hit him with tough-guy talk about prison? "This is gritty and all, Detective, but I have something I need to —"

"Somewhere along the line, Larry decided the Brotherhood made good arguments. So when he got out of prison, he decided to align his business and racial philosophies. Went back to dealing, but instead of cocaine, he moved to crack. That way he was selling mostly to blacks. He used kids, all under sixteen. You know why?"

"Prosecuting them is harder?" The writer in Daniel unable to resist.

"That was part of it. Other thing is, kids can sell in schoolyards. Which let Larry expand his interests. See, he'd give the prettier girls credit for a while. But when the bill came due and they couldn't pay, he'd turn them out. Get them tricking for him."

Waters looked over. "I'm talking little girls, eleven, twelve."

Daniel swallowed. "Sounds like an asshole."

"He was."

"Was?"

"Yes." The cop looked away again. "Three weeks ago he was shot and killed under a bridge on the L.A. River."

The city swam in front of him. Daniel was glad he'd chosen to stand. He fought to keep the reaction from his face, wasn't sure he made it. "Really."

"Yep. Three bullets, a nine-millimeter."

"Why are you telling me this?"

Waters brushed a speck of dirt off his trousers. "The law is a good thing. It's what separates us from animals. But sometimes it's a little strict." He paused. "No one is going to miss Larry Morgan. The world is better with him not in it. But the law doesn't care. If someone were to come forward and confess to killing him, that person would be tried for murder. They would lose everything. They would go to prison, which is not a happy place. And it wouldn't matter that Larry was a piece of shit."

Daniel stared at the horizon. A thousand

thoughts came and went. None of them stuck.

"I saw you on TV the other day. Quite a story." Waters paused. "Funny you didn't mention it when we spoke on the phone."

"You mean when you told me you'd found her body?" The retort came fast and angry.

Waters shrugged. "There's no law that a detective has to tell a suspect the truth."

"Convenient."

"It is, yes." Waters spun so his legs were above the walkway, then dropped off the ledge. He slapped dust off his pants. "Look. We're not going to come after you. Your wife isn't dead, and you're a media darling. You're a very lucky man. If I were you, I would count my blessings. And be careful not to mess up what I had. Understand me?"

Daniel stared. Did he? Could the detective actually be telling him . . .

"I'm going back to work. You and Laney do the same." The cop started away, turned back. "Like I said. A place with no memory."

Daniel watched him go. His mind tracing the conversation, filling in the gaps. The cop knew about the man he'd killed. And if Waters knew about that, then he probably knew about Bennett, too. Two homicides. But he was letting them go.

On the other hand, maybe he was fishing, hoping that Daniel would reveal the murders himself. Only, Daniel had decided to confess, and the cop hadn't given him a chance.

You're missing the point.

It wasn't what Bennett did to you *that made killing him something you could live with. It was what he did to Sophie. That was his unforgivable sin. That justified your actions. When he murdered Sophie, Bennett put himself beyond morality.*

Before, in the river basin, you were the one who went beyond morality. You were the monster. At least, that's what you believed, and why you were willing to turn yourself in. You thought you had committed an unforgivable sin, that you had murdered an innocent man.

But you were wrong. Larry Morgan was as evil as Bennett.

You've spent the last weeks trying to become the man you were before. Problem is, that man is dead. You murdered him on a beach in Maine. And what you had rebuilt of him died again when you killed Bennett.

But only so that you could be resurrected.

Who you are now is up to you.

He turned, pushed himself away from the wall. Walked fast to the parking lot. Behind him, the city sparkled in the midday sun. The sky was cloudless and open.

Laney leaned on the front panel of the BMW. Watching for him. He smiled, walked straight to her without breaking stride, put his arm around her waist, and pulled her close. Kissed her like a free man.

"What did he say?"

"He said . . ." Daniel paused. "That I was reborn."

"Huh?"

"He said it's over."

"Really?" She gave him a quizzical look.

"All of it." He laughed, stepped away, sighed. Shook out his arms. He wanted to jump up and down and holler like a child. He wanted to howl and to cry. But he wanted something even more. "Let's go to bed."

"You got turned on talking to a detective?"

"I didn't say anything about sex." He smiled. "I'm going to sleep."

From the privacy of the upper balcony, Roger Waters observed Daniel Hayes and Laney Thayer. Saw them kiss, heard the man laugh. Watched as they got back in their expensive car and rolled the windows down. The last he saw of them, Daniel had his arm out the window, rolling like he didn't have a care in the world.

They bought it. His little fiction had worked. Good.

With Hayes's conscience taken care of, the chance he'd come forward and confess to the murder was zilch. Who would give up the good life, the movie star wife and the house in Malibu, to get justice for a pedophile crack-dealing pimp? That would take a breed of asshole Waters didn't know, and he had a pretty good catalog on assholes.

The fact that none of it was true, well, Hayes never needed to know that.

There's no trail now. They'll keep quiet. No silly martyrdom. No naïve attempts to clear the slate. They'll keep quiet and count their blessings.

Which means there's nothing to connect you to Sophie Zeigler.

His stomach roiled at that. If only he'd known what Bennett had in mind when he got that address.

Didn't you? On some level?

It didn't matter. Now he was clear. If Daniel had come forward, the whole story would have come out, all of it, and they would have used Sophie Zeigler's murder as a justification for shooting Bennett. Which would have raised questions about how that fucker had found her.

Now there was nothing to tie Waters to her death.

Well, one thing. But he'd taken care of it.

The light out the window was very bright. It seemed like the air was shimmering. There was a tree, a stunted sort of thing, spiny and awkward. Birds perched there, their song just audible through the glass.

The room was plain but clean. A thin plastic curtain screened the view of the hall. Fans in the machines hummed.

Somewhere out of sight, someone said something in Spanish, and someone else laughed.

The man in the bed stared at the ceiling tiles. The world had a Demerol fog to it. Thoughts were disconnected and lazy, drifting in and out, mingling as they chose.

How had he gotten here? He could almost remember, almost . . .

A guy in green scrubs stepped into his room, pulling the curtain aside brusquely. He had dark circles under his eyes and a five o'clock shadow. Too tired to be a doctor, too smug to be a nurse. A resident. The resident began checking the IV tubes, the level of fluid in the bag.

The man in the bed ignored him, chased the memory. It cleared a bit at a time, layers of tissue paper stripped away.

He remembered a voice. A man's voice.

You just won't fucking die, will you?

And something else. What? Something about fingers. And . . . angels?

It was important. Fingernails, fingers do the walking, fingerpicking —

Fingerprints.

I've got your fingerprints and your DNA and pictures of you. Another layer of tissue paper tore away, revealing the face. Detective Roger Waters. His lips tight. The skin of his nose shiny. *You may own me, but now I own you too.*

I get you across the border, we're done. You don't bother them or me ever again.

Los Angeles is off your fucking map, you hear me? Forever.

Ahh. Yes. That made sense.

"*Buenas tardes,*" the resident said, as if he'd just noticed there was a person in the bed. "How are you feeling?"

The man in the bed blinked away the memory, took in the resident's face. Dark skin and dark hair. A good-looking guy, but there was something off about him. Not just the air of exhaustion, or the accented English. Something else.

His pupils. They were dilated.

Dilated pupils meant speed.

Dilated pupils on a resident meant someone was raiding the medical supply cabinet.

Interesting.

"*¿Señor?*" The resident cocked his head. "You are awake?" His voice quick and pinched.

"Oh yes, brother." The man in the bed smiled. "I'm awake."

ACKNOWLEDGMENTS

I'm indebted to a number of people for this book. My deepest thanks to:

My agent Scott Miller, the *man.*

My editor Ben Sevier, who improves everything he touches.

The whole team at Dutton/NAL, especially Brian Tart, Sandra Harding, Christine Ball, Amanda Walker, Rich Hasselberger, Melissa Miller, Carrie Swetonic, and Jessica Horvath.

Dr. Cooper Bart Holmes and Dr. Gene Mindel for patiently sharing their expertise on dissociative fugue states.

My buddies Brett Battles and Gregg Hurwitz, who generously served as Los Angeles tour guides.

Mike Biller, who steered me right on MRI technology while also suggesting I get my own head examined.

Officer Jason Jacobson for schooling me on Tasers and catching a dozen firearms problems.

Phil Wang, formerly of the LASD, who helped me get my Sheriff's Department facts straight.

Dana Kaye, my Maggie and more.

Sarah Self, the queen of Hollywood.

Gillian Flynn, Blake Crouch, Michael Cook, Tommy Heffron, and Alison Janssen, for their early reads and generous feedback.

Joe Konrath, who twice saved my butt on this one.

Sean Chercover, my creative partner and road dog.

The booksellers and librarians — we love you.

Mom, Dad, and Matt, without whom I'd be lost.

And especially my wife g.g. Always, and for more reasons than I have paper.

ABOUT THE AUTHOR

Marcus Sakey is the bestselling author of four previous novels, three of which are in development as films. His fiction has been nominated for or won an Anthony, Barry, Macavity, Strand Critic's Circle, Reader's Choice, Crimespree, Dilys, Crime Shot, Romantic Times, and ITW Thriller Award. He lives in Chicago with his wife. Visit his Web site at MarcusSakey.com, or follow him on Facebook and Twitter, where he posts under the clever handle @MarcusSakey.